Copyright © 2025

All rights reserved

The characters and events portrayed in this book are fictitious. Any similarity to real persons, living or dead, is purely coincidental and not intended by the author.

All brand names and product names used in this book are trademarks, registered trademarks, or trade names of their respective holder. J Frances is not associated with any product or vendor in this book.

No part of this book may be reproduced, or stored in a retrieval system, or transmitted in any form or by any means, electronic, mechanical, photocopying, recording, or otherwise, without express written permission of the publisher.

No part of this publication may be used or reproduced in any manner for the purpose of training artificial intelligence technologies or systems.

Cover design by: Get Covers

CONTENT WARNING

This book is meant for mature audiences and contains content that may be triggering for some readers – including sex, profanity, drug addiction, mental health issues, infant loss, stillbirth, grief, domestic violence and references to suicide.

If you or someone you know is contemplating suicide then please call the helpline on 116 123 or go online to www.spuk.org.uk.

If you are the victim of domestic violence then please reach out to the National Domestic Abuse Helpline on 0808 2000 247 or go online to www.nationaldahelpline.org.uk.

If you are struggling with drug or alcohol addiction and need help then please go online to www.mind.org.uk.

SONG LIST FOR BLAZING INFERNO

Wire to Wire – Razorlight
Open Your Eyes – Snow Patrol
Tchaikovsky's Swan Lake
Always in my Head - Coldplay
Under The Bridge – Red Hot Chilli Peppers
Bad Habits – Ed Sheeran
Christmas Lights – Coldplay
Hypnotised – Coldplay
Street Spirit (Fade Out) – Radiohead
Bad Dreams – Teddy Swims
The Heart Asks Pleasure First from the film The Piano
Paradise - Coldplay
Just Say Yes – Snow Patrol
Have You Ever Really Loved a Woman – Bryan Adams
Oh, Pretty Woman – Roy Orbison
Drugs – The Music
Animals – Maroon 5
Fix You - Coldplay
She Will be Loved – Maroon 5
Sugar – Maroon 5
Mamma Mia – Abba
Take This Pain – Jake Banfield

About the Author

J Frances is in her early forties and is a hopeless romantic who is addicted to books. Her love for books started as a young girl when she used to read book after book, forever visiting the library either with school or with her mum.

With a vivid imagination and a clear passion for writing, she began writing stories on her beloved typewriter until eventually finding the time in her life in her early thirties to write her first ever novel back in 2013. J Frances lives in Lancashire with her husband, two sons and pet dog, Milo.

This novel is the second in the Reclamation Rock Star Series and continues where the first novel left off.

For My Husband and Sons

*This book is dedicated to my precious family. Without the love and support of my boys, this book would not have been written. Thank you for giving me the love, support, time and space that was needed in order to complete book number two in this series of novels.
I love you all from the bottom of my heart.*

J xx

CHAPTER 1

LAUREN

I stare down the long, dimly lit corridor of the hospital as I walk towards the intensive care unit, my footsteps echoing loudly around me. The hospital I notice is unusually quiet and I suddenly feel alone. Very alone. Where is Stacey? She said she would come with me. Desperate to see Jonny, I put all thoughts of being alone to one side and quicken my pace, but the faster I walk, the further away the room at the end of the corridor moves away from me. Feeling panicked, I start to run, but the darkened corridor is endless, stretching out in front of me like a never ending treadmill.

"No!" I scream, wondering if I'll ever see Jonny again. "Jonny!" The walls start to close in on me, the corridor fading into total darkness. "Jonny!" I scream again, but it's no use, nobody can hear me. Nobody can help me now. "Jonny!" I scream for the last time...

Somewhere over the Atlantic Ocean - November 2015

I wake with a start, my heart pounding in my chest, sweat pouring from my brow as I try to focus in on my surroundings.

"Lauren?" Turning towards the familiar voice, my eyes finally zone in on Stacey sitting in the seat beside me.

"Where am I?" I ask, feeling disorientated.

Stacey raises her eyebrows. "We're on a flight over to LA," she says, giving me a strange look. *Of course we are.* Shit, I really am disorientated. "Lauren, are you okay?"

I shake my head at her. "I won't be okay until I get to that hospital to see Jonny."

"Did you have a bad dream?" she asks.

"More like a nightmare," I mutter. Resting my head back against the seat, I close my eyes once more and sigh heavily. "I just want to get there, Stace."

Taking a firm hold of my hand, she says, "We'll be there soon, Lauren, I promise."

****

After what feels like the longest journey of my entire life, our taxi transfer from LAX airport finally arrives outside Ben's LA residence at 8.00 pm. Nestled amongst the roving hills of LA, Ben's home can only be accessed through security gates, beyond which is a very long driveway with trees lining either side.

The property is situated in a highly exclusive and ridiculously expensive area of Beverly Hills, not too far from Jonny's home, so I've been told. Normally, I'd be excited and most likely overwhelmed by this sort of thing but under current circumstances, how big and fancy Ben's house is, is the farthest thing away from my mind at the moment. In fact, now we're actually here, standing outside of Ben's house in the dark as the taxi driver unloads our luggage, I'm beginning to feel anxious about what sort of reception I'm about to get from the lads.

It took some persuading on Stacey's part to get Ben to agree to have us stay with him while we are over here. Two full days to be exact. Two full days of phone calls going back and forth between London and LA while I ran around like a headless chicken trying to rush through our travel documents and sort out our flights. I think in the end, Ben simply took pity on me and eventually gave in. I think he finally realised that he is literally the only way I can even get remotely close to seeing Jonny in that hospital, and so, finally, after much arguing with Stacey, he relented. And here we are. About to face the music.

"Okay?" asks Stacey, pressing the buzzer next to the front door, sealing our fate. *Oh well, no turning back now, even if I wanted to.*

Exhaling loudly, I say, "I just want to get this over with."

A few seconds later and the front door is suddenly wrenched open. Ben stands there across the threshold dressed in a faded black t-shirt and ripped jeans, looking less than pleased to see us. His blonde hair is all dishevelled and he looks as though he hasn't shaved in days.

Scowling between the pair of us, he mutters quietly, "I guess you better come in." Eyeing our suitcases up behind us, he then says, "Don't forget your luggage."

Stacey is about to open her mouth to speak when Ben suddenly turns his back on us and walks off, leaving us to fetch our own luggage. Which is fine. We are more than capable of carrying our own luggage after all, although Stacey doesn't seem to think so.

"How bloody dare he? After everything…"

"Come on, Stace," I say, cutting her off, "let's just get our stuff inside and then we can deal with the next bit." The next bit being me wanting to know when I can go and visit Jonny, if I'll be allowed to visit him at all.

****

"So, let me get this straight, you just expect us lot to somehow get you into the intensive care unit at the hospital without Jonny's dad knowing anything about you visiting?" asks Ben, his face aghast. "Seriously?"

Ben looks over at both Will and Zack and all three of them look between both me and Stacey in turn, pure disbelief plastered all over their faces. Stacey is standing next to them giving Ben the daggers while I am sitting on Ben's bright red leather sofa in the middle of one of his many living rooms with my head in my hands. I feel hopeless. Completely and utterly hopeless.

"Just stop with the sarcasm, Ben, and help us!" snaps Stacey, "help Lauren!"

"Oh, you expect me to help out Lauren?!" shouts Ben, gesturing towards me, "you expect me, along with my friends, to help out the woman who caused our best friend to try and take his own life in the first fucking place!"

"Hey! That was uncalled for!" screeches Stacey.

"Uncalled for? Are you fucking kidding me?!" Ben yells, almost spitting his words out at his former girlfriend.

"Yes, uncalled for!" she yells right back at him, "because none of this is Lauren's fault!"

"Stace…" I mumble, trying to stop the argument between them from escalating any further.

"So whose fault is it then?!" snaps Ben, completely ignoring me.

"Why don't you ask the man you call Band Manager!" shouts Stacey.

Ben frowns down at Stacey as both Will and Zack exchange worried glances with each other. "What the fuck do you mean by that?" asks Ben, his voice slightly quieter than it was a moment ago. When Stacey fails to respond, Ben then looks over at me. "What does Stacey mean by that?"

I sigh heavily. "It's a long story…"

"So tell it quickly..." snaps Ben.

"Hey," says Will, placing a hand on Ben's shoulder, "just calm down a bit and give Lauren some time to explain."

The trouble is, I don't want to explain. I don't want to have to tell any of them any of it. Ever. Which is why I keep my explanation brief.

"Look...Pete hates me, always has done and always will. He wanted me out of Jonny's life for good and he succeeded... that's about the top and bottom of it all really..."

Ben is less than impressed with my answer. "So, that's it? Pete just...offered you some money to stay out of Jonny's life for good and you couldn't say no?" *What the actual hell?*

"What? You think I took money from Pete to stay out of Jonny's life?" I ask, feeling upset that Ben would think that of me. "You think I love money more than I love Jonny?"

"Seems that way to me," says Ben with a shrug. "Am I right?" he asks, turning to both Will and Zack for support. Both of them simply shrug their shoulders in response. Turning back to me, Ben then says, "I think we're all agreed on that."

"Whoa, I didn't agree to anything," says Zack, holding up his hands. Looking over at me, he says, "I just don't know what to think at the moment, Lauren...none of us do..."

"Unless you start talking," says Ben, folding his arms across his chest.

Stacey shakes her head at him. "What the hell is wrong with you? Where is the Ben I met in London? Is he still here? If he ever existed at all!"

Scowling down at Stacey, Ben mutters, "That Ben is so long gone I don't even know *who* you're talking about."

Stacey's face drops in dismay and she draws back from him slightly. Seeing him treat her that way makes me hurt for her. In fact, it pisses me off.

"If you want to be angry with me, Ben, be angry with me, but leave Stacey out of this. None of this is her fault."

Ben sighs. "Whatever, Lauren, just tell us what the fuck is going on."

Standing up from the sofa in anger, I finally let him have it. "All you need to know is that Pete is the one who has done this to his son! He forced me out of his son's life twice and now I'm standing here in your home begging you all to help me see Jonny! Pete can't know that I'm here but I need to see Jonny and I need your help to do that!"

"You can't just walk in here and demand that of us and expect us all to just accept what you're telling us, Lauren! I mean, do you even know what he went through when you left him? Do you know how badly his head went when his mom died? You should have been here with him to support him through it but you weren't! You just left him to deal with it all on his own and we tried to support him! We tried to help him but he just wouldn't let us and now he's lying in a coma in hospital after trying to commit suicide! Fucking suicide, Lauren! And apparently this isn't the first time he's attempted to take his own life either because back in Manchester, when he was with you, he attempted suicide then too!" My word, he couldn't be more wrong. He's got this all wrong.

I shake my head furiously. "Jonny never tried to take his own life when he was with me, it was an accidental overdose. Who told you that?"

"What the fuck does it matter?" snaps Ben.

"Who told you?!"

"Pete told us!" yells Ben, "Pete told us that Jonny attempted suicide because you turned your back on him after he got hooked on drugs, and that Jonny went to him for help when he had nobody else left to turn to..."

I continue to shake my head in anger. "No," I say, "no, you've got it all wrong, Pete has lied to you and he's lied to his own son and he's continuing to lie to every bloody person around him!"

"So tell us the fucking truth!" shouts Ben.

"Hey! Just cut it out Ben and calm down," says Will, trying to diffuse the situation.

"I ain't calming down until *she*..." he points at me when he says that, "...starts telling us the fucking truth!"

"What the hell I ever saw in you once upon a time I'll never know!" yells Stacey, re-joining the conversation. "How dare you treat my best friend this way?!"

"And how dare *she* treat *my* best friend in the way that *she* has done!"

Stacey, Ben, Will and Zack all start to shout together in unison, both Zack and Will trying to calm Ben down while Stacey throws insults at Ben left, right and centre. Finally, it all becomes too much for me.

"Just shut up!!!!" I scream at the top of my lungs. All four of them stop dead in their tracks, shocked into silence. "Jonny is lying in a hospital bed and this is how we're behaving with each other?" Ben is about to speak but I cut him off. "Jonny accidentally overdosed on drugs back when we were together in Manchester because of how grief stricken he was when we lost our baby boy..."

Ben's mouth drops open in shock and Will and Zack look on at me in disbelief. I close my eyes so that I don't have to look at them. I can't look at them right now. It's painful enough as it is without having to look them in the eye as I tell them the worst part of my past.

"We were both so consumed by our grief that we reacted in ways that drove a wedge between us...I pushed Jonny away emotionally and because of that...he turned to drugs to block it all out...so yes, part of his drug addiction was my fault but losing our baby? That wasn't my fault or Jonny's, that was the fault of somebody else entirely..."

Opening up my eyes once more, I look over at all three of them and feel myself beginning to waver slightly, wondering whether to tell them the rest of the story. But these three men standing in front of me are Jonny's best friends, his band mates, his family. If I can't trust them enough to tell them the truth in order to help Jonny then there's no point in me even being here.

Mustering up the courage to finally tell them the truth, I finally say the dreaded words out loud. "Losing our baby was the fault of my own dad...my own dad and his fists..." I render all three of them speechless, Stacey wandering over to me so that she can wrap a comforting arm around my shoulders.

Out of the three of them, Zack is the first one to speak. "Shit...that...that must have been difficult for you both, Lauren...really difficult. I'm so sorry." He clears his throat nervously. "We're all sorry...aren't we?"

Ben frowns over at me. "You and Jonny had a baby together?" I nod.

Wrapping his hands around the back of his neck, Will looks up at the ceiling and exhales loudly. "Shit, this is a lot to take in."

"I'll fucking say," Ben mutters, "but what I still don't understand is how Pete fits into all of this..."

Stacey glares over at him. "Do you have any emotional bone or feeling in your body at all? Has anything that Lauren just said to you even registered with you or are you made entirely of stone?!"

"Stace, it's fine, he's in shock…"

"Like hell he is!" she yells, storming back over to him. "You're a heartless, hurtful bastard and I hate you for feeling nothing!" She shoves hard at his chest. "You're empty inside, Ben Anderson, and I bloody well hate you!"

"Well I'm glad you've got me all figured out, Stace!" he snaps, "and you know what? I'm glad that you hate me, because it makes sleeping with all those women over the last few weeks since we broke up all the more worth it because now, as you hate me so damn much, I don't have to feel guilty about them anymore!" Stacey slaps him hard across the face and then bursts into floods of tears before storming out of the living room. I glare over at Ben. "What?" he says, holding up his arms in defence.

"Seriously? You're asking me *what* after saying what you just said to my best friend?"

"You're a fucking dick sometimes," says Zack, plucking a fag out from his packet of cigarettes. "A fucking dick." Turning to me on his way out of the room, Zack says, "Sorry, Lauren."

Will turns to Ben and says, "You are way out of line tonight, Ben. Way out of line."

"My best friend is lying in a coma in hospital and you've got the fucking nerve to tell me I'm out of line?"

Ben starts to square up to Will but Will is having none of it. Pushing his hand firmly against Ben's chest, Will says, "He's my best friend too. And Zack's. We're all in this together, not just you. Believe it or not, the world doesn't just revolve around you."

With a heavy sigh, Ben chances one more look at me before leaving the room, slamming the door behind him.

"I'm sorry about that," says Will, looking over at me sorrowfully, "and I'm sorry for everything that you've been through. It must have been tough for you both."

I nod. "Yeah, it was tough…more than tough actually…it was the worst time of my life…" Gulping past the lump in my throat, I then say, "Until now…now is officially the worst time in my life because Jonny…Jonny might die…"

Will shakes his head. "Jonny won't die, he's stronger than that. Shit, he's the strongest person I've ever known."

"But he's in a coma…last time, when he accidentally overdosed, he was unconscious when I found him but when they got him to the hospital and got him the right treatment, he came round quickly, but this…it's been three days. Three days and he still hasn't woken up!"

Will hushes me before pulling me into a hug. "He's going to wake up, Lauren," he says determinedly, "and you're going to be by his side when he does."

"But…Pete won't leave Jonny's side, and if he knows I'm here in LA, then…"

"Then what?" asks Will, pulling me gently away from him, "what will Pete do if you go against him?"

I pause for a moment before answering him. "Then he'll release the story of my past with his son to the newspapers, meaning that the entire world will know everything about what happened to us back in Manchester. That's why I gave Pete what he wanted, because I was trying to protect Jonny from his past…*our* past. A past so painful that I couldn't bear to see it splashed about in the newspapers for every man and his dog to read about."

Will sighs heavily. "My god, just who the hell have we been working for all this time? And Pete would really do this to his own son?"

"I know it's a lot to digest, but...Pete's always hated me, so him going to these lengths just to rid me from Jonny's life doesn't shock me in the least. He hated me then and he still hates me now."

"Well, no more," says Will, firmly, "we have to put a stop to all of this and we have to somehow get you into that hospital tomorrow to see Jonny."

"But...how..."

"Just leave it to me," says Will, a look of pure determination on his face, "you leave it to me."

****

The following morning I'm up early so I get a quick shower and go downstairs well before the rest of the house even wakes up. I barely slept a wink all night, instead worrying about Jonny until the early hours of the morning. Which is a shame, because the bedroom which Ben has given me to stay in for the duration of my time here is stunning. As is Stacey's. In fact, everything in this house of his is stunning, not to mention expensive. I'm fairly sure the bedding I sort of slept in last night is more expensive than my entire wardrobe of clothes and believe me, I own a lot of clothes. Too many.

As I wander through Ben's home, towards the back of the house, taking in everything I missed last night, I stumble upon a hallway. And not just any ordinary hallway. Both walls are lined entirely with photographs of the band, along with awards they've picked up over the years, as well as every album they've ever released encased in glass frames. There are four albums in total, the fifth album currently in the making. Well, it was in the making, until....

Shaking away all bad thoughts, I continue to gaze at the hallway of wonder, taking in the photographs of Reclamation that adorn both walls. Most of them are from their live shows, beautiful artistic shots of them on stage as they play their instruments and smile at their fans. One of the shots is of Jonny doing the splits in mid-air with his electric guitar in his hands. He's wearing his trademark leather jacket and beaming with happiness over at his audience. The bright lights of the stage are behind him, illuminating him in all his rock star glory. The text underneath says the photograph was taken in Buenos Aires, Argentina, 2012, back when they did their first ever world tour. They had become so huge at that point that the demand for a world tour was so high, they simply couldn't not do it. I have no doubt in my mind that they would have toured the world again this year, had it not been for Jonny's mum being so ill at the time....

Feeling suddenly overcome with emotion, I reach out my index finger to touch the photograph of Jonny. I slowly trace his hair, his eyes, his mouth. Tears form in my eyes as I think back to how we were together in London, how we were when we first got together as young teenagers back in Manchester. God, we were mad, madly in love without a care in the world. How did we end up here? How the hell did Jonny end up fighting for his life in hospital? What if I lose him? What if he....

Holding back a sob, I close my eyes and take a deep breath in. No, Jonny was a born fighter. He's strong and he's stubborn and he *will* get through this, and I'll be there waiting for him when he wakes up.

I can't look at any more photographs after that, and so I end up walking through to the very back of the house. I am so taken aback by the beauty of the sight that greets me when I step into the back room that I stand stock still on the spot. It's a huge kitchen/diner come living/entertaining area, the vast space seamless in its design as one area weaves flawlessly into another. The best bit though, the true beauty of this part of the house, is the wall of floor to ceiling windows spanning the entire rear of the house. On closer inspection, I can see that they are electrical bi-folding doors, operated by some buttons which I discover on the far side wall near the plush living room area.

I attempt to open up one of the doors and end up somehow opening up all of them. Maybe that's how they work but who knows? Either way, I'm now standing outside on an expansive patio area complete with built in barbecue and designer furniture. There's even a bar over in the far corner. Bloody hell, Ben has certainly splashed his cash on this place. Stone steps lead down to a halfway balcony with yet more furniture and then beyond that...wow.

As I descend the steps all the way down to the very bottom, I am greeted by an enormous rectangular shaped swimming pool. A few sun loungers are dotted around the pool and beyond those are an abundance of trees and shrubs as far as the eye can see. Wow, who'd have thought that Ben would live in a place with such beautiful gardens and greenery. I don't know why but I always had Ben down as a hippy sort of type, somebody who would perhaps have a smaller and much messier home. I know he has lots of money but I just envisaged his home to be more hardcore rock star I guess. Instead, everything in his home has its place and is so well co-ordinated, I would say it's definitely had a woman's touch somewhere along the line. Whether it's a family member or a work colleague or a friend, or even an interior designer, they've certainly done a beautiful job on the place.

I wonder if Jonny's home is similar in design. Either way,

it's most likely to be messy, because Jonny never was one for being tidy. He was always working on his music and out doing gigs and so tidying up and doing household chores never really registered on his radar. I smile at the thought of him. God, what I would give to be nagging at him about his messy ways right now. My smile slowly fades as the grim sight of Jonny lying in a hospital bed comes back to my mind once more.

Sitting down on the nearest sun lounger, my eyes fixate on the swimming pool in front of me. The early morning sun shimmers on the surface of the water and I inhale deeply, trying to find my inner calm again.

"Hey."

Glancing up to my left I see Ben standing behind the sun lounger. Clean shaven and wearing a black Hugo Boss logo vest top with matching knee length shorts, he looks a whole lot better than he did last night. Still, despite how much better he looks and how gorgeous his house is, I'm still pissed with him.

"Hey," I say coldly, before turning my gaze back to the swimming pool.

"I suppose I deserve that," he says with a sigh, before pulling up a sun lounger to sit next to me.

"And a whole lot more where that came from," I say.

He sighs once more. "Yeah, I guess I do."

"For once I'm glad to say we agree on something."

Pulling out a packet of cigarettes from the pocket of his shorts, he plucks one out with his teeth before offering me one. "You want one?"

I shake my head. "No thanks. I've never smoked, although if there was ever a time when I would even consider smoking, that time would be now."

"So take one and enjoy the ride," he says, before lighting up his own fag.

"Thanks for the offer but, I've gone this long without the need to smoke and so I'd like to keep it that way."

"Fair enough." He stuffs his fag packet back into his pocket.

"Have you heard how Jonny is this morning?" Now Ben is here, I need to know any news as soon as possible.

"No change," he mumbles quietly, "although him breathing all on his own without the need for a ventilator is a huge positive in all of this, so let's focus on that positive, Lauren."

No change, but breathing all by himself. No change isn't great but it also isn't the worst news either, and him breathing all by himself without the need for a ventilator is definitely a positive. *He just needs to wake up. Why the hell won't he wake up?*

"So," he says, inhaling deeply on his cigarette, "I came down here to find you to say that I'm sorry for the way I behaved last night, for the things I said and for how I reacted. I could come up with a thousand excuses of why I behaved like I did, but I won't, because sometimes, I really am an asshole, and because I'm such an asshole, I can't come up with an excuse for that."

Squinting over at him, I can't help but break out into a grin. "Yet again, it seems we are in agreement."

"Yeah yeah," he mutters, puffing away on his fag, "lap it up and enjoy the moment why don't you?"

My grin slowly fades. "Oh come on, Ben, surely you can't take that to heart? I was only joking."

"Well, according to Stacey, I don't have a heart, so...."

"The way I recall the conversation from last night, you kind of steered Stacey towards that way of thinking."

"Meaning it's all my fault why she thinks I'm heartless and empty inside?"

"Basically, yes."

Blowing out smoke from between his lips, he leans forward on his knees and stares over at the swimming pool. "Last night, after you lot went to bed, Will came to find me and told me everything that you'd told him about Pete. I felt both angry and ashamed. Angry at that wanker we've worked for for so long and…ashamed because of how I treated you, and…I know none of what happened is your fault, or Stacey's, but I can't help but still feel angry at her."

"Angry at her for what?" I ask.

Blowing out the last of his smoke, Ben then stubs out his cigarette on the flags by the pool. With a heavy sigh, he says, "For changing me."

"Changing you?" I'm confused.

"Stacey and I agreed straight away that we would just have some fun when we were in London together, so we both knew where we stood with each other from the very beginning… but then, I started to feel things, strange things, things that admittedly made me uncomfortable. Anyway, I brushed all those odd feelings off to one side, I got on that plane back home and that was it. Until Jonny told me about his suggestion of her coming over here with you to live in LA. Well, I was ecstatic at the very idea of Stacey being over here permanently but then, it suddenly got ripped away from me. And it got ripped away from me because it was out of my control, and Stacey was never gonna come over here to be with me after you and Jonny split up, and so, the happy scenario I'd started to build up in my mind just vanished. I know we tried for a good while to keep things going over the phone, despite everything that was going on with you and Jonny, but it just wasn't working, and it would never have worked. When we did officially split up, I felt angry and upset and that's when I started to go out on the piss. Night after night after night. And then along came all the women and that was it, I was back to square one all over again."

"Just go and talk to her, Ben," I say gently, "go and tell her you're sorry for the things you said and just make it up with her."

He shakes his head at me. "I will tell her I'm sorry because I truly am sorry for hurting her, but…as for anything else between us, I don't want any complications in my life right now. We all need to focus on Jonny at the moment and all this new information you've landed us with is really going to change things. Not only for Jonny himself, *when* he wakes up, but…for the future of the band, and…anything outside of any of that is just unthinkable."

I nod. "You're right, we all need to focus and pull together as a group but please promise me that you'll go and make it right with her, she deserves that much."

Ben frowns at me. "Of course I'll make it right with her. I'm going to make everything right for everybody here, including you. You get me?"

"Thank you," I whisper, feeling incredibly grateful to him for everything that he and his friends are doing for us.

Suddenly looking pensive, he says, "Will is going to try and get you into the hospital tonight to see Jonny, once visiting hours have finished and Pete has gone home. It's the only time Pete leaves, just for a few hours every night to get some sleep. Will's going to hopefully talk Jonny's bodyguards round into allowing you in to see him but, the whole thing may backfire in our faces and Pete may end up finding out what we're up to. Just be prepared for that, Lauren, okay?" I give him an assured nod, although on the inside, I'm feeling anything but. "Okay, good," he says, and then stands up.

"You do have a heart you know," I say to him, "and Stacey knows that." Ben gives me a reluctant nod before walking back towards the house.

CHAPTER 2

LAUREN

I stare down at Jonny lying motionless in his hospital bed. The machines bleep loudly around him and he's wired up to so many things that I'm nowhere near as close to him as I'd like to be. But the main thing is, I am here, and that is all that matters to me right now.

My hand rests on Jonny's right hand, my fingers gently stroking his fingers over and over in the hope that my touch will somehow breathe new life in to him and wake him up. *Why the hell won't he just wake up?* Because to me, he looks as though he is simply asleep. In a peaceful, restful sleep that he'll soon wake up from. He doesn't even look ill. Not really. Despite looking a little pale, Jonny still looks as beautiful now as he ever did, which makes this so much harder to bear. And I only have ten minutes with him. Ten minutes. That's all the hospital staff would allow to somebody who isn't a blood relative or a lifelong partner or spouse. I am simply a nothing to them. And I deserve to be seen as a nothing, because it is partly down to me as to why Jonny ended up here in the first place.

Stifling back a sob, I lean forwards and take a hold of his right hand. Turning it over as gently as possible, my watery eyes come to rest on the tattoo of my name etched into his skin on his inner right forearm. His first ever tattoo. We had just turned eighteen when we both went along to the tattoo parlour together to get each other's names burned into our skin. I brush the tips of my fingers back and forth over each letter of my name before pressing a soft kiss there.

"Oh Jonny," I whisper in anguish, "I am so so sorry for leaving you again…and I am so very sorry for causing you so much pain that you felt you couldn't cope after you lost your mum… if only you knew why…if I could only get that chance to tell you exactly why…"

I break down then, sobbing quietly next to him as I squeeze the life out of his hand. The machines continue their endless bleeping in the background, Jonny simply lying there next to me, unresponsive and immobile. It's far from the Jonny I am used to seeing. God, please just let him wake up and be okay. I just want him to be okay.

Sniffing back more tears, I say to Jonny, "You were the only one for me, Jonny Mathers…and there will never be another you…ever…so wake up…please just bloody wake up…"

Lifting his hand up to my face, I press his fingertips gently against my wet cheek. Closing my eyes, I whisper to him, "So many tears I cry for you, my love, so very many, that's how well loved you are. And not just by me. By so many other people in your life…so just wake the hell up." My voice cracks and I kiss the tips of his fingers before placing them back down gently on the bed.

No touching, the nurse said. Easy for her to say, so much harder for me to do. How can I not touch him? Leaning over, I study his face intently, making sure I memorise every line, every contour, every single detail of his beautiful features before I get wrenched away from him, possibly for the last time. What if this is the last time I ever get to see him alive? *Oh god, I can't take this anymore, I can't handle it.*

"I love you, Jonny," I whisper, before pressing a tender, lingering kiss to his forehead, "don't ever forget how much I love you."

****

When I arrive back at Ben's house a short while later, I fall to pieces. A million pieces. It takes the work of both Ben and Stacey to calm me down before plying me with whisky. The shock of drinking something I absolutely loathe actually works, the sheer burning of the amber liquid as it slips down my throat and down my food pipe temporarily taking my mind off everything. But not for long.

"I just can't believe I might never see him again…"

"Sssh," says Stacey, gently pulling me against her.

Ben pours me another whisky and I accept it gratefully. "You will see him again, Lauren," says Ben, "I promise."

I grimace slightly as I take another sip of whisky. "But you heard what Tony and Andy said earlier tonight, we put them in a really difficult position because of Pete…"

Ben shakes his head at me. "Tony and Andy work directly for Jonny, not Pete. They are part of Jonny's security team and so they owe Pete nothing."

I sigh. "Even so, the situation is far from ideal and, as the nurse said to me tonight, I'm not family or a spouse or even his…girlfriend, and so…I don't have a right to be there…"

"You're the bloody love of his life," says Stacey, quickly becoming angry, "you have more right to be there than that so called father of his. A father who would sell his own son to the papers just to keep you out of his life for good. Pete Mathers is sick, Lauren, and believe you me, karma will get him…"

"But the time for that isn't quite yet," says Ben, giving Stacey 'the look'.

"Oh, so when is the right time exactly?" snaps Stacey.

I have to hand it to Ben, he more than bites his tongue with his response to Stacey. If she had said that to him last night then he would have bitten her head clean off, but not tonight. With a serious look on his face, Ben says quietly, "Soon, Stace… real soon."

Seeming content with Ben's answer, Stacey visibly calms. I am taking this as a positive sign that they have, as Ben promised me he would do this morning, patched things up with each other. They certainly seem more relaxed in each other's company tonight but what exactly has been said between them, I'm not sure. I haven't really seen much of Stacey on her own today and so haven't had a chance to ask her. Most of the day was spent in the company of the lads and Stacey was holed up in her bedroom on her own for most of this morning and so hazarding a guess, I would say it was at that point when Ben perhaps went to talk to her. Either way, they are making progress, and that's all I can hope for.

****

The following morning, the entire household is thrown into chaos when an unexpected visitor turns up at the entrance gates, buzzing the life out of Ben's entry phone, forcing everybody out of their beds at a stupidly early hour. It's barely even light outside I notice as I quickly wrap my dressing gown around me.

Throwing open my bedroom door, I am shocked to see Ben dashing out of Stacey's bedroom and across the landing to his own bedroom, wearing only a pair of boxer shorts. He emerges from his room a few moments later wearing a plain white t-shirt and some black pyjama bottoms before descending the stairs in a panic, completely oblivious to my presence. Well, so much for Ben not wanting to complicate matters with Stacey. We've barely been here two days and they've clearly already spent the night together.

I decide to grill Stacey all about it later on and instead see what on earth is going on downstairs and so I continue my walk along the landing, until I collide with Stacey as she comes out of her room and walks directly into my path.

"Oh shit, sorry, Lauren, I...didn't see you there." She flashes me an awkward smile and then breaks eye contact with me. Hmm, she's avoiding eye contact with me. Something definitely happened between those two last night.

"That's okay." I smile. "Are you okay?"

Stacey looks back up at me and frowns. "Sure. I'm fine." And then she smiles. "Yes, I'm fine. You?" Yep, she got some last night for sure. She always acts strange when she's trying to keep something from me.

"Look, Stace, I saw..." A loud bang on the front door makes both Stacey and I jump, putting all thoughts of me questioning my best friend right out of my mind. "What the hell?"

Both Stacey and I tear downstairs towards an anxious looking Ben who's pacing up and down the hallway with his hands in his hair. "What's going on?" I ask him, feeling worried, "who's at the door?"

Ben stops pacing and fixes me with a long stare. Another loud bang at the front door, coupled with yelling this time, tells me all I need to know. "Holy shit," I whisper, suddenly feeling sick.

"What?" asks Stacey, not catching on quick enough, "who is it?"

"It's Pete," I whisper, my voice trembling with fear, "he knows I'm here."

Seconds later, Will and Zack come flying downstairs to join us. "What's going on?" asks Will, looking worried.

"Pete's here," Stacey tells Will.

Will's face drops and he immediately turns on Ben. "If you knew it was Pete then why the fuck did you let him through the gates?" he growls at him through gritted teeth.

Lowering his voice, Ben says, "He said he had an update on Jonny when he spoke to me through the entry phone, *that's* why I let him in. As soon as he got to the front door he started going fucking berserk. I'm only glad I didn't open the door before he got to it."

"Shit," says Will, "shit, shit, shit."

"I know she's in there!" yells Pete, before hammering on the front door once more. "And I know you let her see my son!" He bangs on the door again, once, twice, three times. I take a step backwards. The very sound of him makes me want to cower away under a rock somewhere. He scares me. He scares me to death. "So know this! You've all just gone and fucked yourselves because from now on, only *I* get to see *my* son, you understand?!"

Oh shit, I didn't want this. I didn't want any of this. I am just about to step forward to speak up when Ben gets there first. Slamming the palms of his hands against the front door, he says angrily, "We know what you've done, Pete! We know what you've done to Jonny and you're gonna get what's coming to you, asshole, because karma is a fucking bitch!" Ben smacks both of his fists against the front door before taking a step back to regain his composure.

To my surprise, Pete doesn't respond to Ben's threat. Instead, he must retreat, because the next thing we hear is a car door slamming before the squealing of rubber tyres tearing up the gravel of Ben's driveway as he drives off at high speed.

A couple of minutes later, Ben goes outside to check that

Pete really has gone before returning to us in the hallway. Slamming the front door behind him, a murderous looking Ben then balls up his fists before punching the life out of his front door. He doesn't hold back this time, Ben's anger bubbling over to the point of no return.

"Fucking wanker!" he yells, his right fist meeting the door once more.

Looking concerned, Stacey decides to approach him. Placing her hand gently on his arm she says quietly, calmly, "Hey, look at me."

Slapping his palms against the front door, Ben says, "He won't get away with this, Stace, I won't let him get away with it."

"I know you won't," says Stacey. Reaching up, she places the palm of her hand against his cheek and he sighs.

Turning to look at her, he says, "We're Jonny's friends, we're his fucking family, Pete has no fuckin' right to…"

Stacey hushes Ben by planting a tender kiss on his lips before wrapping her hands around the back of his neck, pulling him in for a hug. He accepts her embrace gratefully and I can't help but smile at the pair of them. Ben literally turns to mush around Stacey and it's so wonderful to see. And his allegiance to Jonny knows no bounds. Despite their differences, I can see now that Ben thinks the world of Jonny. They all do. Which is why what Pete is doing is wrong. So very wrong.

"So," says Will, looking deadly serious. "What the fuck do we do now?"

Pulling his lips away from Stacey's, Ben then looks between me, Will, Zack and Stacey. "Now? Now we take no prisoners. And if Pete wants an all-out war then he's got one, because if he thinks for a minute that us lot will go down without a fight then he's got another thing coming."

"So…"

"So we all go to the hospital together today and we face Pete head on," says Ben, "and we don't fucking budge until we get to see Jonny. No matter what happens or what shitty threats he comes out with, we stick together and let it play out. For Jonny."

"For Jonny," says Zack, patting Ben on the shoulder.

Both Will and I exchange glances. "For Jonny," says Will, quietly.

Feeling a little emotional at witnessing the lengths this wonderful group of people will go to for the man I love, I nod gently and say, "For Jonny."

"For Jonny," says Stacey, smiling over at me.

CHAPTER 3

LAUREN

"Now we're here, I'm not so sure about this," I say, feeling sick with nerves.

Ben reverses his Range Rover into an unmarked parking spot in some sort of storage yard situated behind the hospital in LA. It's late afternoon and as the paparazzi have set up camp outside the front of the hospital waiting for news on Jonny, Ben thought it best to avoid the glare of the cameras and instead sneak in through the back entrance.

Pete successfully managed to keep the news of Jonny's condition out of the papers for the last few days before it finally got leaked to the press this morning. And now, they're desperate for answers. Answers to the questions of how Jonny ended up being seriously ill in hospital in the first place. Answers that Pete is not prepared to give right now, and for once in my life, I actually agree with him.

As concerned as Jonny's fans are for his welfare, the vultures that are the paparazzi are just desperate for a news story. A story that sells millions of papers and makes them their money. Needless to say that security has been stepped up threefold around the hospital since the story broke around the world this morning, which in turn will no doubt create even more hurdles for us to jump over in order to see him.

"No turning back now, Lauren," says Ben, turning off the engine. He flashes me a wink through the rear view mirror and

I return that wink with a smile.

"Come on," says Zack, giving me a gentle nudge in the side with his elbow, "let's do this."

Zack is sitting in the middle seat between me and Will and is more than a little itchy to get out of the car and get his mouth around a cigarette, because Zack is the very definition of a chain smoker.

"You just want a fag before we go inside the hospital, don't you?" I jest. Zack smiles and I roll my eyes at him. "And there's me thinking you were enjoying being squished between me and Will in the back of Ben's Range Rover," I say, pretending to be offended.

Zack chuckles before reaching for his packet of fags that he has stored in his t-shirt pocket. "Oh, I loved every minute of being squished in between you two," he quips, before pressing a fag between his lips, "but needs must and all that."

I put Zack out of his misery and get out of the car so that he can enjoy his smoke before going inside the hospital to face the music. Ben, Stacey and Will follow suit, Ben lighting up his own fag before locking his car. "Right, I've been in the back entrance before so follow me."

"Are you sure about this?" asks Stacey, not looking entirely convinced.

"Hey," says Ben, "don't you trust me?" He takes a long pull on his cigarette as Stacey considers her answer.

"Hmm, not quite sure really," she jokes.

He narrows his eyes on her before pulling her in for a quick kiss. "How about now?" he murmurs with a grin, Stacey giggling in response.

I roll my eyes at the pair of them. As happy as I am that these two lovebirds are getting back on track, we really need to focus on the job in hand. "Come on, Ben, no more distractions, let's just get this over with."

"Sure thing, Lauren," he says, grabbing hold of Stacey's hand, "everybody follow me."

****

Ben's master plan works, we get into the hospital without being seen by the paparazzi. We even get as far as the intensive care reception desk. But that's as far as we do get, because not long after our arrival, we're greeted by none other than Pete and his hefty security team.

Dressed in a beige designer suit with a crisp white open collared shirt beneath and looking as smart as ever, Pete may still look the part of a wealthy businessman but on closer inspection, I can see how world weary he actually is.

This stuff with Jonny has really worn on him. Not to mention the grief he must still be dealing with after losing his wife only a few weeks ago. It's a hell of a lot for one person to cope with, and it's beginning to show. The lines on his face, more wrinkles around his eyes and the flecks of grey in his hair are all telltale signs that Pete isn't quite as macho and as strong as he makes himself out to be. That maybe he is human after all. If only he would show it.

Not wanting to cause a major scene, Pete addresses us as politely but as firmly as possible. "I distinctly told you all to stay away from the hospital, and so you give me no choice but to remove you by force."

He signals to the two men standing behind him, none of which are Jonny's bodyguards I notice. I only wonder where Tony and Andy are while all of this is going on. Maybe Pete sacked them after they allowed me in here to see Jonny last night. The two large looking men make a move towards us but

Ben takes his own step forward, towards Pete, so he's right in his face.

Keeping his voice as low as possible, Ben says through gritted teeth, "You throw us out of here by force and I will squeal, Pete. I will squeal like a fucking pig to those paparazzi camped outside those front doors right now. I will tell them absolutely everything that I know about you. What you did to Jonny. Your only son. How you ripped his life from under him, not once, but twice."

Pete suddenly holds up a hand to the two men, signalling for them to stop their approach. Turning to them both he then says, "Leave me." The men frown at each other before reluctantly walking off past the reception desk and through the double doors back into the intensive care unit.

Pete turns back to us, his steely gaze coming to rest on me. "I don't know what Lauren has told you but as you've worked for me for over nine years, and you've known Lauren for a mere couple of weeks, if that, I know who I'd believe."

I get angry then. Really angry. "Are you calling me a liar?" I ask, raising my voice slightly, "after everything you threatened me with back in London, after ripping Jonny away from me back in Manchester, how could you…"

Stacey suddenly pulls me back from saying anything more as the hospital staff sitting behind the reception desk start to notice our little scene beginning to unfold.

Ben glances over at them before resting his eyes back on Pete. "I know who I believe right now, and it ain't you, otherwise you wouldn't be so desperate to stop us from trying to see our best mate when he needs us the most."

"She's bad for him," Pete says to Ben, "she's bad for my son."

"No, Pete," says Ben, shaking his head. "Lauren is good for

Jonny. I saw how they were together in London and he loves her. He needs her. So let her in to see him. Let us all in to see him, one by one, and then we'll leave quietly through the back door just like we came in."

Pete ponders for a moment, looking between all five of us before looking over at the reception staff sitting behind the desk. I fear for one dreaded moment that he's going to say no, because if nothing else, Pete is stubborn. He won't be told what to do by anybody around him and Jonny is exactly the same, maddeningly stubborn and extremely defiant. And Pete always wondered why they clashed so much.

"Fine. You can see him, one at a time, but only for five minutes each. You understand?"

Ben nods his head in agreement. Pete turns swiftly and we follow him past the reception desk and through the double doors into the long corridor that leads to the intensive care unit. Ben gives me a reassuring nod along the way, Will draping his arm around my shoulders as we walk towards Jonny's room. That familiar knot like sensation in my stomach begins to show its presence, gnawing away at my insides as the thought of seeing Jonny lying motionless all over again starts to get to me.

Stopping just outside Jonny's room, Pete quickly ushers away his security team and then turns to us and says, "I stay in the room at all times."

Ben nods his head once more. "Fine." Urging me forwards, he then says, "Lauren, you go in first, I know how desperate you are to see him again." He gives me a small smile, causing my heart to grow that little bit bigger for him. If it wasn't for Ben, I wouldn't even be standing here right now. I owe Ben a hell of lot. More than that. I owe him everything.

Reaching across, I give his hand a quick squeeze. "Thank

you," I whisper.

Stacey turns to me and says, "We'll just be out here if you need us. Okay?" Stacey glances over at Pete when she says that. In other words, 'hurt my best friend and you'll have me to deal with.'

I smile at her. "Thanks, Stace."

Pete pushes the door open and we both step inside Jonny's room. He then closes the door firmly behind him before making a beeline directly for me. "You just couldn't stay away from him, could you?" Oh my word, I haven't even had the chance to look at Jonny yet and Pete is already turning on me.

My eyes instantly fill with tears. "How can you even say that to me?" I blurt out, "how can you even stand there and say that to me when Jonny is lying in a coma in hospital because of something that you did?"

Pete shakes his head at me. "He tried to take his own life because he couldn't handle the grief he felt when he lost his mum. This has nothing to do with you leaving him. Nothing at all."

I look on at him in disbelief. "You honestly don't see it, do you? Or at least, you don't want to see it?"

"See what?"

"How much your son loves me. How much he does actually need me in his life. You made me leave him again, Pete, and look what it did to him! I should have been here to support him when he lost his mum but I wasn't here. Because of you I wasn't here and he fell to pieces because he thought I'd left him again because I didn't love him enough. Because of you!" I swipe at my tears, feeling silently angry with myself for breaking down in front of him.

Pete sighs heavily. "He was mad for you, Lauren. Crazy for

you. I've never seen anything like those types of feelings in my life ever before but you were both so young. *Too* young. And it held him back. *You* held him back from being the very thing that he is now."

I shake my head in anger. "No, Pete. I never held him back. I encouraged Jonny every step of the way. I fell in love with him for so many reasons but one of the main reasons was because of how musically talented he was. *Is*. Even when I fell pregnant I told him I would have travelled around the world with him and our baby if it meant getting him the opportunity that he needed to get himself noticed. I wanted that for him because I loved him and I wanted him to succeed but Jonny never liked being told what to do. Jonny would have done it all by himself but in his own time and on his own terms, but you pushed him. You pushed him and pushed him and in doing that, you pushed him away."

"You distracted him, Lauren. Too much. And all that stuff that happened with your father…"

"Wasn't my fault!" I yell. "Pete, I never asked to be born into a family where I had a violent alcoholic as a father. I didn't ask to be brought into this world so I could live a life of misery after my mum took her own life when I was only five years old. Jonny came into my life like a whirlwind one day and he made me happy. So deliriously happy that I wondered what on earth I'd done to suddenly deserve all of that happiness…and then my dad took all of that happiness away from me when he attacked me and killed my unborn child. *Jonny's* child. *Our* son. *Your* grandson. And then…well, you know how the story ended, Pete, because you ended it yourself…"

For the first time ever in my life, I have left Pete Mathers speechless. Never before have I laid it as bare as I just have done and, I might be wrong, but I swear I just saw some sort of guilt whirling around in his eyes, as fleeting as it was. Maybe

I'm just hoping for him to feel guilty but I swear he's feeling something because his silence speaks volumes. Pete has never ever fallen silent where I'm concerned and I wonder, after all this time, whether Pete will finally relent and give me a chance. A chance to prove my worth, although in all honesty, I shouldn't really have to prove my worth to anyone, least of all him.

Clearing his throat, Pete finally breaks the uncomfortable silence and says, "You've got five minutes with him. I'll wait outside and give you a moment." *A moment?* Pete's giving me a moment alone with his son? After everything he's said and done to me in the past? Well, it isn't much but it's the best I can hope for right now. At least he's finally being amicable.

Nodding my head at him, I say, "Thank you."

No sooner is Pete out of the room and I'm straight over to be by Jonny's side. I can't believe I've been in here for five minutes already without so much as getting a chance to properly look at him. Still lying motionless on the bed, I pull up a chair to sit next to him and take a hold of his hand. "Hey you," I whisper against his palm.

I look on at him longingly, my chest aching at the sheer sight of him. His dark hair is all over the place and he has some serious stubble going on in the chin area but other than that, he looks perfect to me. Perfectly normal. And healthy.

I let out a weary sigh, my eyes beginning to water with tears all over again. "Do you remember when you wrote that song for me, Jonny? Back in Manchester? That song you wrote for me, about me? You named that song *My Angel*." I let out a mournful sob. "You called me your angel, Jonny. And now your angel is sitting here next to you in hospital, begging you to wake up."

I kiss the palm of his hand and then nuzzle my nose against

the tattoo of my name on his forearm. "And you burned me into your skin too. Do you remember that?" My tears fall onto his skin as I let out another sob. "And we once made a baby together," I whisper, "a son, who we named Oliver. A son we lost but a son we both loved so very much." Sniffing loudly, I kiss Jonny's hand once more before placing it back down on the bed. "I'm so sorry, Jonny. For everything bad that ever happened to us...I'm so very sorry."

I look down at the bed, tears streaming down my cheeks as my emotions finally get the better of me. I've been trying so hard to keep it all together, but I can't do it anymore. I don't think I can do any of this anymore.

Reaching towards Jonny's hand for one last kiss, I suddenly notice something. Movement. Two of Jonny's fingers are moving. Only slight movement but they're moving. *Oh my god.* Standing up, I lean over the bed and look into Jonny's face in the hope that his eyes will suddenly flutter open and he'll see me standing over him. But they don't. Glancing back down at his fingers, I see two of them move again.

"Jonny? Can you hear me?" Oh, please let him be able to hear me. Looking down at his hand once more, I see Jonny's fingers move in response to my question. "You can hear me?" More movement, four fingers this time. Touching his fingers gently with mine, I say to him quietly, "I'll be right back."

I fly out of that room like a bat out of hell. "He's moving his fingers!" I shout excitedly.

Pete is the first one to stand up out of everybody, his face one of complete and utter shock. "What did you just say?"

"I said he moved his fingers and when I asked him if he could hear me, he moved his fingers again in response to my question!"

Will, Zack, Ben and Stacey start to hug each other, the sheer relief on their faces clear to see.

"My boy," says Pete, pushing past me in desperation to get to his son.

"I'll get the doctor," says Ben, running across the corridor to call for some assistance.

Seconds later, a male doctor and two nurses dash past us and into Jonny's room, closing the door behind them. Another nurse joins us a moment later, guiding all of us into one of the side rooms where we face an agonising wait.

"I wanted to be in there when he woke up," I whisper, feeling disappointed.

Stacey wraps a comforting arm around me. "You'll see him soon enough, Lauren. I promise."

Squeezing her hand, I say, "I hope he's waking up, Stace, because I can't take another second of him lying there motionless. I just can't."

"He'll wake up, Lauren. I can feel it. You seeing his hand moving is a good sign. A really good sign."

"But what if it's just his reflexes or something? Maybe I just wanted him to wake up so badly that I imagined it?" *Did I imagine it?* No, Jonny was responding to my voice by moving his fingers. So he must know I'm here. Oh, I hope to god he knows I'm here.

CHAPTER 4

LAUREN

Over an hour later, and after what feels like an age, the male doctor finally comes back to talk to us. Ben, Stacey, Will, Zack and I wait with baited breath as the doctor walks into our room. Closing the door behind him, he approaches us slowly. His face is serious but then, he is a doctor after all. Unless it's bad news. Oh, please don't let it be bad news.

"Is he awake?" I ask the doctor, desperate for an answer, "oh, please tell us he's awake."

The doctor looks between all five of us before finally nodding his head. "I'm pleased to tell you that yes, Jonny is awake." I almost drop to the floor with relief, tears of joy springing from my eyes as Stacey cuddles me against her that little bit tighter. "Jonny's father has asked that I update you on his condition…"

"His condition?" I ask, feeling suddenly concerned, "what condition? Is he okay? Can he remember things?"

Thankfully, the doctor is quick to reassure me. "I apologise, I simply meant that his father wanted me to give you all an update on Jonny and I can tell you that from what we have seen so far, the signs are good. He remembers his name, his date of birth, his address. He remembers what he does for a living and the names of his family members and friends…"

"So, that's good, right?" asks Ben, fishing for more information. "That means he's going to make a full recovery?"

"It's early days yet, and we need to conduct more tests, brain scans and such, but for now, he seems to be answering every question correctly that we have asked of him so far…his mental state however is another matter entirely…"

"His…mental state?" I ask, feeling sick with worry.

The doctor falls silent for a brief moment before speaking again. "Jonny is in here because he attempted to take his own life, and he remembers exactly why he is in here…and that he failed at his attempt…"

"Oh shit," I whisper, feeling anguished, "when he woke up, I didn't even think about the fact that he would…remember that. Is…is he…okay?" My question is so feeble under the circumstances but I, along with every other person in this room, was so desperate for Jonny to wake up that we didn't even stop to consider how his mental state would be when he woke up.

"Jonny is extremely tired and weak and needs a lot of love and support to get him through these next few crucial days and then in the coming weeks. His rehabilitation is going to be a lengthy process and one that will ultimately require his input, but he'll only get better if he wants to get better…"

"We'll be here for him, whatever he needs…" I say, feeling desperate.

Holding up his hand, the doctor then says, "Primarily, Jonny's care ultimately lies with his next of kin, his father…"

Ben shakes his head. "Nope. No way, he ain't fit to…"

"Not now," mutters Will, scowling over at Ben. Ben is about to respond but the doctor continues.

"As I said, his father is his next of kin and all the care arrangements for Jonny will go through him, until Jonny is mentally strong enough to make decisions for himself..."

My god, this is worse than I thought. Far worse. If Pete gets his claws back into Jonny by making decisions for him on his behalf then he could prove to be a massive influence over his son. Meaning that I may have zero chance of ever being allowed to see Jonny ever again.

This is like the worst part of our history repeating itself. It's like Manchester all over again. When Jonny was kept locked up in that awful rehabilitation centre meaning that Pete got his chance to send me away out of his son's life for good. He's going to do this to me again. I know he is. But then, I thought I saw a glimmer of something in Pete earlier. Something that made me think that maybe, just maybe, he might change his mind about me. Perhaps it's a long shot me thinking that but right now, I will take any positive thought I can.

"Please can we at least see Jonny, now that he's awake?" I ask in desperation.

The doctor shakes his head. "That isn't my decision I'm afraid. It's really up to his father, however, at this early stage, I would advise limited visitations to begin with."

"So, we can't see him?" snaps Ben, turning angry, "we can't go in and see our best friend?"

The doctor grimaces. "I'm sorry, now you must excuse me, I really must get back to my patient and then I have other patients to attend to also."

Will extends his hand to the doctor and he takes it gratefully. "Thank you," says Will, "thank you to you and your team for everything that you've done for our friend." The doctor nods his thanks and then exits the room, closing the door behind him.

A subdued silence surrounds us all, each of us in shock at

the afternoon's events. What should be a happy occasion has now turned sour and whether it remains sour is all down to one man. The one man who has made my life a misery twice over. The question is, will he make my life a misery for a third time, or will he finally find something within himself to allow me back into his son's life. To allow us all back in. His friends, his bandmates, his family. His love. Well, I was his love. In all honesty, I'm not too sure how Jonny would react to seeing me again.

"But know this, Lauren. Know this, because it's the last thing I am ever going to say to you...this will be the last time you ever leave me because I will never allow you to do this to me ever again..."

The last words Jonny said to me echo loudly in my mind. He said he would never allow me to do that to him ever again. Which means he hates my guts and will never want me back in his life again. Ever. I let out a weary sigh and allow Stacey to pull me in for a proper hug this time. She hushes me gently as the lads stand around us in silence. Even Ben is silent. And his silence speaks volumes. We have been defeated by Pete and we know it, and, like it or not, we're going to have to accept that defeat for the sake of Jonny's recovery. For now anyway.

Another moment of silence passes between us all and then suddenly, the door to our room opens and in walks Pete. I turn to face him as he strolls calmly into the room. Looking between every single one of us, Pete's gaze finally comes to rest on me. "Jonny is..." Pete swallows hard, almost like he's finding it difficult to say the words. My stomach plummets to the floor.

"What is it? Has something happened? Has he fallen into a coma again?" I ask, fearing the worst.

Pete frowns at me. "No, it isn't that..." Pete pauses for a moment, clearing his throat nervously. Jeez, I don't think I've seen Pete look like this ever before in my life.

"Fuck, man, just spit it out!" snaps Ben.

Another nervous clearing of his throat and then Pete says, "Jonny is asking to see you, Lauren." *Oh my word.* I feel as though I've just had the stuffing knocked out of me. Jonny is asking to see me? Pete's told him that I'm here?

"How did he...did you..." I can barely form the words to string a sentence together, that's how taken aback I am. Just a moment ago I feared I may be wrenched away from him all over again but now, he's asking to see me. He *wants* to see me.

Pete shakes his head. "I had nothing to do with this...Jonny asked for you because...he already knew that you were here."

I look around at everybody in shock. Turning back to Pete I say, "He...heard me talking to him...earlier?"

Clearly uncomfortable at this turn of events, Pete reluctantly nods his head at me. "Yes...he heard you, and now he's asking to see you, but be warned, Lauren, when you go in there and see him, just...tread gently." I take offence at that.

"What is that supposed to mean?"

Pete narrows his eyes on me. "It means that he's fragile, Lauren. He's frail and weak and his head is all over the place. He's also very much aware of what he tried and failed to do so please just...handle him with care."

Pete Mathers may be a lot of things but right now, he's genuine. He's genuinely heartbroken over what's happened to his son. He may be able to hide most things from most people but it's clear to me now that he's hurting. And he's hurting badly. Pete's walls are beginning to break down and it's only a matter of time before they crumble to the floor completely.

Pete didn't need to come into this room to tell me that his

son wants to see me. He could have made Jonny believe that he dreamt of me being here in this hospital. He could have then sent me away all over again. But he hasn't. For the first time in his life he's doing the right thing and I'm thankful. So very thankful that I can't even begin to put into words how thankful I am.

"I...I'm...thank you..." That's all I can manage to say. Pete simply gives me a nod of acknowledgement and then stands to one side, allowing me to pass.

"We'll be right here waiting for you, Lauren," says Stacey, giving my arm a gentle squeeze, "good luck." I smile through my sudden pang of nerves. Nerves over how Jonny will react to seeing me again. How his mental state will be and if he'll even want me in his life again.

"Thanks, Stace," I say quietly.

As I walk out into the corridor and over to the door of Jonny's hospital room, I take a deep breath in, mentally preparing myself for what I'm about to face. I try to focus on the fact that Jonny is awake and remembering things. I also try to keep in my mind's eye that Jonny will go on to make a full recovery because of the amazing support network he has around him. Blowing out a long breath, I finally muster up the courage to turn the handle.

****

As I walk through into Jonny's hospital room, making sure to close the door behind me so that we can have some privacy, my stomach begins doing somersaults. I swear it literally takes everything I have inside of me to muster up the courage to turn around and see him. And boy when I do see him, when I first set eyes on him, sitting up in his bed, his dark eyes fluttering open as I make my cautious approach towards him, I almost fall to pieces.

Tears begin to prick at the back of my eyes as I try my best to hold myself together. Because all I want to do right now is throw myself at him and tell him how much I love him and how sorry I am for leaving him when he needed me the most. I want to hold him and comfort him and tell him how relieved I am that he's finally back with us in this world again. I also want to tell him the truth about absolutely everything. But I can't. Not yet. Jonny is far too fragile to hear any of that right now, which is why I am afraid. Afraid of how he's going to react to me being back in his life after abandoning him for a second time.

As I reach the chair by the side of his bed, I look down at Jonny and our eyes meet for the first time in over four months. My heart skips a million beats, his dark brown eyes gazing up into my blue ones. I almost have to pinch myself to believe that this is really happening, that Jonny is really awake and looking up at me from his hospital bed.

He doesn't look very well though. I can see that now. When he was lying here unconscious and in a coma, he looked almost normal and healthy, but now that his eyes are wide open and staring up at me, I can see how much pain he's actually in. Mental pain. The pain of knowing what he tried to do to himself but failed to do. Jonny's pale skin, coupled with the black circles beneath his eyes, make him look tired and world weary, almost like a shadow of his former self. And that makes me feel so sad. So wretched, that I can't hold back the tears for a minute longer. They fall, unbidden, down my cheeks as Jonny looks on.

"I'm sorry," I whisper. Those are my first words to Jonny. My first two words after four months of nothing. And right now, I'm not so sure what I'm saying sorry for. For hurting him and leaving him again? Or for breaking down and crying in front of him when he needs me to be strong? It takes a long moment before Jonny finally opens his mouth to speak to me.

"What are you sorry for?" he asks, his voice sounding a little croaky.

Deliberately breaking eye contact with him, I bite down on my wobbly bottom lip to try and stop myself from sobbing out loud. "Just know that I'm sorry for everything, Jonny," I whisper, "for crying in front of you right now when you need me to be strong, and for…abandoning you again…"

I let out a small sob and collapse into the chair next to Jonny's bed. Placing my face in my hands, I try and hide my tears well away from his penetrating gaze but it's pointless. I've done the very thing I promised myself I wouldn't do, and it's pathetic. *I'm* pathetic.

"Why are you here in LA, Lauren?"

Jonny's question both surprises and hurts me in equal measure, but I suppose I more than deserve it. Hell, I even half expected it. I am, after all, one part of why he's even in here and I deserve to be punished for my actions. But Jonny needs to know the whole truth, about everything. But not yet. He needs to be so much stronger than he is to hear what I have to say, but making Jonny understand any of that is going to be difficult. Really difficult.

Meeting his gaze once more, our eyes lock for a long moment and my chest constricts, my breath catching in my throat. I am so desperate to reach out and hold his hand. To kiss him and touch him and love him. But I don't. Because I'm terrified. Terrified of what his reaction might be. And so I stay seated in my chair with my fingers knotted together instead. "I'm here because I love you, Jonny, and…when I heard about what happened to you…I…"

"Felt guilty?"

"No," I say, shaking my head, "well, yes, I felt guilty but that's not..."

"So you came here out of guilt because you thought somehow or other it would relieve your conscience when I eventually woke up?" asks Jonny, quickly becoming irate. "And what if I hadn't woken up, Lauren? What then? What if I'd have gotten my wish and ended it? Would you have still felt guilty? Felt guilty for the rest of your days?"

"Don't say those things, Jonny," I say through my tears, "I can't even bear to think about that, never mind hear you say it out loud."

"Believe me, Lauren, the pain that you're *apparently* feeling for me is nothing to how I feel inside right now."

"I know it isn't, and it'll never be anywhere near to how you're feeling, but know this, Jonny, there's no *apparently* when it comes to you. I came here because I love you. Always have. Always will. It's *that* simple."

Jonny blinks at me, seemingly unaffected by what I just said. "Real love doesn't abandon you twice in one lifetime, Lauren."

"Jonny, please..."

"Which is why I'd really like you to leave now."

I look on at him in despair, tears still streaming down my cheeks. "Please don't send me away. You woke up from your coma when you heard my voice earlier, that can't be a coincidence..."

"I don't want you here," snaps Jonny, wincing slightly. I immediately panic.

"Are you okay?" I ask, automatically reaching out for his hand. He snatches it away from my grip and sighs heavily, his eyes closing briefly.

"I just wanted to punish you for what you did to me, Lauren…and now I have. So you can go now."

Swiping more tears away from my cheeks, I say, "But…I need to tell you why I left you. I need to tell you the real reason why."

"So tell me why," Jonny sighs, closing his eyes properly this time, as if he's completely disinterested in anything more I have to say.

"Well that's just it, I can't tell you…yet. You need to be stronger before…"

"Same old Lauren," says Jonny, opening up his eyes once more to look over at me. "Same shit, different day."

I shake my head at him. "No it isn't. I swear to you it isn't. You just need to get stronger first…"

"I don't want to get stronger, and I don't want to see you ever again, so close the door on your way out." Jonny turns away from me, resting his head against his pillow before closing his eyes again.

And as much as it kills me inside to do it, I do as he asks of me. I don't want to upset him any more than I already have done, but I make sure I say one final thing to him before I leave. "I love you, Jonny, and I will tell you the truth one day, even if you don't want to hear it…just don't forget that I love you."

Jonny doesn't even react to that statement, instead remaining motionless on his hospital bed with his eyes closed, his head turned away from me.

With a heavy heart, I stand up and walk slowly away from the love of my life. But not for the last time. Because I'll be back for Jonny, whether he wants me to come back for him or not, because I will not go down without fighting for him, for us, and I will not walk away from him ever again.

****

The next week passes slowly on by, the sheer torture of Jonny refusing point blank to see me almost finishing me off completely. It's nothing less than I deserve but, knowing that everybody else around me is allowed in to visit him, even if it's just for a few minutes at a time, is nothing less than gut wrenching agony.

According to the lads, he's making slow but steady progress day by day, becoming more alert and aware of his surroundings and less sleepy than he was to begin with. He's eating and drinking as he should be and all of his tests have come back clear, showing no permanent damage has been done. The only damage as far as everybody around him can see is the mental state he is currently in. Apparently, Pete has been talking about sending Jonny back to rehab but, Jonny has refused to go, and his doctors agree. Thank god. Because the last thing Jonny needs is to go back to rehab.

What Jonny needs right now and what the doctors have advised him to have, is counselling. Whether it's grief counselling to support him after the loss of his mum, counselling for the mental trauma he's currently experiencing following his suicide attempt, or both, Jonny has, yet again, refused all help. Meaning that both doctors and his family and friends alike are feeling sick with worry. Especially as Jonny has been told that he may be allowed home at the beginning of December, which is only two weeks away.

I can't imagine Jonny being anywhere near ready to go home in as little as two weeks, but once the doctors feel as though he is physically fit enough to be discharged, Jonny will be allowed to go home. On the stipulation that somebody stays with him when he gets home. That somebody being Jonny's dad. Meaning that any chance of me getting even remotely close to him over the next few weeks is pretty much zero to none.

I sigh heavily as I continue to watch the video of me and Jonny singing karaoke together in the pub we visited when we stayed in Yorkshire with Ben and Stacey back in July. I found it on one of Reclamation's online fan pages and I keep playing it over and over again. It both comforts and depresses me in equal measure. Seeing how happy we once were after being given a second chance together, only to have me rip it all apart again barely a week later. An errant tear falls from my cheek on to the screen of my mobile phone and I wipe it quickly away, fed up with myself for crying all of the time.

"You really need to stop watching that," says Stacey, plonking herself down on the sun lounger next to mine. "And you really shouldn't be out here at such a ridiculous hour. You do realise it's two o'clock in the morning?"

I sniff loudly. "At least I have an excuse. What's your excuse for being up at this unearthly hour of the morning?"

"Erm, do you really want to know?"

"Actually, no, I don't want or need to know anything, although at a guess, I'd say Ben has a lot to do with it."

Stacey clears her throat. "Anyway, moving on."

"Yes, please do," I say, feeling a stab of pain in my chest as I watch Jonny smiling down at me lovingly on the video. He then kisses me in front of the entire crowd of people around us in the pub and they all begin to wolf whistle and clap, cheering us on to sing more songs. Which we did. It was such a happy day. A day I'll treasure forever.

"Oh, Lauren, please stop torturing yourself with that video and please come back inside. It's far too dark and cold to be out here in the garden. And lonely."

"The swimming pool is lit up and looks beautiful, and for your information, I'm not cold or lonely."

Resting her head back on her sun lounger, she says, "You're right, you're not lonely." Taking a hold of my hand, she gives it a gentle squeeze. "Because I would never allow you to ever be lonely...but you aren't doing yourself any favours by being out here on your own. You're out here wallowing and wallowing is not good."

Prising my hand away from her grip, I shut off the video and then lie back on my sun lounger. "So what if I am wallowing? If it was you in my situation, you'd be doing exactly the same thing as me and don't pretend otherwise."

"Yes, I suppose I would be doing the same thing as you are, but please keep in mind that when Jonny goes home..."

"He still won't want to see me and then his dad will be living with him, making it even harder for me to see him, and..."

"Jonny has his own mind, Lauren, and despite what he's been through and his current mental state, he will not be forced into anything by anybody, especially his dad."

"But his dad can make decisions for Jonny on his behalf, the doctor said so last week when Jonny woke up."

"Ben's already told you that the doctors have only advised that just in case Jonny struggles with making decisions himself. At this moment in time, Jonny is not struggling to make any decisions, as you well know."

I let out an exasperated sigh. "Yes, I know all of that, but I still can't help but fear Pete, of the influence he potentially has over Jonny when Jonny is still so vulnerable."

"Dare I say it but Pete has been quite accommodating since Jonny came out of his coma last week."

"That's the guilt starting to come through, Stace. I saw it all over his face last week when I saw him at the hospital. All this stuff that's happened with Jonny, and losing Judy before that, I think it's affected him far more than even he realises."

Stacey sighs. "Yeah well, I don't really care how he feels, he deserves to feel guilty for the stuff he's done, and a whole lot more to boot."

Turning towards Stacey, I say, "I just want to look after Jonny, and I want to tell him the truth about everything."

Reaching for my hand again, Stacey says, "I'm not sure when, but soon, you'll get your chance to tell him everything. I promise."

"God, I hope so," I whisper, "I truly hope so."

CHAPTER 5

JONNY

I stand on the threshold of my house, wondering whether or not I can take the first step inside. I call it a house because this place is no longer a home to me, if it was ever a home at all. Because a home is where your heart is, where your family are, a place of love and warmth and above all, happiness. No, this house is not my home. And it never really was.

"Jonny? You okay?" My dad walks into the house of horrors and quickly places my hospital bag down in the hallway before returning to my side in the doorway. "You feeling light headed again?"

I feel his hand come to rest on my shoulder, but all I can do is stare into the empty void that is my home, almost like I'm fearfully waiting for it to swallow me up all over again. Just like it did the last time. I shudder at the memories of what went on in here before I....

"Son? Do you need me to take you back to the hospital?"

My dad offering to take me back to that hospital is more than enough to snap me out of my depressing reverie. Like an actor slipping his stage mask back into place, I turn to my dad and turn on the usual Jonny attitude. "No fucking way am I going back to that place. I'm fine. I was just…thinking of the state this place must be in…after what happened…"

"I took care of all that, son. This place is shiny and new again thanks to the team of people I got in to clean it all up."

I immediately go on the defensive. "You got a clean up crew in here? What if they…"

"They won't squeal to the papers, don't worry, that's all been taken care of too. Trust me."

My dad walks back into my house with a smug smile on his face, looking ever so pleased with himself that he really has everything figured out. He waits for me in the hallway, forcing me to finally move my feet and take my first steps into the very place where I really don't want to be.

My dad did offer to have me stay over at his place but that's not even an option in my mind. I haven't been there since before my mum died and there's no way I could go there now. I can't even think about my mum never mind stay at the home she once lived in with my dad. Which is why I had to come back here. To face the music and the harsh reality of what my life has become.

Closing the door behind me, I'm met with an eerie silence from the house, and yet more staring from my dad. "Will you quit with the staring and just be normal?" I snap.

My dad shrugs his shoulders at me. "I'm just worried about you, that's all."

I sigh. "Look, I said I'm fine and I'm fine so let's just leave it at that, shall we?"

My dad gives me a wry smile. "I'm glad to see your fiery personality is still intact."

"And don't forget it," I mutter.

"So, do you want me to carry the bag upstairs for you?" he asks.

I roll my eyes at him. "I think I can just about manage to carry my own bag upstairs, Dad, but thanks all the same."

Picking up the bag, I make my way over to the bottom of the stairs as my dad heads toward the kitchen.

"I'll get a pot of coffee on."

"Yep, you do that," I mutter under my breath, resisting the urge to throw him out right here and now.

I know I sound like I'm being ungrateful, but since I woke up from my coma, my dad has been pretty unbearable. Suffocating in fact. Which is not like my dad at all. It's almost like he's had a personality transplant or something. Mind you, I suppose I did give him the biggest fright of his life by doing what I did....

Another shudder moves through me as I think back to that night when I finally hit rock bottom. I try to shake away the memory but as I reach the top of my stairs and begin to cross the landing towards my bedroom, I feel a chill run down my spine. My heartbeat spikes, blood rushing through my ears as I push open my bedroom door to find that...everything is back to normal.

Brand new dark grey bedding adorns my king size bed in the middle of my room and all my clothing and whatever else that had been left scattered around on the carpet is now gone. In fact, I think my dad's had my bedroom re-carpeted.

Bending down, I brush my hands over the carpet to discover that yes, he's definitely had my bedroom re-carpeted while I've been in hospital. It's the exact same expensive light grey coloured carpet as the original, but I can tell by the pile that it's brand new. I dread to think what the old carpet looked like when he found me lying on it that morning....

I feel my head spin as images of that night begin to flash up in my mind. I take a few deep breaths in to try and calm myself but fuck, being back here in this very room where it all happened is messing with my head far more than I thought it would. In fact, I don't think I can stay in here. Not in my bedroom anyway. I'll stay in one of the other bedrooms for now. Trouble is, there isn't a room in this godforsaken house that hasn't been tainted with my sordid past. Well, all except one room actually. My favourite room of all. My music studio.

Dumping my bag at the foot of my bed, I then dash over to my bedside cabinet and pull open the top drawer. Grabbing the small silver key from the back of the drawer, I then slam it shut and head back downstairs.

Walking over to the door of my studio, I insert the key into the lock. Turning it slowly, I then cautiously open the door. My eyes instantly find my Steinway grand piano, the sunlight just catching it at the right angle, the black polished surface gleaming brightly, almost like it's calling out to me.

Stepping into my studio, I feel an immediate calm settle over me as I take in absolutely everything I love about this room. The piano taking centre stage in the middle of the room, the desk sitting next to the large window in the top left corner that is currently piled high with notepads, pens and scraps of paper. My shelves on the back wall are littered with books upon books on every music composition you could possibly imagine, and my many guitars line almost the entire length of the right wall, placed ever so intricately in their stands with my keyboard standing amongst them. Yes, this room is, and always has been, my happy place. My calm in the many storms that have battered me over the years.

I walk over to my piano and rest the fingers of my right hand on the keys. Closing my eyes, I try to get a feel for the musical instrument that was, not so long ago, almost like an extension of me. I tinkle with the keys playfully, trying my utmost to conjure up the many colours and images in my mind that took flight whenever I played this beautiful instrument.

Opening my eyes once more, I decide that tinkling with the

keys isn't enough. I simply have to play it and find out if my worst fear has been realised. The fear that I may not be able to play the piano like I used to. The fear of picking up my guitar and not remembering the strings. Or worse still, being unable to remember how to write or read music. In my mind, I can still play my musical instruments. In reality, I might not have a fucking clue. The doctors said it might happen. Despite the scans of my brain coming back clear, they still said it is common for people who have been in comas to experience bouts of memory loss. For people to perhaps have to re-learn something that they once upon a time knew like the back of their hand. Like playing the piano.

I sit down on the stool and rest both my hands on the keys this time. Closing my eyes, I think long and hard about what piece of music to play, so hard that I end up giving myself a headache. *Perhaps I'm trying this too soon.* I shake my head. *No, like fuck it's too soon, this piano is a part of me and I will not be beaten by my fear.*

Another few minutes roll on by, my mood taking a downward spiral, but then suddenly from nowhere, I begin to play. I play a piece of music that I remember playing for the first time to a girl I once loved. A girl I still love. With all my fucking heart and soul. Tchaikovsky's Swan Lake. A ballet that Lauren loved so very much. The very ballet that inspired her to be a dancer from when she was just a little girl.

When she realised that ballet dancing wasn't quite for her, she went down the professional dancing route instead, and boy was she good at it. Exceptional in fact. I can see her now in my mind's eye, dancing right here in front of me on this piano top as my fingers flit across the keys at lightning speed. Her passion for dancing ignited my already burning passion for music. She was like the fuel to my fire that I needed so badly. So very badly.

I wince at the pain that flashes across my chest that happens whenever I think about Lauren, my fingers pressing down on the keys that little bit harder. I can't think about Lauren anymore without feeling in pain. And the trouble is, she invades my thoughts constantly. And knowing that she's still over here in LA is doing me no good at all. She hurt me twice over and I can't allow her back into my life again to do it for a third time. Which is why I can't see her again. Ever. *But I want to see her, so fucking badly that it's killing me inside.*

"Oh, there you are."

I rip my fingers away from the piano keys immediately, my eyes flashing open to see my dad standing in the doorway of my studio. "You scared the shit out of me," I grumble.

My dad strolls into the room. "I see you've reacquainted yourself with your piano," he says cheerily, pointing to the musical instrument in question. Smoothing his hand over the wooden piano top, he says, "And boy am I happy to see you play."

Feeling uncomfortable at being so closely scrutinised by my father, I push the stool away from the piano and stand up. "I could really do with a coffee and a fag right now."

I hear my dad tut as I walk past him. "Now, Jonny, you remember what the doctors said, about being more healthy, to help with your recovery…"

"Fuck that, I ain't quitting smoking for anyone." Reaching for the packet of fags in my jeans pocket, I ignore my dad and continue regardless.

My dad closes my studio door behind him as I press the cigarette between my lips. "Cigarettes are bad for you, Jonny," he says, with a look of disdain written all over his face.

"Then why do they taste so good?" I can tell that my sarcastic remark really gets my dad's back up, but he doesn't rise to it this time, instead heading towards the kitchen.

"I think it's time for that coffee I'd started making," he says, finally changing the subject.

Leaving my dad in the kitchen, I head over to the patio doors at the back of the house so I can take my bad habit outside with me. "For once, Dad, I agree with you."

****

I spend a sleepless night in my own bedroom after all, thanks to my dad and his never ending paranoia about my health and welfare. The last thing I wanted to do was to make him even more paranoid about my current mental state and so, I sucked it up and decided to stay put. In my own bed. Surrounded by my own demons. But after waking up for the third and final time at six o'clock in the morning, sheathed in sweat and shaking from yet another harrowing nightmare, I decide that enough is enough and instead head for the shower in my en-suite. The hot water soothes me as it washes away the last remnants of my horrific flashbacks, the recurring nightmares becoming more frequent and far more intense than they were just a week ago.

I'm putting that down to being back here, in the very place where it happened. It's almost like I'm re-visiting the scene of the crime by simply sleeping in my own bed. Perhaps I need to re-think about where I sleep tonight and fuck what my dad thinks about it all. Either that or I spend the next however many weeks getting fuck all sleep while my mental state continues to deteriorate. No, I seriously need to get a handle on my mental health, or at least, I need to appear to everybody around me that I have a handle on it. How I feel on the inside is another matter, but with the music career I have and the life I lead, I can't afford to be out of the limelight for very long.

That is, if our fans want me to come back into the limelight again. The fuck up I made in front of thousands of Reclamation fans back in Chicago when I was as high as a kite after my mum died is not one of my proudest moments. In fact, I'm ashamed of myself for doing it. Trouble is, I barely remember any of it. That's how off my face I was. Social media however worked its wonderful magic of reminding me exactly what I'd done on stage that night, forcing me further into the downward spiral that ultimately ended with me being admitted into hospital.

Finishing up my shower, I dry off and throw on a t-shirt and some sweatpants and head downstairs to the kitchen. I quickly make myself a strong coffee before heading outside into the back garden. It's still a little dark and fairly cool out here but I'm not bothered. I just want to sit outside in the garden by the swimming pool and collect my thoughts for a short while. Even if those thoughts are of nothing other than the shit storm that is currently my life.

Sitting myself down next to the table by the pool, I take a quick sip of my coffee before lighting up my first fag of the day. Leaning back in my chair, I close my eyes and inhale the smoke deeply into my lungs. I feel my body instantly relax as I slowly blow out the smoke from between my lips before taking another long drag.

My mind starts to drift to all thoughts of Lauren again. Just as it did last night, and the night before that, and the night before that. In fact, my mind has done nothing but drift to Lauren since I saw her in the hospital, not long after I woke from my coma. It was hearing Lauren's voice that pulled me back from the brink that day. Before that, I don't remember hearing anything at all. I only remember darkness. Pitch black nothingness that simply terrifies me whenever I think of it.

I puff on my fag that little bit harder as I try my utmost

to force my dark thoughts to the very back of my mind once more, instead focusing on my thoughts of Lauren. My girl. My angel. The angel who brought me back to life simply by just being there. By my bedside. Waiting desperately for me to wake up. And when I did wake up and finally see her, I then pushed her away. To hurt her. Deliberately.

I stub out my fag end angrily into the ashtray and then instantly reach for another one, taking a quick sip of my coffee before lighting up again. I puff away on my fag as my anger begins to bubble beneath the surface. Why the fuck did Lauren leave me all over again? Why? *Because of your past mistakes, Jonny, that's why.* I shake my head in irritation at the one woman I thought would never ever leave me. The woman who I would have sacrificed absolutely everything for. My career, my money. Fuck, I would have sacrificed my very life for her, that's how much she means…meant to me.

I shake my head again, becoming more and more irritated with my thoughts of Lauren. Because this is what she does to me. Every single time. She bewitches me. Beguiles me. She gets into my head and seeps her way into my skin, into my very blood, right through to my soul, and then she pierces my heart with a knife and then just walks away as though I meant absolutely nothing to her.

I notice my fag start to move as my fingers begin to tremble, the anger coursing through my veins like never before, almost burning its way out of the ends of my fingertips. *Get a fucking grip, Jonny, you need to keep it together.* I take another long pull on my fag.

But I can't get a grip on these feelings going on in my head right now, and that's the problem. Fuck me, what I'd give for a fix of coke right now. Just one high that will blot Lauren out of my mind and put my demons to rest temporarily. But what then? What happens when I come down from that high?

And therein lies my huge problem. I shake my head at myself, angry at my weakness. God, I'm pathetic. Totally and utterly pathetic. Stubbing out my second fag of the day, I quickly reach for another.

****

Later that morning, I'm just finishing up eating my bowl of cereal at the breakfast island in the kitchen when I hear the sound of the doorbell ringing loudly from out in the hallway. My dad is at the front door before I even get the chance to stand up from my stool.

"It's okay, son," he calls through to me from the hallway. "I'll get it."

I swear my patience with him is waning already and we've barely lived together for a day. If he isn't asking me if I'm okay every five minutes then he's filling those moments in between by doing other things to "help" with my recovery. Such as ordering in a food shop for me so that I can start on a healthier eating programme to boost my mental wellbeing, and going through my shit heap of a filing pile in the study upstairs so that he can oversee the running of the record label while I'm "otherwise engaged." Not to mention arranging a meeting for some time today with my PA, Lara, presumably to run through absolutely everything that has been neglected these past few weeks.

Yep, my dad has got everything well and truly figured out and running smoothly which leaves me to question, what the fuck am I supposed to be doing with myself while he's obsessively taking control of everything in my life? Sweet fuck all apparently, that's what. And it's driving me insane already. *He's* driving me insane.

A few minutes later, my dad walks into the kitchen, beaming from ear to ear. "You have visitors," he says, a little too cheerily for my liking. Following closely behind him are none other than Ben, Will and Zack. My band mates, my best friends, my amigos. Well, thank fuck for that, some other company other than my dad who is slowly sending me round the twist.

"Hey, dude, how's it hanging?" Ben gives me a friendly slap on the back before we bump fists.

"Not bad...all things considered." I shoot Ben a look and he frowns at me as Will moves in for a quick bump of fists, swiftly followed by Zack.

"It's good to see you at home, man," says Zack, smelling of his usual cannabis like fragrance.

Will looks between all four of us. "Hey, I just realised something. This is the first time all four of us have been in a room together since..." He hesitates slightly. "Well, you know, since before you..."

I give Will a friendly punch on the shoulder. "Yeah, I know." Will smiles. "Well, it's good to see you all," I say, and I really mean that.

Glancing over towards the archway that separates the kitchen from the hallway, I suddenly wonder if they've brought Lauren and Stacey along with them. My chest immediately tightens, as it always does whenever I think of her. Of Lauren. "So, have you three...come on your own?" I ask, trying to sound casual. But I sound far from casual. In fact, I sound pathetic. I really do need to man the fuck up and stop thinking about the one woman who's wholly responsible for reducing me to this broken down wreck in the first place.

Ben raises a suspicious eyebrow up at me. "No, it's just us three. Why?"

I shrug my shoulders. "No reason."

"Oh, really?"

"Yes," I say firmly, "*really*."

"You told her to stay away, Jonny," says Ben.

I deliberately ignore his comment and decide to quickly change the subject. "Do any of you want tea or coffee?" Turning away from them, I walk over to where the kettle is.

"Don't you worry about that, Jonny, I'll sort the drinks," says my dad, suddenly swooping in from behind me and picking up the kettle. "Do you lot want tea or coffee?" he asks, repeating my question as he fills up the kettle with water. I just about manage to bite my tongue as my dad takes control of my life all over again.

Turning back to my friends, who have all said yes to the offer of a hot drink, I give them the "Jonny look" before nodding my head towards the patio doors that lead onto the terrace outside. They wise up to my thinking immediately, my dad totally and utterly oblivious as he busies himself in the kitchen. I swear my dad has never been this domesticated ever before in his life and right now, his behaviour is actually beginning to freak me out.

It's raining outside, and a little cold, but I don't give a shit, I slide the patio doors shut with an almighty thud before turning to my friends for support.

"Jonny, are you okay?" asks Will, looking a little worried.

"Don't ask me that," I snap, "nobody out here ask me that." Pointing my finger back towards the house, I say, "I've had enough 'are you okays?' to last me a fucking lifetime already and I've been back at home for barely twenty four hours." Sliding an impatient hand through my hair, I let out an exasperated sigh. "Will somebody give me a fag already?"

"Yeah, sure," says Ben, quickly springing into action. He pulls out a packet of cigarettes from his coat pocket and I take one gratefully. Zack acts quickly with his lighter, sparking up my fag for me. I take a long pull on my fag before sinking down into one of the chairs under the sun canopy. On a day like today, it can act as my rain canopy.

The other three pull up a chair alongside mine, Ben and Zack sparking up their own fags. Will, who is the only one out of the four of us who doesn't smoke, sits back in his chair and says, "So, your dad becoming overbearing, is he?"

"Overbearing is putting it fucking mildly," I mutter. Taking another long pull on my fag, I say, "I can't even take a piss at the moment without him asking me if I'm okay." They laugh. "You lot think I'm kidding, but I'm not."

"Well, it sure is good to have you back home, Jonny, even if your dad is driving you round the bend," says Zack, chuckling to himself.

"I would say it's good to be home but, as you can see, it currently isn't."

As if on cue, my dad makes his presence known again. Sliding open the door, he then ducks back inside to retrieve the tray of hot drinks before bringing them out to us on the terrace. "You boys sure you don't want to have your drinks inside where it's warmer?"

"Nope," I state, taking a quick puff of my fag, "we're enjoying the fresh air." *And the peace*, I think to myself.

"You call puffing away on those things fresh air?" my dad says with a note of disapproval in his voice. Setting the tray of hot drinks down on the floor, my dad then starts to look round for the table that once lived out here. The very table that got trashed several weeks ago following one of my all-nighters. "Didn't you have a table out here?" he asks me.

I glare up at him. "Once upon a time, there was a table out

here. Now there isn't. The end."

My dad looks less than impressed with that sarcastic remark. "Ditch the sarcasm, son, it never did suit you."

"I beg to differ," I retort, turning away from him as I take another long drag of my cigarette.

My dad sighs loudly. "I'll pretend you didn't just say that to me and I'll go and get the table that's next to the swimming pool. Will, you want to give me a lift?"

Will stands up a little too enthusiastically for my liking and that's when I officially snap. "Will, just sit the fuck down for fuck's sake!"

"Now, Jonny," says my dad, a little too calmly, almost like he's trying to stop a toddler from having a tantrum, "there's no need…"

"Dad, will you just stop?!" I yell, finally losing it with him. Standing up from my chair, I start to gesture wildly with my hands. "You're fucking well suffocating me and controlling everything around me and I can't handle it for a minute longer so please just back off!"

I wince at the sudden shooting pain in my head and collapse back down into my chair, dropping my cigarette on to the floor as a bout of dizziness hits me from nowhere.

"Jonny? Are you okay?" My dad crouches down to the floor to try and support me but I bat his hands away.

"I'm fine," I mutter, holding my head in my hands.

"I'm calling the doctor," he says, suddenly dashing off.

"Hey, dude, you okay?" asks Will.

"I told you to stop asking me if I'm okay," I say through gritted teeth.

"Your dad means well, Jonny," says Will, "he's just worried about you. We all are."

The pain in my head thankfully soon passes and my dizziness along with it. Sitting back in my chair, I look up at all three of them and say, "It's because of my dad why that just happened. If I get stressed or angry then it brings that shit on. The doctors say it should pass with time but for now, I need to stay as relaxed and as calm as possible, but my dad and me right now?" I make a slitting of the throat gesture against my neck with my hand. "Not fucking calm." I rest my head against the back of the chair and close my eyes. "Will somebody please go and tell him to *not* ring the doctor before I commit murder."

Will goes off to find my dad, but soon returns. "Well, he didn't ring the doctor," says Will.

"Good," I reply.

"But only because Lara's just turned up at your front door." Will grimaces and I roll my eyes heavenward.

"For fuck's sake," I mutter under my breath, "could this day get any worse?"

Lara, my PA, suddenly steps out onto the terrace. Wearing her usual five inch heels, barely there dress, and a smile as fake as her tan, she comes strutting towards me like some model on a catwalk. And I absolutely one hundred percent detest the woman. Yes, she works for me and is good at her job, but as a person, Lara is as fake as they come. And if there's one thing I hate about people, particularly women, it's pretending to be something that they're not.

"Hey you," she coos, as though she knows me oh so well. Which she doesn't. Never has done and never will. Ever.

I reluctantly stand up to greet her, giving her a strained smile as she gives me her usual puppy dog eye expression before wrapping her arms around my shoulders in some sort of hug. I keep my arms right where they belong. Beside me. I never want to give Lara the wrong impression, but it never seems to make much of a difference to her. She's still far too over familiar and touchy feely with me, and now, it seems, after my stay in hospital, even more so.

"I've been sooo worried about you, Jonny," she drawls in her deep American accent. "And your dad just said you had a funny turn. Are you okay?" I shoot the lads another look of annoyance and they all turn away in unison, either grimacing or sniggering into their cups of tea and coffee.

Pulling back from the stench of Lara's nauseating perfume and her over familiarity, I somehow manage to keep a lid on my bubbling annoyance and answer her calmly. "I'm fine." My dad suddenly walks back out onto the terrace and I scowl over at him. "As I keep telling everybody around me."

"No doctor required then?" he asks cautiously.

"None required," I say, forcing a smile to my face.

"Great," he says, clapping his hands together. "So, Lara, if you want to come through to the kitchen, we can talk there."

Now, that royally pisses me off. I might still have a long recovery ahead of me but being excluded from stuff that really should include me is something else that only serves to get my back up.

"So, you two got it all covered then? The meeting I mean? A meeting that was arranged behind my back and something you told me about *after* arranging it." I look at my dad when I say that. "A meeting that you seemingly don't want me to be involved in."

Lara hesitates slightly. Looking over to my dad for support, she says, "That's not the case at all, Jonny, you're of course welcome to join us. If you're feeling up to it?"

I scratch at my cheek impatiently. "Mmm, am I up to it? Not really sure." Turning to my dad I say, "Dad, am I up to it?"

He sighs at me. "Now, son, don't get riled up again."

"I'm not riled up," I say, "guys, am I riled up?" I turn to the lads for support and they shake their heads. "See? Not riled up," I state. I turn back to Lara. "So? What gives? What's so urgent that you and my dad felt you needed to meet up together today? You know, just twenty four hours after I returned home from hospital."

Lara's fake happy face drops, her pearly white teeth now hiding behind her Botox filled lips. "Your dad just thought it would be a good idea to issue a statement to the press, that's all."

"Now, Lara, I don't think we need to…"

"No, Lara, continue with what you were saying," I say, cutting my dad off before throwing him a glare from across the terrace.

"We…thought it best to issue a statement to the press. On your behalf. Telling the fans that you're now out of hospital and are recovering well after…"

"After?" I prompt, becoming irate again.

Lara looks down to the floor. "After a long illness."

I press my index finger to my chin, pretending to ponder over their idea for a moment. "Hmm, what do you think of that then, boys? My dad and my PA concocting some bullshit story for the press regarding my welfare while I just sit back and know nothing about it?"

"Sounds like billy bullshit to me, Jonny," says Ben, looking as pissed off as I am.

Looking between Lara and my dad, I say, "You hear that? Ben thinks your story is billy bullshit." Lara bites her bottom lip as she nervously tucks a stray lock of hair behind her ear. "Which is pretty much what I think too." Scowling over at my dad, I say, "So, you weren't really meeting to catch up on the business side of things after all, were you? Instead, you thought you'd release a statement to the press about my welfare without me even knowing a damn thing about it?"

"Look, I didn't want to bother you with it, Jonny. It's far too early to bother you with shit like this but the fans need to know what's going on with their idol, and ultimately, what's going on with the future of the band."

I would say that I'm shocked at my dad for pulling a stunt like this, but I'm not. It has my dad written all over it. Trying best to keep my cool, I stroll over to my dad, look him straight in the eye and say, "Well then, as long as the fans and the media *medically* need to know all about how I am then fuck what I think, right?"

"Jonny, those paparazzi have been camped outside your front gates since yesterday morning and those vultures will not piss off until they get a statement…"

"Fuck the statement!" I snap, "and fuck the paparazzi! In fact, you know what? I'll be releasing a statement of my own, in *my* own words, in *my* own time, and when I'm god damn ready. *My* words, Dad, not yours or Lara's. *My* fucking words."

Clearing his throat, my dad then reluctantly says, "Fine."

I shake my head at him in disgust. "You know, for once, the paparazzi aren't the vultures." Pressing my index finger into his chest, I mutter, "The only vultures I can see right now are the ones circling within these four walls." Turning back towards the lads, I say, "And I'm not talking about you three." I cast a glare over at Lara and then once more at my dad before storming back inside the house. I've had enough of this shit for one day. Fuck, I've had enough of this shit to last me a lifetime.

CHAPTER 6

LAUREN

"Mmm, that smells delicious," says Stacey, referring to the huge Christmas turkey I've just removed from the oven. Pulling back the kitchen foil, I sink my spoon into the juices surrounding the bird and then drizzle them over the top of the meat, pricking it with a large two prong fork as I go along.

"It does smell yummy," I reply, "and it's looking good too, cooking nicely, but it still needs another hour or so I think. Wouldn't want to poison ourselves now, would we? Especially on Christmas Day."

"Lauren, in all the years that I've known and lived with you, you've never poisoned us once so I highly doubt you're about to start now."

Happy that my basting is done with for the moment, I cover the turkey over with kitchen foil once more and with Stacey's help, put it back in the oven to carry on cooking.

As I close the oven door, I take a step back and wipe away the sweat from my brow. "Jeez, that is one big bird. Far too big to feed just the two of us. I've gone well over the top with the size for sure."

"Don't be daft," says Stacey, "there'll be plenty of leftovers for Ben and the lads, they'll demolish that turkey when they get back tomorrow afternoon. Well, Ben will anyway. I'm not sure when we'll next see Will and Zack but when they get back from visiting their families, they'll be straight round, believe me."

Leaning back against the kitchen counter, I sigh heavily. "I'm beginning to wonder why we're even cooking a turkey and celebrating Christmas. There's nothing to celebrate. I'm still well and truly separated from Jonny and your boyfriend has gone to visit his parents, as he should be doing on Christmas Day, but even so, it just highlights even more the fact that we're well and truly alone today."

Stacey gives me a pointed stare. "Girl, we've celebrated Christmas on our own for the last nine years, why should one more year make a difference? And anyway, we've always had a lovely time together and I'm actually offended that you think we're suddenly lonely because we don't have our men in our lives today."

"I'm sorry," I say, feeling a little guilty, "I didn't mean it to come out like that. I've adored every Christmas I've ever spent with you, Stacey Kerr. You're the only family I've ever had and I don't know where I would have been without you over the years. I'm just…disappointed that my visions of the sort of Christmas I thought I would be having this year have not come to fruition, that's all."

Stacey gives my shoulder a gentle squeeze. "Yeah, I know, I had visions for that sort of Christmas too, but…well, we'll just have to make the most of it."

Taking a step backwards into the middle of the kitchen, Stacey starts to wiggle her hips in her most provocative lap dancing way, her sparkling green dress shimmering beautifully under the spotlights. "You know, I really do miss pole dancing," she says, referring to our past job.

I roll my eyes at her. "You seriously miss the Tango Man ranting and raving at us? Or worse still, him perving at us? Something that he used to do constantly?"

"I said I missed the pole dancing, Lauren, not him," she

replies, still dancing away in the middle of the kitchen.

When Jonny fell ill and I said I was coming over here to be by his bedside, Stacey didn't hesitate in quitting her job at Carnal Desires, after Frankie told her no to having any more time off work. Stacey decided there and then that it was time to tell the Tango Man to go and fuck himself good and proper and she took great pleasure in doing that. We both agreed to look for new jobs either over here, if things work out like we hope they will, or, back in London, if we both end up going back home with our tails between our legs. Although so far, I don't think Stacey will be going back to London with any tail between her legs, because the only thing that is getting between those lap dancing legs of hers at the moment is Ben Anderson. And speaking of Ben.

"You know, you are one seriously sexy red headed vixen, Miss Kerr," I say with a chuckle, "no wonder Ben keeps coming back for more."

She wiggles her eyebrows at me. "And he'll continue to keep coming back for more because I am not letting him go to any other female ever again in his life."

"And Ben knows this, does he?"

Stacey stops dancing and places a hand on her right hip. "Oh, he knows it alright. Believe me, Lauren, he knows it. In fact, he gets totally turned on by it."

"Really?" I ask, raising an eyebrow.

Stacey grins. "Hell yes, he does. Surprising I know, considering his colourful history with so many women but with me, he loves that I'm bossy and jealous because he says it's like I'm staking my claim over him and for some reason, that drives him wild."

"Mmm, somehow I feel as though I should have always

known that deep down, Ben would want to be owned by a woman. And there's no better woman on this earth to own him than you, so you stay that way, girl."

Stacey gives me a high five before pulling me in for a hug. "You see? We're doing just fine on our own right now." When she pulls back she gives me a cheeky smile. "And anyway, Jonny doesn't realise what he's missing out on by being apart from you. I mean, have you seen you?"

Grabbing a hold of both my hands, Stacey takes a step back to admire me. "If only he could see you today. That sparkling blue mini dress you're wearing makes you look *seriously* hot. I mean, could your legs get any longer? No wonder you became a lap dancer."

"Oh, very funny, I'd rather forget about that time in my life, thank you very much."

"Oh come on, we had fun along the way."

I smile. "Yes, we did. But I only had fun because of you. If it wasn't for you, I never would have stayed in that shithole."

"Me neither," says Stacey, and we giggle.

The door bell suddenly chiming loudly puts a stop to our giggling, forcing us to look at each other with puzzled faces. "Who the hell could that be?" asks Stacey, suspiciously.

I shrug my shoulders. "No idea." Walking slowly out of the kitchen and into the vast open space of Ben's entrance hall, we approach the front door cautiously. "It couldn't be a delivery, could it?" I ask.

"A delivery on Christmas Day?" says Stacey, "and anyway, how the hell could they have got past the security gates?"

Oh shit, I hadn't even thought about that. "Oh hell, somebody has got past the security gates, Stace, I really don't think we should open the door."

Stacey shoots me an amused look. "Seriously? Could you be any more ridiculous?"

"Erm, take it from somebody who's experienced more than their fair share of strangers on the other side of front doors," I say, referring to Pete Mathers turning up on our doorstep back in London.

Stacey's face drops. "Of course, sorry, I didn't think…"

When the doorbell chimes again, causing us both to jump, Stacey, for some reason, just decides to bite the bullet and open the door. "Stace, I really don't think…"

"Screw it," she says, unlocking the door.

I swear, this best friend of mine has far more balls than any man I've ever met. She's fearless and feisty and just what I need right now because unlike Stacey, I'm terrified of whoever is standing on the other side of that door. It could be some crazed fan or even paparazzi who have somehow managed to slip through the security net to get to Ben's front door. Oh hell, where are Reclamation's security team when you need them?

"Stacey, maybe we should call…"

My words are lost on Stacey as she wrenches the front door open to face our potential crazed fan head on. Our mouths drop to the floor when we see who's standing there to greet us.

"Jonny?" I almost whisper his name.

Jonny is standing there on the other side of the door looking as surprised to see us answering the door as we are to see him standing on the other side of it. Dressed in faded black jeans with rips in the knees and a figure hugging white t-shirt beneath his black leather jacket, Jonny looks so much healthier than the last time I saw him. And hot. Man does he look hot.

He's had a shave and a haircut too I notice. One that I totally approve of. He's had it shaved shorter around the sides but left it longer on top, styled into a textured quiff that I am itching to run my fingers through right now.

"Lauren," says Jonny, suddenly looking a little uncomfortable. Turning to Stacey, he nods and says, "Stacey."

"Hey, Jonny," she says, beaming brightly at him. "What brings you here?"

Honestly, Stacey is so forward sometimes. Mind you, at least she's polite about it, and I suppose, getting to the point straight away. Unlike me, who is dying to hide away behind her right now because I really don't know how to handle this sudden turn of events. Why on earth would he turn up unannounced knowing that I'm still here? And today of all days.

Clearing his throat, Jonny says, "Sorry for making you both wary, I know Ben's security code for the gate so I just let myself in these days." He falls silent for a moment and then continues. "Is Ben here? I was hoping to see him today."

Stacey grimaces. "Actually, he isn't. He went to stay with his parents last night and he's there until tomorrow so it's just me and Lauren. He didn't tell you?"

Jonny shakes his head. "No. He didn't. Although to be fair he didn't really broach the whole Christmas Day subject with me because of…well…you know why."

Stacey turns to give me a look. A look that is clearly telling me to talk to him. Glancing over at Jonny, I just about manage to muster up the courage to say something to him when he beats me to it. "Well, I better leave you both to it and get back home then. I'll…maybe see you again soon." Jonny turns to leave and Stacey elbows me in the ribs, causing me to cry out in protest.

"Sorry?" says Jonny, turning back round, "did you say something?"

Stacey and I exchange a quick look before I finally get a grip of myself and speak up. "I said stay."

Looking suspicious, Jonny slowly walks back over to us. "Stay?"

Clearing my throat, I say, "Yes, Jonny. Stay…stay and have Christmas dinner with us."

"You're cooking a Christmas dinner?" he asks in surprise.

I frown. "Yes, of course. I always cook Christmas dinner."

"And she makes *the* best Christmas dinner ever," says Stacey, really trying to sell the whole staying for Christmas dinner thing to Jonny.

Jonny glances over at me and gives me one of those looks that I've missed so much. One of those lingering looks that I feared I may never see ever again.

"Yeah, I know she does," he says quietly. "Look, I'm sorry…I didn't mean that how it sounded, I just…" Jonny sighs. "Sorry, I…I shouldn't have come here today. I should have just stayed under my rock as I originally planned to do but I had to get out of the house…" Jonny focuses his gaze on the floor and sighs again. "I just…had to get out."

"Well, now that you're here, why don't you join us?" asks Stacey.

Looking up at us, Jonny's uncertain eyes lock with mine once more and I suddenly go to shit in front of him. "Look, Jonny, you don't need to stay if you don't want to. I know things are still awkward between us and I know how today must be for you and I don't want to…"

"I'll stay," he suddenly says, taking me completely by surprise. So much so that I fall instantly silent. "I'd really like to stay," he says, giving me that lingering look once more.

Gulping down my sudden pang of nerves, all I can do is continue to gaze over at him. Gaze over at him and wonder what on earth I have done to deserve this amazing thing happen to me today.

"Sooo," says Stacey, finally breaking the silence, "do you want to come in or stand outside on the doorstep for the rest of the day staring at Lauren?"

Oh my word, could she be any more direct? I so want to kill her right now for saying that. I decide to kill her with my eyes instead. Thankfully, Jonny ignores Stacey's comment, instead managing an awkward smile before stepping inside.

Stacey mouths the words 'Oh my god' to me before stepping inside and closing the door behind us. Oh my god indeed. How today will turn out I have no idea but either way, Jonny is here and he's decided to stay and have Christmas dinner with us, and right now, that's all I can ask for.

****

Jonny follows Stacey and I into the kitchen, Stacey eyeballing me the entire way. In the end I have to force myself to break eye contact with her for fear that Jonny will latch on to our silent conversation. "So, do you want a drink?" Stacey asks Jonny.

"That depends on the drink," says Jonny, "if you're offering me alcohol then I'll have to politely decline."

"You don't want alcohol on Christmas Day?" asks Stacey in mock disgust, "oh come on, Jonny, everyone has to have at least one tipple on Christmas Day."

Before Jonny gets a chance to speak, I leap to his defence.

"Back off, Stace. Jonny has driven here remember and he doesn't need to drink if he doesn't want to. Right?"

I direct my question at Jonny and he nods in agreement. "Lauren's right. I'm driving, and to be brutally honest…I haven't drunk alcohol at all since I came home from hospital. The doctors thought it best I lay off it for a while to aid my recovery."

Stacey and I fall silent, both feeling awkward at the sheer mention of his time in hospital. *Great way to put your foot in it, Stace.* Jonny sees how uncomfortable we are and is quick to reassure us. "But I'm allowed to drink alcohol now I've had the all clear, so I may just have that 'tipple' as you call it, Stacey, with my dinner. That okay?" he asks, trying to lighten the atmosphere once more.

I roll my eyes at him. "You don't need to ask for Stacey's permission, Jonny."

Stacey scowls down at me. "Erm, actually he does need to ask," she says in jest, "because I am the one in charge of the booze after all. It's my job for today. Well, that, and loading the dishwasher after the meal."

Jonny breaks out into a grin and my stomach flips. Seeing him smile after all these weeks without seeing him at all is wonderful. So bloody wonderful that my chest aches with the feeling. God, I feel suffocated by him already. Suffocated by my depth of feelings for him that I can barely breathe. So much so that I find myself having to turn away from him. I go over to the oven to pretend I'm checking on the turkey once more.

"Turkey smells delicious by the way," says Jonny from behind me.

"It does, doesn't it?" says Stacey in agreement.

Clearing my throat nervously, I turn back towards Jonny and

give him a small smile. "Thank you. I just hope it tastes as good as it smells."

He smiles right back at me, turning my insides to mush. Quickly turning back to the oven, I try my best efforts to concentrate on anything other than Jonny, but it's difficult, especially when he's watching my every move. Holy shit, I suddenly wish I wasn't wearing this overly clingy mini dress to dinner now. Why the hell did I choose to wear this today? I mean, it wasn't as if we were going out on the town or anything. Just staying in sitting around a table and eating dinner. But Stacey and I have always glammed ourselves up on Christmas Day, hence the sparkling clingy mini dresses we bought for ourselves when we went shopping together earlier this week.

Oh well, nothing I can do about my choice of dress now, and anyway, Jonny turning up on our doorstep today was a complete and utter surprise. A shock actually. The best shock I've ever had in my life, but right now, I'm feeling all sorts of feelings and emotions again which I've tried so hard to bury over these last few weeks. Weeks of Jonny point blank refusing to see or even speak to me. And now, here he is, standing in Ben's kitchen with both me and Stacey, about to eat Christmas dinner with us. It's all very confusing and overwhelming but I need to get a handle on myself and just deal with the situation. I need to enjoy the moment and whatever today brings. If Jonny wants to spend time in my company then that is a positive step in the right direction. It may mean something but it may mean nothing at all. Either way, I'm going to enjoy the precious time I get with him today. Starting with serving up this three course Christmas dinner I have slaved over for the past few hours.

"Right, Stace, if you could get the champagne glasses out and put them on the table and then help me make the prawn cocktail starters then that would be great. Once they're done then the turkey should be ready and it can rest for a bit before carving."

"Yes, boss," says Stacey, waltzing off with the champagne glasses.

"So, you're having champagne?" asks Jonny.

Closing the oven door once more, I turn back to Jonny and smile. "Yes. Stacey went all out and bought a really expensive one this year too." Blowing a stray curl away from my face, I then say, "But you don't have to drink any if you don't want to, Jonny. Don't start drinking again just to please Stacey…"

"Lauren, I'm not an alcoholic."

"I know you're not," I say with a frown, "I just meant…"

"I know what you meant," he says quietly, and then sighs. "Sorry, didn't mean to go on the defensive."

"Don't apologise. It's fine."

Blowing out a breath, he says, "I guess I'm just worried that if I start drinking again, it might lead to other stuff, even though drinking was never the problem for me. It was the other shit that was the problem."

"I know."

A moment later, Jonny says, "Oh fuck it, I'll have some champagne with my meal."

"You sure?"

Jonny nods. "Yeah, I'm sure. It's Christmas Day after all and one drink won't hurt, will it?"

I smile. "Stacey will be so pleased."

"Stacey will be so pleased with what?" asks Stacey, breezing back into the kitchen.

"That Jonny has decided to have a glass of your *very* expensive champagne with his meal."

"And I should think so too," she says, making Jonny smile once more. Turning back to me, she says, "Right, girl, I'm all yours, what do you want me to do next?"

****

The atmosphere around the dinner table as all three of us tuck into our Christmas dinner a short while later is relaxed and happy. The Christmas music is playing softly in the background and we even pull a few crackers. After enjoying our prawn cocktail starters and a glass of champagne each, we then start on our main course of turkey and all the trimmings and I have to say, even though I cooked it, I really have done a pretty good job of it this year. Even if I do say so myself.

"God, this turkey just melts in your mouth," says Stacey, before making a small moan of pleasure.

I laugh. "*That* good, is it?"

"Mmm, soooo good," she says, and then she giggles.

Jonny smiles at Stacey's enthusiastic reaction to my Christmas dinner. "Well, I might not be moaning with pleasure right now like Stacey is, but I agree with her, this dinner you've cooked today is amazing, Lauren." Mmm, Jonny moaning with pleasure, what I would give to hear that right now. *Okay Lauren, get a grip!*

I smile at Jonny. "Thank you, I'm glad you're enjoying it."

"And speaking of enjoyment," says Stacey, as she retrieves the bottle of champagne from the bucket of ice she placed it in earlier, "how about another glass of champagne, Jonny?"

Jonny frowns, his hesitation over whether he should be drinking more alcohol or not written all over his face. He opens his mouth to speak, just as his mobile phone starts ringing. "Sorry," he mutters, before fumbling about in the pocket of his jeans to retrieve his phone. Looking down at the mobile phone in his hands, his frown deepens.

Not wanting to be nosy but naturally slightly worried, I ask gently, "Everything okay?"

Clearing his throat nervously, Jonny continues to stare down at his mobile for a moment before finally pressing his finger to the screen to cancel the call. "It was my dad," he says quietly, "ringing me for about the tenth time today." Pressing his finger on one of the side buttons, Jonny holds it in for a few seconds before the phone switches off.

"You've turned it off?" I ask, surprised.

"Yep," he says with a sigh, "I've turned it off." Looking over at me, he says, "And you know what? It feels good." Turning to look at Stacey, Jonny then says, "And yes to your answer of having another glass of champagne please, Stacey."

Stacey grins. "That's more like it." Stacey refills Jonny's glass right to the brim.

"So, your dad's become a bit…overbearing has he?" I ask him.

Jonny picks up his glass and says, "Overbearing is putting it mildly. *Suffocating* is probably the more appropriate word to describe him since I came out of hospital. In fact, now I've switched off my phone he'll probably have the police out looking for me next, you watch." Jonny takes a large gulp of champagne from his glass as Stacey continues to refill both my glass, and hers.

"Maybe you should tell him where you are then, just in case…"

"No way," says Jonny with a firm shake of his head, "no fucking way is he spoiling my day. Especially not today."

Placing his champagne glass back down on to the table, Jonny then picks up his cutlery and proceeds to carry on eating his food in silence, putting a swift end to that conversation.

I can feel the change in atmosphere already, Jonny bristling with tension at the sudden elephant in the room. It was always the same between those two, especially where our relationship was concerned. I lost count of the number of rows we had over Jonny being at loggerheads with his father, either over something unpleasant he'd said about me, or the fact that he was constantly interfering in Jonny's life one way or another. I always tried to see the reasoning behind Pete's actions so that I could keep the peace between father and son, but Jonny always saw that as me taking his father's side instead of his. Which was completely untrue. I was always on Jonny's side. I still am. And I always will be.

In an attempt at trying to get the happy atmosphere back from just moments ago, I raise my glass in a toast, just as the beautiful lyrics of Coldplay's Christmas Lights begin to play over the sound system. Lyrics that resonate so much with all of us right now. About fighting and tears, about how it doesn't quite feel like Christmas and how they want to bring their loved one back to them. This is one of my all-time favourite Christmas songs and how very appropriate that this song has started to play, just as I am about to make a toast. A special toast to remember our loved ones who have gone, but who we hold close in our hearts. Forever.

"To a peaceful Christmas…and to our loved ones who are no longer with us."

Jonny looks up at me when I say that, his eyes locking on to mine for a lot longer than what would be considered normal. After a moment, he slowly reaches for his champagne glass. Raising his glass in the air, he says quietly, "To absent loved ones."

Stacey follows suit, all three of us clinking our glasses together in a toast before taking a sip of our drinks. I say sip, Jonny actually throws back the rest of his champagne before asking for another refill. Stacey and I say nothing as she refills his glass again, both acutely aware of the pain that Jonny is currently in. I didn't mean to cause him any more pain by making that toast just now. All I wanted was to give him comfort by at least acknowledging his mum on what I know is a really difficult day for Jonny.

Jonny's mum adored Christmas and always went over the top with the whole Christmas dinner and decorations stuff. She wasn't bothered about the presents, more about the family and friends she was spending time with. Judy was the very heart of what Christmas represents. Love, warmth and kindness. She had those three things in abundance and I really can't even begin to know or understand how Jonny must be feeling right now. I lost my mum when I was only five years old and I barely even remember her because I was so young. The loss of my mum is nothing in comparison to the depth of loss that Jonny must be going through. Which is why I want to be there for him. I so badly want to be there for him, in any way I can be. We may not be together anymore but I can still be there for him, as and when he needs me to be. And today he needs me. He needs us. Me and Stacey. And we're not going anywhere.

****

Several hours and several drinks later, Jonny, Stacey and I are in the midst of playing a card game. Poker to be exact. At which I am losing badly. Mind you, so is Stacey. Jonny is clearly more experienced at the game than we are and is taking full advantage. Either that or we are way too drunk to even know what we're doing. Probably the latter, but either way, we're all having fun and that's all that matters.

Jonny decided to start on the bottles of beer in Ben's fridge after we finished the champagne at the table, which is when Stacey and I started on the prosecco. Once the poker game got started, Jonny wanted to show us he meant business by breaking open a bottle of whisky. He thought that sitting at a poker game with a bottle of beer wouldn't feel quite right and so, he started on the whisky, meaning that any ideas from earlier about him driving home have definitely gone by the wayside.

Mind you, it's not as though he'll be ringing round for a taxi later on. He has a full security team at his beck and call day and night so no doubt one of his chaperones will be coming to collect him at some point. Not that I want him to go home of course. Hell no. I want him to stay. I want him to stay at Ben's and never leave ever again. Because he's had so much fun with us today. He's laughed and chatted away to us and been so relaxed and happy in our company that it still seems hard to believe that there were any bad feelings between us. In fact, I think not talking about our relationship or any of the shit from our past has been the reason for us getting on so well today. Jonny clearly just wanted a day to get away from it all and him coming here was such an unexpected surprise that I still have to keep pinching myself to believe that it's real.

It certainly becomes very real a short while later when Jonny sweeps the board with a full house, clearing out me and Stacey completely. "Oh my god!" screeches Stacey as she throws her cards on to the table in total disgust. "That is money going to money, Jonny Mathers!"

Jonny chuckles away to himself as he scoops the money away from the middle of the table towards him. "What can I say, Stace? The professional beat the apprentices."

I raise an eyebrow up at him. "Care to put a wager on that?"

He stops scooping up his money and sits back in his chair. Setting me with a challenging stare, he says, "You wanna go ahead and lose more money? Then be my guest."

I narrow my eyes on him. "No. What I am going to do though is clear you out completely."

Holding out his arms to the sides, he says, "Then bring it on."

"You're not seriously going to have him another game are you, Lauren?" asks Stacey, "we've practically bet all the cash we had on us!"

Keeping my beady eyes on Jonny, I say to Stacey, "Not quite. I have another purse in my suitcase upstairs with more dollars in. It's under my bed. Will you go and get it for me please?"

"Seriously?"

"Yep," I say. Cocking my head to one side, I grin at Jonny as Stacey reluctantly goes off upstairs to find my purse.

"You sure you wanna do this, Lauren?" asks Jonny, "because I've been in a fair few casinos in my time, whereas you…"

"You think I've never stepped foot in a casino, Jonny? We do have casinos in London you know."

"Have you stepped foot in a casino?" he asks, raising an eyebrow.

I simply shrug at him. "Once or twice."

"Once? Or twice?" He grins.

"I won a lot when I was in there," I say with a scowl.

"At what? The slot machines?" Jonny chuckles to himself.

"I'm glad you find me so amusing, Jonny," I say with an eye roll.

Resting his forearms on the table, Jonny then leans toward me. "Look, if you say you won poker when you visited these casinos you say you visited then fine, but I know you, Lauren.

Inside and out. And I know when you're bluffing."

Jonny gives me the once over with his eyes before his gaze meets with mine again, and I find myself blushing. Damn my pink cheeks. And damn him. He's doing this deliberately to send me off kilter, but I won't be influenced by Jonny's penetrating gaze and his smart mouth. If I have any chance of beating him at all then I need to focus.

Stacey returns with my purse and then all bets are on. We spend over an hour trying to beat the smug bastard who just sits there and happily takes all our money. In the end, as painful as it is to do, I have to give in and fold. I also have to deal with Stacey glaring at me from across the table as Jonny sweeps the money away from us all over again. "Don't feel too bad, ladies, you gave it your best shot."

Stacey huffs loudly. "Yeah, thanks for that, Lauren. You know, if you'd have listened to me earlier then we wouldn't have just lost *another* hundred dollars to the man who already has millions in his bank account!"

Throwing back the rest of my prosecco in order to numb my annoyance at being so stupid, I then say, "Don't sweat it, Stace, it is only a game after all."

She rolls her eyes at me before turning her gaze to Jonny. "Can you believe she just said that to me?"

Jonny laughs. "Actually, where Lauren's concerned, yes I can."

"Thanks very much," I reply sharply.

I receive another eye roll from Stacey before she stands up from the table. "Right, even though I'm annoyed with you, I still love you, and am therefore leaving to go up to bed before I get more annoyed with you. Plus, I'm as pissed as a fart and badly need my bed." Stacey leans down to give me a quick hug.

"Thank you so much for today, it's been fun, and the turkey was a-ma-zing! Love ya." She gives me a quick kiss on the cheek.

Turning to Jonny, she then says, "And thank you, rock star, for spending Christmas Day with us. It's been fun. Well, it was fun, up until you cleared our bank accounts out, but apart from that, I've had a great time. Goodnight."

Jonny smiles at Stacey. "Me too, Stace. Thank you for having me for dinner. Goodnight."

"Goodnight," I call to Stacey as she heads out of the room and up to bed, leaving Jonny and I all alone.

Oh hell, we're alone. After being in Stacey's company all day long, we are now alone together. Shit, I suddenly feel terrified at the prospect of being sat here alone around this table with Jonny. So much so that all of a sudden I have no idea what to say to him. Glancing down at my watch, I decide that the time is a good subject to start with.

"Shit, it's almost midnight." The time of night has in fact shocked me. The day has gone by so fast that I really can't believe Jonny has been here for a whole ten hours.

"Midnight? Shit, I better get home before I get in trouble with my dad."

I glance up at Jonny who is looking more than amused with himself. "Very funny. You taking the piss out of me?"

"Actually, I'm not taking the piss out of you. More out of my dad. Well, at his expense anyway."

"He's really suffocating you, huh?"

"Just ever so slightly," says Jonny, his face turning serious. He clears his throat nervously. "Anyway, the less said about that, the better."

I nod. "Yeah. Of course. Sorry."

"You don't need to apologise," says Jonny. I give him a small smile and then look away from him. And then descends an uncomfortable silence. Looking down at my lap, I begin to knot my fingers together.

"I want to thank you for today, Lauren." I look up at Jonny once more. His gaze is fixated on the middle of the table as he pushes around one of the playing cards with his fingers. "Because what you and Stacey gave me today was priceless." As Jonny's eyes meet with mine again, I feel my breath catch in my throat, the familiar ache in my chest almost causing me to cry out with the sheer pain of it.

"And...what..." Shit, I can barely get my words out to speak to him. "What did we give you today, Jonny?"

Jonny blinks. "Inner peace. And I haven't had that for a very long time."

I deliberately break eye contact with him, instead staring at my hands again. I can feel the sudden tension mounting between us and I can't handle it for much longer. Not when I know that Jonny is so not in the same place as I am. Nowhere near. He can't possibly be. Not after everything that passed between us before today even happened. Unless him being here today has changed all of that. Perhaps he can find it somewhere in his heart to forgive me for doing what I did. But Jonny possibly forgiving me wouldn't bring an end to our problems. Far from it. Because Jonny still needs to learn the truth about why I left him, and once he learns that truth, he may turn his back on me once and for all.

No, I've decided that no good can come of this at all. At least not tonight. As desperate as I am to just break down and throw myself at him, I wouldn't be doing myself, or him, any favours. This has been a happy day and my drunken self is not going to ruin it.

Tearing my gaze away from my hands, I muster up the courage to look over at Jonny again. Smiling, I say, "Well, I'm glad that we gave you the inner peace that you needed, Jonny. Today has been a happy one and I'm glad that we were able to make you smile on what I know must have been a really difficult day for you."

Jonny swallows hard and then gives me a small nod of thanks. Another moment of silence passes between us and that's it, I can bear it no longer. "So, I…best be off to bed."

Suddenly looking uncomfortable, Jonny says, "Sure, yeah, it's late. In fact, I better ring Tony to come and get me." Scraping back my chair, I stand up from the table and find myself swaying slightly from the bubbles of champagne and prosecco still working their way through my system. "You okay?" asks Jonny, suddenly looking concerned.

"I'm fine," I say, shrugging him off. Jonny gives me a reluctant nod before reaching into the pocket of his jeans for his mobile phone. "Look, why don't you stay the night?" Holy shit, did I really just say that out loud? I have the alcohol to thank for that! Jonny looks up at me in surprise but I'm quick to explain.

"I just meant that you could sleep in one of the spare rooms, that's all. Stacey is staying in Ben's room and I'm in one of the spare bedrooms, but there are still two other bedrooms that are standing empty…of course you know that already, being Ben's friend and all…" Shit, I'm blabbering, and I know I'm blabbering, but somehow or other, I find myself still needing to fully explain my drunken ramblings to Jonny. "Sorry…I just thought that…as it's so late you could…you know what? Forget I said anything…" I quickly push my chair under the table and turn to leave.

"I suppose I could stay," he suddenly says, forcing me to turn back round. Standing up from the table, he looks down at his mobile before looking up at me again. "In all honesty, I can't really face going home to my dad tonight, especially as I've had a skin full. It would only end in an argument, or worse, and… well, I don't want him to spoil what's been a really lovely day."

I swallow past the lump in my throat as Jonny gazes over at me from across the table. "It was an unexpected surprise you turning up on Ben's doorstep today…but I'm glad that you did."

"Me too," Jonny says, his eyes still well and truly on me.

Feeling claustrophobic in his presence, I find myself bidding him a quick goodnight. "Well, I better go up to bed. Goodnight, Jonny."

Jonny suddenly recovers himself. Finally breaking eye contact with me, he reaches for his packet of cigarettes from the table and says, "Sure, yeah, I'll just go and have a quick fag outside before I turn in myself. Goodnight, Lauren…and thanks again for today."

"You're welcome. Goodnight."

CHAPTER 7

LAUREN

Closing my bedroom door behind me, I breathe a sigh of relief as I lean back against it, grateful to be upstairs and finally away from the sheer suffocation of being around Jonny all day long. I inhale deeply, taking a long, steadying breath in as I try to calm my beating heart, which is thumping so hard against my ribcage, I fear it may beat right out of me.

Glancing around the darkness of my bedroom, I decide not to switch on the light for fear of it making me feel even woozier than I already do. Jeez, I really am drunk. More drunk than I first thought. Which is why I need to get out of this overly clingy dress and just get into bed. I struggle with the zip on my dress at first, almost falling over as a result. I eventually manage to get out of the damn thing and leave it on the floor, along with my underwear.

Pulling on my pyjama shorts and vest top, I then climb into bed. I get out of bed about a minute later, instead deciding to take my makeup off and brush my teeth. I hate going to bed with a face full of makeup and a furry mouth and even in my alcohol induced state, I somehow just can't bring myself to do it. It only takes me five minutes and then I'm back in bed again, nice and comfy and ready for sleep. I close my eyes and snuggle under the duvet, thinking of the wonderful Christmas Day I've had with both Stacey and Jonny. The most unexpected Christmas Day I could have ever imagined, but one I'll never ever forget.

****

I wake a short while later to a noise in my bedroom. The noise of a door opening, and then closing again. Rubbing the sleep away from my eyes, I slowly roll over to see the silhouette of an intruder standing in the shadows by my bedroom door. Still feeling a little disorientated from waking up so suddenly, I slowly sit myself up in bed, squinting over at the shadowy form on the other side of the room. The shadowy form of a man staring right back at me. I gasp out loud as I suddenly realise who my midnight visitor actually is.

Slowly stepping out of the shadows and into full on view, is none other than Jonny. A sorrowful looking Jonny gazing over at me in bed. He says nothing, instead continuing to stare over at me as I stare back at him. In shock. Complete and utter shock that he's really here. In my bedroom. *Holy shit.*

Gulping down my sudden bout of nerves, I consider whether or not to say something, but decide against it. I think it best that I say nothing and let Jonny do the talking. If he wants to talk that is….

After a moment, he starts to walk slowly towards me, his eyes never leaving mine the entire time. He comes to a halt beside the bed and then just stands there in silence, gazing down at me. Goosebumps race across my skin, my breath catching in my throat as Jonny's eyes sweep over me, once, twice, three times. When his gaze locks with mine once more, I almost cry out in pain as the sheer force of my feelings for him hit me head on like a freight train. A freight train barrelling towards me at break neck speed that I have no hope of stopping, even if I wanted it to.

Pulling back the duvet, I quickly drag myself up onto my knees and make a grab for him at the same time that Jonny makes a grab for me. Trapping my face in his hands, he presses his forehead against mine, his brows creasing together, almost as if he's in pain. Physical pain. "I spent ten years without you in my life," he whispers, his voice barely audible, "but these last few months without you have felt like longer."

He sighs heavily against my mouth and I run my fingers through his hair, revelling in the feel of him in my arms after spending so long without him. Hell, I nearly lost him. Jonny tried to take his own life and I'm partly responsible for that. I hate myself for it, for putting him through so much pain and leaving him all alone when he needed me the most.

I slowly trail my fingers down his cheeks as his fingers trail down mine, his eyes glistening with unshed tears. Unshed tears for the mum he lost. Unspoken grief for his mum that he can't even begin to deal with. Jonny has been through so much in such a short space of time and he shouldn't have had to deal with any of that alone. *I should never have left him alone.*

"Jonny…I…"

Jonny places his index finger over my mouth, silencing me. "Let's not do that, Lauren. Not right now," he whispers, as if reading my mind. "All I want to do right now is feel." Pressing his forehead harder against mine, he closes his eyes on a sigh. "Because I've felt nothing since you left me again. Absolutely nothing. And then when I woke up from my coma and I saw you, I…I suddenly felt everything…because without you I feel nothing, without you I *am* nothing, and I can't bear to be without you for a second longer."

Jonny's mouth crashes into mine so fast that he almost knocks me over with the sheer force of his kiss. I gasp loudly in surprise but am quick to respond, wrapping my hands tightly around the back of his head and holding him firmly against me. Tears of relief begin to break free from my eyes and I sob into his mouth, my emotions finally beginning to bubble over and get the better of me.

Gently wiping away my tears with his thumbs, Jonny then kisses my damp cheeks one by one, before returning his mouth to mine. He kisses me with such desperation, such hunger, that it leaves my knees feeling weak and my body feeling alive. Truly alive.

My skin sets on fire as I feel him grow hard against me, heat pooling between my legs as Jonny's desperate hands begin to work their way around my body. In fact, Jonny is so desperate that he doesn't know where to touch me first. His hands are everywhere…in my hair, on my face, my shoulders, my breasts. Absolutely everywhere. It's like he's trying to remember what he once had, moulding his hands over every curve and contour of my body as he continues to take my breath away with his kisses. So many kisses.

We kiss for what feels like an eternity, the pair of us barely coming up for air, too afraid to let go of each other after being apart for so long. Too long. Our breathless pants are the only sounds to be heard in the quiet of my bedroom, the blanket of darkness surrounding us, enveloping us in its warmth and comfort. We kiss and we touch, but most of all, we *feel*.

I reach for his t-shirt and pull it up and over his head. I deliberately press my palms against his hard chest, my fingers crawling their way along the inky edges of his many tattoos. Jonny is trembling beneath my fingertips as I slowly make my way around his torso, his grip on my body becoming more forceful.

Jonny snaps one of the straps on my pyjama vest as he drags it up and over my head in desperation. He then kneels down on the edge of the bed before dragging one of my breasts into his mouth. I moan softly, my head falling back in pleasure as Jonny sucks on my nipple hard. His fingers begin to circle their way around my other nipple, pinching it every now and again, just how I like it. I trail my fingers into his hair and rock back and forth gently against him as he suckles away at my breasts, over and over like he can't quite taste them enough.

Jonny's groans become louder as I rise and fall beneath him and I begin to pant in desperation. Sheer desperation for more. "Jonny…" I pant, "…please…"

Finally tearing his mouth away from my breasts, Jonny then tugs at my hair as he drags my mouth back to his. I desperately fumble to reach for the zipper on his jeans but Jonny takes matters into his own hands. Suddenly picking me up from the bed, he then throws me backwards on to the mattress before tearing my pyjama shorts off of me.

I gasp in shock at the sudden movement, but quickly regain my composure when Jonny starts to strip off his jeans right in front of me. He deliberately locks eyes with me as he unbuckles his belt before slowly pulling his zipper down. I bite down on my bottom lip as I drink him in in all his naked glory.

Shoving his jeans and boxer shorts to the floor, Jonny stands proud by the side of my bed, his dark brown eyes burning into mine as I deliberately allow my legs to drop open, giving him a full on view and an invitation. An invitation for more. So much more. Jonny's lust fuelled gaze rakes over the entire length of my naked body as I lie there and wait for him, aching with need and desperately wet.

After a moment, he slowly crawls his way on to the bed and on top of me. Bracing his hands above my head, Jonny's eyes linger on my face for a moment before he reaches down to kiss me. And boy do I kiss him back. I grab the back of his head and open up my mouth to him, our tongues teasing each other in a slow waltz, Jonny gently pressing the head of his cock against my entrance.

I moan softly against his lips and then push my hips up towards him, silently begging him to put an end to my misery.

The misery of being without him for so long. Jonny lets out a low growl before slowly, oh so slowly, thrusting himself inside me.

We both cry out in unison, our eyes fixated on each other as Jonny fills me to the hilt. I swear I almost black out with the feeling, fresh tears filling my eyes as I cling on to the back of his head for dear life. Jonny's mouth drops open in pleasure as he slowly pulls himself out of me before thrusting back into me again, harder this time.

"Ah," I moan, before closing my eyes.

"Look at me," says Jonny suddenly, firmly. My eyes flash open again and Jonny is frowning down at me. Brushing a gentle hand through my curls, he says, "I want your eyes on me the entire time."

Gazing up into his blazing eyes, I gently cup his cheek and then lean up to kiss him, to reassure him. "Make love to me, Jonny," I whisper against his lips.

Resting my head back on my pillow, I do as Jonny asks of me, I gaze up into the eyes of the man I love as he makes slow, passionate love to me. It's so honest and open between us, neither of us hiding away from the other one, both looking at each other with so much love and adoration that I feel as though I might break apart in his arms. Shatter into a million tiny pieces as my emotions run riot and get the better of me.

Running my fingers through his hair, I whisper, "I love you, Jonny."

Hearing my declaration of love seems to spur Jonny on. With a loud groan, he then rests his forehead against mine as he begins to increase the tempo of his thrusts, causing me to cry out. I throw my head backwards as I begin to lose my mind, giving myself over to him completely, but Jonny quickly looms over me, forcing me to look up at him once more.

"Don't look away from me, Lauren," pants Jonny. "I need you to look at me."

Jonny then grabs a tight hold of the top of the wrought iron headboard behind me as he plunges himself deeper inside me, over and over and over again, so fast and so hard, that my head begins to spin.

"Jonny…" I breathe. Curling the fingers of my left hand around one of the wrought iron spokes on the headboard behind me, Jonny then moves his right hand on top of mine, linking our fingers together around it.

"Oh god," I moan, making a grab for Jonny's head with my other hand, "oh god…Jonny…"

Jonny then kisses me hard on the lips, plunging his tongue inside my mouth and swallowing my moans as my body convulses around him. I come hard and fast, my body thrashing up against his, meeting him thrust for thrust, greedy for more and desperate to milk Jonny of everything he has.

Releasing my hand from around the headboard, I then move both my hands around the back of Jonny's head this time. I keep my eyes well and truly on him until he can bear it no more. Tugging hard on my long curls, Jonny suddenly yanks my head backwards and towers over me, his eyes blazing down into mine as he comes with a loud groan of release. I watch as the man I love comes apart in front of my very eyes, the sheer strength and intensity of his orgasm taking him to the brink.

"Lauren…I…" Jonny's words are lost as his orgasm suddenly becomes too much for him to handle. Collapsing in a heap on top of me, I hear a mournful sob right before I feel Jonny's face buried in my neck.

It isn't until a moment later, when Jonny finally pulls his

face away from my neck to glance up at me, that I realise he is crying. Something that Jonny has never done ever before when we've made love. And that concerns me. A lot. "Jonny? Are you okay?"

As Jonny's breathing gradually begins to slow, he turns to me with his tear stained cheeks and whispers, "No, Lauren, I'm not okay, but I think you already know that."

I do know that, because it is abundantly clear to me right now that he isn't okay. And it crushes my insides to know that. "I'm sorry that you're not okay, Jonny," I whisper. Brushing a hand through his hair, I say, "Do you want to talk about it?"

He instantly shakes his head. "No…no I don't." Reaching for my hand, he then links his fingers through mine and presses a soft kiss against my inner wrist. "I just want to stay in this moment with you," he whispers, "for as long as I possibly can." Cupping his cheek with my free hand, I lean up and gently kiss the last of his tears away, just as Jonny did with me only moments before.

Some time later, we make love all over again, well into the night, before tiredness finally takes its hold, Jonny falling fast asleep in my arms as I hold him close against my chest. And for the first time in months, I fall into a peaceful, restful sleep knowing that the love of my life is back in my arms once more.

****

I wake up the following morning and to my surprise and absolute delight, I find Jonny lying in the bed next to me. He is wide awake, staring over at me intently with those beautiful dark brown eyes of his. The early morning sun is peeping through the shuttered blinds, casting a warm comforting glow over the pair of us.

"Hey," he says to me quietly.

I blink at him, still completely taken aback by the fact that he's still here this morning. In my bed.

"Hey," I whisper back to him.

"You look surprised to see me," he says, his eyes still fixated on mine.

Feeling a little embarrassed, I avert my gaze away from his. "I…I guess I am…surprised. I thought that perhaps after last night, you might have…"

"Regretted you this morning?" says Jonny, finishing my sentence for me.

"Sorry," I mumble. "I know that's shit of me to think that."

Jonny sighs. "Actually, it isn't shit of you to think that. I… well…"

Glancing back up at him, our eyes meet once more from across the bed. The intensity of Jonny's gaze punches me right in the gut, reminding me of just how much I love and adore this man lying next to me. There is a slight gap between our naked bodies but we are still led side by side, face down, both hugging our pillows and looking at nothing else in the room other than at each other.

Jonny continues. "What I'm trying to say is that I don't blame you for thinking that, after how I've been treating you and how angry I've been…but after yesterday with you and Stacey, and then last night with you…" Jonny pauses momentarily and swallows hard. "Last night was amazing, Lauren," he whispers, his brow furrowing slightly. "And it was amazing because for the first time in months I felt alive again. Truly alive."

God, I just want to grab a hold of him and make him feel alive all over again. I want to cradle him in my arms and make love to him over and over. I want to show him how much he means to me by worshipping the very ground that he walks on. Hell, if he wants me to throw myself at his feet and beg for mercy and forgiveness then I will. I will literally do anything for this man. Anything it takes to have him back in my life again.

I am about to respond to his wonderful declaration when Jonny suddenly speaks again. "But whether I feel alive with you or not, Lauren, I still have doubts. Huge doubts…about you, about us, and about why you left…and I can't change those doubts or the anger I still feel towards you, no matter how hard I try…"

"I am sorry, Jonny," I say, cutting him off. "I am truly sorry for doing what I did to you back in Manchester, for doing what I did to you this time…"

"But sorry doesn't change anything," says Jonny, glancing away from me. Looking down at the bed and at the gap that lays between us, he sighs heavily. "When I first woke from my coma and you came to see me in my hospital room, you said something to me." Jonny's eyes find mine once more. "You said that when the time was right, you would tell me the truth about everything." Holy shit, he remembered. I did say that to him. I begged for him to understand why I left but had told him that I could only tell him when the time was right. When he was strong enough.

"I dismissed you that day in hospital," Jonny continues. "I'd not long been awake from my coma, you were suddenly there standing by the side of my hospital bed saying the usual sorry speech that you'd said to me the first time round back in London…and I was so angry that I just didn't want to listen." Jonny falls silent for a brief moment, his eyes desperately searching mine. Searching for the truth after being denied of it for so long. Too long.

"But I want to listen to you now, Lauren," he whispers. "I'm ready to listen."

It's now or never. Jonny is finally giving me the chance to tell him the truth. To reveal the shocking and ugly truth of what his dad did to me. To us. Jonny is going to struggle to deal with it all but he needs to know. He needs to know absolutely everything. Everything that happened back then, and everything that's happened since then. It will ruin the relationship he has with his father but I can't run away from the truth anymore. And the truth will hurt him. I just don't think even he knows exactly how much.

"The truth is ugly, Jonny," I whisper, feeling suddenly teary and emotional. "It's really really ugly."

Shifting slowly over towards me, Jonny closes the gap between us once and for all. Cupping my cheek in his hand, he whispers, "Ugly or not, I need to hear the truth, Lauren. I *have* to hear it."

Taking a deep, shaky breath in, I close my eyes and begin to tell Jonny everything. The whole truth. Nothing but the truth. So help me God.

CHAPTER 8

LAUREN

Jonny is sitting at the end of the bed with his head in his hands, tears of anger and hurt rolling down his cheeks as I finally finish telling him the painful truth about his dad. He has remained silent throughout, listening intently, as the pain of my words pierced right through him, slicing his skin and seeping into his very heart.

Seeing him like this, in so much pain, makes me ache for him. All I want to do is wrap my arms around him and comfort him, but I don't. Because Jonny needs his space right now. Space to wrap his head around it all. He needs to allow himself some time to really process what I have told him.

"I can't believe it," he finally whispers, his voice sounding pained. "My dad…he was the one who…my dad did that to us…to me?"

Jonny's head suddenly whips round to look at me. His eyes are wild and angry, all bloodshot and wet with tears. So many tears. "My own dad did that to his own fucking son?!" Jonny spits out venomously, before turning his face away from me once more. Swiping an angry hand over his face, Jonny then begins to rock back and forth on the bed, his hands shaking uncontrollably as his anger begins to boil over.

I really don't know what to do or say to comfort him, and I don't think anything I do or say will help him anyway, but I can't just sit back and say nothing while he falls to pieces right in front of me. "I'm sorry, Jonny," I whisper, feeling utterly wretched for him.

"Don't fucking apologise for him," says Jonny, almost choking on his tears. He shakes his head and then looks over at me sorrowfully. "Don't apologise for anything that he did," he whispers. With the heels of his hands, he rubs at his tear stained eyes in frustration. "Did my mum know about what my dad did?" he suddenly asks me.

"No. Definitely not."

"How can you be so sure?" Jonny asks, desperate for an answer.

I sigh. "Because…when your dad put a stop to me being able to visit you in rehab, I then went storming round to your mum and dad's house to question him. He answered the door and on seeing me standing there, he quickly ushered me away from the house and on to the street, well away from the eyes and ears of your mum. When I started to raise my voice and make a scene to try and get your mum's attention, he…"

"He what?" Jonny presses. "What did he do? He didn't hit you, did he?"

I am quick to answer. With a shake of my head, I say, "No. Your dad was never physically violent. He…he said that if I went round to their house again, or if I attempted to talk to your mum either on the phone or in person, then…he would never allow you out of rehab. Ever. He said he would keep you imprisoned in there until I left Manchester…"

I feel a flash of pain in my chest when I think back to that day. Pete's threat to keep his son locked away in rehab forever may have seemed extreme, but where Pete Mathers was concerned, nothing was extreme. I know for a fact that he would have followed through on that threat. He would have kept Jonny locked away in that god awful rehab centre for as long as it took to get rid of me from his son's life.

It was one of the cruellest, coldest things in my life that I have ever had to witness. A father imprisoning his own son, without that son knowing a thing about it. A father who apparently wanted to get his son clean and off the drugs and yet, a father who was willing to drag out that drug addiction for as long as it took for him to succeed in getting rid of me. I therefore had to cut and run as soon as possible. In order for Jonny to be free of his addiction and free from rehab once and for all, I had to leave Manchester for good. I literally had no choice. Pete Mathers gave me no choice.

Jonny shakes his head in disgust. "Jesus Christ, my dad really is the chief fucking manipulator, isn't he? The bastard...the mother fucking bastard." Letting out a weary sigh, Jonny then says, "I should have known that you wouldn't have just upped and left me like he told me you had done. Can you believe that he actually told me that you just fucked off and left Manchester without so much as a goodbye note?"

Jonny places his head back in his hands, and that's it, I'm done in. I can't leave him for a minute longer. Shuffling my way along to the end of the bed, I reach for him and pull him against me. He comes willingly, burying his face into my neck as he wraps his arms tightly around my back.

His sobs come thick and fast and all I can do is cling on to him for dear life, hushing him gently and comforting him in his hour of need. This is the second time only in my life where I have seen Jonny crumble to pieces right in front of me. The first time was when we lost our unborn son. The most heartbreaking time in our lives that we ever had to get through together. And not long after that harrowing time, Jonny's dad did this to us. To him. To his only son. My heart bleeds for Jonny, just as it has bled for him all these years.

As Jonny's sobs begin to slowly ebb away, I continue to brush my fingers through his hair until he stills. Pulling his face away from my neck, Jonny's reddened eyes meet with mine and I almost cry out from the pain and anguish I see swirling around in them.

Pressing his forehead against mine, Jonny then cups my face in his hands and sighs loudly against my mouth. "You didn't leave me because it all became too much for you," Jonny whispers, his voice almost breaking with emotion. I shake my head at him, my eyes blurring with tears. "And you do love me," he whispers, as if to reassure himself. "You really do love me."

"Oh, Jonny, of course I love you," I whisper desperately. Grabbing a tight hold of his face, I say, "Always have. Always will."

Jonny sobs loudly into my mouth, his hands crushing against my face as he pulls me hard against him. And I cling on to him just as tightly, desperate to tell him how much I love him, how much I've always loved him. It's emotional and raw, the pair of us completely opening up to one another after so many years of unbearable pain without each other. Jonny never fully knowing the truth or understanding why I left him.

And now that he knows the truth, the whole, ugly truth, it seems that Jonny is intent on nothing other than making love to me. Shoving me gently backwards on the bed, Jonny places his hands on either side of my head and then parts my legs with his knees. Gazing down at me as though I am the only thing in the world that exists to him, Jonny then slowly thrusts himself inside me. Deep inside. I gasp loudly at the feel of him, fresh tears filling my eyes as Jonny closes one of his hands around my cheek.

"Never again," he whispers. "He'll never do that to us ever again."

Jonny kisses me tenderly, his fingers gently stroking the skin of my cheek as he starts to slowly move inside me. I moan softly, completely overwhelmed by this tender moment between us, Jonny's reeling emotions making him completely vulnerable to me.

The tears roll down his cheeks as my body bows beneath his, Jonny's slow, gentle thrusts sending me soaring. Soaring high above the clouds and into heaven itself. Last night was emotional between us, but this, right now, this is different. This is open and honest and raw. Completely raw. Jonny and I are consoling each other with our love, consuming each other to the point of madness.

We can barely hold on to our sanity, both clinging to each other and moaning uncontrollably as the intensity of Jonny's slow thrusts send us skittering off into the stratosphere, where nothing else on earth exists except for this feeling of utter euphoria. Where love and pleasure crash together in a heady mix of two souls intertwining and becoming one.

Jonny grips my hair tightly between his fingers and I press his forehead forcefully against mine as we both come together with a loud moan, sobbing our absolute hearts out as the last ten years of hurt and pain come pouring out of us. I feel the warmth of Jonny's juices flood my womb and I wrap my legs around his waist that little bit tighter, holding on to him for as long as I possibly can.

I pull Jonny's head on to my chest afterwards, his tear stained cheek resting in the dip between my breasts. I tangle my fingers into his hair and he sighs in contentment. "Oh, how I've missed this," whispers Jonny, his voice almost breaking with emotion. "I've missed this closeness with you, Lauren. So much. So damn much."

Brushing a tender hand through his hair, I whisper, "I'm

sorry that I gave in to your dad, Jonny...I'm sorry for being so weak..."

"Will you stop apologising for him, Lauren," says Jonny, firmly. "I don't want to hear you apologise for him ever again. Do you understand me?"

Jonny looks up at me, anger flaring in his tear stained eyes, and I pull my hand away from him, upset with myself for angering him, for spoiling our moment. This perfect, unexpected moment that only yesterday, I would never have predicted. Not in a million years. And yet here we are. Together again. In this perfect moment. *Our* perfect moment.

"Understood," I say to Jonny, before resting my hand in his hair once more.

With a nod of his head, Jonny says, "Good." He then leans up and plants a tender kiss to my lips, leaving me breathless.

When he pulls away, Jonny then rests his head on my chest again, his fingertips drawing invisible circles around the well of my throat. I shiver with delight at the barely there touch. "Anyway, I should be the one who's sorry," he says to me quietly. "For not seeing him for what he really was all along. For being blind to his manipulation..."

"Jonny, you were in rehab the first time round, you couldn't possibly have..."

"I wasn't in fucking rehab this time round though, was I? And somehow he still managed to fly all the way over to London behind my back to..." Jonny sighs in frustration, his eyes closing for the briefest of moments. I place what I hope is a reassuring hand on his cheek and he turns his face into my palm. "Oh, Lauren, I'm sorry," he whispers, his emotions reeling all over again. "I'm sorry for what my dad did."

"Don't you start apologising for him, Jonny," I say to him

gently.

"But that newspaper article that he got printed about me, the one with all those women, to get you to break up with me, and the threat of selling the story of our past to the newspapers, I mean, what the fuck was he playing at?" says Jonny angrily.

"Hush, baby," I whisper to him. Placing a finger over his lips, I say, "That newspaper article that got printed about you is completely irrelevant, Jonny. I admit it hurt to see it at the time but it would never have driven me away from you. Nothing could ever drive me away from you…"

"Except for my dad," snaps Jonny with a scowl.

Ouch, that admittedly hurt, but no less than I deserve given the current situation. Dropping my hand on to the bed, I deliberately break eye contact with him. "I'm sorry…"

"I told you not to apologise for him, Lauren," says Jonny, biting my head off again.

Feeling a little hurt at his sudden anger towards me, I decide to turn away from him, but he instantly pulls me back before I can roll away. "Fuck…Lauren, I'm sorry. I didn't mean to aim my anger at you. Baby, look at me…please."

At the feel of Jonny's hands on my face, I can't help myself, I turn back to look up at him. Jonny's guilt-ridden eyes meet with mine and he quickly scoops me into his arms and pulls me against his chest. "I'm sorry," he breathes into my hair. "I'm a fucking idiot."

"You're not an idiot," I say to him softly. "You've just been badly hurt by the one man who isn't supposed to hurt you. Unfortunately, I know exactly how you feel in that department."

Running his hands through my hair, Jonny whispers, "I know you do, baby. Your dad was even shittier than mine." *Shittier is putting it mildly*, I think to myself. He sighs into my hair. "Well, no more," vows Jonny. "I swear that I will never allow any other person on this planet to come between us ever again. I swear on my life."

****

When Jonny and I finally emerge from the bedroom a short while later, we find Stacey downstairs in the kitchen, tidying up all the mess from the day before.

"Well, well, well, I would say good morning to you both but as it's now officially gone noon, I'll say good afternoon instead," says Stacey, a knowing smile spreading across her face. "Although from the noises you two were making earlier, I'd say it was a *very* good morning for you both too."

She winks at the pair of us and I practically kill her with my eyes, feeling suddenly embarrassed about the fact that Jonny is standing right here with us. Stacey couldn't care less though, and she makes it known. Rolling her eyes at me, she says, "Oh, stop it with the glaring, Lauren, I'm really happy for you two, and anyway, Jonny doesn't care if I heard you both this morning, do you Jonny?"

Jonny smiles over at Stacey. "Normally, I would pretend to care, just for Lauren's sake, but right at this very moment, I really really don't." Snaking his arms around my waist from behind, Jonny plants a tender kiss on my cheek. "Because I am the happiest man on the planet right now," he murmurs against my skin, and I giggle. I can't help it. I still feel like that teenage girl around him sometimes.

"You see?" says Stacey, gushing excitedly. "Christmas miracles really do happen after all!" Clapping her hands together, she then says, "Just wait until I tell Ben, he'll be so pleased you two have finally resolved your differences."

"No differences to resolve, Stacey," says Jonny, planting

another kiss on my cheek. "Because none of what happened was Lauren's fault."

"Oh, so you've finally told him?" Stacey asks me, her eyebrows raised in surprise. "Oh, I'm so relieved. Jonny, you have no idea how harrowing it's been for Lauren…"

"Whoa! Hang on a second…you know?" Jonny asks Stacey, his grip around my waist loosening. *Oh shit.* I'd completely forgotten to tell Jonny about our friends already knowing the truth about his dad. I'd spent so long this morning telling him all about it that I'd forgotten to then tell him that our friends already knew.

"Jonny, wait, I was meant to tell you this morning, but I forgot…"

"You *forgot*?" asks Jonny, suddenly looking angry with me. Looking between me and Stacey, he backs away from me slightly. "And who else knows apart from me then? Just Stacey or anybody else?" Feeling suddenly awkward, Stacey looks away from Jonny and instead fixates her gaze on the kitchen floor. Meanwhile, my nerves begin to get the better of me and I start to fidget on the spot.

"I asked you a question, Lauren," mutters Jonny. "Who else knows?"

Taking a deep breath in, I finally muster up the courage to look up at him and I'm met with a glare in return. "I…I'm…"

"They all know, don't they?" snaps Jonny, saying out loud what I couldn't. "Ben, Will, Zack, Stacey, all of them know the truth about my dad already? While I've been sitting around for weeks at home, seeing my friends, talking to them about you and wondering what the fuck went wrong with you and all this time…they knew!" Jonny shakes his head in anger. "They fucking knew all along when I didn't!"

"Jonny, it wasn't like that…in order to get over to the States to see you, I had to tell them the truth…" I try to reach for him, but he backs away from me.

"Save the excuses, Lauren!" Jonny shouts. "Because I've heard enough excuses fall out of your mouth to last me a fucking lifetime!" And with that, Jonny turns on his heel and storms away from me. I don't even bother to go after him as I know my attempts at calming him down would be fruitless.

"Oh shit, Lauren, I'm sorry," says Stacey, looking ridden with guilt. "I just assumed he knew but I shouldn't have and I'm sorry."

I sigh heavily. "It's been a long morning, Stace, and I just… I completely forgot to tell him that you all knew. It slipped my mind. I didn't mean to upset him, he's got more than enough to deal with at the moment…"

Tears, unbidden, begin to roll down my cheeks, and Stacey is quick to act. She pulls me into a great big hug and allows me to get everything out of me. I sob into her shoulder as she hushes me quietly. Poor Jonny. I feel awful about everything that has happened. Will he forgive me for this now? Lord knows I don't really deserve much more forgiveness from him. I've asked for him to forgive so much of late that I wonder whether he has much left in him to forgive. Only time will tell.

CHAPTER 9

JONNY

I don't believe this is happening to me. I don't fucking believe it. Not only is my dad the sole reason behind the love of my life leaving me, not once, but twice, but now I find out that my friends knew all about it before I did. Will, Zack and Ben, all three of my best friends who were sat with me just a few days ago in my back garden, smoking fags and chatting about the normal shit we all chat about, already knew the truth. That my dad is a mother fucking bastard who is about to get what's coming to him.

Fuck, I'm angry. Angrier than I've ever been in my entire life. Well, almost. I can't really compare any level of anger to how I felt when I found out that Lauren's father had beaten her up to the point of almost killing her. She'd fallen down the flight of stairs outside our flat he'd said. Even though her face was so badly bruised from his fists that I'd barely recognised the girl I'd fallen madly in love with. And how that deranged, murderous bastard could even deny kicking her several times in the stomach after punching her in the face and then pushing her down the stairs, I really don't know. But he did.

I wince at the memory, Lauren's battered and almost lifeless body being lifted on a stretcher and into the back of an ambulance. My desperate screams and cries for them to save her, to save him…my unborn son. *Our* unborn son. But it was too late for Oliver. Far too late. Because my precious child was already dead. I just didn't know it until a short while later.

I gulp down the acid like bile that has suddenly made its way up into my throat, those horrific images from long ago now whirring around in my mind and making me feel sick. Physically sick to the pit of my stomach. I try desperately to push away those painful memories from my past, but it's difficult. So fucking difficult. Especially as I've left things hanging with Lauren after we argued earlier. I'm so angry with her though. Angry that she told my friends the truth about my dad first before she told me. Angry that she kept the fucking secret from me for so long. Shit, I'm furious. And I don't want to be furious with Lauren, but unfortunately for her, at this moment in time, I can't help myself.

I need to take a hold of my fury right now though, and I need to aim that fury at my dad when I finally face him. Gripping the steering wheel even tighter, I push the accelerator of my Porsche right to the floor and speed up, the determination to square up to him being my main focus right now. Because I have to focus. I *need* to focus. I need to face the bastard and make him pay for what he's done to me. His only son. Well, my dad won't know what's hit him when I arrive home in about ten minutes' time. Because I will make sure he lives to regret the day he ever took Lauren away from me….

****

I pull up outside my house and kill the engine of my Porsche. I'm seething with fury and my hands are shaking badly, the adrenalin over finally facing my dad pumping its way through my veins. But I need to get a grip on that adrenalin. Before I go in there and start ranting and raving at him, I definitely need to get a grip on it, because if I don't, I know for a fact that I will hurt him. And believe it or not, I don't want to be that son, the son that hurts his own father. No way. I will not be pushed to the limit because of him and his unforgivable actions. I've been pushed to my limit before, and not by him….

Shaking my head out of the darkness that is my past, I manage to somehow regain some sort of composure and slowly but surely, I climb out of the car and walk over to my front door. Plunging the key straight into the lock, I turn it and push open the door.

Stepping inside my hallway, I immediately hear my dad's voice, bellowing at somebody on the other end of the phone I presume. He's in the kitchen I think, ranting and raving about the fact that he hasn't heard from me and he wants something doing about it. Fuck, he's probably on the phone to the police. He hasn't heard from me for twenty-four hours and now he's reported me as missing to the police I bet. This is the kind of over-the-top shit that I'm really sick of. I told him I was going out yesterday to visit friends. I didn't tell him who or exactly where I was going but I told him I wanted to be anywhere but in here with him. And he's done nothing but bug the fuck out of me ever since, just like he's been doing for the last few weeks since I left the hospital, trying to control my every movement, where I go and who I go with. Well, he's about to lose that control over my life in spectacular fashion.

I deliberately slam the front door shut behind me so that my dad will hear it. I only have to wait a few seconds before he comes storming through the archway and into the hallway from the kitchen. His mouth drops open in shock when he sees me standing by the front door, but then the usual furrowed brow returns and he starts his usual rant.

"Jonny! What the hell?! I've been going out of my mind with worry!" he yells at me, like I'm a teenage boy who ran away from home and has caused him nothing but hassle.

I stand there motionless, pinning him to the spot with an icy glare. Not seeming to notice my stance, my dad turns his mouth back towards his mobile phone and shouts, "Look, forget it, he's just turned up! Lucky for you because otherwise I would have had your ass fired for being so useless!"

He ends the phone call and then raises his arms in the air as he walks toward me. "Where the hell have you been, Jonny?!" he demands, "I told you that while you're recovering, you need to keep in touch with me at all times…"

"Why did you do it?" I snarl at him, waiting for him to react to my question.

As I expected, my dad doesn't understand the question, a deliberate ploy by me just to unnerve him, to send him off kilter, so that he loses that cock sure arrogance that bugs the absolute shit out of me.

"What?" he asks, suddenly looking confused, "why did I do what, son?"

At the sheer mention of the word *son*, I lose my shit with him. "Don't call me son!" I snap at him angrily, "don't call me son ever again after what you did!"

The penny seems to suddenly slot into place, my dad's confused expression quickly giving way to realisation. The stark realisation that I finally know the shameful truth about what he did.

My dad's initial response is to remain silent, presumably to allow himself a bit of time to process this sudden turn of events. His silence though just infuriates me even more, forcing me to question him yet again.

"I asked you a fucking question!" I shout over at him, my hands now balled up into tight fists beside me. "Why. Did. You. Do. It?" I deliberately annunciate each word so that he can see just how angry I actually am. But my dad's response isn't one I was expecting. It's one I should have expected from him though. And let's face it, with my dad, nothing should come as a shock to me anymore, not after what he's done.

"So, she finally got to you, did she?" he says to me, regarding me with contempt, "after all these years, she finally got to you." I assume the 'she' he's referring to is Lauren. Fuck, that makes my blood boil even more. How dare he refer to the love of my life as nothing more than a 'she'.

I take a menacing step towards him, flexing my fingers over and over, as if in readiness for battle. "Her name is Lauren," I mutter, taking another step in his direction.

"Look, whatever is going round in that head of yours right now, I can assure you, I did it for you, son. Everything I've ever done in my life has been because I wanted the best for you..."

"I told you not to call me son!" I shout as I barrel towards him at breakneck speed.

Because I can't hold back any longer. His reaction has only served to fuel my rage, and for that, he deserves to feel pain. He needs to feel the pain he put me through all those years ago. He needs to feel the unbearable pain he's putting me through right now. And for some reason, my dad doesn't cut and run. Or maybe I don't give him time to run, because one minute I'm storming towards him like an uncaged animal and the next, I'm grabbing him by the scruff of his shirt and plastering him up against the hallway wall.

The nearby vase of flowers on the side table suddenly smashes to the floor in the kerfuffle as my dad tries to fight me off, but it's no use, I'm far too strong for him and with youth on my side, he doesn't stand a chance.

"How could you do it to me?!" I scream into his face. "Your own son!" I yank his shirt hard and I slam him into the wall once more. He grimaces, his face twisting up in pain.

"That girl nearly ruined your life!" he shouts back at me defensively, "and I couldn't stand back and watch her ruin it completely!"

"Fucking bastard!" I take a hold of his neck and hold him firmly against the wall as he struggles hard against me.

"Oh, go on then, Jonny," my dad splutters, goading me. "Do it. Beat me up. Hurt me. You're good at doing that, aren't you?"

Suddenly, a vision from my past comes back to haunt me, the face of Lauren's father cowering away from me as I came down on him hard, blow after blow, the anger and the raw grief over the loss of my son because of what he did, pushing me over the edge and turning me into somebody else entirely.

I remember for the briefest of moments about not wanting to stop hurting the man who took my unborn son away from me. I remember the feeling of being completely and utterly out of control, as though possessed by some other unworldly being who wanted nothing more than to see the murderous bastard suffer for what he had done.

But then I had an epiphany. A moment of realisation where I pictured what my life would be like if I did in fact carry on hurting the man who murdered my unborn son. And so I pulled back. I pulled back and stopped myself. And then I walked away, leaving the bastard writhing around in enough pain to make damn fucking sure he wouldn't hurt my girl ever again. And believe me when I say, I would do it all over again to protect the woman I love. Fuck, I would do it a thousand times over if it meant protecting Lauren from his brutality. Because that's the kind of man I am. I love with every fibre of my being and I protect the people I love. I don't hurt them. Any of them. Not even my dad.

Loosening my grip from around his neck, I step away from my dad, deliberately putting a bit of distance between us. I exhale loudly as I watch him clawing at his neck, coughing and spluttering and muttering some expletives under his breath.

Jesus, I could have really hurt him. That's how blinded by fury I was just now. Furious or not though, this bastard is still my dad. Or at least, I used to think he was anyway.

"Get out of my house," I mutter to him as I shake out my hands.

"Don't you see what she does to you?" says my dad, coughing loudly. "Don't you see how dangerous she is for you?"

"You're the fucking dangerous one!" I bellow at him. "You're the cause of the last ten years of heartache for me! I've spent an entire decade without the woman I love because of you, and then, when I finally find her again, you try to prise her away from me all over again! And Lauren was never anything else other than nice to you and Mum. Nice, kind and honest. But you never liked her because of where she came from, because of the dad she had, but Lauren never asked to have a dad like that. Lauren never asked for a father who beat her with his fists on a regular basis. All she asked for was to be safe and loved. That's it. Nothing more, nothing less. But you just wanted me to succeed no matter what. You wanted me to have a music career and become rich and famous and whatever else, just to satisfy your own desperate need for success. Well, Dad, you did it. You finally got me where you wanted to get me and look at me now!" I thump a balled up fist against my chest. "Fucking look at where it got me!"

My dad just shakes his head at me. "You can't blame me for the person you turn into when that woman is in your life. You lose your head around her and you go off the rails..."

"I went off the fucking rails without her! My head went to shit when Lauren walked away from me again, and then when Mum died, life without either of them wasn't even worth living! That's why I tried to take my own life, Dad! That's the god awful truth of all of this and it's all your doing!" I point an angry finger at him. "It's all your doing and I want nothing more to do with you, do you understand? As of this moment, you are out of my life for good. You are no longer my dad, you are no longer the band's manager, and as for the record label, I'll be seeing you in court over that..."

"Oh, so you think you can just buy me out of the record label, do you? You think I'll just...sell my half to you oh so willingly?" My dad sneers at me. "Well, in your wildest dreams, Jonny. Because if you think for a minute I'm going to let you take away what I've spent the last ten years working so hard for, then you're very much mistaken."

My dad's threat is unnerving, but it isn't enough to deter me from my mindset. Which is to rid him from my life completely. "You'll be hearing from my lawyer," I say to him, firmly. "Now get the fuck out of my house and don't ever come back. I'll send your belongings over with Tony because I want you out and I want you out now."

Finding some new found confidence, my dad strolls over to me on his way out. "You'll live to regret this, Jonny. Believe me."

Turning my face to look him right in the eyes, I say to him, "I highly doubt that. Now get out." When he doesn't move, I shout the words at him this time. "I said get out!"

My dad gives me one last disapproving look before he finally walks out of my house, and out of my life, forever. At the sound of the front door slamming, I then crumple into a heap on the tiled floor of my hallway. And that's when the gravity of the entire situation really hits me. It hits me head on like a tornado, almost ravaging me in its wake.

Pain sears through my head, the trauma from my suicide attempt coming back to haunt me. Images from my past begin to flash before my very eyes all over again, like they did earlier on in the car on the drive over here, only this time, they feel a hell of a lot stronger than they did before.

I see Lauren being bungled into the back of an ambulance, unconscious, my stillborn son all wrapped up in blankets after he was delivered by emergency caesarean section while Lauren remained unconscious and in a critical condition.

I see her dad's face looking up at me in fear as I beat him senseless with my fists after finding out what he'd done. I see all of it, every part of my painful past, and it consumes me from within, utterly destroying me. I howl in pain as the images rip through my psyche, my forehead now pressed against the cold, hard tiles as I try my utmost to fight them. But the harder I try at pushing them away, the stronger they seem to get.

I scream at the floor, my hands gripping my head as the agonising pain engulfs my mind completely. I need the drugs. I need my fix. I need something to take this overbearing pain away. But I can't go back down that road, not now I have Lauren back in my life.

Lauren. My girl. My love. I try so badly to bring her beautiful face to my mind, but my attempts are futile. The painful memories win the battle and in the end, I give myself over to them, until the pain becomes too much for me to bear. And that's when the darkness takes its hold, wrapping itself around me like vines, strangling the very life out of me until all I see is black. Nothing else but black....

CHAPTER 10

LAUREN

"He's had a what?" I ask, desperate for answers from the doctor.

"I'm afraid he's had what we call a nervous breakdown," Doctor Owens says, grimly, "it usually happens when a person becomes so mentally overwhelmed by everything in their life that they can't possibly function properly as they normally would do. And with Jonny only just on the road to recovery from his recent suicide attempt, his refusal to accept any further help when he left our care has, I'm afraid, led him to this point."

"Oh shit." Of course Jonny refused to accept any help. Initially he did anyway. I assumed, albeit naively, that once the hospital had discharged him, Jonny would then have to accept the help on offer.

Shit, my head is in a complete spin as I try desperately to process what Doctor Owens is telling me. I feel Stacey squeeze my arm in support, Ben, Will and Zack all standing behind us in the side room of the hospital. A similar room to the one we were standing in just a few weeks ago when Jonny first woke from his coma.

Doctor Owens looks between all five of us and says, "When we discharged Jonny from hospital, it was on the understanding that he would seek treatment for his mental health, that he would get the counselling he so desperately needs to get him better…"

"Well a fat load of help that was to Jonny!" I yell, finally losing my shit with the doctor, "how could you discharge him if he was still so clearly unwell? I thought he was only allowed to be discharged once the help was put in place!"

Putting his hands up in the air, as if in protest, Doctor Owens instantly leaps on the defensive. "When you deal with somebody as high profile as Jonny and his father, you are simply left with no other option other than to give them the advice in the hope that they will take it. I think it is well known just how stubborn Jonny can be."

"Jonny should never have been left in the care of his father!" I shout, "because look at what it's done to him!"

Stacey pulls me back from getting in Doctor Owens' face, Will stepping into the fold in a bid to calm me down. "Look, we're all clearly upset over Jonny, but this isn't Doctor Owens' fault. We all know where the fault lies, and it isn't with anybody in this room." Will places his hand on my shoulder and gives me a sympathetic smile. "Isn't that right, Lauren?"

Wiping an errant tear away from my eye, I give him a reluctant nod. "Yes, that's right. I'm sorry, Doctor Owens, for my outburst, I'm just…I…"

Unable to finish my sentence, I suddenly burst into tears, Stacey quickly scooping me into her arms and hushing me gently. The shock of Jonny being found led out cold on his hallway floor has finally gotten to me.

I shudder at the moment we received a worrying phone call from Tony an hour earlier, Jonny's bodyguard finding him unconscious and unresponsive when he arrived at Jonny's residence. And it was sheer luck that Tony even turned up at that point. If he'd have turned up any later, who knows what could have happened.

Needless to say that this sudden turn of events has kicked Christmas well and truly away for this year, the lads all coming to the hospital this afternoon as soon as they heard the news; Ben, Will and Zack all leaving their Christmas celebrations with their families straight away so they could be here for Jonny.

"Look, Doc, I think what we all need to know is, how can we actually get Jonny the help he really needs?" asks Ben, forcing me to pull away from Stacey's hold. Sniffing loudly, I look over at Doctor Owens who looks between us all once more.

"I'm afraid that's down to Jonny himself," says Doctor Owens with a sigh, "only he can decide if he wants the help that is offered to him. But what you all can do, as his friends, is to continue to love and support him in his time of need. I'm sure that with his dad now out of the picture so to speak, Jonny will hopefully listen more and respond to the offer of treatment in a more positive way…"

"You think?" asks Ben, looking none too pleased with Doctor Owens' response. "No offence, Doc, but if that's all you're offering to Jonny in order to help him, then…"

"I'll talk to him," I say, cutting Ben off. Wiping the last of my tears away, I straighten my back and try my utmost to muster up some inner strength from somewhere.

"Oh, and you really think *that's* going to help him?" says Ben, snapping at me angrily, "because he's oh so happy with you and us right now after finding out we all knew about his dad when he didn't!"

"Hey!" shouts Stacey, glaring over at Ben, "don't speak to Lauren like that! If anybody can talk Jonny round, Lauren can!"

"So, this is what it's going to be like between us from now on, is it? You fucking firing your mouth off at me if I so much as say one cross word to Lauren?" snaps Ben, looking seriously pissed off with Stacey. "Because if it is and this is what our relationship is gonna be like, then I'm out!"

"Oh really, you're *out*?" says Stacey, placing her hands on her hips. "Just like that, you're *out*?"

"Fuck yeah, I'm out!" shouts Ben, before storming past Doctor Owens and out of the room. The door slams behind him and we're all left wondering what the hell just happened. Doctor Owens suddenly looks really uncomfortable and it's left to Will again to simmer the remaining tension in the room.

"Erm, sorry about that, Doctor Owens," says Will, looking a little embarrassed. "We're just all really worried about Jonny, and tensions are running…a little high." Will shoots a quick glance over at me before turning back to Doctor Owens. "But the most important thing right now is getting Jonny better again, so, when can we see him?"

"You can go in and see him shortly, but I suggest one visitor at a time. Perhaps it's best if his lady friend…Lauren, is it?" Doctor Owens looks at me apologetically.

"Yes…Lauren," I manage to croak out, "my name is Lauren."

Doctor Owens nods his head at me and says, "Perhaps Lauren can visit Jonny first and then we'll see how he is after that. We don't want to overwhelm him with too many people all at once, and I think a couple of people in this room…and out of it…" He looks at Stacey when he says that. "…need to cool themselves off first before visiting him at all."

Stacey nods her head and then turns away in embarrassment. Poor Stacey, she was only trying to speak up for me but then, at what cost. Maybe Ben is right to be a little annoyed with her. Maybe Stacey does stick up for me over him when there's no need for her to do so. Ben's anger with me is merely because of him worrying over Jonny again. It happened the first time round, and I know it's how Ben seems to deal with things. He shouldn't mis-direct that anger but again, I do understand how he is feeling right now. God knows I feel it too. We all do.

"Thank you, I'll go in and see him first," I say to Doctor Owens before he leaves the room.

Turning to Stacey afterwards, I say, "Hey, don't be angry with Ben. He's just worrying about Jonny. Go and talk to him… please?"

Stacey rolls her eyes at me. "He can stew for all I care," she replies sourly, "he's such an asshole." Before I get the chance to reach out and comfort my best friend, she too storms off in a huff and I'm left in the room with only Will and Zack.

"Well, that went really well," I say to them both.

Zack grimaces and then automatically reaches for the cigarette from behind his ear that he'd placed there earlier. "Sorry, Lauren," he mumbles. Placing said cigarette in his mouth, Zack then gives my arm a quick squeeze as he walks past me. "I'm taking five."

The door closes behind Zack and I look up at Will in disbelief. "Does Zack ever say anything more than a few choice words? Doesn't he have an opinion on anything?"

Will shrugs his shoulders at me. "Don't be offended by him, Lauren. Zack is Zack. He's a modern-day hippy who is so laid back that he doesn't even know what day it is sometimes."

"That'll be the pot smoking that's doing that," I say, "but putting all of his laid back shit to one side, doesn't he worry about Jonny and everything that his friend is going through at the moment?"

"You sound kind of annoyed with him."

"That's because I am annoyed with him!" I snap. "I'm annoyed with all of you actually!"

Will frowns. "You're annoyed at me? What did I do?"

I sigh heavily. "Nothing," I say to him quietly, "you did nothing…and neither did I."

"Well, what could we have done?" asks Will, his gorgeous, sun-kissed face all screwed up in annoyance. "With Pete at the helm, what the hell could any of us have done?"

I think this is the first time I've ever seen Will annoyed. Besides Zack who is practically horizontal, Will is the calm one of the band, the one who always manages to talk people down and diffuse any situation he's presented with. He's also the one who is the most supportive, always offering help and kindness whenever and wherever it is needed. Which is why it was unfair of me to say what I just said to him, and I am quick to apologise.

"I'm sorry. I didn't mean you personally, Will. I just meant… shit, I'm sorry."

Will sighs at the sight of me tearing up again and mutters a curse under his breath before wrapping a comforting arm around my shoulders. "It's okay, I know you didn't mean it. And I promise you now that all of this is going to be okay."

"Oh, I hope you're right," I whisper, my voice quivering with emotion. "I sincerely hope you're right."

****

Jonny is sitting up in bed when I walk into his hospital room a few minutes later. His eyes gently flutter open at hearing my footsteps approaching and I smile down at him warmly. I stop at the side of the bed and reach for his hand. He links his fingers through mine and gazes up at me sorrowfully, the dark shadowy circles beneath his eyes and the pale complexion on his face a tell-tale sign to me that all is not well with him. To the right of him is a saline solution bag which is attached to a stand, the fluid pumping its way into Jonny's body via the tube in his arm. God, what a mess. Why is everything such a mess?

"Hey," Jonny says to me quietly.

Gulping down my emotions, I try my best to smile my way through the tears that are threatening to fall, but it's difficult. So difficult. "Hey," I say, my voice barely a whisper.

"I gave you another fright today, didn't I?" asks Jonny.

I nod my head, tears now swimming around in my eyes as I fight so hard to control my emotions in front of him.

"I'm sorry," he whispers painfully. His face is filled with regret and I can see his eyes glistening with unshed tears. "I'm so sorry for putting you through more of this shit."

Leaning over him, I cup my hand gently against his cheek. "You have nothing to apologise for. I'm the one who's sorry for not telling you about your dad sooner. I'm the one who's sorry for my part in all of this, but most of all, I'm sorry for not being there when you really needed me the most."

Jonny sighs heavily, his eyes closing in pain. "I confronted my dad and he…he wasn't even remorseful about what he had done, and I got angry…I…I had him pinned up against the wall…"

"Hush, baby," I whisper, trying my best to console him. "Don't get yourself all riled up again over him. Please, Jonny… none of what happened is your fault."

Jonny opens his eyes once more, the painful expression on his face and the sorrow swimming around in his eyes almost crushing me to death on the inside. "I…I can't handle the truth about what my dad did to us, about what he did to me.

I can't fucking handle it. I can't handle any of it." Tears break free from his eyes and I trap his face in my hands, pressing his forehead to mine.

"I hate to say this but you need help, baby. You have to get help this time…promise me that you will accept the help this time." My voice breaks with emotion and my own tears begin to fall thick and fast, Jonny now sobbing hard into my neck.

"Help me, Lauren," begs Jonny, his voice sounding all muffled and desperate. "Please help me."

CHAPTER 11

LAUREN

"Wow, you've really cleaned this place up," says Jonny, looking around his hallway in total amazement. Wandering through to the kitchen/dining area, he raises his eyebrows in surprise at the changes I've made to his already beautiful home. In fact, looking around at the additions I've made, mainly feminine touches such as flowers in vases, huge cushions and some new throws on the sofas, a few ornaments about the place and a new chic looking lamp over in the corner, I think I've perhaps gone way over the top here. It is Jonny's home after all. Not mine. At least, not quite yet anyway. "Well, you really have made your mark, haven't you?"

"Oh shit, you don't like it, do you?" I say to him, panicking slightly, "I've gone over the top with the whole trying to make it homely for you, haven't I? Oh, Jonny, I'm sorry."

The last thing I want to do is take over the place and upset Jonny even more in his already fragile state of mind. This is his first day home from hospital after residing there for the last week and after he asked me to move in with him the other day, the first thing I set about doing was wanting to make his home warm and welcoming again. Looks like I failed in spectacular fashion.

Jonny turns to face me and frowns. "Are you for real right now?" Sweeping his arm out in front of him, he gestures towards the newly furnished room in front of us and says, "What you've done in here, in this room alone, is…well it's…it's the exact thing that I've been wanting in my life again since the day I lost you the first time round." I gaze up at him lovingly and he pulls me into his embrace. "This room I am now standing in with you already has love and happiness written all over it and that's because of you, Lauren. Nobody else, but you."

Trailing my fingers into the back of his hair, I reach up and press a tender kiss to his lips. "I love you, Jonny Mathers," I whisper. He smiles the biggest smile I've seen on his face in what feels like an eternity. A real smile that reaches those beautiful, loving brown eyes of his that I've missed getting lost in so badly. So very badly.

Moving in here without actually having Jonny here to move me in with him has been the strangest time. But thankfully I've had plenty of helpers at my disposal to help me with said move. Stacey, Ben, Will and Zack have all been on hand to help me throughout the last week and I wouldn't have been able to do it without them. All of them.

The running tension and flared tempers between us all in that hospital room from last week have now been forgotten about, the arrival of the New Year 2016 being the perfect excuse to put the last shitty year behind us for good. And what better way to start off the New Year than by making a proper home with my man. It's going to be a long road ahead for Jonny in terms of his recovery but I'm here now to help and support him with that. Because I'm not going anywhere this time. I'm going to make damn sure of that.

"I love you too, Lauren Whittle," murmurs Jonny, kissing me softly.

I melt against him and hum my approval. Oh how I've missed his lips on mine, the feel of his arms wrapped tightly around my waist as he holds me against him, the smell of his aftershave and the sheer taste of him. I've missed absolutely everything about him.

"God, I've missed you," whispers Jonny, suddenly breaking our kiss and instead enveloping me into a great big hug. He buries his face into my neck and I hear him inhale deeply, his hands now interlinked around my lower back. We stand there for long moments, basking in the scent of each other and the comfortable silence around us. This is exactly what Jonny needs right now. Warmth, comfort, peace, but most of all, love. Well, he'll be getting all of those things, that's for sure, and he'll be getting them in spades.

"So, do you want to see what I've done with the rest of your house?" I ask, finally breaking the silence.

Jonny pulls away from me slightly and smiles down at me. "Oh, I absolutely would love to see what you've done with the rest of the house. One thing to remember though from now on. Please refer to this as 'our' house. 'Our' home. Not mine. What was once mine is now yours too. Ours. Forever. Do you understand?"

I nod at him gently. "Our home, Jonny…forever."

****

We spend our first day at home together going through all the rooms and sorting stuff out and Jonny finally reveals his in-house music studio to me, the only room that had been locked up until today. Jonny is very precious about his studio and so keeps it under lock and key when he isn't in it. Which is completely understandable, considering how much the equipment in that room is actually worth. I was completely awestruck when he first took me in there, the vast space absolutely packed to the brim with musical instruments and pretty much anything else remotely music related.

The grand piano is the focal point of his studio though, and I honestly cannot wait until I get to see Jonny playing on a grand piano again. Besides his concert last summer, I haven't seen Jonny play that beautiful musical instrument since we were first together back in Manchester, so needless to say I am itching to see him play. *Patience is a virtue, Lauren, patience is a virtue.*

When evening arrives, I cook us a nice easy meal that we eat in front of the television together. Within an hour of eating however, Jonny is tired and so we head up to bed. I've changed the bedding in his room and I've bought him some new pillows that I hope will make him feel more comfortable as he said he hasn't been sleeping well in here since his suicide attempt. My stomach lurches at the very thought of those two words, never mind the implications behind them. It's almost as though I have a reality check every time I think of what Jonny tried to do to himself. It sickens me to the very pit of my stomach and I can't bear to think that he was in here, in this very bedroom, when he did what he did.

I switch off the bedside lamp and climb into bed to lie next to Jonny when he suddenly sits up like somebody has electrocuted him. "Turn the light back on," he says, sounding panicked, "Lauren, turn the light back on now." Feeling alarmed that something is very wrong, I quickly roll over and click the lamp back on.

"Jonny, what is it?" I ask worriedly, turning back to face him.

His eyes quickly scan the bedroom before he looks over at me. "I just...I can't sleep in the dark at the moment...okay?"

Oh shit, I had no idea. Absolutely no idea that he's suddenly scared of the dark after...oh shit. "Oh, baby, I'm sorry," I whisper, leaning over to console him. He edges away from me and instead lies back down on the bed and rolls over on to his side, effectively turning his back on me. I pull my hand away in disappointment, feeling upset at the rejection. "Jonny..."

"I don't need your sympathy, Lauren," snaps Jonny, cutting me off, "I just…I'm tired and I just need to sleep. Goodnight."

Feeling a little dejected and teary at Jonny's sudden abruptness, I simply nod my head at him, even though he can't see me. "Goodnight, Jonny," I whisper through my tears, "I love you."

****

I am woken up in the middle of the night by Jonny, shouting out for help and thrashing about uncontrollably next to me. I find myself half buried under the duvet as Jonny starts to claw at the sheets in horror, his eyes bulging out of their sockets with fear as he fights desperately to get them off him. Pushing back the duvet cover, I quickly spring into action.

"Jonny, it's okay," I say to him, as calmly as possible. Getting on to my knees, I sit back on my haunches and gently grab a hold of Jonny's arm. He reacts badly to that, quickly snatching his arm from my grip, a look of terror on his face. His eyes look all glazed over, as though he is in a trance, stuck in the middle of a terrible nightmare that he cannot get out of.

"Jonny, it's me. It's Lauren," I say softly. When I reach for him again, he shakes his head and then scrambles to get away from me. In doing so, he falls off the side of the bed and crashes to the floor in a heap. I crawl my way on to his side of the bed in a panic and I look down to find Jonny fighting with fresh air.

"Get off me!" he shouts to nobody. "Get off me!"

Climbing off the bed, I end up sitting on top of Jonny in an attempt at getting him to see me, instead of what he thinks he is seeing. You aren't supposed to wake a person up when they are dreaming but I need to restrain him at least, I need to calm him down. Taking a firm hold of his arms, I manage to hold them in place for a brief moment so that I can lean down and talk to him.

"Jonny, it's me, it's Lauren," I say, much louder than before. "I need you to see me."

All of a sudden, Jonny stops trying to fight with me as my voice finally breaks through the sleep like trance he had been under. Looking around the room in confusion, his eyes gradually find their way back to me. "Lauren?" asks Jonny, sounding out of breath. "What happened?" He looks afraid, like a frightened young school boy who's just woken up from a terrible nightmare. "Are you okay?" Jonny reaches up to touch my face, studying me intently. "Did I hurt you?"

I shake my head at him. "No, you didn't hurt me, Jonny," I whisper. Leaning over him, I clasp his face in my hands and press my forehead to his. He is absolutely dripping in sweat and his body is trembling all over. In all my life, I have never experienced anything like this with Jonny ever before. And it has terrified me. "You just had a really bad nightmare," I whisper, trying to keep my emotions out of my voice. "But it's over now," I say softly, "and I'm here."

I caress the tips of my fingers along the clammy skin of his cheek and Jonny closes his eyes on a sigh. "I'm sorry you had to witness that," he whispers hoarsely, "I'm so sorry."

"Sssh, baby, it isn't your fault. None of this is your fault."

Jonny opens his eyes once more and fixes me with a long stare. I stay leaning over him, brushing my hand through his hair as he slowly begins to calm down. "I'm glad you're here with me, Lauren," says Jonny, "I'm so glad that you're here."

"I'm not going anywhere ever again." I press a soft, tender kiss to his lips, and he sighs. "Do you want to tell me what the nightmare was about?"

Looking suddenly uncomfortable, Jonny glances up at the

ceiling and blows out a shaky breath from between his lips. "It's…it's the same one every single time. I'm…I'm being buried alive…" I draw a sharp intake of breath and wince. My poor Jonny. My poor poor Jonny. "And I'm just surrounded by darkness, and…these shadow like creatures or demons or whatever the hell they are keep pulling me down into the ground further and…no matter how hard I fight against them…I can't get myself out, and that's…that's why I can't sleep in the dark at the moment, because of the recurring nightmares."

"Oh, baby," I whisper, "I hate that you've been going through this all on your own." Gazing down at him, I cup his cheek in my hand. "How long have you been having these nightmares, Jonny?"

His eyes find mine once more and he looks up at me sorrowfully. "They've been happening from the very first night after I woke up in hospital. They were more like flashbacks at first but, since I came home from hospital, those flashbacks got worse and turned into these recurring nightmares. The only nights when I haven't had them was on Christmas night when I stayed over at Ben's with you and when I was back in hospital this week. It's…it's being in here that's making them worse, Lauren. It's like being back at the scene of the crime and I don't know what the fuck to do about it."

"We're going to get you the help you need, Jonny. I promise. First thing tomorrow you need to call those numbers that the hospital gave to you and you need to book yourself in for your therapy sessions…"

"You know I hate all that psychobabble shit, Lauren," says Jonny, dismissively.

"It isn't psychobabble shit, Jonny…."

"So, you really think some stranger sitting in a chair across from me is going to just suddenly heal all my mental health issues do you?" says Jonny, beginning to get irate with me.

"No, Jonny. I don't think that at all. What I think is that they are going to work really really hard with you to get you better. It's going to take time to work through all the shit that's been going around in your head but if you put in the hard work as well as them, you will get to a much better place than where you are right now. That's what I think."

Jonny sighs in irritation. "Well, I only wish I had your optimism, Lauren. Forgive me for being so fucking cynical."

He tries to move away from beneath me but I'm having none of it. Holding firm, I make a grab for his face. Turning his gaze back to mine, I say, "Hey, look at me. Jonny, look at me."

With a heavy sigh and a roll of his eyes, the stubborn man that is Jonny Mathers finally stops trying to move out of my hold and instead admits a reluctant but silent defeat.

Moving my face close to his, I say, "You're going to get through this. *We* are going to get through this together. And do you know why we are going to get through it? Because you promised me you would accept the help this time. You made me a promise in that hospital and I'll be damned if you go back on that promise, because you're far too important to me, Jonny Mathers. Do you hear me? *You* are important and *you* matter."

A few tears begin to roll down my cheeks as my emotions over Jonny's mental wellbeing finally get the better of me. I can't hide my worry from him any longer and Jonny looks up at me guiltily, his hand now reaching up to cup my cheek in his palm. "Oh, Lauren, I'm sorry," he whispers, his voice now shaking with emotion, "I swear to you on my life, right now, here in this very room where all this shit happened to me, that I will *not* break my promise to you. I will get the help and support I need, and I will fight to get myself better. Okay?"

Nodding through my tears, I whisper, "Okay."

"Okay?" asks Jonny, double checking that I really believe the promise he just made to me.

I nod my head again. "Okay."

Wiping my tears gently away with his thumbs, Jonny then pulls my mouth down on to his and kisses me passionately. I plunge my hands into his hair and open my mouth to him, allowing his tongue to caress tenderly against mine. He moans softly and moves his hand around the back of my head, his fingers trailing into my hair and tugging on my soft curls. I whimper with need, the familiar warmth already building between my thighs as I feel Jonny grow hard against me.

"Jesus, Lauren," Jonny breathes, his voice sounding strained. Deepening the kiss, Jonny then rolls us over so that I am on the floor beneath him.

Suddenly desperate to feel his skin against mine, I tug at the hem of Jonny's t-shirt and pull it up and over his head in one swift movement, revealing the montage of tattoos on his torso. They are sheathed in sweat after his nightmare moments before and I find myself unable to resist reaching out to touch them. And when I do touch them, god when I do, that is Jonny's undoing. It's as though that one touch from me ignites the fuel to his fire. Making a grab for my face once more, Jonny returns his lips to mine in desperation and I part my legs for him. He insinuates himself between my thighs and shoves the lace of my slinky black nightie up my legs with one of his hands.

I begin to pant and beg for more as I feel the tips of his fingers skim their way along my inner right thigh. Dragging his lips away from mine, Jonny then braces himself above me with his free hand, the fingers of his other hand mere centimetres away from my clit.

"Jonny," I breathe, gazing up into his smouldering dark browns, "please…"

I am desperately wet and barely able to contain myself, Jonny's fingers moving slowly, oh so slowly along, to that sweet, tender spot between my legs that is begging to be touched. For his touch and his touch alone. But that one touch from Jonny that I am craving so badly never arrives.

I see the sudden change in his eyes right before he rips his hand away from my body. Looking around the bedroom at his surroundings, it's as though Jonny has suddenly realised where we are and for some reason, that bothers him. That bothers him a lot.

"Jonny? What is it?" I ask, concerned. "Is it the nightmares again?" Pulling my nightie back down to cover my nakedness, I then sit myself up to face him. "Hey," I whisper, grabbing a gentle hold of his face, "what is it?"

Smoothing his hands down my arms in a show of affection, Jonny lets out a heavy sigh. "I'm sorry, Lauren. I can't do this with you in here. I thought I could…but I can't." Jonny looks down at the spot between us where his thighs cover mine. "I'm sorry."

Brushing my knuckles back and forth over his jawline, I say to him, "Is it because of the nightmares?"

Jonny glances up at me, his mouth set in a grim line. "It's because of everything." Everything? What does that even mean?

"But I don't understand, what…"

"Can we just not do this right now," says Jonny, pulling out of my hold.

Why the sudden change in demeanour, I really don't know. We were talking and kissing and consoling each other, and then, from nowhere, he just shuts down on me when we're being intimate. Something that has never happened ever before. I must remember though that Jonny is very delicate at the moment, and I have to be careful about how far I push him. Because if I push him too far with too many questions then he'll just shut himself off from me completely, and that's the last thing I want.

"I'm going for a fag," Jonny mutters as he drags himself up from the floor and away from me.

I look on at him in dismay as he pulls on his t-shirt and heads for the bedroom door. I manage to hold on to my tears until he closes the door behind him, and then I can't help it. The tears return from earlier, in full flow, as I sit here on the floor feeling rejected. I know Jonny didn't mean to make me feel this way and I know that he isn't well, but it doesn't stop me from feeling like he doesn't want me. It hurts like hell and I honestly don't know how to deal with it. Because I really felt like we were getting somewhere today, Jonny confiding in me about his inner most feelings and worries. But now I feel like we've gone backwards again, and I have absolutely no idea what to do about it.

****

The next few days roll on by without either of us discussing what happened in the bedroom that night. I decided to leave Jonny be, in the hope that whatever is going around in his mind will finally find its way out of his head and be shared with me. The days have been long and hard, and Jonny has been very quiet and depressed. He did however make the important phone calls I asked him to make and his appointment with the counsellor who is going to be working with him has been made for the end of the week. This one thing alone gives me hope, and hope is all I've got right now. Well, that and my best friend of course.

"So, you two aren't…"

I shake my head at Stacey before she even gets the chance to finish that question. "Let's not say things out loud that other people might hear," I say quietly to Stacey, shooting her a glare.

She rolls her eyes at me. "Oh for goodness sake, Lauren, the boys are outside, they can't hear a word we're saying…"

"They can't hear a word *I'm* saying, Stace. You on the other hand need to lower your voice." I glance over at the patio doors for the fifth time in as many minutes, making absolutely sure that they're properly closed. Which of course, they are.

"My word, you are so paranoid this morning, Lauren. What the hell is with you?"

Circling my way around the breakfast island in the kitchen, I head back to the coffee machine to make a fresh pot. "After everything I've just told you, you're seriously asking me what is with me this morning?"

Stacey follows me to where I'm standing by the coffee machine. "I meant by how paranoid you are, Lauren. Obviously I understand your situation with Jonny…"

"No you don't," I whisper, my voice wavering with emotion. "You really don't."

I rip into a new packet of ground coffee that I've just pulled out of the cupboard and I end up tearing the entire top of the packet off, grains of coffee spilling out all over the kitchen worktop and the floor. I cry out in frustration and throw the packet on to the floor. "Oh, for fuck's sake!" I shout, my emotions finally getting the better of me.

"Hey, calm down," says Stacey, pulling me away from the

mess. "I'll clean that up while you go and take a moment. Okay?"

"A moment to do what exactly?" I snap, "to wallow in yet more sadness that I'm already wallowing in?" I start to flail my arms around the kitchen in despair, tears now swimming around in my eyes as I try and fail to stop myself from crying. "Because that's what I'm doing here. I am wallowing in shit and I don't have a bloody clue how to put it right!"

At the raising of my voice, Stacey quickly springs into action by pulling me away from the mess in the kitchen. Steering me out of the kitchen completely, she walks me through the hallway and towards the back of the house where there is a nicer sized, more private living room where we can talk properly. It's what Jonny calls 'The Snug' and it certainly lives up to its name. With a log burner over in the corner, a large dark grey shag pile rug in the middle of the room and two cream coloured cosy sofas set around it, this room is the exact haven that I am looking for right now.

Closing the door behind us, Stacey marches me over to the nearest sofa and sits me down. Plonking herself next to me, she then wraps a comforting arm around my shoulders and pulls me in close. I cry quietly on her shoulder for a few moments, Stacey just cradling me softly in her arms until the tears slowly ebb away. I feel a bit better afterwards, as though I have expressed the last few days from my system.

"I'm sorry things are so shit for you at the moment," says Stacey.

With a loud sniff, I say, "It's not shit for me. It's shit for him. It's shit for Jonny."

Stacey sighs. "I know it's shit for him, and I know it's shit for you, and I know you're sick of me saying it to you, but you will get through it. And when Jonny starts his therapy, that's another step in the right direction. A huge step. Especially for him."

"I know," I whisper, "it's just…he's like a shadow of his former self, Stace. He keeps having recurring nightmares, he isn't sleeping properly, and he won't come anywhere near me either, after what happened between us the first night he came home from hospital…" I sigh heavily.

"Look, I know it's unusual for Jonny to pull away from any sort of intimacy with you, but if his head is in a bad place then nothing is going to be easy for him, especially when it comes to his inner most feelings and emotions…"

"But we were being intimate with each other. We were talking and he was opening up to me and we were kissing and touching and then all of a sudden, from nowhere, he just…he just pulled away from me and I don't know why."

"Have you asked him?"

"I asked him initially and he didn't want to talk about it and so I haven't plucked up the courage to ask him since. I don't want to upset him any more than he already is."

"Well, unless you broach the subject with him, how are you going to fix things with him? And how is he going to get better if you aren't talking properly to each other?"

Pulling out of Stacey's hold, I place my forearms on my knees and look down at the floor in dismay. "I have no bloody clue," I say, feeling completely helpless.

The door to 'The Snug' suddenly opens and I look up from the floor to see Jonny walking into the room, closely followed by Ben. "Hey," says Jonny with a frown, "I heard you shout and then I came in and noticed the spilled coffee in the kitchen and you two were nowhere to be seen. Are you okay?" He looks worried. And Jonny feeling worried is something I am trying to avoid at the moment.

Standing up from the sofa, I manage to force a smile to my face, hoping against hope that Stacey will join me. "I'm fine… I just…spilled coffee all over the floor and got annoyed with myself, right Stace?" I turn to Stacey who quickly stands up and plasters on the fakest smile I have ever seen in my life.

"Erm, yeah, yeah. Dizzy Lauren and her coffee and boy does she need that coffee this morning, Jonny, because man is she grumpy."

I practically kill Stacey with my eyes when she says that to him, Jonny looking between the pair of us as if we have completely lost our minds. Ben sniggers from behind Jonny and Stacey clouts him around the head as she moves past Jonny. "And speaking of her being grumpy, I think I best get the kitchen cleaned up and another pot of coffee on the go. You can help me with that can't you, Ben?"

Ben screws up his face in protest but soon gets the message as Stacey hauls him out of 'The Snug' and back into the hallway, leaving both Jonny and I alone, presumably to talk.

"I assume from that little performance that you're not actually okay after all," says Jonny, quietly, closing the door behind him, "but I think I already knew that." Our eyes meet from across the room, Jonny's gaze locking on to mine in that oh so familiar way I go absolutely wild for. "I'm sorry that I'm making you feel sad, Lauren." He swallows hard, his Adam's apple bobbing in his throat as he does. "I hate that I'm dimming that light within you that used to shine so brightly. I fucking hate it." He sighs.

Walking over to where Jonny is standing by the door, I reach out for him and he steps into my embrace willingly. "You're not dimming anything inside of me, Jonny," I say to him, "I promise that you aren't."

Pressing a gentle palm against my cheek, Jonny sighs once more. "Of course I am," he whispers, "and you don't deserve that. You don't deserve any of the shit I'm currently putting you through."

"Jonny…"

My words descend into silence as Jonny suddenly kisses them away. His lips are warm and soft and I find myself wanting more than just a kiss. So much more. What I would give for him to just take me right here, right now, in 'The Snug'.

I don't even care that our friends are nearby either, that's how desperate I am for some intimacy with the man I love. Because intimacy and being close to Jonny are the very things that have always been there for us. Even throughout the darkest moments of our past, Jonny and I have always had that deep rooted connection to one another like nothing else I've ever experienced in my life. Which is why I am left feeling hurt and confused all over again when Jonny suddenly rips his mouth away and takes a step backwards, deliberately putting distance between us.

"Jonny, what's wrong?" I ask, frowning over at him. I take a step in his direction but he shakes his head and holds his hands up in the air, effectively stopping me from getting close to him again.

"Don't," he says firmly, shaking his head again.

Feeling crestfallen by his changeable and downright hurtful behaviour, I raise my eyebrows at him and take a reluctant step backwards. "And you wonder why I'm feeling sad?" I say to him, fresh tears now brimming at the back of my eyes. "You wonder why you're dimming that light inside of me when you won't let me anywhere near you?"

Jonny looks over at me in shock. "But…you just said that I

wasn't dimming your light…"

"Well I lied!" I spit out at him furiously. "I lied to protect your feelings but what about *my* feelings, huh? What about mine?!" I swipe angrily at my tears as Jonny looks on at me in despair.

"I'm not trying to hurt you, Lauren, I'm…"

"Then what the hell are you doing? Because I'm trying here. I'm trying so damn hard and I just don't understand what exactly it is that you need me to do! What do you need me to do? Please just tell me what I need to do to get you to be close to me again!"

"Look, you don't understand," he says sadly, "I just…I can't…" With a heavy sigh, he looks down at the floor, as if ashamed of himself, but for what, I really don't know.

My chest aches at seeing him so tortured over something that is clearly bothering him, but I have to focus on my anger right now, because if I don't, my emotions will take over again and we'll be back to square one. "You can't what? Tell me what it is that you can't do?"

Jonny is quiet for a long moment, his eyes still fixated on the floor, as if deep in thought about what to say to me next. I can tell that he's fighting with himself over whether or not to tell me what's going around in his head.

Eventually, he speaks. "This place…this house…" He pauses momentarily, swallowing hard as he continues to struggle to find the right words. "All of it is…tainted with a past that I'd rather forget…"

"Jonny, we all have a past…"

"I did some fucked up shit here, Lauren," says Jonny. "And I can't…I won't…fuck, I don't want to expose you to any of what went on here before you came back into my life…"

"None of that matters to me, Jonny…"

"Well it matters to me!" snaps Jonny. Pulling his gaze back to mine, he thumps himself in his chest with his fist and says, "It matters to *me*."

Taking a cautious step towards him, I say calmly, "What I'm trying to say to you, Jonny, is that I love you, and all that matters now is the life that we make here together. The past is the past…"

"Not for me it isn't," mutters Jonny. Shaking his head, he says, "And I won't allow you to be poisoned by my past…"

I frown. "You think living here in your house is poisoning me with your past?"

"Yes, I do. Because this house is fucking ridden with it. Absolutely ridden with every dark part of my past that I just want to forget. This house poisons me with my past and I will not allow it to poison you too…"

"But…" I look up at him in confusion. "I don't understand… what are you saying to me exactly?"

"That I need to get the fuck out of here and sell this house before it sends me completely mad."

"But…Jonny…" Ignoring me, Jonny reaches for the door handle and yanks the door open. I follow him into the hallway. "Jonny, wait." I reach for his arm but he shrugs me off. "Jonny, where are you going? We need to talk about this more…"

Turning back to me, he says, "I'm going for a fag with Ben, and then I'm contacting my realtor."

"Your realtor?" I ask, not having a clue who or what he's talking about.

"Estate agent to you, Lauren. I'm putting this house on the

market for sale immediately."

He's going to sell his house? Jeez, now I really am worried about the state of his mind. This is such an extreme reaction to everything that's happened to him over the last few months. So extreme that I have absolutely no idea how to handle this sudden turn of events. "But…"

"No 'buts', Lauren. This is happening. You want me to start to get better? Then this is the start of me doing that." Jonny backs out of the hallway and into the kitchen, presumably to go and find Ben so he can have that fag he just talked about. Well having his usual fag is one thing, but selling his house? Just like that? Surely he won't go ahead with it…will he?

CHAPTER 12

JONNY

"So, dare I ask, how did it go?"

I swallow down a mouth full of pasta and look over at Lauren sitting at the dining table across from me. I can tell from how quickly her eyes darted back to her food that she's nervous about broaching the subject with me. I hate that I have that effect on her. I can be such an unapproachable bastard sometimes.

"The therapy session went better than I expected it to. It was awkward to begin with but then once the initial awkwardness wore off, it was okay."

It actually wasn't okay at all. I hated every second of the hour I spent with the overly sympathetic counsellor I had to sit with earlier this evening. His name was Brian and he was your typical counsellor - middle aged, neatly styled beard, big round glasses, balding on top with some gingery wispy bits of hair at the sides and around the back of his head. His dark brown trousers and flowery like shirt really finished off the middle aged hippy look to perfection. Brian was absolutely everything I typically can't stand in a person, and yet he was nice. I liked him. I just didn't like the talking in depth about my feelings part of the session.

"You hated it, didn't you?"

I stop twirling the pasta around my fork and look up at Lauren in surprise. How does she do that? Read me so well? I both love and hate that magical gift she has in equal measure. With a heavy sigh, I admit to the lie. "I hate it when you do that, but yes, okay, I admit it, I hated it. I hated the whole opening up to some stranger shit but…in all honesty, I actually quite liked the guy. Well, once he cut out the sympathy shit with me that is. Once I told him exactly how it was to be between us, the air cleared and he was…well he was likeable."

Lauren smiles softly. "Wow, that's surprising, but very positive…"

"Don't get too excited yet, Lauren, it was the first session. I may like Brian now but I may end up hating or killing him by the end of session two."

Lauren giggles, and I can't help it, that wonderful sound finally brings a long overdue smile to my face. "You think I'm kidding?" I joke, before piling another forkful of food into my mouth. "By the way, this homemade pasta you've cooked for us tonight is fucking amazing. Best thing I've had in my mouth for a while."

I can't help my smart mouth when it comes to innuendos and suggestive talk but right now, that remark I just made is bang on the money. A sad fact that is all of my own doing. And how my balls haven't exploded from not getting some Lauren loving these past couple of weeks, I really don't know, but hopefully I won't have to put up with the agonising wait to be inside of her for much longer, now that the house is officially on the market for sale.

"That could easily be remedied, Jonny," says Lauren, suggestively.

That naughty glint is back in her eyes and when her tongue darts out of her mouth to deliberately lick the pasta from her fork in what feels to me like extra excruciatingly slow motion capture, I have no choice but to shut her down immediately.

"Lauren, don't," I warn, narrowing my eyes on her.

"What?" She shrugs, feigning innocence, her eyes meanwhile twinkling mischievously as her tongue darts out to the fork of food once more.

"You know what," I say firmly, before dragging my eyes away from Lauren and her seductive ways. Trying desperately to focus on the remaining food on my plate, I somehow manage to compose myself and my raging hard on, blocking all thoughts of screwing Lauren on top of this dining table from my mind. "Not here. Not in this house of sin."

"Oh come on, Jonny, the house has only just gone on the market, it might take ages to sell and then we'll need to find the one that we want. You can't possibly predict how long all of that is going to take…"

"Lauren, I have the money to buy another house tomorrow if I want. We don't need to sell this one first before buying another one. We'll start looking soon."

"So, you're going to buy another multi-million dollar house? Just like that?"

I glance up and am met with a frown. "Sweetheart, you can buy any house you want. Multi-million dollar or a few hundred thousand dollars. Whatever makes you happy."

Lauren raises her eyebrows at me. "So you're leaving this decision to me?"

I frown. "No, of course not. We're going to choose a new house together. I'm just saying that if you want all the glitz and the glamour of getting the house of your dreams then we can have that, or if you want something more down to earth and minimalistic just like the good old days back in Manchester then we can have that instead. Whatever you want, I want. I just want what we buy to be ours. This place isn't ours and it never will be. The sooner we're out of here, the better."

Placing her fork down on to her almost empty plate, Lauren reaches for my hand from across the table. Squeezing it gently, she says, "And I love that you are willing to buy any type of house to make me happy, whether it be glamorous or not so glamorous, but I want to contribute to our life out here, Jonny. Once Stacey and I have finally given notice on our lease at our apartment back in London and flown over the rest of our stuff, I want to settle out here and get a proper job. Maybe even get the job I've always dreamed of doing one day...."

"And I want all of that for you too. I can open so many doors over here for you..."

"Thank you, but I want to forge out a career for myself, whatever that career turns out to be. I don't want to make something of myself just because of who my boyfriend is..."

"And that is what you will do. You will shine like the brightest star in the sky when you go and tread those boards on Broadway one day. All I'm offering is to open some doors for you. Nothing else. London has nothing on LA when it comes to being cut throat in the music and entertainment industry, believe me."

"And whilst that's lovely of you to say, I want to be realistic about my job prospects out here. As much as I want the whole dream career thing, I have to be prepared for the fact that it may not happen..."

"Bullshit. It will happen. And it will happen because you are a beautiful, talented lady who doesn't have a fucking clue just how beautiful and talented she actually is."

Lauren gives me one of her mushy looks before rising from her chair and walking over to where I'm sitting. Clasping my face in her hands, she leans down and presses a soft, tender kiss to my lips. I sigh into her embrace, my hands finding her hips and resting there, the tips of my fingers twitching desperately to do more than just rest.

"I love you," she whispers, between kisses. I hum my approval of her declaration and begin to fight the fight within myself once more as my erection rears its frustrated head.

Thankfully, the sound of the doorbell chiming saves me from the bell, literally, Lauren pulling away from me at the sudden interruption. She looks over towards the archway that leads out into the hallway. "Who could that be?"

I roll my eyes at her. "Sorry, sweetheart, my powers of being able to see through walls and doors are a little fuzzy today."

Looking back down at me, she says, "Oh, very funny. You know what I mean. That was the doorbell chiming, not the security gate buzzer..."

"Which means it's either one of four people," I say, rising from my chair. "Take your pick, is it Ben, Will, Zack or Lara... or maybe a bird or a plane or even superman..." Lauren batting me on the arm has me chuckling softly. "Sorry, baby, I couldn't resist. Look, stop panicking about who is or isn't at the front door and let me go and answer it."

She sighs. "Fine, I'll stop panicking, but forgive me for being curious about who it is at this time of night. It's gone eight o'clock and we never get visitors at this time of night. Well, not unless it's been pre-arranged..."

I give Lauren another eye roll before I head out of the dining area, through the kitchen and into the hallway. She follows quickly behind me. "It's probably Tony or Andy, don't worry," I say to her over my shoulder.

I'm left to eat my own words when I open the front door to find my dad standing on the other side of it. I put my arm out automatically to protect Lauren standing beside me, shoving her gently backwards. "Lauren, go back into the kitchen," I say to her quietly whilst staring down my dad. For once in her life, Lauren doesn't argue with me and instead, quietly retreats back into the house somewhere.

"Jonny, I…"

"What the fuck do you want?" I snap, cutting him off. "And more importantly, how the fuck did you get through the security gate when I changed the code?"

Holding up his hands, as if in defence, he says, "Look, that doesn't matter…"

"It fucking matters to me!" I shout, stepping outside and getting right into his face. "Because like I said to you the last time I saw you, I don't want you in my life anymore, you got that?!"

"Look, Jonny, I heard you were in the hospital again recently and I just had to come and see if you were okay. Both Lara and I have been worried about you…"

My eyebrows shoot up in shock. "Lara gave you the code to my security gate?"

My dad lets out an irritated sigh. "Look, Jonny, she works for me too, she works for the label…"

"Like fuck she does!" I yell. "And what else has Lara done for you I wonder?!" When my dad hesitates, I push him for more information. "Well?!"

"Look, don't blame Lara for the things I've done. As an employee I asked her to do them and she did them…"

"Lara released that story to the press about me and all those women, didn't she? On your say so?" When my dad begins to squirm on the spot, I know I'm on to something. "And she was the one to cancel the shows too, wasn't she?" When my dad continues to say nothing, I just laugh out loud at the complete and utter sap I have become. I have been well and truly taken advantage of here when I've been at my most vulnerable. "Of course she did," I continue, "because who was better placed to do that other than the PA of the leading man himself?"

My dad sighs. "I told you, as an employee of the label, she did those things for me because I asked her to."

"And as I just told you, she works for *me*!" I jab my fingers into my chest to get my point across to him. "Not you. Or at least she did work for me anyway, until she broke my trust! She'll be fucking lucky to keep her job after this!"

"Oh come on, Jonny, don't be ridiculous!" my dad snaps, finally losing his temper. "I gave her no choice, I had to come and see you..."

I shake my head at him, almost laughing to myself at the lengths this man will go to in order to get what he wants in life. "Of course you gave her no choice, Dad, because why would you? Just like you never gave Lauren a choice!" I can't help it, my anger begins to boil over and I end up shoving him in the chest, causing him to stumble backwards slightly. "Now I'm giving *you* no choice, Dad. Get the fuck out of my life forever and do not come back! You hear me?!"

"Just give me a chance to explain!" he shouts over at me.

"Explain?" I say, approaching him slowly this time. When I reach him, I say to him quietly, "I think you explained everything crystal fucking clearly to me when we last saw each other..."

He shakes his head at me. "Some of the stuff I said was unforgivable, I know that, I was just angry..."

I take a step backwards and begin to laugh at him. "Oh, *you* were angry, were you?"

My dad sighs in irritation. "Oh for fuck's sake, Jonny! No matter what I say or do from now on, it won't ever be right for you, will it?!"

"You're damn right it won't be! Because as I recall, you threatened to make me regret cutting you out of my life the last time we saw each other. You showed no remorse over the things you had done and you still spoke of Lauren as if she was a piece of shit on the bottom of your shoe, so forgive me for not wanting to hear you out after everything you've said and done. Now, for the last time, get the fuck off my property and out of my life for good."

My dad looks up to the heavens, his eyes closing briefly. "I shouldn't have said those things to you. Look, Jonny, you're my son. My one and only son, and I want to make things right with you…"

"The only way you can make things right with me is by turning back time to about ten years ago and changing the things you did back then." When my dad gives me nothing more than an eye roll in response, I then say, "No? You can't do that? Then we're done here, Dad. For good this time."

"I see you've put the house up for sale?" he asks, completely ignoring my request for him to fuck off.

"The selling of this house doesn't concern you," I say, turning my back on him.

As I walk back towards my front door, my dad says, "I was actually going to wish you luck with the house sale…"

"I don't need luck from you," I throw back at him over my shoulder. "Now get out of my life and stay away from us." I try to ignore the pang of guilt I feel when I say that to him, but it's there, taunting me from within. I just have to learn to push it down and ignore it. My dad has well and truly burned his bridges with me this time and I will never allow that man back into my life ever again.

"Goodbye Jonny."

My dad's sombre farewell affects me far more than I expected it to, the burning ache in my chest forcing me to harden my outer shell so that my emotions don't get the better of me. Balling my fists together, I dig my fingernails into my palms, focusing all my energy on the pain I'm inflicting upon myself instead of the pain in my heart. Because my heart does feel pain over my dad. Whether I want it to or not.

The minute I step back into the house and close the front door, Lauren rushes over to me in the hallway. "Jonny, are you okay?" She reaches up to my face with her hands but I turn away from her and walk off. I can't handle her sympathy right now. I can't be pulled into her arms and crumple into a heap of tears and upset over that bastard I once called my dad. I can't and I won't.

"Jonny?"

Guilt swamps me, hearing Lauren calling to me from behind as I continue to walk away from her. "Not now, Lauren," I say to her, a little harsher than I intended to.

She stops following me then, and I can only imagine the look on her face right now. Which is exactly why I don't turn around to look at her. I just need to be alone. Alone in the only place that I can be alone. My music studio. Pulling the key from my jeans pocket, I insert it into the lock and open the door. Stepping inside, I take a deep breath in and close the door slowly behind me.

CHAPTER 13

JONNY

With my head in my hands on the piano top, I sigh in frustration. *Why can't I think properly? More importantly, why the fuck can't I write anymore?* Letting out an aggravated shout, I slam my palms on my piano top and look up to the ceiling. Why me? Why did this shit have to happen to me?

Ever since I returned home from hospital the first time round, when my dad was living here, I haven't been able to write songs. Or music. The colours that used to dance around in front of my very eyes as the lyrics and music found me are no longer there. My head is instead drowning in darkness, the blanket of black fog sheathing my very mind and cloaking it to the point where thinking about anything is difficult. So fucking difficult. And the more frustrated I become, the darker that fog becomes.

Glancing over at the clock on the wall, I see that it's two o'clock in the morning. Shit, have I really been down here for so long? And while I've been in here, my so called haven, I have done nothing but play songs I've either already written, or songs by other artists. That's it. I have fuck all else to show for the time I've been locked up in here whilst poor Lauren has been left all on her own for the entire night. She didn't even come in to say goodnight to me earlier on and I can't say I blame her, after the way I dismissed her. A huge wave of guilt crashes over me and I shake my head at my actions.

Resting my fingers back on the piano keys, I close my eyes,

taking a deep breath in before I start to play once more. My fingers flit over the keys with speed as I fight back against the dark chasm of my mind, my emotions beginning to spiral as I play a piece of music that was from one of my mum's favourite films, The Heart Asks Pleasure First from The Piano. It's been a long time since I played this piece and the last time I played it, I played it for her. For my mum.

Eyes still closed, I try desperately to swallow down my emotions and instead throw myself into playing the music, my fingers moving tirelessly across the keys as though they have a mind of their own. This is where I lose myself completely in my music. As though the piano is a very extension of me. And it is. God damn, it is. This wonderful instrument is a part of me now and I could never live without it. Just like I could never live without *her*.

I gasp in surprise as my eyes flutter open to find Lauren standing in the doorway of my music studio gazing over at me. It's as though my mind has conjured up this beautiful mirage standing in front of me and for a few brief seconds, I actually think I am imagining her. That is until she starts to walk slowly towards me, her pure white satin dressing gown flowing behind her.

She is a vision to behold in the dim light of my studio and I find my fingers coming to a complete halt on the piano keys as I draw in a shaky breath, her sheer beauty completely knocking me off course and putting my piano playing well and truly off the mark. Lauren is the only woman in the entire world who has ever been able to weave that magic over me. Always could, and always will.

"Hey," I say quietly, extending my hand out to her.

She takes it gratefully and moves her face down to mine so we're nose to nose. Looking me deep in the eyes, she murmurs, "Hey, yourself."

Pressing a soft, lingering kiss to my lips, she then moves in between me and the piano before sitting down on my lap, her legs astride mine. Unable to keep my wandering hands to myself, I slowly untie her dressing gown, allowing it to fall open so I can gain access to her hips and that wonderfully juicy ass of hers. I mould the beautiful curves of her ass cheeks against my palms, eliciting a cute little giggle from Lauren as I do.

"God, I love that sound," I murmur, before planting a kiss on her lips. "And fuck have I missed it." I kiss her once more before pulling her against me in an embrace. "Oh, I'm sorry, Lauren," I whisper, feeling terribly guilty, "I'm so sorry for dismissing you earlier after my dad visited. I shouldn't have cut you off like that and locked myself away in here all night long. I'm so so sorry."

Pulling back slightly, Lauren looks me straight in the eyes and hushes me gently. "Sssh, baby, no apology necessary. Although I do think that you and I really need to stop apologising for the shitty fathers in our life." My girl has a point.

Nodding gently, I say to her, "You're right, baby, we do."

With a determined nod, Lauren says, "So we start now, Jonny. No more apologising for the shit that our fathers have brought to our life and the shit they may still bring. Agreed?"

I nod. "Agreed."

Lauren smiles and then slowly leans in for another quick kiss. When she pulls back, she then places her cheek against my chest and I wrap my arms tightly around her back. We sit there in the quiet stillness of my studio for a moment or two, just enjoying the closeness of each other.

These are the moments I have missed the most in my life.

Having the woman I love cradled gently against my chest as she breathes in and out, feeling happy and contented with life. I only wish I could feel as happy and contented as I used to, and in these quiet moments with Lauren, I still do feel that way for the most part, but there are so many things in my life that just aren't quite right at the moment and my mind will not rest until they are sorted out. Things that are bothering me so much that I can't even write a fucking song. Not one lyric. And speaking of losing my song writing prowess, I suddenly find myself opening up about it to Lauren when I'd previously been unable to.

"I can't write songs anymore," I suddenly blurt out, as if Lauren had already been listening in to those thoughts whirring around inside my head.

She suddenly pulls away from my chest and frowns at me, her face crinkled up in concern. "What?"

I sigh heavily. "I…I seem to have lost the ability to write songs, music, or anything remotely related to song writing in general."

"But…" Lauren still looks a little taken aback by my sudden confession. "When?" she asks, her eyes searching mine, "since when?"

Letting out another sigh, I say, "Since I first came home from hospital when my dad lived here with me, I…" I pause momentarily, not really wanting to say these things out loud and feeling weak for actually admitting to any of it. "I find that no matter how long I sit in here for, no matter how much piano or guitar playing I do, the lyrics and the notes just…well they just won't find me…or I can't find them. Either way, I'm fucked. I'm about two thirds of the way through writing a new Reclamation album and now I can't write one fucking note, not one fucking lyric, because all I see right now, Lauren, is darkness. Pitch fucking black. The vivid colours and the lyrics

I used to see dancing right in front of my very eyes are now all gone, replaced with nothing other than a huge black abyss that will not leave me. When I close my eyes, I see black, when I first open my eyes in the morning, I see black. Tonight, sitting down here on my own in this very studio, all I could see was black. Black. Black. Fucking black."

Feeling ashamed and embarrassed, I turn away from Lauren and look down at the floor but she reaches out for my face and turns it right back again. "Hey," she whispers. Gazing deeply into my eyes, as though she is gazing into my very soul, Lauren says, "What do you see now, Jonny?"

Swallowing down the huge lump that has suddenly formed in my throat, I whisper back to her, "I see a rainbow. The rainbow in my many storms."

Placing her forehead gently against mine, Lauren then cradles my face in her hands and whispers, "You see, Jonny? There is still colour in your life, still colour in your mind and your very soul. You just have to stop looking so damn hard to find it."

I draw back slightly at hearing those beautiful words, my eyes suddenly misting over with emotion. How does she do that? How can she make me feel so much better by saying just a few words? Words that have pretty much rendered me speechless but have really sunk in. Because Lauren is right. I do have to stop looking so damn hard. I have to stop trying so hard. And then maybe, just maybe, if I stop pushing my mind too much into trying to write something, the lyrics and the music may come and find me instead.

"God, I love you," I breathe, "I love you so fucking much that it hurts. It physically hurts me." I almost wince at the pain I'm feeling in my chest right now. That all-consuming pain and suffocation I feel whenever I get lost in a moment like this with her.

Lauren looks at me tenderly, her fingers gently running their way through my hair. "I feel the same physical pain as you do, Jonny. I love you so much that I don't know what to do with that feeling sometimes."

"Let me make love to you," I suddenly whisper, deliberately brushing the tips of my fingers over her left nipple through the satin of her nightie. "Let me make love to you, Lauren. Right here, right now."

Before she even gets the chance to respond, I suddenly make a grab for Lauren's face, pulling her lips on to mine as my emotions finally begin to unravel. Our kiss is full of fire and passion and Lauren is as greedy for me as I am for her. Because it's been too long. Way too long since I've been inside my girl, and I'm not about to let this house of sin get the better of me for a minute longer. I need Lauren tonight more than I've ever needed her and I'm going to savour every single inch of her.

I quickly push her dressing gown over her shoulders. The white satin material slips easily down her arms and then drops gently to the floor, pooling around the legs of the piano stool beneath us.

Suddenly conscious of how fast things are moving between us, I break the kiss. Pulling back from her slightly, Lauren then shoots me a questioning look. "Do you not want to?" Lauren asks me breathlessly. "Is it the house thing again?" Fuck, Lauren has this all wrong.

I quickly shake my head at her and reach for her face once more. "No, baby, of course not." I press a reassuring kiss to her lips before explaining myself. "I just want to savour you, Lauren. And as much as I love the rush of ripping off your clothes and getting inside you as quickly as possible, I just want to savour every single second of this moment between us right now, because it's been way too long."

She rolls her eyes at me. "And whose fault is that?" Okay, she's got me on that one.

I give her a reluctant nod. "Yeah, okay, the fault lies entirely with me, but just so you know, where we are right now, in this music studio of mine, this is the only room in the entire house that hasn't been tainted with the sins of my past and therefore the only room that is the exception to the rule."

"And you're telling me this now? After refusing to have sex with me in this *house of sin* for the last couple of weeks?"

"Oh shut up and kiss me," I growl, silencing Lauren in an instant. She melts back into me oh so easily, her lips parting to allow my tongue access. I stroke my tongue gently against hers and she moans softly, pulling me hard against her. Placing one hand around the back of her head, I hold her firmly against me as my other hand reaches for the thin strap of her nightie. Slowly, oh so slowly, I push the strap over her shoulder, following its trail down the entire length of her arm with my fingers. She gasps against my lips and I feel her shiver at the barely there touch. Jesus, I am so hard for her right now that it's taking every ounce of restraint within me to not just pin her against the piano top and fuck the living daylights out of her. *Easy Jonny, easy, you want to savour her tonight, remember?*

Breaking apart for a moment, Lauren suddenly lies back slightly so her upper back is resting against the piano top behind her. With one breast now exposed and ripe for the taking, Lauren then bites down provocatively on her bottom lip as she lowers her gaze to her other breast which is still covered. *Hmm, what my baby wants, my baby gets.*

Lauren watches me intently as the other strap of her nightie follows the same, achingly slow journey as the other one, the tips of my fingers grazing gently against her soft, flawless skin. Lauren lets out a breathy moan as her other breast is gradually exposed to me, both of her nipples now as hard as bullets and standing to attention just begging for me to give them some Jonny loving. And boy are they going to get some Jonny loving tonight, that's for god damn sure.

I start with her left breast, taking the entire peak into my mouth. I suck on it hard and Lauren lets out a loud moan of pleasure, her entire upper body sagging beneath me in relief. Relief that the dry spell between us is finally coming to an end. And what an end it is going to be. Because I need to show her right now how much I have missed her. I need her to know how much I love and adore her and how I literally worship the ground she fucking walks on. And I can do that with my mouth, my hands, my body. Oh the things I intend to do to her tonight. Because now that I have had that long awaited taste, that long awaited taste of Lauren I have been craving for, there is no going back for me. I am gone. Well and truly gone.

Shoving her ass up on to the piano keys behind her, I allow the worshipping to truly begin. I take time over my girl, licking and kissing her breasts, squeezing the nipples between my thumbs and forefingers as her ass presses down hard against the piano keys beneath her. Her loud groans of pleasure mix with the off key sounds of my piano, the heady combination of the two things I love the most in the world turning me on like I've never been turned on in my entire life. Of course this isn't new to us, getting hot and heavy on a piano. Hell no. We've done this before in our past. Many many times. But in this moment, right here, right now, after the long journey we've had to get back to this point, to each other, it feels like nothing I've ever experienced with her ever before.

And my feelings are so strong that I can feel my restraint with her slipping already. I can feel the overwhelming desire to be inside her and it rages through my veins like a blazing inferno. The same blazing inferno that inspired me to write the song about us. The song that launched Reclamation as a band and scored us our first number one hit. The song I poured absolutely everything into writing after she left me in Manchester. When she left me. When Lauren left me. Because of *him*. Because of *him* forcing her to leave me.

Anger suddenly bubbles beneath the surface but before I allow the agonising pain of what my dad did to me spoil our moment, I instead turn to the one woman who I know will heal that pain. Dragging my mouth away from her breasts, I quickly move up to her lips and practically drown myself in the taste of her. And she reciprocates.

"Oh, Jonny," she whispers in between kisses, my name on her lips a plea. A plea for more. And hell is she going to get more. So much more.

Standing up from the piano stool, I break our kiss momentarily as I slowly tug on Lauren's nightie, the satin garment following the same journey as her dressing gown did just moments before. She then stands in front of me completely naked, looking up at me seductively from under those long blonde lashes of hers, her beautiful ocean blue eyes fixated on mine as her breasts rise and fall rapidly, her breathy pants beginning to kick up a notch. I lose every last shred of restraint in that moment, Lauren looking up at me in that way I love so god damn much. Too much.

With a desperate groan, I suddenly sweep Lauren right off her feet, instead placing her down none so gently on top of my piano. She gasps at the sudden movement as I catch her a little off guard but she soon recovers, quickly reaching for the zipper on my jeans. I pull off my t-shirt at the same time as Lauren yanks down my jeans and boxer shorts in one swift movement, me kicking them off as they land at my feet, along with my socks.

No sooner have they gone and I am catching her beautiful mouth with mine once more, the pair of us clawing at each other with our hands as though we are still reaching for more clothes, when in actual fact, we are just reaching for each other.

The silence of my music studio is punctuated only by our breathless pants and moans and the tinkling of the piano keys under Lauren's feet as my fingers begin to play Lauren like the beautiful musical instrument that she is.

She lies back on my piano top as I spread her legs wide and pleasure her with my fingers, my mouth, my tongue. Arching her back away from the piano, she gives herself over to me completely as I make her wriggle and writhe beneath me, her thighs trembling against my face, my tongue merciless in its quest to send my girl into heaven itself. I just can't get enough of the taste of her, the feel of her beneath my fingertips, the sound of her breathy moans and her pants for more. More? She wants more? *Fuck.*

"You wanna come, baby?" I whisper breathlessly against her clit, "you want more of this?" I give her clit a slow, teasing lick and she lets out a long drawn out whimper.

"Jonny, I want…I want…you…"

Somehow managing to find the strength to prop herself up on her elbows, a flushed looking Lauren glances down at me, where I'm positioned between her thighs. She then watches me as I continue to go down on her. I watch her watching me and I swear to god that this is one of the most intimate and erotic moments I've ever experienced with Lauren, and believe me when I say that there have been many.

Watching her shake and shudder and moan my name loudly as she watches me finally bring her to orgasm with my mouth is almost too much for me to bear. I grunt and groan along with her and she bucks against my mouth until I've finally drawn every last ounce of pleasure out of her. She falls back against the piano top with a soft thud and I take great pleasure in lapping up every last taste of her. She tastes like the amber nectar that she is, all sticky and sweet and so fucking addictive.

I decide to give Lauren a moment to come back down to earth after rocking that immense orgasm out of her, thinking that I've most likely tired her out too prematurely, but I should have known better. As soon as I'm up on my feet, Lauren is snaking her long, curvy legs around my waist, pulling me towards her. "Did I ever tell you that you have the mouth of a rock god, Jonny Mathers?" She bites down on a deliciously saucy smile.

Sweeping my greedy eyes over her damp, naked body, I take great pleasure in the fact that Lauren is ripe for the taking all over again. As well as complimenting me on my god like qualities in the bedroom department. "No, you didn't," I say to her. Grabbing a firm hold of her hand, I suddenly pull her up into a sitting position, her legs now wrapped tightly around my waist and my cock ready for action. "And I may have the mouth of a rock god, but believe me when I say that my mouth is nothing to what my dick can do."

"Oh, is that so?" Lauren giggles mischievously.

I narrow my eyes on her in jest. "You know full well that it's so," I murmur against her lips. I smile, right before I put my godly like mouth back into action all over again by planting one hell of a kiss on her lips.

Lauren responds instantly and pulls me against her forcefully, deepening our kiss, the urgency from moments before now returning once more. Feeling her hands in my hair, her legs wrapped around me and her lips on mine just sends me crazy. Bat shit fucking crazy.

"I'm done waiting," I growl, breaking our kiss briefly so I can watch as I finally, after what feels like a fucking eternity, put myself inside her. We both moan together as I thrust into her, all the way in until I can go inside her no further. "Fuck…you feel so…fuck…Lauren…"

Lauren tightens her legs around me once more and places her hands around my lower back, pulling me into her, once, twice, three times. Slowly. Oh so fucking slowly. Placing my mouth against hers, I let out a shaky breath as I grab a hold of her hips, matching her slow thrusts with my own. Her mouth drops open in pleasure, her lust filled gaze fixated on our connected bodies as we begin to really make love on top of my piano.

The keys begin to play their staccato melody as I thrust in and out of Lauren, over and over, at a most agonisingly slow pace that simply blows my fucking mind. I watch her head fall back ever so slightly, her lids hooded as I make her pant and moan and mewl.

Beads of sweat begin to form on her skin as I really start to up the tempo between us, our beautiful soft melody now making way for a much harder bassline, a fast paced frenetic rhythm that neither of us can get enough of. Harder and harder we go, Lauren thrusting herself against me as desperately as I'm thrusting into her, our bodies slapping loudly together as we begin to build ourselves up to one hell of a crescendo.

Lauren makes a sudden grab for my face as she breaks apart in front of my very eyes. Her loud cries of pleasure fill my music studio as I make her come hard, and it all becomes too much for me to bear. I keep her pinned to the spot, my hands still firmly on her hips as I slam myself home inside of her so she can take as much pleasure from me as she can possibly get. Swallowing her cries with my mouth, it only takes a few more thrusts before I am completely and utterly done. In fact, I am undone. That's what I am right now.

I curse loudly as I finally reach my climax, emptying myself into her as Lauren continues to kiss the very life out of me, begging me to never stop doing what I'm doing to her. I break apart in front of her, kissing her desperately, still thrusting inside her, my emotions raw and open as everything that's happened to me of late hits me head on, all at once. I allow Lauren to pull my face into her neck and boy do I cling on to her. I cling on to her for dear fucking life and I never ever want to let her go again.

****

We lie on the floor of my music studio afterwards, wrapped up in the soft linen bed sheets that I went to get from one of the spare bedrooms upstairs. Throw a few fluffy pillows and a double mattress into the equation and Lauren and I now have our very own haven down here. Literally.

I stare longingly into her beautiful blue eyes, the tips of my fingers slowly peeling back the bed sheets and skimming their way down the entire length of her spine, pausing at the dip in her lower back where they begin to draw circles. I flash Lauren a mischievous grin as I watch her try her absolute best not to wriggle, but it's no use, she wriggles anyway and then bursts into a fit of giggles. I chuckle along with her. "I know this normally drives you crazy but I thought it drove you crazy in a horny type of way, not an amusing, laugh out loud, wanting to run away from Jonny type of way."

She flashes me a shy smile and then pushes her face into her pillow as I really go to town on making her wriggle. "Stop it, Jonny, it's driving me crazy," she protests, but I ignore her feeble protests and continue my playful attack. Pulling the pillow away from her face, she looks over at me and grins. "For some reason, you doing that tonight is tickling the hell out of me and I can't bear it…"

Her words are lost as I set about tickling her in plenty of other places, which drives her even more insane. I watch in amusement as she rolls over on to her back in an attempt to shake me off but I just roll right along with her.

We roll around for ages, laughing loudly and tickling each other. It's the most we've laughed in so long and it feels like we are purging ourselves of the last few hellish months. I really do feel like I'm in heaven right now, locked away with the woman I love, safely cocooned and protected from the rest of the world and its many pressures and upheavals. I would give everything up that I have right now in my life just to exist in this moment with her. Absolutely everything. Because that is what Lauren is to me. My everything. My entire world. Nothing else outside of these four walls exists to me. Only her. It was only ever her.

That thought in itself is sobering and my laughter eventually fades away, as does Lauren's, the pair of us gazing at each other once more in that way that makes my chest constrict and my throat close up. I swallow down a lump in my throat as I brace myself above her, my hands on either side of her head.

God, she's beautiful. So fucking beautiful. Her long blonde curls are spread out around her head in all their glory, her shiny locks of hair flowing over my hands as my fingers tangle their way into the soft, silky strands. The blues of her eyes hook me in once more and I find myself literally drowning in them. Drowning in her.

"God, I love you," I breathe, feeling overcome with emotion all over again, "and I know I keep saying it to you, over and over, but I just want you to know. I *need* you to know, just how much I do love you. And…I want what's happened in here between us tonight to cement that love, Lauren, because I need you to know that I am still me. I am still the Jonny you fell in love with all those years ago…and I…"

I take a moment to compose myself, Lauren still gazing up at me lovingly and waiting patiently for me to continue. "I want you to know that I will give it all up. The band, the lifestyle, the money. Hell, I'll give all my money away tomorrow if you want, if it means spending the rest of my life with you and living a happy life together instead of constantly being in the spotlight. I am only ever at my happiest when I am with you, Lauren."

My eyes search hers desperately, looking for the hint of a reaction to a decision I have literally just made in this moment. A decision I truly stand by. Because I am at my happiest when I am with Lauren. Always was and always will be. Not so sure that Lauren thinks the same way as I do though, looking at her furrowed brow right now.

"Jonny...I..." She hesitates, almost like she's trying to find the right words to say to me. "I want everything you just said too..." I smile with relief and reach down to kiss her but she pushes me gently back. "But..." I draw back from her in surprise.

"There's a but?" I can feel my happy mood already beginning to dissipate.

Running a hand through my hair in reassurance, Lauren says, "You adore your music, Jonny, and you know you do..."

"I adore you more..." I start to protest but she silences me with her fingers.

"I am not being the sole reason as to why you suddenly walked away from your music career, Jonny. Hell, you and the rest of Reclamation have barely got started. You can have both and still be happy."

I shake my head in determination. "It's not the band or the music that's the issue here, Lauren, and you know that. It's all the shit that goes with being famous that I've come to loathe. I love our fans, you know I do, but I can't deal with the rest of this lifestyle anymore. I just can't...and I won't..."

Rolling off Lauren, I instead lie on the mattress next to her and look up at the ceiling. I feel as though I've just had the very happiness knocked right out of me. *Why doesn't Lauren want to run off into the sunset right along with me?* I thought that was what she wanted. Lauren suddenly turns onto her side and props herself up with her elbow, her other hand coming to rest on my chest, her fingertips brushing ever so softly against my tattoos. My cock stirs from beneath the sheets down below but I ignore it…for now anyway.

"Don't be mad at me, Jonny," says Lauren, quietly.

I blow out a breath from between my lips. I still don't look at her. "I'm not angry with you, I'm…disappointed."

"Will you look at me please?"

Like a petulant teenager, I give Lauren an eye roll before I reluctantly turn to look at her. Placing her hand against my cheek, she looks into my eyes earnestly and says, "I love you, Jonny Mathers. I love you with every fibre of my being. Which is why I cannot let you give up on your music career because of me…"

I cut her off. "It isn't because of you, Lauren, it's because of the shitty lifestyle that goes with it, the constant paparazzi waiting for me around every corner, the rumour mill, the digging into my private life, both past and present. Need I go on?" I look away from her. I'm beginning to get pissed off now. Lauren of all people should understand. Why the fuck doesn't she understand?

"We can change all of that, Jonny."

Sitting myself up on the mattress, I shake my head at her. "No we can't."

Being the stubborn mule that she is, Lauren sits herself up right next to me. Pinning her eyes to the side of my head, she waits for me to look at her but I don't, I still avoid her gaze. She continues to talk at me anyway. "Yes, we can. You of all people can do anything they set their mind to. You can change your entire relationship with those vultures out there." I glance over to see her pointing towards the front of the house.

With a shake of my head, I say, "You are so naïve to this sort of life, you really are."

"Don't patronise me!" she suddenly snaps, forcing me to look at her once more. "Don't you dare patronise me in that way, Jonny Mathers! I may not have lived my life in the spotlight so far but I know for a fact that not all famous people out there live their lives in that spotlight. You are the one person who can change all of that. You can change how they view you or don't view you at all. You can go about your life with me in private because once you settle down into that life with me, you will become boring to them. The paparazzi live for gossip and stories that sell. You settling down with the woman you love won't sell papers. You going out on stage being drugged up to high heaven and going out finding a different woman every night is what sells newspapers, Jonny, not being settled with me. I swear to you that they will eventually lose interest and move on to somebody else."

Lauren looks angry with me right now and I have to say, what she just said to me has pretty much left me speechless. Well, almost…. "Telling it like it is then, in all its gory detail." I'm referring to her referencing my drug addiction and previous reputation with the women of course. It still stings whenever I'm reminded of what I did before Lauren came back into my life.

She suddenly looks guilty. "Sorry, I didn't mean to bring those things up…I was just…trying to make a point."

"Point well and truly made," I mutter. Pulling my knees up to my chest, I then place my elbows on them and rest my forehead in my hands. With a weary sigh, I suddenly feel defeated all over again.

A moment later, I feel Lauren's arm winding its way around my shoulders, her head coming to rest on my shoulder. "I'm sorry," she whispers, "I didn't mean to burst your bubble."

"*Our* bubble," I say, correcting her. I'm not letting Lauren off the hook that easily.

Placing her mouth against my bare shoulder, she lets out a defeated sigh of her own. "I just want you to be able to have your music career, a happy relationship with me, and be left to do all of that alone without constantly being followed around by people who want to deliberately get a piece of you so they can make some money out of you."

"Yeah well, we don't always get what we want, Lauren. On the surface, being rich and famous is supposedly what most people dream of having but, the grim reality of it all is that money really cannot buy you happiness, believe me."

"Hey," she says to me, gently coaxing me to turn to look at her. Bumping her nose up against mine, she looks me straight in the eyes and says, "Don't you think that I of all people know that already?"

I nod. "I know you do. I wasn't meaning you when I said that."

Resting her head back on my shoulder, Lauren says, "Yeah, I know."

Lauren falls quiet for a moment, lost in her thoughts as much as I'm lost in mine. In all honesty, deep down, I don't want to actually walk away from the band or from my music career, I just want the outside world to stop following me around and splashing my private life about like it's a soap opera. Maybe Lauren's right. Maybe once I settle down into a happy, contented life with her then they'll get bored and leave me alone.

"I need time to think about what we've discussed in here tonight," I finally say to her.

Turning her face into my neck, she then places her hand on the side of my head and presses me against her. "Then let's take some time away from it all to think about your future. *Our* future."

Gazing down at her, I think I may know where she is going with this. "Are you perhaps suggesting that we go on holiday somewhere far far away with nothing but golden sands to roll around on and endless oceans to splash about in with only each other for company?"

A cheeky smile suddenly creeps its way across Lauren's lips, that happiness finally returning to her eyes, our difficult conversation from moments before finally ebbing away. "You read my mind, Jonny Mathers."

I grin like the cat who got the cream. "Finally, we agree on something." She giggles, and my cock twitches. "Oh, sweetheart, you know what happens to me when you giggle."

Lauren squeals for dear life as I push her gently backwards on to the mattress, tickling her in every area of her body that makes her squirm and wriggle like mad beneath me. I just love seeing her smile and laugh with me, that happiness we had from so long ago finally returning. I can't wait to get away for a while with my girl. I haven't had a holiday in years and the thought hadn't even crossed my mind until Lauren mentioned it just now. Wow, an entire holiday with the woman I love, far away from anybody and everybody. Sounds like pure heaven to me....

CHAPTER 14

LAUREN

Three weeks of paradise is what Jonny promised us. Three entire weeks. And four days in to our three week break and Jonny has delivered exactly that. A paradise beyond anything else I have seen in my life.

Tucked away on a tiny island somewhere in the Maldives, Jonny has hired out an entire villa for us. And what an amazing villa it is. Our bedroom, which is situated at the very front of the villa, has a full wall of windows which open up and lead out onto our very own private sun terrace, complete with plush sun loungers, parasols, and all manner of fancy outdoor furniture. Beyond the terrace are a few stone steps that lead down on to our very own private beach, and the view of that beach from our bedroom is truly breathtaking.

Not only do we have our own beach, but we also have our very own plunge pool. Hidden amongst lush plants, shrubs, and the most colourful flowers I have ever seen, the plunge pool is situated just to the left of our villa. Like a beautiful hidden gem, the plunge pool is the perfect place to really get lost on this island. Especially if you want to get lost with a certain someone….

Jonny holds me firmly against him as I come with a loud moan of release, the water of the plunge pool lapping gently around us as I slowly ride out my orgasm. Jonny buries his groans into my neck as he finally reaches his own climax, thrusting up into me hard as he comes inside me for the second time this morning. Well, that's what holidays are for, right?

"Oh, baby, that was fucking amazing," Jonny murmurs breathlessly into my neck, "as always." He presses a soft kiss there before gently easing me off him. I smile at him as he pulls me in for a cuddle.

"And as always, Jonny, you are so welcome."

He laughs. "Four days away in paradise and you're beginning to sound more and more like me."

"And that's a bad thing?" I say to him.

"Fuck no," he says with a grin, "definitely not a bad thing at all."

"I always knew you loved yourself," I hit him back with a quip.

Narrowing his eyes on me, he says, "That smart mouth of yours may get you in trouble if you carry on talking like that, Lauren Whittle."

"Mmm, the hostage in trouble with the kidnapper? I kind of like the sound of that."

He gives me one of his mischievous grins. "I kind of like the sound of that too," he murmurs against my lips.

I let out a little giggle as Jonny's hands begin to roam their way around my body again. "I'm sure you giggle deliberately," he says, giving my bottom a quick squeeze beneath the water.

"Erm, excuse me..." My voice is lost on another giggle.

"See? There you go again."

I try to wriggle out from his grip as I protest my innocence. "Well, I wouldn't be bloody giggling if you weren't intent on tickling and touching up my most sensitive parts now, would

I?"

"I'm just fine tuning you, sweetheart."

"Fine tuning me? What am I, Jonny? One of your musical instruments?"

"Oh, baby, you are the sweetest musical instrument of them all. Playing you is like nothing I've ever played before in my entire life."

Cocking an eyebrow up at him, I say, "Okay, smooth talker, so if I was an actual musical instrument, which one would I be?"

"Oh, without a shadow of a doubt, you would be a guitar."

"A guitar?" I ask, unsure of where exactly he's going with this.

"One hundred percent, you would be a guitar," he says, his eyes twinkling mischievously.

"Okaaay," I say slowly, "so why would I be a guitar?"

Moving his hands away from my bottom, Jonny then slides them up my thighs, towards my hips. "Well for starters, the body of a guitar is curvy…really curvy." Jonny smooths his hands over my hips beneath the water, his fingers trailing back and forth over my skin, causing me to bite down on my bottom lip. "And like a guitar, you are exactly that, curvy…in all the right places." I grin, enjoying this flirtatious exchange we've got going on between us.

"Carry on," I say, encouraging him.

"And then," he continues, coasting his hands down my legs as far as they will go beneath the water, "there's the neck of the guitar." He bites his bottom lip as he gently lifts up my legs and wraps them around his waist under the water. "The neck of a guitar is long, smooth, and polished to perfection, just like these flawlessly perfect pins of yours."

"Oh yeah?"

"Hell yeah," he whispers, his mouth now just millimetres away from mine. Droplets of water fall from his dark hair on to my face, his dark brown eyes smouldering with promise.

"You forgot about the strings, Jonny. What about the strings of the guitar?"

"Oh, I haven't forgotten about the strings, sweetheart."

"You haven't?" I tease.

"Absolutely not," he says, as he suddenly moves his hands all the way down to my feet. "You see, technically speaking, if you were a guitar, your feet would be classed as the head of the guitar."

My brow crinkles up in confusion. "My feet would be the head?"

Jonny's mouth pulls into a suggestive smile. "Yes they would, because the strings are situated between the head and the body of the guitar." Jonny moves his hands back to my hips. "Body." His hands then slowly glide their way back down my legs. "Neck." Finding my feet once more, Jonny then says, "Head." But Jonny doesn't stop at my feet this time. Oh no. He carries on going, finishing off his guitar lesson with me in a way like only he can.

I take great pleasure in watching Jonny's fingers just beneath the surface of the water as they go on an achingly slow journey, drawing invisible lines from my feet, all the way up the insides of my legs to between my thighs. I gasp out loud as his fingers come to rest *there*. "Strings," he whispers. His lust filled gaze sears into mine and I suddenly find myself wanting all over again.

With my legs still wrapped around his waist and his hands

between my legs, I arch my back against the side of the plunge pool and thrust myself into his hands, silently begging him for more. So much more. "I think this guitar has been fine-tuned enough, Jonny Mathers, this guitar needs to be played all over again and it needs to be played right now."

"Oh, baby, I love it when you talk my language," he says with a sexy smile.

****

Jonny and I decide to spend the rest of the day lazing around on the beach, soaking up the sunshine. I'm busy reading my new book and sipping at a cocktail when Jonny suddenly decides to go and take a dip in the sea.

"You coming?"

He squints over at me from his sun lounger. Slipping my sunglasses down my nose, I appraise the beautiful sight sitting before me. Jonny is looking more and more like his normal self with each passing day. His newly sun kissed skin has given him a much healthier glow and the grey shadowy circles beneath his eyes have now started to fade away, thanks to him getting lots of rest and respite, and better quality sleep.

It's been an entire month since we decided to take a holiday and in that month, Jonny has really started to show signs of improvement in both his physical and mental health. Obviously, taking a holiday in paradise is really helping with his recovery but in the month before this holiday, although it hasn't been easy at times, he really has started to take the help offered from the people that really care about him. His friends, his counsellor, and of course, little old me.

Smiling over at my man, I say, "As tempting as your offer is, I'm really enjoying the sunbathing, the cocktail, and my book right now."

He pretends to look hurt and offended by my rejection. "You're saying no to Jonny Mathers?"

I laugh at his playfulness, revelling in this side of Jonny that I have seen so much more of recently, especially since coming to this beautiful island. "I really am saying no to you, Jonny Mathers. Who'd have thought it?"

"Shit, I really must be losing my touch," he quips, grinning. "But, your loss, baby."

He stands up from his sun lounger and stretches out his arms above his head, giving me one hell of a view of his newly tanned torso. And what a view it is. His tattooed arms and chest are practically gleaming at me in the afternoon sun, the bronzer I happily applied to his skin earlier really showing them off in all their glory. Hmm, maybe it is my loss after all.

"Enjoying the view, sweetheart?" Jonny's face breaks out into a conceited grin and I shake my head at him in mock annoyance.

"Love yourself much?" I jest, rolling my eyes at him.

"Of course," he says, "but you love me more." Bending down, the smug idiot then plants one hell of a kiss on my lips before pulling away and walking off towards the sea.

Shoving my sunglasses back up my nose, I can't help but smile as I watch him saunter into the crystal clear waters of the Indian ocean. He looks so happy and relaxed as he immerses himself beneath the gentle waves that are lapping against the shore. I sigh in contentment. This is exactly where I wanted the pair of us to be. Back in our happy place. Not necessarily here on this paradise island but back in our happy place in our relationship. Which we are.

It's taken some time to get here though, given the many uphill battles we've had to face together. Some of those battles haven't as yet been won but those ones will take some time. Such as his former drug addiction, which is still silently crippling him on a daily basis. He may not know that I see it, but I do. I see the shakes and the anxiety when he becomes overwhelmed and afraid, I see what the flashbacks do to him, and I see what that addiction still does to him. Every single day.

The other difficulty is the strained relationship he now has with his father. I have to admit that Pete has actually tried to reach out to Jonny many times over the last month, but Jonny is having none of it. Pete has therefore backed off and gone quiet, which wasn't what I was expecting from him at all. Originally, he threatened court action against Jonny over the music label they co-own together but has since thrown in the towel and told Jonny he can have everything and that he wants nothing in return. Which seems very strange to both me and Jonny.

Part of me thinks that maybe it's a deliberate plan of silent manipulation, Pete fading away into the shadows leaving Jonny to start stewing over things to the point where he starts to feel guilty about not seeing him and therefore reaches out. The other part of me thinks that maybe, just maybe, for once in his life, Pete's actually being genuine. Although I'd never say that out loud to Jonny. If anybody so much as mentions Pete's name at the moment then Jonny shuts them down immediately. He doesn't want to speak or even think about his dad and for now, I respect that.

It sounds ridiculous, but part of me would love nothing more than for Jonny to make amends with his dad. Even after everything Pete has done, I would still love to see that happen. Having already lost his mum, Jonny only has one parent left and I know that Pete has hardly been much of a parent to Jonny in so many ways but I do hold a silent hope that one day, in the future, Jonny might find it somewhere within himself to forgive his dad for everything that he did to us. To him. It's a far reaching idealistic sort of future I have going on in my mind and will most likely never happen, but I do hold out hope. I have to have hope, because without it, that would mean Jonny and I not having any parents in our life at all, and that makes me feel sad.

It makes me feel even more sad knowing that one day, should Jonny and I decide to start a family, any children we may have wouldn't experience that whole grandparent relationship that every child should get to experience. Unfortunately, I didn't even experience it. I'm happy to say that Jonny did, but both of his grandparents have long since passed and now, here we are. Back together at least but both damaged and changed as a result of our fathers.

I shudder at the very thought of my own father. The evil bastard who I know for a fact is still living and breathing, even after everything he ever did to me. I wonder sometimes whether there is an actual god out there somewhere, when a man like him somehow still gets to exist and then a beautiful woman like Judy, Jonny's mum, got ripped away from this world by a disease as cruel as cancer. It all seems so wrong somehow, and yet, completely out of our control. Sadly.

Anyway, I need to put a stop to these depressing thoughts right now and instead focus back on my book. I manage to do just that for a while, until a dripping wet rock star suddenly looms over me with a huge grin on his face. He literally crawls his way on to my sun lounger, covering me in nothing but salty seawater and grains of sand.

"Jonny!" I squeal in shock, trying to bat him away with my book.

"Oh come on, Lauren, stop being boring and get your ass in that beautiful ocean with me. You've been reading from the minute we came on to the beach. Surely, it's time to get wet with me. Pun intended."

I chuckle. "Jonny Mathers, you are incorrigible!"

"I'd rather go with sexy or demon like in bed but... incorrigible it is!"

My book and sunglasses are suddenly snatched away from me and the next thing I know, Jonny is hauling me up from my sun lounger and throwing me over his shoulder. I scream of course but he ignores me and continues to stride towards the ocean, laughing loudly at my pointless protests. Wading into the balmy waters of the Indian ocean, Jonny then finally releases me from his hold, throwing me backwards, none so gently, into the sea.

Another scream of protest from me before I finally manage to pull myself up into a standing position in the water. Rubbing the salty seawater from my eyes, I am eventually able to focus my scowl over at Jonny who is still grinning like the immature man that he is. "You are so dead for that, Jonny Mathers. So dead."

"Yeah, but you'll have to catch me first, sweetheart." And with that, Jonny turns and starts to swim away from me. Oh, so it's going to be like that now, is it? Playing a little game of catch me if you can or tig as we used to call it at school.

"Oh, bring it on, Mathers!" I shout over to him as I start to swim as fast as my arms will take me. "Bring it on!"

****

I turn over in bed and stretch my arm out to feel for Jonny, only to find that he isn't there. My eyes fly open and I am immediately worried that he isn't in bed with me like he should be.

Taking a quick glance around our darkened bedroom, I notice that the windows are slightly open at the front of our villa, a warm, gentle breeze blowing its way inside. The shutters which have been drawn apart to allow access to the outside area move back and forth against the windows, the low flapping noise most likely to have been the culprit for waking me from my slumber. That and the empty bed of course.

I frown over at the open windows. I do worry about him when he wakes up in the middle of the night. He hasn't been doing it quite as often as he was a month ago but every now and again, he still finds it difficult to sleep and so gets up and takes himself off somewhere, usually to play the piano or go for a cigarette when he's at home.

Pulling back the bed sheets, I stand up and slip my stripy pink and white sliders on to my feet before heading outside on to the terrace. Jonny isn't there either. Squinting into the darkness of the beach in front of me, I soon find what I'm looking for. I see the glow of a cigarette in the distance and I can just about make out the silhouetted form of my rock star, sat down on the sand looking out towards the ocean.

I walk down the stony steps on to the beach and take in the beautiful sight in front of me. The full moon is out in all its glory tonight, basking Jonny in its warm, comforting glow. The endless ocean in front of us sparkles under the light of the moon and I suddenly realise why Jonny decided to come out here tonight. For whatever reason, whether it be a nightmare or just the fact that he couldn't sleep, who wouldn't want to see this wonderful scene in front of us at least once in their life.

I come to a silent stop just to the right of Jonny. Folding my arms, I continue to gaze at the ocean ahead even as I feel Jonny's gaze coming to rest on me. He doesn't seem surprised to find me standing next to him on the beach at some unearthly hour of the morning. He probably felt my presence long before he even saw me. It's always been the same with us two.

"Hey," he eventually says.

"Hey, rock star," I say, finally sitting myself down on the sand next to him. Leaning over, I press a gentle kiss to his lips which he receives gratefully. When I pull back and look into his eyes, even in the darkness with only the moon for light, I can see that he looks worried, or at the very least, unsettled. "What's the matter? Did you have another nightmare?"

Frowning, he then looks back out at the ocean before taking a long pull on his cigarette. After a beat, he then says, "It wasn't a nightmare this time, Lauren...it was..." He blows out a nervous breath along with his smoke before continuing. "It was my mum."

I raise my eyebrows in surprise. "Your mum?"

He nods his head gently, his eyes still dead ahead. "Yeah... I..." He hesitates, looking a little uncomfortable. "I had a dream or a vision, whatever you wanna call it. As clear as day. My mum was standing in my dressing room at a concert, bathed in white light, dressed in one of her usual outfits she used to wear whenever she got the chance to attend one of my concerts." I sit there quietly, trying to take in what Jonny is telling me. "When I got up from my chair and walked over to her, she smiled at me and then turned towards the door to my dressing room...and then she pointed at the door."

Stubbing his cigarette out in the sand, Jonny then finally turns to look at me, his face one of disbelief. "I think she was trying to tell me something, Lauren. I think she was trying to..." Jonny bites back a sudden wave of emotion, taking a minute to compose himself. Moving closer to him, I place my arm around his shoulders and pull him in close.

"It's okay, Jonny, you don't need to continue if you don't want to..."

"No, I want to," he whispers. Clearing his throat, he then says, "I think my mum was trying to tell me to go back to doing what I love the most." Locking eyes with mine, he then says, "And we both know what that is."

Gulping back tears which have suddenly sprung from nowhere, I then clasp Jonny's face between my hands and place my forehead against his. "You think she was telling you not to give up on your music career? To go back to the band, to playing live? To finish your US tour?"

"Oh, even better than that, sweetheart, I think she was telling me to start a whole new tour. A fresh start. A new chapter."

"You do?"

He nods his head at me. "Oh yeah, I do."

Sweeping my thumbs back and forth beneath his beautiful eyes, I say to him, "Tell me more."

"Because not only did my mum point over to the door, she then walked over to the door and opened it for me."

I almost can't believe what I'm hearing. Never before in my life have I heard or personally experienced anything like this. An ethereal like vision of a loved one who has passed on who is trying to reach you from wherever they are.

"Oh my god, Jonny…" My words are lost, my emotional state finally beginning to get the better of me.

"And beyond that door, was the whole world, bathed in nothing but colours. Bright, vibrant colours swirling around just calling out to me…and then when I took a step towards that door, I looked back to smile at my mum who smiled right back at me before pointing again. I then looked away from her, took a step through the door, and that was it, I woke up."

"Oh, Jonny, that's the most…well, it's the most wonderful thing I think anybody has ever said to me. Your mum…trying to reach you…from beyond the stars…"

"She not only reached me, she…shit, I don't know what the hell happened but since I woke up about two hours ago, I've written a song…"

Oh my god, now I am shocked. Jonny has finally written a song. After going three entire months since his overdose without being able to write a single musical note or lyric, his mum has finally found him and somehow or other, Jonny has taken inspiration from that vision and has written a song. I am speechless right now. Literally speechless.

"Jonny, I…"

"I know, right?" Jonny shakes his head in disbelief and then looks back out at the ocean once more. "You know, I never ever believed in an afterlife. I always used to think that once you were gone, you were gone, but then my mum died and I…well, I struggled in my own head to deal with the fact that she was gone and it horrified me that I'd never ever see her again. I still struggle with that fact. Every single day. But then this…this vision of her tonight, it was so real, Lauren. So real."

Placing a hand against his cheek, I deliberately turn his face towards mine. "That's because it was real, Jonny." I then rest my hand against the bare skin of his chest, over his heart. "Because she's still in here," I whisper through teary eyes, "and she will always be in here, wherever you go, for the rest of your life. Your mum will never ever leave you, Jonny. I can promise you that."

Jonny lets out a ragged breath, his eyes now shining with tears as he gazes down at me. Running his fingers through my curls, he then says, "I love you, Lauren Whittle, and I want you with me always. I want you to tour the world with me and the band. I want you to buy a house with me and make it into a home of our very own, but, most of all…" He glances away from me briefly, looking out at the ocean again before resting his gaze back on me. Pausing momentarily, he then takes a deep breath in, as if preparing himself for something. Something huge.

"Lauren Whittle, you were with me for four and a half years of my life the first time round and I didn't do then what I am about to do now, but I should have done."

I frown. "Jonny, what are you…"

"Stand up," he suddenly says to me.

"What?"

"Please will you stand up for me, Lauren? I have something very important to ask you." *Oh my god, surely not. He can't be. Can he?*

My nerves are now shot to shreds but I do as he asks of me. I slowly, on very wobbly legs, stand up from the sand, dressed in nothing other than my white satin nightie, and look down at him. Jonny then moves from a sitting position, into a kneeling position. *Oh shit, this is really happening. I cannot believe this is really happening.*

Looking up at me with the most loving and honest eyes I have ever seen on a man, Jonny takes a gentle hold of my left hand and says the words that at one time in my life, I never ever thought I would hear.

"Lauren Catherine Whittle, love of my life, my absolute everything, will you do me the honour of becoming my wife?"

Oh my god, this is really happening! Right here, right now, on this beautiful moonlit beach in the Maldives at some silly hour of the morning, the love of my life has gone down on one knee and is asking me to marry him. Could life get any more perfect than this? I am both surprised and shocked at this unexpected, but oh so romantic, proposal of his.

When we came on this holiday, I never thought for a minute that Jonny would propose to me. In fact, marriage never even crossed my mind. And it never did. Because all I ever wanted was just to be with the man I love, and him with me, but now that he's kneeling down in front of me, looking up at me as though I am the only woman in the world that exists to him, marrying Jonny is the exact thing that I want and need in my life. Jonny is all I need, and boy are we going to take on the world together, just like we were meant to do in the very beginning.

"Of course I'll marry you, Jonny," I say to him, the huge smile on my face literally making my cheeks ache, "yes, yes, yes!"

Jonny's smile makes his face light up with sheer happiness and he suddenly stands up and swoops me up into his arms, kissing me like he's kissing me for the first time all over again. He spins me around on the beach and I squeal with happiness, Jonny laughing madly at me. It is our happiest moment I think, a moment we will both treasure in our hearts forever. Just him and me against the world again. Me and him. Always.

CHAPTER 15

JONNY

Lauren Whittle has said yes to becoming my wife. The love of my life has accepted my unexpected proposal and made me the happiest man alive. And the proposal was unexpected. So unexpected that even I didn't know I was going to do it, until I was in that moment with her. And boy are there going to be so many more special moments with Lauren, especially now I've made it official by asking for her hand in marriage.

Her hand in marriage. Wow, I can't fucking believe it. That I, Jonny Mathers, have finally manned the fuck up and asked my girl to marry me. Lauren Whittle is now my fiancée and the sooner I get a big rock on that wedding finger of hers, the better. Because I want to show her off to the world for the truly beautiful, kind, talented woman that she is. Lauren deserves the whole world and a hell of a lot more after what she's been through in her life, and I am the lucky son of a bitch who has been given that privilege to give her just that.

And what a privilege it is right now to make slow, passionate love to the woman who has said yes to becoming my wife. As soon as she said yes to my proposal of marriage, I just had to consummate that acceptance by bringing her back to bed and worshipping every last inch of her.

I literally made her weep as I allowed my tongue and fingers to really work her over, getting her so riled up to the point where we both had to stop with all the foreplay because we just had to make love to each other. Desperately.

With her back to my chest, we are sitting up on the bed, Lauren grinding down slowly on my cock in the darkness of our bedroom as I snake an arm around her body from behind. Reaching for her left breast, I pinch the nipple gently between my thumb and forefinger, eliciting a soft moan from my girl as she turns her face upwards toward me and leans in for a kiss.

Our tongues slash together in a hot, wet kiss as our bodies become one, Lauren's right hand reaching up behind her so she can pull me harder against her. Our moans meld together, our mouths greedy for more, Lauren working herself up and down on my cock a little faster than moments before, just enough to really get me going.

While my left hand continues to worship her breasts, my right hand decides to go south of her belly, to my favourite place in the entire world. Sweeping a finger over her clit, Lauren jolts against the barely there touch, and I let out an agonised groan as I feel how wet she is down there, at how our bodies fit together so perfectly. Fuck, she is just so beautiful. Beautifully wet and moulded around my cock to absolute fucking perfection.

Sweet Jesus, I won't last long. Not tonight. The knowledge that we've now made a lifelong commitment to each other is sending me wild for her even more than usual. In fact, I can't take this slow paced tempo for a minute longer. I need it harder and I need it now.

"Harder, baby," I growl into her mouth.

Lauren doesn't need telling twice when it comes to commanding her in the bedroom. She loves it when I boss her around and talk dirty to her and, as predicted, she gives me exactly what I want. Lauren wants it too of course. Fuck, does she want it as much as I do.

Lauren soon has the pair of us clinging on to each other

desperately as we ride out our orgasm together. Our loud groans and breathless pants cut through the darkness of our bedroom, the humidity of the weather doing its work on us as beads of sweat cling to our bare, clammy skin.

I swear I am literally drowning in her right now, Lauren seemingly unwilling to stop until we are both more than satisfied that we are done. The trouble is, with Lauren, I am never done. And neither is she. We go on for a few more minutes, grappling with each other, kissing madly, deeply, thrusting, and reaching for more. So much more.

Lauren lets out another breathy moan as she comes hard all over again and I slam up into her one final time before placing my arms around her body from behind and stilling us.

"Sssh, baby," I whisper against her lips, "I've got you."

Lauren is panting madly, her chest heaving against my arms as she finally gives in and begins to relax against me. Eventually, she speaks. Or at least, she tries to anyway.

"Shit…that was…" Lauren's words are lost as she fights to catch her breath.

"Earth shattering?" I mumble against her cheek.

She lets out a little laugh. "I was going for out of this world amazing but, earth shattering pretty much sums up what I was trying to say."

Planting a tender kiss on her cheek, I then hug her even tighter against me. "You don't need to say anything to me, sweetheart, your body tells me everything I need to know."

I can't help but reach down and feel for where our bodies are still joined together, the bedsheets beneath us sopping wet with our arousal. "Jesus, Lauren, I want you again already and I'm still inside you," I whisper against her cheek, my eyes closing briefly, as if in pain. Pain from the endless torture of being in love with a woman so madly, so deeply, that it scares the absolute shit out of me. I swear that sometimes, I actually feel agonised over the depths of feelings I have for this woman. I wonder if other people who are in love feel this way, or whether it's just me. Just us. Because I swear that Lauren feels it too.

As if reading my thoughts, her eyes suddenly flick up to meet mine and even in the darkness of our bedroom, I can see right through those beautiful deep blue eyes of hers. I can see into her very soul. I always could. "I feel the same, Jonny," she eventually whispers to me, "always have done, always will."

A short while later, we make love all over again, Lauren led on the bed beneath me this time as I thrust gently into her. It's tender and loving and fuck is it all-consuming. A heart bursting, soul splintering moment of love between us as I take us over the edge and into the stratosphere once more. We both come apart at the seams and then collapse into each other's arms afterwards, momentarily spent. For now at least.

We lay on the bed afterwards, Lauren's damp, naked body pressed tightly against mine. Lauren is busy drawing lazy circles around the tattoos on my chest as my fingers trail featherlight touches along her shoulder and arm. Lying here in the dark with Lauren, just in the peace and quiet of our surroundings at some ridiculous hour of the morning, is the very tonic I need in my life right now.

Before coming away on holiday, I couldn't sleep in the dark at all, or at least, I could rarely sleep in the dark anyway. I have my suicide attempt and coma to thank for that. But somehow or other, being here on this island with the love of my life, my future wife, has changed all of that. I feel happy and relaxed and…safe. Sounds odd that a world famous rock star who seemingly has everything in the world would somehow feel scared of things but, famous or not, I am merely one man. A human. And I have started to accept the fact that I can break. Fuck, I did break. I broke apart in front of the eyes of the entire world and it is that very thought I am terrified of.

I'm scared about going back out into the world and being in the glare of the paparazzi again. I'm terrified of being followed around and Lauren being followed right along with me. I'm worried about the disappointment on the faces of my fans right now as they become ever more impatient about my whereabouts, because I never did issue a statement. I never stood up and took charge of my failings and I never put them in the picture about what had happened to me.

In some ways, it isn't any of their business, my private life is my private life. But, they are my fans, and I adore my fans. Without them, I wouldn't be where I am today. I carry on making music not just for myself and my own love of the job but, for them too. I feel like I've let them down by saying nothing at all, by staying silent and hiding away, leaving them to think all sorts of things about what could have happened to me. To me and the band.

This is partly why I just want to walk away from it all and never look back. But can I really walk away from it all? From the thing I love? And after seeing my mum in a vision tonight, pretty much telling me to go back to the band that I've come to know and love as my family, can I really still walk away from all of that like it all meant nothing to me? Like my band, my best friends, my family, meant nothing? I sigh absently.

"Are you okay?" Lauren's sweet voice cuts through my negative thoughts, thankfully pulling me back to the present and into our peaceful surroundings once more.

"Of course I'm okay," I lie. Well, I'm not really lying. I am okay. With Lauren, I am always okay. I just don't like how my mind has suddenly wandered to negative thoughts once again.

I really need to listen to the advice of my counsellor more and work on that negative thought process that still catches me off guard, but me being me just plays ignorant most of the time when it comes to stuff like cognitive behavioural therapy or whatever the hell it's called. I know I promised Lauren I would continue with the counselling sessions and anything else that gets thrown my way, but I can't honestly say that I do absolutely everything my counsellor advises me to do. Not that I would tell Lauren that of course…..

"Baby, you sighed. A great big sigh."

Shit, did I really sigh out loud? I thought it was in my head. I think fast so as not to get a grilling from Lauren. "It was a satisfied sigh," I say, trying my best to avoid the Lauren Whittle inquisition. "It was my 'I'm relaxed post amazing sex with my new fiancée' satisfied sigh." She laughs at that but then shakes her head.

"You are so full of it, Jonny Mathers."

"I'm full of you, and you of me, I know that much." I hit her back with a suggestive quip and she rolls her eyes at me.

"Jonny, talk to me…please. Something is bothering you, I can tell."

I let out an exasperated sigh this time. One I am fully aware of. "Lauren, can we just enjoy this moment please? Enjoy our post lovemaking afterglow and the fact that we are now officially engaged."

"We're only officially engaged when you put a ring on it, Mathers." Oh, so Lauren's smart mouth is coming out to play now, is it?

"Oh, is that so?" I ask, narrowing my eyes on her. She smiles.

"Yes, it's so."

"I thought you weren't at all materialistic," I joke.

Reaching up, she brushes a tender hand through my mussed up bed hair. "Very funny. You know full well that I am far from being materialistic. Hell, I'd put a ring pull from a can on my finger if it meant cementing my commitment to you."

That stops me in my tracks, the jokey like smile now fading away from my face as I look on at Lauren lovingly. She really would wear a ring pull from a can on her finger, because that's how much she loves me. She doesn't want expensive diamond rings and glamorous fancy weddings that cost hundreds of thousands of pounds. She just wants me. Me and me alone. Nothing more. Nothing less.

Trailing my fingers into her mass of blonde curls, I say to her, "And that's exactly why I love you more than anything or anybody else that walks upon this earth." I reach across to plant a soft, tender kiss to her lips. When I pull back, I say, "But just so you know, you will be getting a big diamond engagement ring on that finger of yours, because I want to do things properly. So, Lauren Whittle, you will get your diamond ring and you will get a big dream wedding, if that's what you want…"

"Jonny, I don't want or need a big dream wedding. I just want you…and a modest, but pretty, diamond ring that means something to me. To us. I don't want you spending thousands of pounds or should I say, dollars, on a piece of jewellery, just because you can. I want my engagement ring to signify the beginning of our journey towards getting married, the beginning of our next, wonderful chapter together. That's all I want. Okay?"

I blink at her in wonder, sometimes doubting whether this woman is actually real or whether she's just a ghostlike figment of my over active imagination. "You are real, aren't you?" I ask her in disbelief. "Because I really couldn't handle it if you weren't."

She flashes me one of her most wondrous smiles, the one that really reaches her eyes and settles into her skin, her very soul. *My* soul. "Oh, I'm very real, Jonny. I've been real from the moment we met when we were just fifteen years old. And I'm here to stay. Forever. You hear me? Because this is it this time. No more doubts. No more interfering fathers and no more running away. It's just you and me against the world, Jonny. Remember?"

Cupping her cheek in the palm of my hand, I say the very words that I first said to her all those years ago, "You and me against the world, baby. Just you and me. Always."

****

"Oh, so you're blindfolding me now?" Lauren looks on at me in amusement. "Seriously?"

"It's the only way to keep any surprise hidden from you. If you don't have the blindfold on, you'll see the surprise too soon."

"Where did you even get a blindfold from anyway? I'm curious." Trust Lauren to ask a question like that.

"You seem more interested in the blindfold than the actual surprise."

She laughs. "Oh no, definitely not. I can't wait to see my surprise, you've been teasing me about it all day long."

She's not wrong there. I wanted to do something really special for Lauren today. Since proposing to her in the middle of the night last night, I decided I wanted to make a really big deal out of that proposal by officially celebrating it together, just the two of us. I want to do things properly and make a huge fuss of her and so, my idea was born. Thankfully, the staff here at where we are staying have been amazing in getting it all sorted out for me, with one or two ideas and additions thrown in by me of course.

"Of course I've been teasing you about it, that's all part of the fun and the build up to the surprise. So…" I grin down at her and hold the blindfold up in front of her face. "You coming to see this surprise or what?" She raises a suspicious eyebrow up at me and my grin widens. "You look stunning by the way. Absolutely stunning."

And she does. Dressed to kill in a short electric blue strapless dress, Lauren's curves are a sight to behold as the material of the dress works its wonders on that beautiful body of hers. With her sun kissed skin, smoky eyeshadow, nude lips and dampened blonde curls fresh from her shower, she literally knocks the stuffing out of me. I sometimes wonder what the hell I did to get so lucky, being with a woman as beautiful as her, but then, she seems to say the exact same thing about me.

"Well, thank you for the compliment, rock star, although I would have preferred to have worn this dress with the high heels that are supposed to be worn with it, as opposed to my flip flops."

I chuckle. "I told you, high heels aren't really suitable for where we're going tonight, however, I'm more than happy for you to wear said high heels in the bedroom later on…"

"Now why doesn't that surprise me?" she says, with a hint of sarcasm in her voice.

I narrow my eyes on her. "Don't pretend that you wouldn't enjoy it."

She smiles up at me suggestively and then glances back down at the blindfold in my hands. "Maybe my high heels aren't the only thing I'll be wearing later on, Jonny…"

"Well I really hope they will be the only thing you'll be wearing once I've finished with you," I hit her back with a quip.

She rolls her eyes heavenwards. "I was talking about the blindfold." Oh, I see where Lauren is going with this. Hmm, I like her thinking. I like it a lot.

Biting down on my bottom lip, I say, "How have we never tried this before?"

"I have no idea." Looking up at me, I can see from her eyes that all sorts of dirty thoughts are suddenly running through her mind. They mirror my thoughts exactly. "But now that you're standing there holding this thing out to me, I kind of like the thought of it." See? We're like two peas in a pod, Lauren and I. We were so meant to be.

Placing my index finger under her chin, I tilt her face up towards mine. Planting a soft, wet kiss to her lips, I then pull back and whisper, "Hold that thought, sweetheart, because I promise you that I'll make good on it later on."

Her eyes sweep over my face as she sinks her teeth into her bottom lip. "And I'll hold you to that promise, Jonny Mathers. Believe me."

Oh I believe her alright. In fact, if we don't get out of here right now then we won't be going anywhere and Lauren won't be experiencing any surprise other than me shoving her backwards on to the bed, blindfolding her and absolutely ravaging the living daylights out of her. *Easy Jonny, save the good stuff for later. Focus on the here and now and the surprise you've got planned for Lauren.*

On that note, I decide to instead walk behind her so she doesn't distract me any more than I already am. "You ready?" I whisper into her ear. She nods. I then slowly, ever so slowly, place the black blindfold over her eyes. She gasps in surprise.

Or is it arousal? I'm not entirely sure, but one thing I am sure of is that my cock is more than twitching right now. Shit, I really need to get out of here before I get carried away.

Taking a firm hold of Lauren's hand, I lead her out of our villa and towards the beach, being careful not to rush her or trip her up along the way. "You okay?" I check in with her, making sure I'm not walking too fast.

"I'm all good," she says with an excited smile, her eyes still well and truly hidden away behind the blindfold. My heart leaps in my chest at seeing her so happy and excited.

Turning my attention back to our private beach in front of us, I look towards the ocean and in the distance I see a man waiting in a speedboat ready to take us on our journey. My stomach flips excitedly. This is it. Time for Lauren's surprise. And what a surprise it is going to be….

CHAPTER 16

LAUREN

It seems to take an age, being on the speedboat with Jonny, waiting for my surprise. I can't even enjoy the sights from the boat as Jonny insists on keeping my eyes well and truly covered until we reach our destination.

When we do finally arrive, I hear Jonny thank the driver for us before picking me up and out of the boat and then placing me down on the ground, or should I say, the sand. Of course we're on another beach. Where else would we go on this beautiful island?

I hear the boat speed off into the distance as Jonny gently guides me along the sand. My curiosity is really beginning to get the better of me. "Well I sincerely hope that whoever just brought us here on that speedboat is coming back to pick us up later on."

"Maybe I've stolen you away to another part of the island for the entire night," Jonny says, chuckling to himself.

"Hmm, I wouldn't mind if you did do that actually…anyway, enough of the torturous keeping me waiting, Jonny Mathers, please can I see what my surprise is now?"

Jonny walks us a few more steps before finally coming to a complete stop. "Actually, yes, you can see what your surprise is now. I must say that I admire you for being _so_ patient all the way here by the way." I note the sarcasm in his voice and I just shake my head at him.

"I think I've been more than patient, thank you very much."

Jonny laughs and then brings his hands up to the back of my head, readying himself to untie the blindfold. "You ready?" he whispers into my ear. *Am I ready?*

"Of course I'm ready!" I shout excitedly. "Now come on, Mathers, put a girl out of her misery, will you?!"

Seconds later, Jonny finally loosens the blindfold from around my eyes and I am met with the most beautiful scene. I bring my hands up to my mouth in shock as I take in the surprise. A surprise that Jonny has clearly worked so hard on setting up for me.

I glance around the beach in front of me, the sand sprinkled with an array of bright red rose petals and tealights. A small white table and two antique style posh looking chairs are set up for the pair of us with a huge candelabra in the centre of the table.

Also on the table is a bottle of champagne that looks as though it is chilling away nicely in a bucket of ice with two champagne flutes sat either side of it. Everywhere I look there are candles upon candles and as I glance over my shoulder toward the ocean, that's when I see it. The very thing I am sure Jonny brought me here for. The most breathtaking sunset I have ever seen.

"Oh my god, Jonny…" I am lost for words as I watch the sun begin to descend beyond the horizon, as though it is dipping into the very ocean itself. The sky is a burning glow of red and gold and the crest of the waves sparkle beneath the sun's rays. Jonny stands behind me and slips his arms around my waist.

Placing his chin on my left shoulder, he looks out at the sunset and says, "This is what I wanted you to see, because where we're staying, on the other side of the island, is where the sun rises. Here is where the sun sets. And I wanted you to see the sunset at least once before we leave this beautiful haven."

"Oh, Jonny, this is perfect," I whisper, my eyes still fixated on the beautiful sunset right in front of us, "it's the most beautiful thing I have ever seen in my life."

"I disagree," Jonny whispers, forcing me to turn my head to look up at him. "*You're* the most beautiful thing I have ever seen in my life, Lauren. This sunset comes in at a very close second." I smile up at him. "Happy engagement night to us, future Mrs Mathers." Jonny presses a soft kiss to my lips.

"Happy engagement night right back at you, Mr Mathers," I say back to him.

I reach in for another kiss before the pair of us turn back to watch the last of the sun's rays sink into the ocean. We stand there in silence for a while, taking in the changing colours in the sky as the sun finally goes to bed for the night. I don't recall ever feeling as relaxed and as happy as I feel right now. Even more so when my new fiancé eventually decides that it is time to wine and dine me.

He leads me over to the table and pulls out one of the chairs for me. I sit down and then watch in curiosity as Jonny suddenly disappears behind me. Moments later, Jonny returns with a male waiter following directly behind him. I smile to myself. Of course he had some help setting up all of this. And no wonder. You can barely see the sand on this beach because of all the rose petals and the tealights scattered around us. That certainly explains why I haven't seen him for most of the afternoon. He has been a very busy man indeed and I love him even more for it.

As Jonny finally joins me at the table, I lean over and give him a quick kiss on the lips. "Thank you for this, Jonny. I absolutely love it."

He grins back at me like a loved up loon. "Oh, there's plenty more to come, sweetheart, because my waiter friend here, Layan, is going to be serving up the most delicious food you have ever tasted. Isn't that right, Layan?"

Layan, a smartly dressed young looking man with olive skin and a mass of curly black hair nods his head at me and smiles politely. "Yes," he says, "me serve beautiful lady."

I smile back at him and say, "Thank you, Layan, you're too kind."

He beams brightly at me and Jonny and then proceeds to open up our bottle of champagne. Pouring the champagne into our glasses, Layan makes sure he hands me my glass first. Such a gentleman. "Thank you."

Layan then hands a glass to Jonny and says, "You enjoy drink. Me come back with food when ready."

He nods his head and smiles at us before turning on his heel and retreating back into the large beach hut behind us, which I have to admit I've only just fully noticed. I've been so swept away by the whole romantic gesture that I haven't really taken in my surroundings as yet.

"Layan is very polite and friendly," I say to Jonny, "he got a whole restaurant of food and chefs back there or what?"

"Layan is lovely. He's one of the locals, as you will probably have gathered from his limited English. And yes, in that hut behind us is where all the magic is happening right now. There are two chefs on site and another two waiters on hand to help out with our meal and whatever else we want for the entire night."

"So, we are staying overnight then?"

"I thought it best, as opposed to going back to our villa on the other side of the island via speedboat in the pitch black later on."

"Hmm, probably a good idea. Although…"

"Although?" Jonny asks, raising an eyebrow.

"What about our clothes and toiletries and stuff from our villa?"

Jonny grins lasciviously. "Firstly, we won't be needing any clothes when I get you back to our room later on." I chuckle at that. "And secondly, don't you worry about a thing tonight, I have everything covered and sorted out."

"You old romantic, you," I say to him.

"See? I told you there was still some of the old Jonny inside of me somewhere. You just…had to dig a little bit deeper to find him."

I gaze across the table into his eyes and cup his left cheek in my hand. "I love you, Jonny Mathers."

Resting his hand over mine, Jonny says, "I love you too, Lauren Whittle." We slowly come together, kissing each other gently, tenderly, Jonny's hand reaching into my hair ever so softly. When he pulls away, he says to me, "Now how about we toast our engagement properly?"

Raising his champagne glass in the air, he says, "To us, and to a very happy future together."

I raise my glass in the air and clink it gently against his. "To us and our happy future."

We both take a sip of our champagne and then kiss once more, finally sealing our happy moment together and making it official. We are engaged at last and I am so happy that I want to scream it from the rooftops and tell the entire world but, for now, just keeping this happy moment between ourselves will do just nicely.

The rest of our romantic evening is truly magical as the waiters and the chefs wait on us hand and foot. The food is top class cuisine and is like nothing I've ever tasted before and they bring out plate after plate, constantly looking after us and making sure absolutely everything about the evening is perfect and special. The champagne is literally on tap and one of the waiters even starts strumming away on a Spanish guitar for us later on. Jonny loves that and soon pulls me away from the table so that we can have a dance on the sand, near the water's edge.

As the waiter plays away on his guitar in the background, Jonny sways me gently in his arms as the waves from the ocean gently lap at our feet. The tealights shimmer in the distance behind us and some of the rose petals blow across the sand as the soft evening breeze picks up. This is my most perfect moment with Jonny and I want to remember this for the rest of my life.

"I want to remember this night with you forever," I say to Jonny, "this is my perfect moment right now. If I never get another perfect moment then I want you to know that this moment right now is it. Complete and utter perfection."

Jonny caresses his hands over my lower back as we continue to sway to the music. His eyes look back and forth between mine, as though he is trying to memorise absolutely everything about my face, about this moment, this oh so perfect moment that he has created for us. He looks at me with so much love and adoration that it makes my chest ache.

"This is the start of our next chapter, Lauren, and there are going to be plenty more perfect moments for us along the way. I can promise you that."

I reach up to give him a kiss and he then pulls me against his chest as we continue to sway gently to the music. Jonny rests his chin on top of my head and there we stay, in our perfect moment, dancing away in each other's arms, for as long as the world will allow us.

CHAPTER 17

LAUREN

"Oh my god! You're engaged? Arghhh!" Stacey squeals loudly with excitement, jumping up and down on the spot like a mad woman as Jonny and I deliver our happy news.

Ben looks on at the pair of us in shock at first, before turning his eyes on Stacey who is now pulling me in for a great big hug. "Oh, Lauren, you have just made my day! In fact, scrap that, you have just made my entire year! I am so happy for you both!"

I can't help but jump up and down right along with my best friend as the rest of the lads start to congratulate Jonny, one by one. Will is first to shake hands with Jonny, swiftly followed by Zack and then lastly, Ben, who still looks like he's been shocked into silence by the news.

Reaching over to Jonny, he gives him a friendly slap on the shoulder and then says, "I can't say I'm not shocked that you're finally nailing yourself down to one woman for the rest of your life but...I'm seriously happy for you, dude. If anybody deserves happiness after the last few shitty months, then it's you, and I really mean that."

Jonny looks really humbled by Ben's response to our engagement and his smile is genuine. For once in their life, both Jonny and Ben are actually having a serious moment together.

I pull away from Stacey in surprise as I watch Jonny give Ben a manly hug. A proper man hug where they slap each other's backs and everything, before quickly pulling away. It is a very brief exchange but an exchange nonetheless. It makes me smile.

"And as for you, Lauren Whittle," says Ben, turning to me this time. "You better be ready for what's coming." Oh, here we go.

"And what would that be, Ben?" I ask, my curiosity piqued. I am not sure whether this will be a serious response or a joke coming my way.

"Married life of course. It won't be easy being married to him, you know. I swear the press and the fans are going to go nuts when they hear the news. Just be prepared for that, Lauren."

I am just about to speak when Jonny speaks for me. "Oh don't worry, Lauren and I have everything covered in that area. Right, baby?" *Do we?*

Instead of asking questions, I decide to play along and smile my biggest smile. "Of course, we have everything under control, Benny boy, don't you worry about that. Nothing outside of these four walls can come between what Jonny and I have. Paparazzi included. This time is for keeps."

Jonny walks over to where I'm standing and pulls me into his side. Kissing me on top of my head, he says, "Abso-fucking-lutely this time is for keeps. I am getting a ring on this woman's finger and sealing the deal and as soon as that engagement ring is on, I'm going to shout from the rooftops…in fact, no, I'm going to shout from the top of the fucking world that Lauren has agreed to become my wife, because I want everyone out there to know what she means to me." Gazing down at me, he then says, "What *you* mean to me. I want everyone to know what you mean to me, Lauren."

As lovely as that declaration is, it's a far cry from what he was saying to me back in the Maldives the day before yesterday, and what he's been saying to me in the Maldives every single day from the moment he proposed just over two weeks ago. About how he wanted to keep the happy news just between us and our friends for the time being and how he wanted our private life to stay private for as long as possible. Why the sudden change of heart and the seemingly urgent need to announce our engagement to the world, I really don't know, but I admittedly don't feel overly comfortable with it. I don't want to admit that though, not right now anyway, and so I smile my way through the little niggle that is now gnawing away at my gut and instead lean up to kiss my fiancé on the lips. Our friends all whoop and whistle loudly, Ben shouting at us to get a room.

"Well, I think this happy news calls for champagne, and lots of it!" shouts Stacey.

Jonny pulls his mouth away from mine and looks over at Stacey. "I couldn't agree with you more, Stace. I'll get Tony to sort out some champagne and get it delivered as soon as possible."

"Sounds like a plan to me," says an eager looking Stacey.

****

Later that evening, both Jonny and I pop the cork on four bottles of champagne, the six of us all indulging in some ridiculously expensive bubbles. I told Jonny to get prosecco. Jonny decided to get expensive champagne. He said it was a celebration of our engagement and so what could I possibly say to that?

We are sitting in 'The Snug' at the back of Jonny's house, all chatting happily together as we sip at our champagne. Jonny and I are filling our friends in about the holiday and Jonny's proposal on the beach, Stacey gushing at the romance of it all.

The early March weather in LA is quite cool at the moment

and so the large log burner in the corner of the room is now lit and roaring to life. I'm feeling the cold even more tonight after spending three weeks in the Maldives. The weather there was glorious every single day; hot and sunny and not a cloud in sight. It was sheer bliss, and telling our friends all about it is just making me miss it even more. Especially as we've now come back home to this 'house of sin' as Jonny keeps calling it. It never bothered me at all until it started bothering Jonny, and now all I can think of whenever I am here is what happened before I came back into his life. Of the fact that he tried to take his own life under this very roof. I hate that I'm now thinking these things and I'm doing my best not to think about them, but it's difficult. The sooner we move house, the better.

Jonny and I were meant to start looking at houses a month ago, but then we went away on holiday and the house hunting never even got off the ground. Now we're back in LA, Jonny has said that choosing a new home together and buying me an engagement ring are the first things on his mind and so I am hoping that we can get started on searching for a house as soon as possible. Especially as Jonny has now insisted that we permanently sleep in his music studio downstairs, as opposed to his bedroom, or anywhere else in the house for that matter. And as amazing as our first night in his music studio was all those weeks ago, it's not a proper bedroom and it never will be. Sleeping in there does have some benefits though, especially when Jonny decides to ravish me on top of his piano or bang me senseless against his book shelves. Yes, for now, I will focus on those *benefits* and they will be what get me through these next few weeks or months, up until we find a new home together.

"So, you taking Lauren engagement ring shopping tomorrow, or what?" Stacey's voice pulls me back from my thoughts and I see she is already grilling Jonny on what his next move is going to be. Jonny just chuckles at my best friend.

"Maybe not tomorrow, but don't you worry, Stace, it's all in hand. Lauren is going to get the engagement ring that she deserves and a brand new home with her husband to be." Wow, it's almost as if Jonny has been reading my thoughts tonight. I swear he's telepathic sometimes.

"And I can't wait to choose both of those things with you, Jonny," I reply, smiling over at him as though he is the only person in the room with me right now.

"You know, you two are starting to make me feel sick," says Ben, looking disgusted.

"Oh shut it, Anderson," says Stacey, taking a quick sip of her champagne, "it's about time we had some happy news to celebrate around here. They can be as romantic as they like." Ben rolls his eyes at Stacey and she gives him a shake of the head in return.

"So, have you had any interested parties in your house since you put it on the market?" enquires Will.

Jonny nods. "Yeah, apparently we've had quite a bit of interest while we've been away on holiday. I'll pick up on all of that tomorrow with my realtor though. I swear I've got so much to catch up on. Since being out of the limelight and being...unwell, I've let things slide, and I really need to get my head back in the game and get a plan underway as to what I, and we, as a band, are going to do next."

I can tell that Jonny is already beginning to worry about what comes next now that our holiday is over with. He's excited about moving house and the engagement of course, but that will only distract him from everything else for a short amount of time. I worry that he is going back into all of this too soon though, and as much as I want him to get back in the game and get back to doing what he loves, I want him to take baby steps to get there. I don't want him to leap back into things too quickly and then end up right back where he was just a few weeks ago.

Before we went away, he was talking about quitting music altogether and now he's suddenly wanting to run towards it at break neck speed. Perhaps I am over worrying but after what he's been through these last few months, I don't think that worry will ever go away. Not for a while at least.

"Well, whatever you decide to do next, Jonny, we're behind you, one hundred percent," says Will, "right lads?" Ben and Zack nod their heads in agreement. "And there's no pressure from any of us to rush back into anything either. Whatever you need to do or however long you need, we will support you."

"I know you will, and I'm really grateful to all of you for helping me get back to where I am right now. I still have a long road ahead of me, I know that…" Jonny glances down at me when he says that, "…but I feel that I'm gradually getting stronger day by day and hopefully, in the not too distant future, we can get back out there and get touring again."

My stomach lurches at hearing Jonny say those words, but the lads look really pleased about the prospect of going back on tour again. I can't say I blame them, it has been a while and their last tour of the US was of course cut short when Jonny went off the rails and did what he did. Just thinking about what happened back then makes me feel sick to the pit of my stomach. I really can't imagine Jonny going back up on a stage as yet. He's still riddled with anxiety about everything that happened to him and yet, here he is today, putting back on the stage mask for our friends when he doesn't need to.

Our friends have seen Jonny at his absolute worst, as he has just acknowledged, and yet Jonny is now painting this oh so perfect picture all over again. Just like he used to. I am so happy that he is now well on the road to recovery and of course I want him to get back out there and start touring again, but not yet. I know he said in the not too distant future but what does that even mean? How long exactly is he going to give himself before stepping back into the limelight? A week? A month? Six months? I don't understand where all of this is suddenly coming from and as much as I don't want to burst this positive bubble of his that he has somehow created overnight, I do feel as though I need to speak to him about this. Not now, obviously, but later on when our friends have gone home, I will find the time to talk to him then. For now though, I just want to enjoy the company of our friends who we haven't seen in over three weeks.

"Oh, I forgot to tell you," says Stacey, "I managed to finally sort out the stuff from our apartment back in London. I got the rest of our stuff flown over here and it's currently in one of Ben's spare bedrooms. The lease has now ended and everything has been signed and sorted out. We are now as free as the birds in the sky, girl!"

Stacey leans over from where she is sitting on the sofa opposite me and clinks her champagne glass against mine. "Sounds like another reason to be drinking this champagne to me," I say excitedly, "thank you for doing all of that, Stace. I admittedly forgot all about it."

Stacey shrugs her shoulders. "It was no bother, and anyway, you were kind of preoccupied getting all loved up on a beach somewhere over in paradise. Lucky cow."

"I can't lie to you, Stace, it was literally paradise out there. I didn't want to come home."

"Me neither," Jonny suddenly murmurs into my ear, and I giggle.

"You know, all this soppiness is really forcing me to want to drink," says Ben, pulling a face. "You got anything stronger than champagne? As in whisky or rum? Fuck, anything that will take the edge off of you two."

Everyone around us laughs, and then Stacey pipes up again. "Hey, this is just the beginning of the whole romance chapter for them, Ben. Wait until the actual wedding day, and then just when you think the whole romantic soppy stuff is over with, they'll have babies."

At the sheer mention of babies, my smile automatically fades away. I can't help it. I try to force the smile back to my face but I fail miserably because unfortunately, the whole baby situation is a huge trigger for me. A trigger back to my past and the unbearable pain I went through when I lost my son. My Oliver.

Jonny notices my change in demeanour straight away and places a reassuring arm around my shoulders. Pulling me against him, he says, "But we don't need to talk about any of that right now do we, Stace? For now, let's just live for the moment and celebrate the here and now, yeah?"

"Oh absolutely. To the here and now and to your engagement!" shouts Stacey, not realising at all what she's said. Thankfully. I'd rather she didn't notice because the last thing I want is to draw attention to it. I hate that I still get triggered by it and that it still hurts me, all these years later. I suppose not dealing with grief properly at the time would do that to someone. It certainly had its lasting effects on me anyway. Jonny too. And speaking of Jonny, he dealt with that situation just now in the best possible way and I turn to him and kiss him gratefully.

"Thank you," I say to him quietly.

"What for?" he asks, keeping up the pretence in front of our friends, just in case they overhear what we're saying.

Placing my mouth against his ear, I whisper the words, "You know what for."

****

Stacey and the lads leave just after 9.00 pm as both Jonny and I are exhausted and well and truly jet lagged from the long flight home. We only arrived home yesterday afternoon but neither of us slept well last night because of the time difference messing with our body clocks.

I take a shower and then change into my warmer, more snuggly pyjamas. The weather may not be as cold here in March as it would be back in the UK but it's certainly a lot cooler than where I was just two days ago. I am having serious Maldives withdrawal symptoms.

Wrapping my fluffy white dressing gown around me, I then head out of Jonny's bedroom and downstairs towards his music studio. It seems so silly, showering upstairs in his en-suite, going through my night time routine in his bedroom, drying my hair in his bedroom, getting dressed in his bedroom, to then have to go all the way downstairs to go to sleep in his music studio. I get it of course, and I completely understand why Jonny doesn't want to sleep in there anymore. I hate the thought of even being in his bedroom now myself after what he tried to do to himself in there. I hate the thought of all the other things that went on in this house too, however much I try to put them out of my mind, but, despite all of that, I would still sleep in there if he could.

As much as I love his music studio, actually sleeping in there every single night on a mattress on the floor isn't really appealing to me right now. I just want to snuggle up together under a huge duvet on an actual bed and fall into a peaceful sleep in Jonny's arms, just like we did every night when we were away on holiday, minus the duvet of course, the weather was far too hot and humid for one of those.

On entering his music studio, I immediately spot my rock

star over in the corner. He is sitting on a stool, leaning over his desk and staring intently at what looks to be a notepad that is laid out in front of him. He is strumming a few chords on his guitar and he looks oh so studious and very serious, not to mention sexy, let's not forget how sexy this man of mine actually is.

He is dressed in his usual night time attire, a clingy white v-neck t-shirt which allows me to at least ogle one or two of the tattoos on his upper chest, as well as the sleeves of them on his arms. He wears his light grey pyjama pants as though he has been sewn into them, his perfectly taut bottom straining against the material as he leans forward in his stool to look down at whatever it is he is studying, presumably music notes or lyrics from the looks of things.

And while Jonny is busy creating a brand new masterpiece, I am busy doing nothing. Well, not exactly nothing. I am doing *something*. Or at least, Jonny is doing a whole lot of *something* to me anyway, that familiar tingling between my thighs and the ache in my chest growing stronger by the minute.

I swear I could stand here all night long and study Jonny from afar but unfortunately, my presence is soon noticed by the man himself who in turn, stops what he is doing and smiles over at me. "Hey there, beautiful. Like what you see?" Trust Jonny to follow up a compliment with a smug remark like that.

Closing the door behind me, I turn back to my man and shrug my shoulders. "Hmm, I suppose," I say, pretending to act all casual and nonchalant as I walk towards him.

Jonny's lips pull into a smile once more. "I'll pretend you didn't just say that to me."

Jonny's hands drop away from his guitar and he instead allows it to hang on its strap around his shoulders as he pulls me in to his side for a hug and a quick kiss. "You cold tonight? You're not normally so...dressed." Jonny tries to peek inside my fluffy dressing gown but I gently push his face away.

"Erm, excuse me, what is that supposed to mean?" I ask, pretending to be offended. Or maybe I am offended.

He chuckles. "What I meant to say is that you are wearing far too many clothes for my liking." Jonny reaches for the tie on my dressing gown but I bat his hands away.

"Erm, you just insulted me, Jonny Mathers, and now you're trying to get into my knickers? I don't think so."

I fold my arms across my chest and give him one of my best scowls. I know he was only joking but sometimes I just love to wind him up for the sake of it. It makes for great entertainment.

"*Erm*, Lauren, I hardly need to *try* to get into your knickers, and anyway, by the looks of things, I'd need to get through five layers of clothing first."

I am just about to launch into an angry tirade when Jonny gives me one of his eye rolls before yanking me up against him. "Oh give it a rest, Lauren, I was kidding." He puckers up his lips to give me an apology kiss but I turn my face away so his mouth meets with my cheek instead.

"Mmm, your cheek tastes amazing," he murmurs against my skin, and I can't help it, I start to smile at the conceited idiot. "God, what do they put in your face cream? You taste of sugar and spice and all things nice..."

I burst out laughing when he says that and I finally give in to the loved up lunatic that he is. Jonny sees my laughter as a weakness and soon ceases the opportunity to start kissing me all over again. His deliciously hot mouth melds with mine and my resolve begins to weaken.

Oh, I could more than get carried away with Jonny right now, but before we go to bed tonight, I really want to talk to him about my worries from earlier. I feel as though I should get anything that bothers me off my chest straight away so that Jonny and I are no longer keeping secrets from each other. I want us to be honest and open and talk about anything that is upsetting or worrying us. Only then can we fully be rid of our painful past and start afresh.

It takes every ounce of restraint within me to break a kiss as hot as this one is, but I somehow manage to prise his wandering hands away from my body and take a step back. He looks up from his stool at me questioningly. "You okay? What's wrong?"

Brushing an affectionate hand through his hair, I say, "Nothing's wrong with me, I just want to talk about something from earlier, that's all."

Something registers in his eyes straight away when I say that to him. "You mean when Stacey mentioned the baby word? She didn't mean it, Lauren. I don't think she even realised what she'd said, but I'm sorry if it upset you, I know it's a difficult subject and probably one we will eventually need to discuss but you don't need to worry about it, I'm certainly in no rush to have children right now..."

"It's not about that, Jonny, but...good to know where you stand on that subject..."

"Oh shit, I'm sorry, I didn't mean..."

"Jonny, I wasn't being sarcastic. I meant what I just said, I'm not in any rush to have children and I can't even think about babies or...anyway, that's not what I wanted to talk to you about."

"Okaaay," says Jonny, drawing out the word and looking a

little unsure about what I'm about to say to him.

Pulling up the other stool beside him, I sit myself down and set him with a long stare. "When you were talking to Stacey and the lads earlier, you mentioned about going back on tour in the not too distant future. What did you mean?"

Jonny's eyebrows pull into a frown. "I meant exactly what I said, in the not too distant future…."

"And how long is the not too distant future exactly?"

Jonny scratches at his neck in irritation at my sudden line of questioning. "I don't know, early next year maybe. Why?"

"So we're talking more like a year as opposed to months then…"

"Of course more like a year, a tour takes ages to plan, you know that. Why the concern?"

I raise my eyebrows in surprise. "Really, Jonny? You're asking me why I'm concerned?"

Jonny suddenly remembers himself and instead of flying off the handle and going into defence mode, he actually takes a beat to think about what he just said. With a weary sigh, he says, "Of course, I'm sorry, I didn't think."

A moment of silence passes between us before Jonny speaks again. "You think I'm jumping into things too soon?"

I hesitate before I answer him. The last thing I want is to put Jonny back into a negative thinking pattern. I love that he's now feeling more positive about things but I just want him to navigate through the next few weeks as carefully as he possibly can. "No, I wouldn't quite put it like that, Jonny. More like, don't jump into things but walk into them? If that makes sense?"

I watch as my words sink in with him, Jonny giving me a

small nod of understanding. "Yeah, that makes sense."

"And also..."

"There's an also?" Jonny's eyebrows shoot upwards in surprise.

"Don't panic. It's only a minor thing really."

"Which is?"

"Why do you suddenly want to tell the entire world about our engagement when just a couple of days ago, you wanted to keep it private between just us and our friends?"

Jonny sighs, appearing to be deep in thought. "Because even though I said I wanted to keep our private life private and our news a secret, the other part of me is just sick and tired of hiding away behind these four walls. And I want to set the record straight with my fans and the paparazzi too, because as soon as we step outside back into the world again, they will start printing their usual shit about me and I can't deal with that again, Lauren. I want them to have the truth from the outset. I want them to know that I am now engaged to the woman I love and that I'm finally settling down. In fact, I've been meaning to talk to you about this since we arrived home but I just haven't had chance as yet..."

"Talk to me about what?" Now I am curious, and also a little worried.

"I want to release a statement to the press. My own statement, in my own words...about everything that has happened to me over the last few months..."

"You want to tell the world about your suicide attempt?" I ask, feeling horrified at the very thought. Jonny grimaces when I say those words out loud, reminding him of the very thing he'd rather forget. "I'm sorry, I shouldn't have...I shouldn't have said that out loud..."

"No, it's okay," he says, looking away from me, his eyes now fixated on the floor. "I don't want you to keep walking on eggshells around me when it comes to talking about what happened. What I did. Shit, if I'm going to tell the world about it then *we* should be able to talk about it."

My chest constricts in pain as I think back to one of the worst times in my life, seeing Jonny lying in a coma in a hospital bed, not knowing whether he would live or die. Seeing him now, sitting across from me with his guitar slung around his shoulders and his notepad out in front of him, his song writing prowess having finally returned, it makes me so grateful that someone out there or something saved him from the brink. Something brought Jonny back to me and back into this world and sadly, that doesn't happen for everybody. Not everybody gets a second chance at life and in this moment, right now, Jonny is getting his second chance. His second chance to get back out there and shine.

Standing up from my stool, I close the distance between us and pull Jonny's head into my chest. He nuzzles his face against the fluffy material of my dressing gown and I feel his arms thread their way around my back. "Oh, baby," I whisper into his hair, "of course we should be able to talk about it, I just…hate the thought of upsetting you…"

Jonny gazes up at me, his eyes all misted over with emotion. I touch his cheeks tenderly with the tips of my fingers and drink in absolutely everything I love about him. His mussed up jet black hair, his long dark lashes, the melting brown eyes that pull me in whenever I look into them, his perfectly straight nose and that full, wholesome mouth. I will never tire of looking into this face. Ever.

"Don't ever worry about upsetting me, Lauren. You are the one person in the whole world who I can talk to about anything. I know that sometimes, in the past, I may not have always opened up about things straight away, but going forward, I want us to be on the same page and I want us to talk about things when they bother us."

I smile down at him. "That's exactly what I want too."

Jonny smiles up at me and then continues. "And the whole me telling the truth to the world thing isn't just about me setting the record straight, it's also about bringing awareness to both drug addiction and men's mental health. I've been thinking long and hard about this while we were away on holiday and after going through what I've been through, I want to try and help others out there by talking about what seems to still be a taboo subject. Men like me feel like they have to be 'the big strong man' all the time, like they can't show their feelings or emotions, but you…you always brought about so many feelings and emotions within me that I simply couldn't not feel them. The trouble is that despite how I felt on the inside, I still always felt I had to hide behind the bad boy persona I created when you left me. I've always hidden behind the facade of being so tough and unbreakable, like the rock star bad boy everybody wanted me to be. But, no more. When I release this statement, I want the people out there to finally see me for… well…me."

I look down at this wonderful man and find myself falling in love with him all over again. *Wow. Just…wow.* "You know when I sometimes say to you that I can't possibly love you any more than I already do?"

Jonny bites down on a cheeky smile. "Yeah, I'm vaguely aware of you saying it to me once or twice before today."

"Well, I do. I absolutely love you more now than I did before you made that amazing speech. Because you are the most wonderful, loving, kind and thoughtful man I have ever known and I support you every step of the way with this, Jonny. Every single step. And I promise that you'll never be alone again in your life. Ever. Because you've got this. *We've* got this."

Our mouths suddenly smash together in one huge wave of emotion as our feelings for each other begin to overwhelm us. Jonny sighs into my mouth as I cling on to him desperately, not ever wanting to let him go. It isn't long before Jonny's guitar gets put to one side as he hauls me up from the floor into his arms and leads me over to his grand piano. Ah, the piano. It's been a while….

CHAPTER 18

JONNY

"Are you for real right now, Jonny? After everything that she did, you seriously want to carry on employing Lara as your PA?"

"Just hear me out, Lauren, will you?" I reply.

"Hear you out?" Lauren scoffs. "Why should I bother? It sounds like you've well and truly made your mind up to me!"

As predicted, Lauren is pissed at me. Royally pissed at me actually. And I can't say I blame her, my decision to keep Lara on as my PA is probably a risky manoeuvre, but I've been mulling this over in my head since returning from our holiday, and I think once Lauren hears me out, she'll understand.

"When I said hear me out, I meant as to the reason why I want to give her a second chance."

Lauren starts flailing her arms about in anger. "Oh my god, Jonny, she doesn't deserve a second chance! Have you forgotten what she did to you?!"

"Of course not…"

"Well I think you have!" she shouts, "I think you've forgotten that she went behind your back and told your dad the new gate code for your house when you changed it and didn't want your dad to have it. Not forgetting that she was going to put a press statement together with your dad, *behind your back*, about you, and release it to the papers without even discussing it with you first…"

"Lauren, will you just…"

"And let's not forget what she did *before* both of those things, when she released that sordid news story to the world in order to break us up! And she also cancelled those five shows on your US tour! That's sabotage at the highest level!"

Shit, I knew Lauren would be angry about this whole Lara thing but she's taking anger to a whole new level this morning. Don't get me wrong, I can be one hot headed son of a bitch at times but then I sometimes forget that Lauren can be too. Hot headed, stubborn and immovable. Because once she gets her bee in a bonnet about something that really means something to her or upsets her, then that is usually it, but not this time. I am standing firm on this subject and if she allows me to speak for just a minute or two, I can explain why I am all about giving Lara that second chance.

"Are you going to let me speak or not?!" I snap back at her. Giving her a taste of her own medicine might be just what she needs to calm down.

"Oh, screw you, Jonny!" she yells into my face before storming out of the kitchen. *Or maybe not.*

Feeling irritated that our morning is already dissolving into an argument after we've spent the last few weeks in the Maldives living blissfully together without so much as a cross word, I suddenly begin to wonder why the fuck I am carrying on with my music career after all. Day one of being back to reality and it's already going to shit. Okay, I need to deal with this situation and I'll deal with this right now. Lauren can storm away from me all she wants, but I won't let this rest until I've said what I've been trying to say to her for the last few minutes.

I storm after her through the house, finally finding her in

'The Snug' at the back of the house. She is sitting down on one of the sofas when I enter the room but she soon stands up when I walk over to her in a rage. "You going to let me finish what I've been trying to tell you for the last ten minutes or you gonna carry on ranting?!"

Holding her arms out to the sides, she yells, "If I get to choose then I choose to rant!"

I swear to god, she frustrates the absolute shit out of me sometimes, and it's beginning to show. I really don't want to lose my temper with her right now and have a full scale argument but if she carries on winding me up deliberately, then an argument is exactly what she is going to get.

"You wanna piss me off more than you already are doing? Is that it?" Sweeping an angry arm around the room, I say, "Go on then, carry on with your rant! Holiday and engagement celebrations well and truly over this morning I see!"

"What?!" She screws up her face at me and then folds her arms in a show of defiance. "So you think just because we've been all 'loved up' for the last few weeks that that means I can't stand up to you and tell you exactly what I think about one of your employees! You think I can't have an opinion anymore?"

Lauren does the old air quote gesture when she says the words 'loved up', and that really pisses me off. I hate air quotes at the best of times but when Lauren does it, it absolutely infuriates me.

"Oh stop talking bullshit, Lauren!" I shout back at her. "You're putting words into my mouth now that I simply never said, and don't air quote me either, you know I hate that!"

"Almost as much as I hate Lara for doing what she did to you? I highly doubt it!" she screams.

Letting out an exasperated sigh, I rub my hands over my face in irritation and take a breather for a few seconds. All this shouting at each other is doing me in and my head is beginning to hurt. I don't deal with stress as well as I used to, not since my coma, and any form of shouting or screaming and my head begins to let me know that it's time to calm the fuck down.

With my hands still covering my face, I take a few deep breaths in and out, trying to find my inner calm, just like my counsellor advised me to do in a situation that I find stressful.

Lauren's anger soon turns to concern as she runs over to me immediately. "Jonny? Are you okay?" She slowly prises my hands away from my face and looks up at me guiltily. "I'm sorry for shouting. Are you okay?"

I give her a reluctant nod. "Yeah, I just…my head still hurts if I get really angry or stressed. Since the coma…"

"Yes, I know," she whispers, her hands now clasping at my face as her concerned eyes search mine in desperation. "Of course I know. I should have remembered…oh, Jonny, I'm sorry," she says, looking guilt ridden, "I just got carried away with myself and it's only because I'm worried about you. I worry about you trusting somebody and then that somebody breaking that trust, like Lara did. How can you possibly trust her again after what she did?"

I nod towards the sofa. "Let's sit down."

Lauren takes a gentle hold of my hand and pulls me down on to the sofa with her. She looks a little apprehensive after our argument but at least she has now calmed down and is prepared to hear me out. "Okay, I'm listening."

With a nod of my head, I begin. "What Lara did was unacceptable, and I acknowledge that and I am going to talk through all of that with her, give her the benefit of the doubt and the chance to explain herself." I pause momentarily, being careful as to how I word things so as not to unintentionally offend or upset Lauren. "But I honestly believe that my dad was the one who put pressure on Lara to do all of those things. I think he gave her no choice and most likely threatened her into doing his dirty work…"

"Maybe, but what if he didn't and what if she did those things willingly?"

"Did you do those things willingly when you left me?" I didn't mean it to come out like that, the question just came from nowhere, almost like an automated response on an email. And now Lauren looks upset.

"Why would you say something like that to me?" she asks, her eyes now misting over with tears.

I quickly try to explain myself. "I'm sorry. I didn't mean that how it came out. I just meant that you of all people know only too well the chief manipulator that my dad is. Look at how he got you to leave me not once, but twice over. Think back to how he made you feel and the things he said to you, the threats he made."

Lauren sniffs loudly as a few tears begin to roll down her cheeks. I didn't want to make her cry, that wasn't my intention at all, but unfortunately, I had to say those things to her to make her realise why I want to give Lara a second chance. I reach across and wipe away her tears with my thumbs. "I'm sorry if hearing that upsets you, baby, I just wanted you to understand, that's all."

She nods her head at me and then turns her mouth into my hand. "I know," she whispers, "and believe me, I do understand. I understand better than anyone about how manipulative your dad can be. I just…I just want you to be careful, Jonny, that's all."

"Well of course I'll be careful, I've got you beside me, watching her every move." That lightens the mood a little, I get a small smile for that one.

"Oh, I'll be watching her like a hawk, believe me."

"I have no doubt," I say. Bringing her hands up to my mouth, I kiss them softly before pulling her into a hug. "So, you'll be there this afternoon when Lara comes over to go through this press statement with me?"

Pulling back slightly, Lauren looks up into my face lovingly and says, "Of course I'll be there with you, Jonny. Every step of the way."

****

That afternoon, Lara arrives at the house, looking like her usual dolled up, fake Hollywood self but minus the overly confident smile this time I notice. She looks at me meekly as I open the front door to greet her, knowing full well that her job is well and truly on the line today and that this is the last chance saloon for her, so to speak.

"Hey, Jonny," she says quietly.

Not wanting to give her false hope, I don't smile. I simply nod my head at her and stand to the side to allow her across the threshold and into my hallway. Lara is just about to step inside when Lauren turns up next to me, folding her arms across her chest in a show of defiance, effectively blocking Lara from entering. Lara comes up short, stopping in her tracks as she lays eyes on my new fiancée.

I sometimes forget that they have in fact met each other before. Only briefly. When I was on tour in London last summer. The first time they met was very brief and, needless to say, a little awkward. But this meeting right now? Now this is awkward. Really awkward. I did ask Lauren if she would wait until I brought Lara through to the kitchen so that I could re-introduce them properly, but clearly Lauren has other ideas.

With a look of confusion on her face, Lara still tries to at least extend a greeting to Lauren. "Hey…I think we've met before, I'm…"

"I know we've met before and I know exactly who you are," says Lauren, coldly, cutting off Lara completely. "And I'm also fully aware of what you did to Jonny and the trust that you broke between him as your employer and you as his employee." Wow, she's going straight in for the kill. I would stop her, but… I think she has a right to be pissed and Lara needs to know what she did wrong in all of this.

Lara looks taken aback by the frosty greeting and struggles to know what to say in response. "I'm…I…" Looking up at me, she says, "Jonny…I'm…"

"Don't look at me, Lara," I reply with a shrug, "you can't expect to come here this afternoon after all these weeks and expect to be welcomed with open arms after what you did…do you?"

Lara's cheeks begin to turn a dark shade of pink and she starts getting all nervous and flustered. "Of course not…I'm…"

Turning my back on her, I say, "This is my fiancée Lauren, by the way. You briefly met her down in London last year. So lovely that you get to be reacquainted with her. Do come in."

I throw Lauren an amused look on my way past and I can just about see the ghost of a smile playing at the corner of her lips. She's loving this. Admittedly, so am I, but not in a heartless or nasty way, I think we've just got to the point where we are both fed up of being screwed over by so many people in our life. Lauren's dad, my dad, and now Lara. We are so done with being messed about by so many that a small part of us just wants to take that back this afternoon and let Lara have it. But even I can empathise with Lara and the situation she was most likely put in by my dear dad, and I'm sure that Lauren will empathise too…here's hoping.

All three of us end up in the dining area, just off the kitchen, where Lara pulls up a seat at the table and then sets about getting her laptop and paperwork out of her briefcase. Lauren and I sit down opposite Lara and I immediately begin my line of questioning.

"So, explain. Why did you do it, Lara? All of it?" Even Lauren looks surprised that I'm diving straight into it and muddying my hands already but, I want answers from Lara and I want them now.

What I find most surprising is that Lara doesn't dissolve into a puddle of tears at my bluntness. She instead switches on her laptop, runs a hand through her long black hair and then straightens her back, as if steeling herself before answering. "Firstly, I want to say that I'm sorry for doing what I did, for breaking your trust…"

"Oh please," says Lauren, "like we didn't see that pathetic apology coming…" I look down at Lauren and shake my head at her and she rolls her eyes at me. "Fine," she sighs, folding her arms in annoyance. Looking back at Lara, I nod my head for her to continue.

Clearing her throat, she says, "No, Lauren is right, that was pathetic. Starting off with an apology was…well, it was predictable and pathetic." Lara looks over at Lauren and gives her a nod of the head. "And I get why you're angry with me. Completely. And if you want to fire me, Jonny…" Lara's eyes swing back to me. "…then I don't blame you. You have every right to fire me and if you do, I promise that I'll be out of your hair for good, but…I want to help you. Both of you."

My brow crinkles up in confusion. "Help us?"

Lara nods. "Yes. I want to help you get back on track. With everything…"

"You'll only be allowed to help get Jonny back on track by explaining yourself, Lara," interjects Lauren, looking less than pleased with how this conversation is going.

"Of course," replies Lara, swallowing nervously. Sitting back in her chair, she then starts with her usual annoying hand expressions, something she does a lot of when talking endlessly. "When your dad approached me about releasing that story to the papers, the one that…"

"We're fully aware of which story it was, Lara," I say, interrupting her. I glance down at Lauren to check she's okay. I hate that my sordid past got aired in public but more importantly, the effect it had on Lauren, the effect it still has on Lauren. From what I can tell, she looks okay…I think. Looking back at Lara, I give her a nod. "Continue."

Looking sheepish, she says, "Of course, sorry." Gathering herself once more, she continues. "I told him that I thought it was wrong and that I didn't want to do it, that I wouldn't do it…but then…" Lara breaks eye contact with the pair of us and starts to fidget around in her seat, as if she's on edge about something.

"Then?" I press, becoming impatient with her. I just want everything out in the open now and done with. I have no time for pussyfooting about and any shred of empathy I felt for her earlier is beginning to evaporate. And fast.

"He said that if I didn't do it, he would release something on me, something from my own past, something that… something that I'd rather not come out."

Shit, my dad really is the master of all manipulation and it would seem that wherever I turn at the moment, somebody somewhere has been at the receiving end of that manipulation. I bet if I dug even deeper, I would find many more people over the years that he has manipulated into doing whatever he wanted them to do. Bastard. For the first time since all of this stuff about Lara came out, I actually feel a bit sorry for her.

"Okay, so he threatened you in pretty much the same way he threatened Lauren then?" I ask, my voice a little softer than it was before.

"Not quite the same way, Jonny," Lauren says, appearing unaffected by Lara's words. I get why she feels animosity towards Lara, really I do, but surely Lauren of all people can understand Lara's situation a whole lot more than anybody else. Even more than me.

"Lauren…"

"No, it's okay Jonny," says Lara, cutting me off. Looking directly at Lauren, she then says, "Look, I get it. You don't like or trust me and I get it, and I hope one day that I'll be allowed to re-build that trust with Jonny and hopefully build up some trust with you too, but in order to do that, you need to know what Pete had over me…"

"No." Shaking my head, I hold up my hands to stop her. "You don't need to tell us any details…"

"I had a baby when I was just sixteen years old and I gave that baby up for adoption," Lara says, stunning both me and Lauren into silence. "That baby is all grown up now, a teenager, happy and settled in a new life with a loving family that I'd always hoped for him. I…well I got somebody to look him up for me because I wanted to know that he was living the life that I wanted for him, and he is, so…that's why I didn't want Pete unearthing any of that about my life. Not for the sake of me but…for the sake of the son I gave up who now has a happy and contented life and knows nothing at all about me. I'd rather it stay that way."

Both Lauren and I exchange shocked glances, neither of us

knowing exactly how to respond to a bombshell quite like that.

"So, that's why I did everything that Pete asked of me. Morally, I knew it was so wrong but I just couldn't risk it. I also felt like I couldn't come to you, Jonny, because again, your dad said that if I went to you, he would release the story anyway, so…"

"Jesus Christ my dad really is a piece of shit," I mutter. I shake my head in anger, needing a moment to allow this information to really sink in.

"I'm so sorry all of that happened to you, Lara," says Lauren, softly, "sorry that you had to give your baby up for adoption at such a young age because you felt like that was the only option, and I'm sorry that you felt like you had no choice but to say yes to the man that I said yes to myself, one too many times." I turn to her in surprise. "But I do understand why you did it." Lauren looks up at me sorrowfully. "Unfortunately I understand completely."

Shit, this is not what I was expecting at all, and not at all how I expected this afternoon would go with Lara. I let out a weary sigh and take a hold of Lauren's hand. I press a soft kiss to her palm in a show of love and support and then I turn back to Lara. "I'm sorry too, Lara. For everything that you went through at such a young age and for what my dad threatened you with. Unfortunately, both Lauren and I, more so Lauren than me, know only too well just how manipulative my dad is, but, from this moment on, no more."

Lara nods and lets out a long breath that she's clearly been holding on to. "No more. And, I can make sure that no more comes your way, Jonny."

"How so?" I'm curious.

"I've been preparing for today in the hope that we could come to some sort of a resolution over this and I think that if we get something drawn up, something legal from your lawyers, I don't think your dad would ever be able to make threats like he's done in the past, or at least, if he did and followed them through, he would have the biggest lawsuit of the century thrown at him and in all honesty, I don't think your dad wants that. In fact, when I last saw him, he looked defeated, like he's finally realised the impact of what he's done and he actually feels guilty for it."

"Well good, he fucking deserves to feel guilty and a whole lot more. You said you saw him. When?" I feel unnerved by the fact she's seen him recently, especially as we're trying to re-build some trust here.

"He came to the label while you were away on holiday. I was in the office on the day that he turned up and he came in looking for you. He said you weren't at home and you weren't answering his calls and so he was getting worried. I simply told him you had gone away for a few weeks and that you were doing fine, nothing more than that."

"And then?"

"And then he cleared out his office of all his things and left."

I raise my eyebrows in shock. "He cleared out his office?"

"Yep." Lara nods. "And I haven't seen him since."

"Yeah, well, he may have cleared out his office but that won't be the last we see of him. There's too much legal shit to sort out with the label and then there's so many loose ends to tie up."

The very thought of how tangled up in my life my dad actually is just makes my head ache. Shit, the enormity of it all is suddenly coming very much into focus, which is why I wanted to stay in the Maldives with Lauren forever. I didn't really want to come back to the harsh reality of facing any of this shit with my dad, or the running of the label.

My anxiety begins to bubble away beneath the surface and I can feel myself getting twitchy for a fix. A fix of the very stuff that I am trying so damn hard not to touch ever again. The highs I used to experience on the shit I sniffed up my nose were just a temporary fix to the crap going on in my life and I won't allow that addiction to pull me back in. I've gone without drugs now for four months and I will not go back there. *Focus on something else Jonny, focus.*

Squeezing hard on Lauren's hand, I re-focus all of my energy on the very thing that I think will aid me on my road to recovery. By helping others. By telling the truth. I say to Lara, "Right, well, now that we've cleared all of that up, I want you to do something for me. I want you to release a press statement. A very important press statement."

Lauren squeezes my hand right back and says the very words that she said to me just last night. "You've got this Jonny. *We've* got this."

****

"As you all know, I have been in hiding now for the last four months, and I spent some of those months in and out of hospital. I now want to explain to everyone, in particular my fans and my fellow musicians in the music industry and others alike, about what happened to me, in the hope that it will somehow go on to help others who have faced similar difficulties in their own lives. Normal, everyday people, like I once was, like I still am, on the inside at least."

"The truth of the matter is, I tried to take my own life in November last year, following a ten year battle on and off with a crippling drug addiction. The reasons for my suicide attempt are both personal and private to me, however I wanted to finally share the truth with the world about how close to death I actually came, so that I can strive from this day forwards to try and help others who feel as though they also have nothing else left in their lives to live for. If you ever feel like there is nothing else left in your life, please remember that there is always hope. It is okay not to be okay, and it is only now, since being in recovery from my suicide attempt, that I can say those few words out loud to myself and actually accept them for what they are."

"For so long, I put on that stage mask and carried on going, being the bad boy rock star that everybody wanted me to be. The truth behind the stage mask was that I was actually broken. I broke into a million pieces and then my loved ones and friends around me were the ones to pick me back up and get me the help I so desperately needed. So I say now to all of those people out there who are struggling, please talk to others around you, seek that help and get support, reach out as much as possible and somebody somewhere will help you. I want to try and help others, like me, who are still struggling. People with drug or alcohol addictions, people with depression and high anxiety, people who are suicidal and are suffering badly with mental health conditions. And the only way I feel I can do that, is if I carry on with my musical journey."

"Turning now to the future of the band and my ongoing battle. Reclamation are still very much a band and will continue to be for as long as we feel like we are giving something back to our fans who have supported us since the very beginning of our journey. I want to apologise to all of those fans that saw me at my very worst when on the US leg of the tour with the band in Chicago last year, just before I hit rock bottom. I was on my latest high at the time and it was only after that concert that I knew I simply couldn't carry on anymore. I also want to say how sorry I am to all of the fans that missed out on that tour when I fell ill and got admitted into hospital, but rest assured, the US tour will be reinstated at some point in the future and all people who got refunds for the earlier concerts that were cancelled will be given priority access to the new tour dates when they go on sale."

"Reclamation are also in the midst of writing and recording a new album and a release date for the new album will be announced in due course. A comeback concert is also going to be arranged to coincide with the release of our new album and that will be a one-off concert that will be filmed and screened worldwide as a thank you to our fans for their loyalty throughout what has been a very difficult time for both me personally and the other three band members. All proceeds from this concert will be donated to both a cancer charity, in memory of my beloved mum, Judy Mathers, and a number of mental health charities, in the hope that others can get that help and support they so desperately need. I am one of the fortunate ones, having so many people in my life I can rely on to support me and get me through these difficult times. The other band members, Ben, Will and Zack have been extremely supportive of me throughout my battle so far and they have stuck by me through thick and thin, because when all said and done, Reclamation are more than just a band, we are a family, and as a family, we stand together and face any storms that come our way."

"And speaking of storms, it is with great happiness that I now share with you something wonderful to come out of all of this. Because during the ferocity of the storm I suddenly found myself battling my way through back in November, I found a rainbow. My rainbow. The girl from my early days, long before I even joined the band, the one who stepped up on to that stage with me at the O2 arena in London last year and sang her heart out right along with me. Lauren. My beautiful rainbow, Lauren. Who has recently accepted my proposal of marriage and has agreed to become my wife. I am absolutely ecstatic about finally being able to settle down with the love of my life, at being given this second chance to be happy, and I am in a much stronger and happier place now than I've been for a very long time. All I ask is that everybody out there, fans and media alike, be happy for me, for us, as we embark on our new life together, and to be allowed some privacy along the way."

"Thank you to everybody out there who has listened to this

press statement, which I felt was important to make. These are my words and my words alone. Thank you to all the fans for your unwavering support to both myself, and the band. Reclamation are still here, and will be here to stay for a long time to come."

"Love to all, and stay strong, better days are coming - Jonny Mathers."

I almost tear up at hearing that, Lara reading my press statement live on one of the American news channels this morning, not to mention all the social media platforms that were geared up ready for the live stream. The media were going absolutely nuts last night when they first heard that I was releasing a press statement after all these months of silence. And not just any press statement, a statement written by my own hand, in my own words, and then read out live on television by Lara. I did consider doing a press conference with Ben, Will and Zack, where I was going to read the statement out myself, but then my anxiety kicked in and I therefore put that idea well and truly to bed.

I'm not ready to get out there and be in front of the world's media just yet. Not in a forced setting anyway. Obviously they'll be following my every move again now I've released that statement, but that's to be expected. I can handle being followed around for a while, just about, but being sat in front of cameras and talking to the world's media is not appealing to me at the moment. I just hope that I can eventually get out there and perform again to an audience, in front of cameras and fans and god knows who else, because if I can't, then I've got a great big fucking problem on my hands.

Because I have now promised a comeback concert to celebrate the release of our new album, in the not too distant future, most likely next year, and I badly need to be ready to perform again. The question is, will I ever be able to perform live again? My anxiety is through the roof at the very thought and I know I still have lots to work through with my counsellor but I still can't help but worry about whether I will actually be able to get back to doing what I once loved. Performing live.

It may have seemed like a silly idea to announce something as big as doing a comeback concert when I'm still feeling pretty low in the confidence stakes, but I had to set myself a deadline. Mentally, I will have to work towards that deadline and I will hopefully have an entire year to build myself up to it.

The new album is thankfully nearing completion now that I've found my writing prowess again, and then we have to record the album and release it. The planning for the comeback concert will then follow and the rehearsals for playing the new songs live will start shortly after that. It's a hell of a lot to get my head back into, and that's just all band related stuff. From a personal point of view, I now need to take my girl engagement ring shopping, plan a wedding and somehow move house. Shit, I feel exhausted already, although having Lauren by my side, knowing how organised she is, helps to settle some of the anxiety that I'm currently trying to cope with. And speaking of Lauren….

"Well, Jonny, I think you've done yourself proud by writing that press statement, not to mention how brave you are for actually putting yourself out there like that. Lara did a really good job of reading it too, she's actually beginning to grow on me. She's very good at her job, from what I've seen so far anyway."

I go overly dramatic on the whole shocked faced thing when I turn to Lauren. "Fuck me, did I really just hear you say those things out loud about Lara? The woman who, just a couple of days ago, you wanted me to fire off without so much as giving her a second chance?"

She narrows her eyes on me. "Yeah, okay, rock star, take the piss all you want and mock me, but that was for good reason.

I had your back and I will always have your back, no matter what. Lara, it appeared at the time, was a threat to you and your music career, until we discovered she wasn't and found out the truth. I respect her for telling us the truth without holding anything back. I only wish that I'd done that with you last year in London, when we first got back together..."

"That doesn't matter anymore, Lauren," I say, reaching down to give her a quick kiss on the lips. "All that matters is that you're back with me now and that we're happy. That's all I care about."

She smiles. "Yeah, me too."

"And speaking of being happy..." I reach for her left hand and hold it up in the air between us. Pointing to her wedding finger, I say, "Isn't it about time that we 'put a ring on it', future Mrs Mathers?" She lets out a small squeal of excitement and then throws her arms around my neck, knocking me backwards on to the sofa. I laugh and hug her against me tightly. "Excited much?" I jest.

Pulling back, she beams at me and says, "Excited doesn't quite cover how I'm feeling right now, but...are you sure? About taking me engagement ring shopping I mean?"

I frown, not quite catching on to what she means. "What do you mean? Am I sure?"

"I mean, taking me shopping so soon after releasing your press statement? They'll be camping outside the gates already, Jonny. In fact, they already are, I saw Tony earlier and he told me. I think they rocked up in the middle of the night when Lara told the media yesterday evening that you were going to be releasing a press statement this morning." She grimaces. "Sorry."

Despite my anxiety levels notching up a level at the thought of the media camping outside my front gates once again, I simply shrug off Lauren's concerns. "I don't give a shit about them, Lauren. Hopefully, they'll be happy for us. And let's face it, they'll soon get bored and slope off again, like they did the last time round when I hid myself away for months once I got out of hospital…"

"That was different, Jonny. Once the initial media frenzy outside the hospital died down and you returned home, they knew you weren't well and that you weren't living your life in the spotlight anymore, and so they eventually got bored and went away…but now…now you're making a comeback, you're newly engaged, you're more interesting to them again…"

"Really not helping me in the anxiety department right now, baby," I mutter, my excitement over the prospect of taking Lauren engagement ring shopping beginning to dissipate.

"Oh, I'm sorry," she says, suddenly looking guilty, "I didn't mean to make you feel more anxious, I just…well I just don't want you to suddenly feel overwhelmed when we step outside together for the first time, that's all…"

"We'll be being driven around by Tony and Andy in the back of a car with blacked out windows, it's hardly walking through the gates and into the crowds of the waiting paparazzi now, is it?"

"Yeah, I know, but I just keep thinking back to how mad it was back in London, when you were staying at that posh hotel and the crowds of fans and the media outside just kept growing and growing in size. You were so stressed out with it all, understandably. Hell, I was too. I just want you to feel at ease and not get yourself all riled up about things, that's all."

God, I love it when she gets all worried and concerned about me, it makes me feel so loved and looked after. I am so lucky to have her back in my life. So fucking lucky. Which is why I now need to face my fears and get back out into the world again, and there's nobody else I'd rather be doing that with, other than her.

Placing a finger under her chin, I tilt her face up to meet my gaze. "Whenever I'm around you, Lauren Whittle, I can do anything, *be* anything. With you by my side, I can and will face the world again. So, I will ask you again. You coming engagement ring shopping with me this afternoon or what?"

I'm met with the biggest grin I think I've ever seen on the face of the woman I love more than life itself. "With you by *my* side, Jonny Mathers, how can I possibly say no to that?"

CHAPTER 19

LAUREN

Dozens of flash bulbs go off as we hunker down in the back of the Range Rover and drive past the swathes of paparazzi waiting outside the front gates for just a glimpse of the man they have been waiting so long for. But that moment never quite comes for them, thanks to the blacked out windows of the Range Rover protecting us. We can see the crowds of waiting photographers, the flashes of their cameras, and we can hear them cheering and shouting his name loudly as Tony tries his best to drive through them as quickly as possible, but thankfully, they can't see us.

Jonny is holding my hand so tightly that my fingers are beginning to go numb. Tearing my gaze away from the madness that is going on outside the car, I instead look over at my rock star who is now sitting back in his seat with his eyes closed.

"Hey, are you okay?" I ask, feeling concerned. I knew this was too soon for him. Far too soon. But Jonny being Jonny wouldn't have any of it. He set his mind on taking me out to buy me an engagement ring today and he wouldn't be swayed otherwise.

Blowing out an overly long breath, Jonny's eyes slowly flutter open and he looks over at me. "I'm just trying to breathe through it, baby, like my counsellor has taught me to do."

I am just about to respond when the car comes to a sudden

and abrupt halt, forcing both myself and Jonny forward, our seatbelts snapping us back against the leather seats.

"What the fuck?" Jonny says, leaning towards Tony who is sitting in the driver's seat in front of us. Andy is sitting in the passenger seat next to him, looking just as pissed off as Tony at the sudden emergency stop.

"Shit," mutters Tony, "sorry, Jonny, some overly enthusiastic fans with a banner just stepped right out in front of the car."

Both Jonny and I peep through the gap between the front seats to look discreetly through the front windscreen. A group of girls are standing in front of the car with a huge banner in their hands. The banner reads, *Welcome back Jonny! We still love you!*

Tony is about to pomp his horn at them but Jonny puts his hand out to stop him. "No, it's okay, Tony. They're just excited to see me back out in the world and are wishing me well. Just drive through slowly, no horn needed. Okay?"

Tony nods. "Right you are, boss."

Jonny nods in return at Tony and then sits back in his seat, breathing a sigh of relief. "That's lovely," he says to me quietly, "that those fans have waited for me and shown up to wish me well." I give his hand a gentle squeeze. "And that's why I want to do this, Lauren. They are the reason why I want to get back out there and carry on with my music, with touring. I need to get myself better and get strong again, and I will. With you beside me, I will."

Pulling my left hand up to his mouth, he plants a soft kiss against my palm and then smiles over at me. "But first things first…" Kissing my hand again, on my wedding finger this time I notice, he then says, "…let's put a ring on it, shall we?"

***

I seem to recall telling Jonny that I absolutely, one hundred percent, did not want a really expensive engagement ring. But how could I say no when he whisked me off to Tiffany & Co on none other than Rodeo Drive! That really expensive street in Hollywood that featured in one of my all-time favourite films, Pretty Woman, where Julia Roberts got to shop until she dropped, courtesy of Richard Gere.

Well, Jonny is my Richard Gere today it seems, because not only has he gone and bought me the most beautiful engagement ring, but he's also pulled out all the stops and taken me on a huge shopping spree for some new clothes, swiftly followed by lunch at a posh restaurant in Beverly Hills afterwards to celebrate.

I could literally hear the lyrics of Roy Orbison singing Oh, Pretty Woman in my ears as I got driven around from shop to shop, Jonny splashing his cash, and me well and truly lapping it up. For someone who isn't at all materialistic, I have to admit that I have more than enjoyed our trip out today and I can't pretend that I haven't loved being spoilt rotten. But looking down now at my brand new sparkling 1.25 carat diamond Tiffany set engagement ring as we sit in some really expensive restaurant where a bottle of champagne alone costs almost as much as half a month's rent did back in London, I suddenly begin to feel a little guilty. Guilty about how this lifestyle is already reeling me in.

"You okay, Lauren?" I look up to see Jonny staring over at me from across the table in the restaurant. I give him a reassuring smile and a nod.

"Of course, I was just…admiring my new ring. Thank you again, by the way, it's beautiful."

Jonny smiles and then flashes me one of his trademark winks. "A beautiful ring for my beautiful fiancée." I smile at the compliment. "You want some more champagne?" Jonny picks up the bottle of champagne from the bucket of ice standing next to the table.

"Yes please," I say, gratefully. As Jonny pours the champagne into each of our glasses, I decide to broach the slight niggle that has me feeling suddenly guilty. "Jonny, is this what life is going to be like for us from now on?"

Jonny finishes up pouring the champagne and then looks over at me with a questioning look plastered across his handsome features. "How do you mean?"

"I mean, you spending copious amounts of money on me for no reason and me feeling a little out of my depth. Not that I haven't enjoyed my shopping trip with you today. It's been amazing. So much so that I'm already beginning to feel as though I am going to be easily pulled in to this glamorous lifestyle around here."

Jonny frowns. "I spent money on you today because I wanted to celebrate our engagement and I wanted to spoil you. Back in our early days in Manchester, we were lucky if we had money to even pay the rent, never mind anything else. I never got to spend money on you back then because we barely had any. Now, I can make up for all of that by spoiling you whenever I want…"

"You have nothing to make up for, Jonny. I told you, all I want is you. And as much as I love all of this glitz and glamour and the not having to worry about where the next pay packet is coming from, I can't help but feel that it's…wrong somehow."

"Wrong?" Jonny looks confused. "How do you mean, wrong?"

Holding up my hand, I point at my engagement ring and say, "This ring is beautiful, Jonny, absolutely stunning, and I love it, but it cost so much…"

"The cost is irrelevant. You would have picked out that ring had it been ten dollars or two hundred thousand dollars…"

"And the clothes you bought for me?"

"I'm making up for all the birthdays and Christmases I missed in the years that we weren't together. Next question." Jonny seems to be getting a little pissed off with me now and that wasn't my intention. Not at all.

I sigh. "I'm sorry, it's just…well, take this bottle of champagne for example, it cost almost half of what I used to pay in rent back in London."

Jonny's turn to sigh this time. Sitting back in his seat, he swipes an irritated hand over his face and says, "So, after finally forcing myself out of the house to take you on this amazing shopping trip I had planned, you're now sitting there telling me you don't want any of it?"

Oh, he has this all wrong. "That's not what I'm saying at all…"

"Then what are you saying?" he asks, "because I'm feeling a little confused here. You say you feel guilty over the money I've spent on you today but do you feel guilty about the money I spent on the holiday we had back in the Maldives?"

I'm about to answer but he cuts me off. "And what about the house we are currently living in, and the new one out there somewhere that we are going to buy, a house of our own. Will you feel guilty when we buy that too? And what about the wedding? And any other things I decide I might want to buy you in our future? What about those things? Do you just want me to spend absolutely nothing on you for the rest of our life? Because if that's what you're asking me to do, then…"

Leaning forward on the table, I say, "Of course that's not what I'm asking you to do at all."

"Then what are you asking? What are you saying to me, Lauren?"

Sitting back in my chair, I fold my arms across my chest and think long and hard about my next words carefully. "I'm just saying that this sort of lifestyle is very overwhelming and, as predicted, I knew it would take a lot of adjusting to on my part, but, what I'm most afraid of is…becoming somebody else. Somebody that I don't recognise…"

Jonny takes a moment to allow my words to sink in before responding. Leaning across the table, he reaches for my left hand and gives it a gentle squeeze. "You could never be anybody else other than the person you already are. And you are *the* kindest, most beautiful person with the biggest heart that I've ever known. This lifestyle admittedly changed me, Lauren, but only because I didn't have you in my life at that point to ground me. Now that I have, consider me well and truly grounded, but, grounded or not, you can't expect me to live as we once did back in Manchester. You can't expect me to never spend some of my money on you, on us. If it makes you feel any better, I do give a lot to charity and I'm going to be giving a whole lot more to charity once that comeback concert lifts off the ground next year. I do want to do more to help people, and I want you to be helping them right along with me."

I squeeze his hand right back and I smile over at the wonderful man that he is. His words seep into my skin, right into my heart, and they stay there, warming me from the inside out. "I will be right there with you, Jonny, every step of the way." He smiles back at me. "And I'm sorry, for appearing ungrateful. I just want to remember where I came from. Always. Even if I don't want to remember the man who was supposed to be my father, I still want to remember my roots, and be grateful for the good parts I had in my life back then. The good parts all include you, by the way."

He flashes me his usual cocky grin. "Oh, I didn't think otherwise, sweetheart." I roll my eyes at him and he chuckles. "So, you're okay now? We're okay?"

"Oh, we're more than okay, Jonny Mathers. We are bloody well perfect."

We both lean across the table to give each other a kiss, and at the exact moment our lips meet, a lightbulb flashes from nowhere, startling us both and taking us completely by surprise. We turn to see a lone reporter standing just a few feet away from our table, camera in hand, clicking away at the pair of us. Jonny's happy face soon evaporates when he clocks the reporter, who is trying his absolute best to get as many intimate photographs of us as he possibly can before he scarpers.

Jonny scrapes his chair back in anger and starts to stride over to the nosy reporter but he shoots off too fast. Some of the restaurant staff come dashing over to Jonny when they see him looking less than impressed that a member of the paparazzi with a camera has somehow got into the restaurant without being seen.

"What happened to being allowed privacy in here? That's what we were promised when we came in here," says Jonny, losing his temper. "I want to see the manager. Now."

I try to talk Jonny down about getting the manager out to complain but he won't hear of it, instead laying in to the poor man about the fact that the paparazzi can seemingly just swan into an exclusive, upmarket restaurant oh so easily. Jonny is right though, as somebody has well and truly slipped up here today. Either that or they were paid to allow the reporter through. Either way, Jonny tells them in no uncertain terms that we won't be dining in here ever again. He pays the bill and then we leave, leaving half a bottle of very expensive champagne behind us.

The drive home is awkward, Jonny bristling with anger after the incident at the restaurant. Thankfully, we had already eaten our meal, but that doesn't change the fact that our happy day has since been tainted. Tainted by the reality of Jonny being back out in the limelight for the entire world to see. Of course we knew something like that would happen. Maybe not quite as up close and personal as it was today, but, we expected to be followed around. However, I think the shock of the intrusion has thrown Jonny completely off kilter.

He is sitting next to me in the back of the Range Rover, but he's worryingly quiet. And he's on edge. I can tell. He's staring out of the window, not even looking at me. He isn't even holding my hand. Resting his face in his left hand, he has his elbow pressed against the side of the car door while his other hand rests on his right knee. I can see the tremors in both his legs and his hands. Jonny's anxiety is getting the better of him already and we've only been out of the house for half a day.

I knew it was too soon to go out but he just wouldn't listen to me. But, why shouldn't he go back out into the world again? He had to face his fear at some point, and he can't hide away forever. How on earth do you take baby steps when going back out into the world again? It's either go out and deal with it or become a hermit for the rest of his days. It's such an uphill struggle for him though, and it's sheer torture watching him go through that daily struggle.

Reaching across for his hand, I try to curl my fingers around his but he moves his hand away. "Not now, Lauren. I'm not in the mood."

Feeling a little bit like I've just been kicked in the guts, I say to him, "Jonny, we've had a lovely day, please don't let that one incident spoil it."

"It's already been spoilt. When a reporter took photos of us during what should have been a private and intimate moment. You were right earlier, we should have stayed indoors after all."

I sigh. "Look, we expected to be followed around…"

"I expected to be followed around. What I didn't expect was to be crept up on during a celebratory meal which was meant to be a happy and private moment between me and my new fiancée. Fucking vultures, the lot of them. Those photos will be splashed across the front pages of the tabloids tomorrow morning."

"Jonny…"

"I don't want to talk about it anymore, Lauren," snaps Jonny, "I just want to get home."

The tremor in Jonny's right leg is really beginning to show now and I can see that he's beginning to spiral. Chancing another go at calming him down, I reach out and place my hand on his trembling knee, but he swiftly moves it away. "Please don't," he says quietly, avoiding eye contact.

I sit back in my seat and then turn away in a sulk. Staring through my own car window at the beautiful palm tree-lined streets of Beverly Hills, I wonder how much more either of us can take of this so called 'normal life' we are now living. It's like a rollercoaster ride. One minute we are climbing to the very top of the hill, riding the highest of highs with one another, both happy and excited about the endless possibilities our future could hold. The next, we are at the very bottom of the exact same rollercoaster, being swallowed up by a gaping black hole wondering how the hell we ended up there. It is both exhilarating and exhausting, all at the same time.

For me personally, I just want to live a normal life with the man I love. But, I also really want Jonny to carry on with that music career he has spent so long working hard at. A pity we can't have both of those things without the constant press intrusion, but like I said to Jonny only recently, they will eventually get bored of him, and me. Once they've had their fill of me of course. I don't expect to get thrust out there into the world without them tearing me apart first, piece by painful piece. I'll just have to suck it up and deal with it. For both myself, and for Jonny.

When we arrive home a short while later, the paparazzi and the fans alike are still outside the front gates, just waiting for yet another glimpse of their rock star, returning home from what should have been a happy day out with his new fiancée. Like they didn't get enough of a glimpse of him earlier on. Nothing is ever enough for these greedy reporters. I don't mind the fans being here but the reporters just piss me off. They are so damn well intrusive.

More bulbs flash at the blacked out windows as Tony drives us slowly through the throng of people. Seeing the cameras flashing away at us all over again after the incident in the restaurant earlier just adds to Jonny's already foul mood. He lets out a weary sigh before turning his face away from the window. Reaching into the pocket of his leather jacket, he pulls out his packet of cigarettes in readiness for jumping out of the car. Jonny makes it a rule to never smoke in the car but I can see that he's desperate for a smoke right now. So much so that his trembling fingers can't get the cigarette out of the packet quick enough. In his haste to get his fix of nicotine, Jonny ends up dropping the cigarette in the footwell.

"Shit," he mutters angrily. I reach across to help him pick it up but he just brushes me away again. "Just leave it, Lauren. I can get it myself." He doesn't even look at me, instead swiping the fag up from the footwell and placing it in his mouth.

As soon as Tony pulls up in front of the house, Jonny is out of the car and lighting up that cigarette quicker than it takes me to unfasten my seatbelt. When I do eventually get myself out of the car, Tony and Andy open up the boot to help me inside with my shopping bags. Jonny doesn't stand on ceremony for either me or my shopping. He instead shoots off around the side of the house, presumably to the back garden, as fast as his feet will carry him, puffing desperately on his cigarette.

I ask Tony and Andy to just dump my shopping bags in the hallway. I don't need them to help me any more than they already have done. I thank them and then see them out. Locking the front door behind me, I glance down at my shopping bags and wonder whether to just leave them there so I can go and find Jonny in the garden. After a moment, I decide to carry them up to the bedroom instead. I think I need to leave Jonny to cool off for a bit. Once he's calmed down and smoked several cigarettes, I'm sure he'll feel a bit more relaxed. Not entirely sure about that but I can hope. And hope is all I've got right now.

****

I'm busy sorting through my new purchases when Jonny suddenly bursts through the bedroom door about half an hour later. Looking through the dressing table mirror, I watch as he slams the bedroom door behind him. Turning round to face him, I am met with an anxious looking Jonny.

"Jonny? Are you okay?" My question seems feeble, given the way that he is pacing up and down the bedroom floor right now.

Shit, I thought leaving him alone would have calmed him down, not made him worse. While I've been up here doing sweet nothing, he's been downstairs feeling like this. I haven't even had the chance to properly tidy up in here either before he came blustering into the room. The bed is littered with my shopping bags and I was just about to unpack the new bottle of perfume that Jonny bought for me earlier. Placing the bottle of La Vie Est Belle back into the bag on the dressing table, I turn back to Jonny.

"Baby, what's wrong?"

"What's wrong?" asks Jonny, looking exasperated at my question. "What's wrong is that you were right, Lauren. I went out into the world today far too soon and now? Now I've gone to shit because of what happened in that restaurant earlier. I need…I need…"

Jonny rubs a nervous hand back and forth through his hair as he continues to pace up and down. I think about approaching him but think better of it. The last couple of times I tried to comfort him in the back of the car, he pushed me away and didn't want to know. Still, I need to know what I can do to help him.

"What is it that you need, Jonny?"

Running both hands through his hair this time, Jonny's anxious state is seemingly beginning to get the better of him. "What do you think I need?" When I don't answer him, he suddenly stops dead in his tracks. Looking over at me from across the bedroom, he holds out his arms, as if surrendering himself to me. "I need a fucking fix, Lauren! That's what I need!"

"Jonny…"

"Oh, go on, say it. Tell me that I don't need the drugs at all. Tell me that I just *think* I need them when I actually don't!"

"I wasn't going to say that," I say back to him, feeling a little hurt by his assumption that I think he's all better.

"Oh, really?"

"Yes, really. Jonny, I know you're still struggling. I see it every single day. I see the trembling in your hands and your fingers as you get anxious and fight that inner fight not to give in to that pull that those drugs still hold over you. I know that you have good days and bad days, and moments where you feel like the only answer is to turn to that fix, that ultimate high. But you can't give in. Not now. Just look at how far you've come. It's been four months since you woke from your coma and you haven't given in, so please don't give in now…"

"You don't know what it's like, Lauren," says Jonny. "You have no fucking clue!"

This is pointless. Utterly pointless. No matter what I say or what I do, it's wrong. So bloody wrong. "You know what?" I say, finally losing my patience with him, "you're behaving like an asshole. Because I'm the one person who does actually understand, the one person who does have a fucking clue! I lived with you the first time round, remember? So don't you dare stand there and tear into me because you're so desperate for your fix of that shitty white powder! Tell you what, why don't you go ahead and give your dealer a call? Put us both out of our misery!"

Jonny stands there looking shell shocked at my angry outburst as I impatiently delve into my handbag on the dressing table. Pulling out my mobile phone, I hold it up in my hand and thrust it towards him. "There you go, Jonny. Give them a call right now. Why waste any more time in feeling as shitty as you do. Give them a call and get that fix you so desperately need!"

Jonny scowls and shakes his head at me, as if he is truly disgusted by my suggestion. That only serves to fuel my anger even more. Taking an angry step forward, I shove my mobile phone into his chest. "Go on then!" I yell at him. "Do it! Do it right now!"

Shaking his head once more, he bats my hand away and says,

"No."

"No?" I ask in mock surprise, taking a few steps backward for dramatic effect.

"Stop it," he mutters angrily.

Oh, so he wants to stop now, does he? Well tough, he isn't getting off lightly, not this time. He has forced my hand into being extreme with him and if this is the only way to get him to stop wanting that fix then so be it.

Raising my eyebrows up at him, I say, "But I thought you wanted your fix, Jonny? Your ultimate high!"

Jonny goes from zero to about a hundred miles an hour within seconds when I shout that at him. He storms his way over to me like a hurricane blasting its way through a quaint little village, wreaking complete and utter havoc and leaving nothing but devastation in its wake.

"Oh, I do want my fix, Lauren," he growls, as he begins to back me up against the dressing table behind me. Angry dark brown eyes blaze down into my blue ones, Jonny's breathing coming thick and fast as he literally prises my mobile phone from my hand. He throws it on to the bed in frustration. I am about to protest but I suddenly find myself being caged in against the very same dressing table.

"Jonny, what are you..."

"And that fix right now is you..." *What the hell?* Before I know what's happening, Jonny is trapping my face in his hands and kissing me like he's a wild animal who's been starved of his prey for far too long. And hell if it isn't hot. Like, seriously hot.

"Holy shit," I breathe, Jonny now tearing down my jeans and knickers in desperation. I claw at his t-shirt, dragging it up and over his head as my anger from moments ago turns into pure need. A desperate need for Jonny to be inside me. Right now. I need him now.

Yanking the zipper down on his jeans, I pull them down along with his boxer shorts, just far enough for Jonny to be able to free his erection. Picking me up from the floor, Jonny then shoves me on to the dressing table behind me. Bags of shopping and bottles of perfume go flying off the dressing table and on to the floor as Jonny plunges himself inside me. And he doesn't hold back. Not one bit. He fucks all the anger and desperation out of himself, and I lie back against the mirror and do exactly the same as him.

I grip the edge of the dressing table tightly, moaning loudly as I watch Jonny lose himself in me in the only way he knows how. Because this is the fix he really needs, the ultimate high that he craves. And it was always me. Long before the drugs came along, he only ever needed me. I just had to push him that little bit further just now to make him remember that, because I will not allow Jonny to cave in and give himself over to that shit anymore. I am Jonny's addiction and I always will be. It's him and me, me and him. And together, we are something else entirely. A heady concoction of love and lust. Two crazy ass individuals who have a deep rooted connection to each other that is wild and untamed, and completely unpredictable.

I slap the palms of my hands against the mirror behind me as we both find our release, Jonny growling out an expletive as he empties himself into me. I throw my head back and scream at the top of my lungs, Jonny fucking the last remnants of our argument away. The pair of us hold on to each other for a few moments afterwards, trying desperately to get our breath back.

As soon as Jonny pulls himself out of me however, an air of awkwardness seems to descend between us. Jonny looks uncomfortable as he tucks himself back into his jeans, almost like he's angry with himself. Clearing his throat nervously and without making eye contact, Jonny says, "I'm...sorry about that, I don't know what happened..."

With a roll of my eyes, I somehow manage to sit myself up on the dressing table before jumping down to retrieve my knickers and jeans from the floor. "You broke your rule, that's what happened."

"My rule?" He looks confused.

Pulling my knickers back on, I sigh. "Your rule about only having sex in your music studio?"

Realisation dawns and he mutters a curse under his breath. "Shit, I didn't even think...shit. Are you okay?"

Holding out my arms in exasperation, I say, "You just fucked my brains out on the dressing table in your bedroom, Jonny, so yes, I'm more than okay. In fact, I am so satisfied right now that I think I'll sleep for a week."

"Don't make jokes out of an intimate moment with me, Lauren," says Jonny, not seeing the funny side of my remark at all.

"Oh, come on, Jonny, I was only trying to make light out of the situation." When Jonny stays silent, I give him another eye roll before walking over to where he is standing in the middle of the bedroom. Placing my hands on his bare chest, I gaze up into his eyes and say, "Look, you were desperate for a fix and so I gave you that fix."

Shaking his head, more at himself than at me, he says quietly, "I shouldn't be using you to get my fix, that's not right..."

"You weren't using me to get your fix. You wanted me. I wanted you. And anyway, I'd rather you had your fix of me than shoving that shit up your nose again..."

Reaching for his t-shirt from the floor, he pulls it back on and then sighs heavily. "It shouldn't have happened like that, but I...I was so fucking angry with you for pushing my buttons. So angry. But I should have known better and just walked away..."

Is he for real right now? I don't understand why he's suddenly feeling so guilty about something that we clearly both enjoyed. "Jonny, I was angry with you too, but then that anger turned into something else and I enjoyed it. *You* enjoyed it. What's the problem?"

Blowing out a weary breath, Jonny says, "This isn't how I should be dealing with my addiction problem, Lauren. You know it. I know it. It happened the first time round, remember? And look where it got us. Look where we ended up?"

Oh, this isn't what I was expecting at all. This is all beginning to make sense to me now, and now I feel awful. Awful that Jonny thinks I'm not taking any of what just happened between us seriously when I was just trying to make him feel better. I had no idea he was feeling like this because of what happened in our past. That painful past of ours that keeps rearing its ugly head at every given turn.

Taking a step towards him, I try to reach for him, to comfort him, but just as he did earlier in the car, he pulls away from me. "Jonny..."

"I'm going for another smoke. I'll...see you in a bit..."

"Jonny..." I try to call him back for a second time, but it's no use, he walks out of the bedroom and closes the door behind him, leaving me to wonder how the hell our perfect afternoon has descended into this. This chaos that is now my life. Our life. All I want is a hint of normality, but I'm really beginning to fear that our life is never going to be normal ever again.

****

An hour later, I find Jonny in the back garden, sitting by the swimming pool puffing away on a cigarette and sipping at a coffee. The sun has just set and the darkness is beginning to descend. The sunken spotlights both in and around the pool give off a warm, inviting glow and the water shimmers as I walk slowly on by. I really do love it out here. It's so peaceful and tranquil, like a little haven where I could quite happily spend my time reading and swimming, and sunbathing too once the warmer weather arrives. Yes, outside is lovely. Inside however is another story. Because the inside is tainted with Jonny's past. A past that he'd rather forget.

"Hey," I say to him quietly, unsure whether or not I should pull up a chair and sit down next to him.

Reluctantly, he turns to look up at me. "Hey," he replies, before swiftly looking away from me and instead returning his gaze to the swimming pool.

Jonny continues to puff away on his cigarette as I decide to sit down next to him. He can't get rid of me that easily. If he does want to get rid of me that is. "Mind if I sit with you for a while?" I ask, double checking that he's okay with me being here.

Jonny frowns over at me and then shakes his head, almost in disbelief at my question. "Really? You're seriously asking me if I mind you sitting with me? Am I that unapproachable?" Jonny takes one final drag of his cigarette before leaning over the table to stub out his fag end in the ashtray.

I let out a heavy sigh. "No, of course not, I just thought that you might have wanted to be alone…I don't know…"

"I hate being alone," says Jonny, his gaze now fixated back on the swimming pool, "I just…needed to cool off for a bit after what happened earlier, that's all."

"And now that you have…are you…are you okay?"

Turning back to me, Jonny fixes me with a serious stare. "The truth is, I don't know. What happened earlier, in the bedroom…"

"Jonny, it's okay…"

"No. No it isn't okay. I mean, it was…of course it was fucking incredible…the sex always is between you and me. And what you do to me, how you make me feel, how you drive me so fucking crazy, the way you stand up to me…I both love and hate that about you, but…how we were earlier just reminded me of back then, back in Manchester, when we were so fucked up after everything that happened, how high I used to get, how you…always still wanted me in spite of my drug addiction…" Jonny sniffs loudly, his voice trailing off as he tries to fight with his emotions. "I am so ashamed for putting you through that and I…I can't bear the thought of putting you through that again…"

"Oh, Jonny," I whisper, my voice sounding a little wobbly. Reaching for his hand, I give it a gentle squeeze. "You didn't put me through anything. I was the one who turned away from you. I was the one who caused you to turn to something else instead of being able to turn to me. You wanted to talk about it but I didn't. I hurt us, Jonny. Me. I did it. I caused it. All of it."

"No," says Jonny, shaking his head. "No."

"Yes," I say, tears now forming at the back of my eyes. "It was my fault. It was all my fault."

I can't help it, I burst into tears. Jonny quickly springs into action and hauls me up from my chair and into his lap. Wrapping his arms tightly around me, I cling on to him for dear life and sob into his neck. Jonny soothes me gently, cradling me in his arms until I have absolutely no tears left to cry. Of all the things I expected to be doing today, crying wasn't one of them. What started out as a happy day choosing my engagement ring has somehow descended into heartbreak. And I really don't know how much more heartbreak I can take.

"Shit, this wasn't how today was supposed to go," whispers Jonny, planting a kiss on my forehead. "How the fuck did we end up like this?"

I take a moment to gather myself before I speak, Jonny wiping away the last of the tears from my cheeks. "I don't know, but what I do know is that we can't keep holding on to the painful parts of our past. I also know that we can't live our life out here together by being afraid of going outside into the world."

"And whilst I agree with what you're saying, I just don't know how to do it. I don't know how to move on from our painful past. I don't know how to step outside into the world again without going to shit. What happened today, that photo they took of us…"

"Was a happy one," I say, cutting him off.

Jonny frowns. "What exactly are you saying?"

"That photo they took of us today was a happy photo, Jonny. Whether it was intrusive or not, that photo will be splashed about in the tabloids tomorrow and it will have nothing but happiness written all over it. Am I right?"

Jonny looks deep in thought for a moment, as though he is contemplating what I'm saying. "I guess…I guess you're right. I hadn't thought of it quite like that before."

In all honesty, neither had I. But now that I have, I think I'm on to something. Something a little more positive I hope. "Me neither, but surely to goodness they can only print something nice about seeing us kissing over dinner. Not even a nasty reporter can turn that into something else. At least, that's what I'd like to think anyway."

Jonny nods. "Yeah…yeah you're right. It'll be a nice article I'm sure."

"So?" I press, wondering where we go from here.

"So?" Jonny looks unsure about what I'm asking of him.

"So, what now, Jonny? What next? Are you going to reinstate your ridiculous 'no sex other than in your music studio' rule all over again? Or are we going to just say fuck it, move back into your bedroom, and then have as much sex as we possibly can on every surface imaginable whilst we start looking for a new house?"

Narrowing his eyes on me, I finally start to see a bit of humour returning to his features. "Are you asking me to break my own rules all over again, Lauren Whittle?"

Biting down on a suggestive smile, I say, "Oh come on, Jonny, you never were one for abiding by the rules. In fact, when we were together the first time round, I seem to recall you breaking every single rule that was ever bestowed upon you."

Jonny chuckles. "Yeah well, I seem to recall that you were the one breaking all of those rules right along with me."

I shrug. "It takes one rule breaker to know one."

Brushing a tender hand through my hair, Jonny says, "Yeah, I guess it does." Sweeping his loving gaze over my face, he then kisses me softly, his lips lingering on mine for a long moment. "I love you, Lauren Whittle, soon to be Mrs Lauren Mathers."

I smile against his mouth, loving the sound of what will one day be my married name on his lips. "I love you too, Jonny Mathers. I love you too."

CHAPTER 20

JONNY

Over the next few weeks, things become really full on with the constant press attention, the paparazzi seeming to have permanently set up camp outside the front gates of my home. Despite the intrusion, most of the articles that have been printed about us so far have been nice ones. The personal photo that was taken of Lauren and I kissing in the restaurant that day got printed on the front page of one tabloid in particular, her engagement ring on show for the entire world to see. And since that photo got printed, our life as we know it has been completely and utterly nuts. I think the photo, coupled with my detailed press statement that got released before that, has got the fans and the paparazzi alike worked up into a real frenzy.

According to Stacey, the social media is just a never ending train of headlines about us, and mostly, I tend to ignore said headlines and newspaper articles about myself, but because Lauren is now back in my life, I'm finding myself unable to not read them. I feel that I need to constantly protect her and look after her, and thankfully, so far, most of the articles have been complimentary, wishing us both well and congratulating us on our engagement. Of course there have been the odd few negative ones here and there, mostly about the fact that somebody like me couldn't possibly want to settle down with just the one woman, and that the engagement will be broken off soon enough and I'll be back on the market again.

Those sorts of articles I can live with, and Lauren too. It's the articles that write about personal things and make hurtful comments that bother me, and believe me, I will be monitoring all social media and tabloids from a distance, for the time being anyway. If they start hurting Lauren, they will have me to answer to and I will not hesitate in releasing more press statements or even going live with an interview if any of them decide to stoop to that level. I highly doubt that they will, but having been on the receiving end of negative press attention for the last few years of my life, nothing would surprise me.

These last few weeks with Lauren may have been a whole lot of crazy, but there have been some wonderful moments in between, like finally choosing our first home together, spending time with our friends, and me seeking more and more of that help and support from my counsellor, putting in the effort that I promised Lauren I would do.

I do feel as though I am finally beginning to feel the benefits of those all-important therapy sessions, and for someone like me, that's a huge step. At one time in my life I would never have even considered therapy or counselling. In fact, I would have laughed it off in my usual macho way, thinking that talking to strangers and working through my shit with them wouldn't even come close to sorting my head out. But, here I am, just a few weeks later, already feeling a lot more positive than I was about things.

I do think the fact that Lauren and I have now managed to find our dream home together has helped a lot with that too. When we finally made the time to go looking at houses, it certainly didn't take us long to find the one that we really wanted. A home that we will finally be able to call our own and one without all the bad memories that come with this one. Hopefully, the buyer wanting my house will want to close the deal sooner rather than later, paving the way for Lauren and I to finally start our life out here in LA together properly.

And with the good stuff that has happened, there always seems to come the bad. Since the news broke of our engagement, my dad has reared his ugly head on no less than five occasions, each exchange between us becoming more and more heated. If he isn't trying to get me over the phone then he's turning up at my house unannounced, buzzing at the front gates furiously as the waiting paparazzi look on. And of course, the good old reporters have had their field day with that subject too, endless articles being printed about this apparent feud I now have with my dad, the fact that he hasn't been allowed into my home and is seemingly no longer the band's manager.

The fact that it's all true doesn't make me want to tell the truth about any of it. Because, both for my sake, and my dad's, I'd rather our feud be kept out of the tabloids. I may be angry with him and hate his guts for what he did to me and Lauren, but I will not feed my dad to those vultures. He is still my dad after all and even though I profess to hate his guts, really and truly, I don't. I still love him. I hate that I love him, but I still love him nonetheless. And that hurts. It really fucking hurts.

"Oh my god, I can't believe we're finally here, Jonny!"

I turn to Lauren who is sitting next to me in the back of the Range Rover. She looks as excited as a young kid on Christmas morning.

I smile over at her. "You are such a kid at heart, aren't you?"

She gives me one of her 'are you for real' looks, and says, "Erm, Jonny, we've just arrived at Reclamation Records, as in, *your* record label, the place where you make all the musical magic happen. How on earth do you expect me to be?"

I laugh at her child like enthusiasm and reach across to give her a quick peck on the lips. I love how excited she gets about my music and my career, she was always so supportive of my musical talents, right from the very beginning, which is why this means so much to her. She's been badgering me for weeks about bringing her to the record label to show her around, and finally, after working through more of my shit and trying to re-build my confidence about going out and about, I decided to man the fuck up and just do it. I really need to get back into the saddle anyway and there's only so much I can work on in my music studio at home.

As I've been writing constantly these last few weeks, I'm pretty much done with writing our new album. I've even written the bare bones of the music to all the songs as well. Which is why now is the ideal time to get back to the place where all the magic happens. Reclamation Records. The music label I formed with my dad way back when.

When we first started out as a band almost ten years ago, we were originally signed to a small label, Speedy Records, but as our band rapidly grew in popularity, we became so big so quickly that we outgrew that label within two years. That led on to me and my dad forming our very own label, Reclamation Records, and we've been signing other bands and musicians ever since then.

I have to admit that my dad really did work his ass off to get the record label to where it is today. He was always so good at spotting new talent and he found it refreshing, helping bands or musicians start from nothing, building themselves up to really be something. I feel an ache in my chest at the thought of never being able to experience that sort of thing with him ever again. We may have bumped heads often, but the record label was the one thing that bound us together, the one thing that we had most in common, where we worked together pretty well. He's still very much attached to the label of course, legally anyway, but soon, he won't be, and that admittedly makes me sad.

Fuck, what I would give for things to be different. Why did he have to go and do what he did? I could have forgiven most things but what he did with Lauren, I honestly don't think I'll ever be able to forgive and forget. I just can't get my head around any of it, and that is one of my major obstacles at the moment that my counsellor is trying desperately to work through with me. Trouble is, whenever my counsellor mentions my dad, I simply shut him down. I'm ready to work through most of the shit that's going around in my head right now but where my dad's concerned, I don't think I'll ever be ready.

I swallow down the unexpected lump of emotion in my throat as I look through the car window and set eyes on the large white building in front of us that houses Reclamation Records. This is the first time I've been here in over six months, the first time I'll be walking through those big red doors in the knowledge that my dad and I are officially done working together. Shit, this is effecting me far more than I ever expected it to.

Thankfully, Lauren's squeal of excitement when she spots Stacey in the car park in front of us, jumping out of the passenger side of Ben's Range Rover, is enough to distract me from my spiralling emotions. I wanted to give both Lauren and Stacey the full tour of our record label today, both of them as giddy and excited as each other. Ben decided to drive here himself, and whilst I would have loved to have given Lauren her first ever ride in my Porsche, both Tony and Andy still thought it best that we play it safe and continue to have them drive us around until things with the paparazzi have calmed down. I reluctantly agreed, but in all honesty, it's probably better for my anxiety that we keep it this way, for now anyway.

No sooner have we got out of the car, and both Lauren and Stacey are running over to each other in the car park, the pair of them squealing like teenagers, hugging each other and jumping up and down with excitement. Ben puts his fingers in his ears in a sign of protest but I think it's cute. These two are as thick as thieves and I adore Stacey. She has been, and still is, like a sister to Lauren, and I think she is the sole reason why Lauren made a good life for herself down in London. The support that Stacey has given Lauren over the years has known no bounds and for that, I think she's wonderful.

Needless to say that Ben thinks she's pretty wonderful too, the pair of them still going strong. I really hope that they last the test of time as I'm really happy for them both. Well, as happy as I can be for Ben when he's not pissing me off. Most of the time it's just banter back and forth between me and him but every now and again he'll push my buttons a little too far and then we'll end up clashing. That hasn't happened for a good while now though and I think that's down to Stacey and her weaving some special magic powers over him. Not that I'm complaining. A happy and much calmer Ben makes for a happier and much calmer me, so that can only lead to good things, especially when it comes to recording our next album.

"Do you two wanna calm the fuck down or what?" groans Ben, his fingers still in his ears, "jeez, I swear I've gone deaf."

"What?" I jest, putting my hand to ear, as if straining to hear him. I can't help myself with Ben sometimes. As soon as he opens his mouth, I cease the opportunity to take the piss. It's all part of the banter of course, and winding Ben up gives me yet another distraction from my earlier thoughts about my dad.

Pulling his fingers out of his ears, Ben just scowls over at me. "Oh, Mr Comedian is back out to play again, is he? I would say I've missed him but, I haven't, so get back in your box, Jonny."

I snigger. "Oh come on, I've only just got out of it."

"Now now, ladies," says Stacey, chuckling at the pair of us, "play nicely together today, won't you?"

"Ladies?" asks Ben, looking disgusted. "I'm all man and more."

I'm just about to come back with yet another smart ass quip when Lauren turns to me and silences me with her fingers. "Save it, Jonny," she says, trying her best to be serious, but she doesn't fool me, I can see that slight hint of a smile playing on her lips.

Puckering up, I kiss her fingers before taking a hold of her hand and pulling her in for a hug. "And there's me thinking that you were in my corner," I murmur against her lips, and she smiles.

"Always," she whispers, her eyes twinkling up at me mischievously.

I kiss her again, on the mouth this time, Lauren responding to me instantly, her hands reaching around to the back of my neck, her fingers crawling into my hair. God, she tastes amazing. I swear I will never ever tire of the taste of her, the smell of her, the feel of her lips on mine, her body pressed tightly against me...

Coughing loudly, Ben says, "Thanks for shutting him up for me, Lauren, but seriously, you two need to get a room."

Pulling my lips oh so reluctantly away from the woman I love, I gaze down at Lauren even though I'm responding to Ben. "Oh, we have many many rooms at our disposal, Ben. So many. And we've literally christened them all."

I smile down at Lauren and she gives me the usual eye roll, as though she is absolutely appalled at my smutty remark when in actual fact, I was just speaking the truth. We have now officially christened every single room in my house, and boy are we going to be christening many more rooms together when we officially move into our new home. I can feel my dick twitching at the very thought of having Lauren in a place that we will soon be able to finally call our own. I have waited so long for that moment and for me, that moment can't come quick enough.

"Nice, Jonny, real nice," says Ben, even though he loves the smutty talk just as much as I do.

"Oh, it was a lot more than nice, it was…"

"And that's the end of that conversation," says Lauren, silencing me once more, with her hand fully covering my mouth this time.

"Spoil sport," says Ben in protest, "the conversation was just getting interesting."

Stacey huffs loudly. "Actually, Ben, it really wasn't that interesting. But what Lauren and I would find a whole lot more interesting than this conversation is actually being given a tour of the record label like we were promised." She folds her arms across her chest in annoyance and then looks over at me.

Pulling my mouth away from behind Lauren's hand, I raise my eyebrows up at Stacey. "You and Lauren are a force to be reckoned with, aren't you? Shit, have you seen the look your best friend is giving me right now, baby?"

Lauren turns round to look at Stacey who is currently giving me the daggers. I honestly love winding her up as much as I love winding up Ben. Bad of me I know, but both Stacey and Ben love it really. Lauren grins at her best friend. "We certainly are a force to be reckoned with, Jonny." Linking her arm with Stacey's, Lauren turns back to me and says, "So I'd take heed of her warning if I were you and get this tour of your record label underway."

Both Ben and I exchange amused glances, the pair of us loving the whole double dating type banter that we've got going on with our girls. It's almost always a permanent fixture with us four these days. "You reckon they still deserve the tour, Ben, or what?"

I get a shove in the chest from Lauren for that remark, swiftly followed by an elbow in the ribs from Stacey as they walk past me. Ben and I then fall into step with one another as we saunter slowly behind our girls, both making eyes at the women we love.

"You know, I love how feisty they both are," says Ben, eyeing up Stacey's ass as she struts toward the front doors of the building with Lauren in tow.

My eyes are well and truly on Lauren and her ass too. As the weather is getting warmer, Lauren has been wearing more and more dresses and playsuits, most of them short and leaving little to the imagination, much like the tight fitting emerald green playsuit she is wearing right now. Not that I have a problem with her outfits. Because Lauren has the curviest figure and the longest legs that I've ever seen on a woman in my entire life. A figure that was meant to be on show. She is beautiful both inside and out. The only real problem I have with it is that I constantly feel like a horny fucking teenager around her, meaning that my dick is rarely not twitching when I'm with her. Pathetic I know, but I really don't care. I love her more than life itself, and to have that connection with someone, a connection so intense and deep rooted, makes me the luckiest son of a bitch in the world. A fact I will happily scream from the rooftops one day, most likely the day when she finally becomes my wife.

That's something else that we need to start planning too, that all-important wedding of ours, but something that we haven't quite got round to as yet. *All in good time, Jonny, all in good time. Good things come to those who wait, remember?* Fuck yes they do. And I have waited a very long time for Lauren. Too long. Thank god that long wait is now over with.

"You and me both," I say to Ben, my gaze still well and truly fixated on Lauren's juicy ass, "you and me both."

****

Lauren and Stacey are surprised to find both Will and Zack waiting for us beyond the bright red double entrance doors. I thought that the tour of the record label wouldn't be quite complete without the entire band being present. Not only that, as we haven't really existed as a band for almost six entire months, I really wanted us all to be here today. Because this moment means a lot to me. A hell of a lot. Reclamation are not only my best friends, but they're my family too. They're like the brothers I never had, fighting my every corner and supporting me unconditionally, and I them. I will never ever forget the help that they extended to Lauren and Stacey when they first flew over here to see me. They believed in Lauren when even I didn't and they gave her a chance, a chance to find her way back to me and tell me the truth about everything, and for that, I owe them everything. Absolutely everything.

"Hey, my man," says Zack, giving me a man hug and a slap on the back. "Nice to be back home again."

Giving his shoulder a squeeze, I say, "I second that. It really is good to be home with you all again."

As Zack takes a step back, Will then steps in and we do the old slap on the back manly greeting as I did with Zack just a moment ago. "This place sure is right where the heart of Reclamation is, Jonny," says Will, smiling. Looking round at the rest of the group, he says, "Am I right?"

"Damn fucking right," says Ben, slapping his hand against

Will's in that familiar way they almost always greet each other with. They then do their whole grabbing of the hand thing before bumping fists and pulling away. Shit, I really have missed this. Will's right, being back here at the record label, it really is the beating heart of Reclamation and I can already feel a twinge of excitement at the prospect of recording new music. I should have known all along that this place could breathe new life into me, I just had to find the lyrics and the music before stepping back in here. Now that I have, bring it on.

"Right, time to show these two beautiful ladies what Reclamation is really all about," I say. Taking a firm hold of Lauren's hand, I then say to her, "I hope you're ready to be bombarded by people."

"Bombarded?" she asks, looking a little confused.

I chuckle. "Well, this place is not only home to us as a band but I employ over a hundred people. We're still a small enough record label to be classed as independent, but our little workforce has grown a lot over the last few years, and you and Stacey are about to meet that workforce. You ready?"

"Jonny, we were born ready," says Stacey, becoming increasingly impatient with all the waiting around. "Right, Lauren?"

Lauren smiles. Turning back to me, she then says, "In the words of Jonny Mathers, abso-fucking-lutely."

The grand tour is everything that I want it to be for both Lauren and Stacey, but most especially, for Lauren. I can't even begin to explain the love I feel for her as I watch her eyes light up as she takes in her surroundings. From the artist development department right through to the marketing team, Lauren is just in absolute awe of the place, firing question after question at my employees, making conversation with anyone and everyone who she comes into contact with.

I don't think I've ever seen her as alive and as hungry for something as I am witnessing with her right now.

And just when I think she couldn't possibly be any more in awe of the place than she already is, I go and show her the very last floor. The top floor of the building where all the magic happens. Reclamation's very own music production department and recording studio.

I throw open the door, knowing full well that I've saved the best floor until last. Lauren gasps in shock as she takes in what I call the 'Aladdin's Cave' of musical instruments. I swear that every single musical instrument that has ever been made is in this room. The room stretches across the entire length of the building, all sectioned off according to the group or 'family' that the musical instruments belong to, such as strings and percussion, electronic or brass.

Weaving our way slowly through the family of instruments leads us to the very end of our journey, to the very studio itself. Spanning almost the entire length of the back wall is a huge window, and beyond that window is where Lauren is absolutely dying to get to. Honestly, the excitement on her face right now is a memory that will be seared into my mind forever.

"Oh my god, Jonny, I can't believe that I'm really here. Please pinch me to make sure that what I'm seeing right now is actually real, because I honestly don't believe that it is."

Lauren brings her hands up to her mouth and I wrap an affectionate arm around her shoulders. Pulling her against me, I kiss the top of her head, inhaling her incredible scent. I don't know what shampoo she uses on her hair but man is it intoxicating. Almost as intoxicating as the woman herself.

"Will a pinch on the ass make you believe it's real?" I jest, using humour as a way of bringing her back down to earth.

Lauren bursts out laughing. "Oh, trust you to turn even the most innocent of comments into something smutty."

I give her ass a big pinch and she squeals in protest. "You think it's real now, baby?"

Making a grab for her once more, I then lift her up from the floor and spin her around on the spot. She throws her head back and giggles like the mad teenage girl she once was. Hell, she still is that mad teenage girl, on the inside. Just like I'm still the horny teenage boy that fell head over heels for her, and not just on the inside, as my overly twitchy cock likes to keep reminding me.

"Oh, Jonny, this place is a-ma-zing!" she shrieks.

I laugh. "Just wait until you see what's beyond that window."

"So quit spinning me around on the spot and show me," she says to me, all too impatiently. "And where's Stacey got to? She's missing out on the best part of the tour."

"Actually, I have to confess that I asked Ben to take her on a little tour of their own, just for half an hour. I wanted you to see the recording studio for the first time with just me. Is that okay?"

Pressing the palm of her hand against my cheek, she gives me one of her lingering looks that steals my very breath away. *Shit, what is she doing to me?* "Jonny, it's more than okay. I think it's sweet and romantic."

Looking around me, I say to her jokingly, "Sshh, keep your voice down, don't want any of my employees that might be walking on by thinking I'm going all soft on them…"

"Well, that comes with age, Jonny, and you are thirty years old now so you are getting on a bit…"

"Erm, if my memory serves me correctly, you actually turned

thirty before I did, and anyway, less of the old. I'm far from being old, and my dick is living proof of that."

I get another eye roll for that remark. "How you can go from being all sweet and romantic one minute to having a mouth like a toilet the next, I really don't know."

"But you love it," I murmur, reaching in for kiss. Lauren giggles and then pushes my face away, far too excited about seeing the recording studio than she is about kissing me. I reluctantly put her back down on the floor and she runs off in front of me, towards the steps that lead up to the studio.

"Last one up there is a big girl's blouse!" she shouts, laughing.

I give chase and run up those stairs like a bat out of hell, but Lauren had an unfair advantage over me by setting off first, so technically, it's a draw, and I tell her as much. "You do realise that you cheated just now," I say to her in jest, "so we'll call that a draw."

"Oh, Jonny, this place is...oh my god..."

Lauren doesn't care about who won what right now as she finally takes a step inside Reclamation's recording studio. Speechless, and clearly emotional over being here, Lauren slowly makes her way right into the beating heart of our band, her eyes taking in absolutely everything about the place, the control room in which we are standing in, the isolation booth that is situated at the back of the studio where we record all of our vocals. Audio mixing consoles and computers are the main feature in the control room, this being the place where the audio engineers mix and manipulate the music, as well as routing the sound.

Lauren walks over to the main console that sits in front of the large window, giving her one hell of a view of the room we were standing in just a moment ago. Sweeping her fingers across the equipment, I can tell she is itching for more. So much more. "You want to take a look in the isolation booth? Maybe play around with a microphone?"

Lauren throws me an accusatory glance over her shoulder. "You being smutty again, Mathers, or do you actually mean a microphone?"

I can't help but laugh at that question, but to be fair to her, I can understand why she asked that of me, but for once in my life, I was actually being serious, and not at all smutty. "I would say I'm offended by that suggestion but I'm actually not."

Flashing me one of her cheeky smiles, she walks over to me and says, "Now why doesn't that surprise me?" When she reaches me, she places the palms of her hands on my chest before reaching up for a kiss. When she pulls back, she says, "So, you going to show me your microphone or what?"

"Tell you what, I'll show you mine if you show me yours."

"Oh, you're hilarious, Jonny."

Narrowing my eyes on her, I say, "And you're a fucking tease."

Biting down on her bottom lip, she says, "If we carry on like this, nobody will be seeing any microphones or isolation booths."

Lauren's right, I think we've joked around with each other enough, time to put my girl out of her misery. "Oh come on then, let's get this over with."

Lauren claps her hands together in a show of excitement and I make a grab for her hand once more, leading her through another door at the back of the studio which takes us into the infamous isolation booth. As Lauren feels her way around the microphones and the booth itself, I start to reflect over the many happy times I've spent in here over the last few years.

"We recorded our third and fourth albums in here," I say, suddenly feeling nostalgic. "Our third album was the first album we released under our very own label, and boy did it feel amazing. Even more amazing than when we released our first two albums. There was something more special about releasing it out of our very own studio, our own label. Maybe it was the fact that we worked so much harder to write and produce it."

Lauren looks over at me and smiles. "This place is amazing, Jonny. And you did work hard to get to where you are today. Really hard. Your music, the band, and this place…this place is everything you are, it's everything you always were, it's everything you'll always be. Without you, this place wouldn't even exist. You made this, Jonny, and I am so proud of you for it. You made it. You really made it."

Wandering over to join her by the microphones, I wrap my arms around her waist and pull her against me. "No, Lauren. *We* made it. We made it to this point together, and if somebody had asked me a year ago if I thought for a minute that we would be standing here together in this recording studio of mine in LA, I would have said 'in my fucking dreams', but as it turns out, sometimes those dreams that we think will never ever happen, actually do."

Threading her hands around the back of my neck, Lauren then reaches up and kisses me. "Hell yes, they do," she whispers, "they really really do."

****

We spend the rest of the day at the record label, showing Lauren and Stacey absolutely everything they could possibly want to know about what made us the band we are today. I show Lauren my office and our working area, and I also take her through to say hi to Lara and the public relations team who are no doubt busy planning our next social media move.

I know Lara really wants us to get back on our website and on our Facebook page so that we can start reaching out to our fans again by posting regular updates. She thinks that will make our comeback a lot more personable, plus there are dozens and dozens of messages on there apparently just waiting for me to go through and read them. Messages of well wishes and sympathy after I went public with my mental health battle, thank you notes from fans saying how I've inspired them to seek help for their own personal battles.

Lara really has been trawling through a lot of these messages on my behalf and hearing from her about what some of these messages are about has made me even more determined to get back into the limelight again. Knowing that I have that never ending support from my true fans is exactly why I love doing what I do. Those genuine fans out there are why I keep on going, and I really do need to sit down one day soon and go through those messages. I can then respond to them accordingly, probably over social media, so that I can address them all with one great big message of thanks.

I honestly can't wait to get this comeback concert in the diary as that will be my greatest way of thanking them all, as well as eventually picking up the tour once again. The tour won't be quite like the original tour was though. It'll be even better. I'll make damn sure of that. Because we'll be making some really important changes to our original tour by incorporating our new album. An album that is yet to be recorded. But before we can even begin to think about recording our new album, I promised myself that I would do one last grand thing for both Lauren and Stacey today. The best part of the tour for them by far, or at least, I hope they think so anyway.

I watch as both Lauren and Stacey are brought back into

our music production department on the top floor after I sent them off with one of the lads from our marketing team earlier. I wanted to get set up in here on our various instruments so that we could put on a special, intimate performance for them both here today before we leave for home later.

I'm sitting at the piano in the middle of the room, Ben and Will standing either side of me with their respective bass and rhythm guitars slung around their shoulders. Zack is sitting at his drum set just behind us, perched on his stool with his drumsticks in his hands, ready to rock with the rest of us for the beautiful ladies in our lives.

"Oh my god, what's all this?" says Lauren, walking towards us with a look of pure shock on her face.

"Holy shit, are you…" Stacey starts to speak but then seems to go all fanlike on us, something that happens quite regularly with Stacey when we're all together as a band. Placing her hand on her chest, she takes a few deep breaths in and out before managing to finally compose herself enough to speak. "Are you four really going to perform for us? As in, right now?"

Her and Lauren exchange shocked glances, both seemingly as speechless as the other one. I smile over at the pair of them. "Of course. We couldn't give you a full tour of the label without finishing off with a song or two now, could we?"

Lauren and Stacey seem to suddenly dissolve into a complete puddle of mush right in front of us, both completely taken aback by the grand gesture. Lauren looks a little emotional and overwhelmed as she places her hand over her heart, gazing over at me with so much love and adoration that I find myself feeling suddenly overwhelmed right along with her. Stacey is now fanning her face as she starts to bubble away with excitement. Honestly, if I could frame this moment right now then I would. Because this is exactly the reaction I was hoping for. For us as a band to be able to play live here today and give the women in our life something to really enjoy and smile about. Here's hoping we haven't gone rusty…

CHAPTER 21

LAUREN

To have been given an exclusive tour of Reclamation's record label has been amazing for both Stacey and I today, but the real icing on the cake is happening right now in front of us, as all four lads, Jonny, Ben, Will and Zack, put on an extra special performance just for us two.

I'm both emotional and ecstatically happy as I stand and watch the love of my life play his absolute heart out on the piano with his best friends standing by his side, playing their hearts out right along with him. Stacey and I stand with our arms around each other, swaying along to the music and singing along. As the slow songs eventually turn into the faster, more upbeat numbers, Jonny then turns to his electric guitar instead, all four of them really upping the tempo as both Stacey and I really get our groove on.

It's the most fun we've had in ages and we all enjoy it so much that we end up back at Ben's house afterwards so we can carry on the party we started back at the label. The drinks are well and truly flowing and Ben cranks up the sound system in his back garden, the music filtering through the outdoor speakers as we all sit together on the patio. Ben's outdoor bar is certainly going down a treat today, both Stacey and I indulging in a few cocktails as well as the never ending bottles of prosecco that keep being flung our way. Throw an outdoor barbeque into the equation and the day is nothing short of perfection. We drink until we are merry and we eat until we can no longer move.

As the day turns into night, the party moves down to the swimming pool and a drunken Stacey somehow manages to convince a rather drunken me to borrow one of her bikinis so that the pair of us can have a splash about in the pool. We receive a whole load of wolf whistles from all four of them as we run and jump into the water.

Jonny and Will then decide to serenade us, by sitting themselves down next to the pool, their legs dangling in the water as they strum away on their acoustic guitars. Ben ends up running and jumping in the pool along with us and Zack sits cross legged just next to Jonny and Will with a little bongo drum in front of him. He plays the bongo in perfect timing with Jonny and Will's guitar playing. They play song after song of their own, before eventually accepting requests.

Coldplay and Snow Patrol are at the top of my request list, The Scientist, Fix You and Run all sounding beautiful being played in acoustic. Stacey's requests veer more towards one of her other favourite bands, Maroon 5, She Will Be Loved and Sugar being among her favourites. The cheesy numbers soon follow and there's nothing quite like hearing a huge pop song like Mamma Mia by Abba being played purely on the acoustic guitars with a bongo drum for backup.

We make complete idiots of ourselves, dancing and splashing about in the water, singing several Abba hits at the top of our lungs. Hell, if I saw my drunken self auditioning for a Broadway show right now, I'd send me packing. Thankfully, I can sing and dance a whole lot better when I haven't had too much alcohol. Tonight is all about the fun though and after all these months of nothing but heartache and stress, I finally feel like this is the start of something fresh and new, something happy. The beginning of the next chapter. For all of us.

****

I wake up the following morning with the hangover to end all hangovers. A hangover so bad that I can barely move my head to look over at my rock star who is still lying fast asleep next to me. I don't even remember how we got home last night. I just know that we are home because this is definitely our bed. I make the mistake of turning over to cuddle up to Jonny, a wave of nausea suddenly rising up from nowhere, a burning heat creeping its way up my cheeks, making me feel so hot and clammy that I simply cannot lie here for a minute longer.

I scramble out of bed like a bat out of hell, only just making it to the en-suite toilet in time. I wretch over the toilet for long moments, my stomach expelling absolutely everything and anything it had left in there. Well, this is nothing less than I deserve. I'm old enough to know better and mixing my drinks last night was lethal and so not clever. I was having such a good time though. We all were.

Hell, even Jonny was pissed last night. I remember that much at least. Mostly because I haven't seen him let his hair down and relax for so long. The last thing I remember, after the guitar playing and the pool dancing stopped, was all the laughing. Jonny and I were just laughing at each other, at our friends, with our friends. So much laughter and a whole lot of fun was had last night, but too much alcohol was involved. Way too much.

"Hey, you okay?" Jonny's groggy voice comes from behind me. I'm still clutching to the side of the toilet bowl, wondering whether or not it's finally safe to let go and sit back. Taking a few deep breaths in and out, I decide that the nausea has finally subsided. I quickly flush the toilet, wipe my mouth, and then slide my bum across the cold floor tiles towards the wall on my left. Resting my head back against the tiled wall, I let out a weary sigh and then glance up at Jonny who admittedly looks as bad as I feel.

"I'm never drinking alcohol ever again," I groan, my head still banging endlessly.

Jonny grimaces. "Yeah, not gonna lie, I feel like shit too." Jonny then joins me on the bathroom floor, and there we sit for a good while, my head resting on his shoulder, neither of us having the energy nor the desire to move anywhere.

"How did we get home last night?" asks Jonny.

Despite my splitting headache, I smile at that question. "I thought the very same thing when I first woke up. In fact, I wasn't even sure if we were in our bed at first. For some reason, I thought we'd stayed at Ben's."

"I bet Tony and Andy saw us in a right state last night. I dread to think what we must have been like in the car on the way home."

I chuckle at that. "I think by now that you can more than rely on Tony and Andy for their discretion when it comes to doing their job properly."

"Yeah, it kind of comes with the territory. They're a good pair though. Been with me from the very beginning. There's no two employees I trust more than Tony and Andy. I trust them with my life."

"And I can see why."

Turning his head towards me, Jonny's lips find my forehead. "This feel better?" he asks softly, pressing a gentle kiss there.

My eyes close on a sigh. "A little, but I think I need a whole lot more than a kiss to the forehead right now. I'm thinking more along the lines of really strong painkillers and a nice relaxing bath."

"Tell you what, I will go and get the painkillers and then I'll run you a nice hot bath, on one condition."

I cock a suspicious eyebrow up at him. "And what condition might that be?"

He flashes me a mischievous smile before nuzzling his nose up against mine. "That I'm allowed in the bathtub with you?"

I pretend to really consider his request, Jonny narrowing his eyes on me in jest. After a moment, I say, "Oh, go on then, I'll allow you in the bathtub with me…but no funny business, Mathers. Trust me when I say that my head nor my stomach will handle anything other than complete and utter relaxation right now."

Jonny pretends to look offended for a moment before finally relenting. "Don't worry, baby, I have to admit that for once in my life, the hangover has well and truly won this time. When I said I felt like shit, I really really meant it."

"Well let's hope and pray that the painkillers and the bath work their magic on us then."

****

After brushing my teeth and swirling mouthwash around my mouth to clear away the god awful taste of stale vomit, I then sink into a lovely hot bubble bath with my man. Jonny is sitting behind me, his chest to my back, his tattooed arms wrapped tightly around me. Having said that, I can barely see any tattoos on his arms at the moment, thanks to Jonny going a little overboard with the whole bubble bath thing.

"You think you could possibly have put any more bubble bath in here or what?" I ask in amusement.

I feel Jonny smile against my cheek. "Yeah, I was just thinking that myself. Thinking how I might actually lose you in all these bubbles in a minute."

I chuckle. "As long as we can get lost in the bubbles together,

I don't much care."

"I'll certainly try my best," he replies with a laugh. "You feeling a bit better though? Is the bath helping?"

Actually, the bath really is helping me, and thankfully, the painkillers are too. "I'm happy to report that yes, the bath is helping me, and my headache is already beginning to ease thanks to the tablets I took."

He presses a kiss to the side of my left temple. "Yeah, mine too. Just think, we'll be ready for a full on cooked breakfast by the time we get out of here."

"You think? My stomach still isn't so sure about food as yet."

"Trust me, food is the cure to all hangovers. Haven't you learnt that yet?"

I smile. "You sound just like Stacey. Whenever she saw me suffering with a hangover, she'd always cook me a huge breakfast to make me feel better. I always used to protest about eating it but afterwards, I did always feel better. She's a wise woman that best friend of mine."

"She certainly is," says Jonny, pressing another kiss to the side of my head. "You know, I love how close you both are, the friendship you have with her. Stacey really is one of the kindest and most genuine people I've ever met, and you always know where you stand with her…"

"Oh yes, she doesn't mince her words, that's for sure," I say, and we both laugh.

Stroking his hands up and down my arms under the bubbles, Jonny then says, "You know, I really want you two to make a proper life out here in LA for yourselves. As in, forging out a career for yourselves. I'm not too sure what Stacey wants to do in terms of a job or a career but, there are so many opportunities out here for both of you. I obviously know what you want to do career wise, what you've always dreamed of doing, but, have you thought any more about what your plan is now that things with us are settling down a bit?"

I angle my head so I can turn to look up at him behind me. "I haven't had a lot of time to think about it properly, and we've got so much coming up, what with moving house being on the horizon and of course, a wedding which we need to start planning..."

"I know, but, you've been out here for six months now and since we got back together, you've been doing nothing else other than helping me to get better..."

"And I'd do it all again in a heartbeat..."

"I know," says Jonny, bumping his nose against mine. "I know you would, baby, but now...now it's time to start thinking about what *you* want. Besides moving house and planning our wedding, what is it that you really want to do out here?"

"Wow, that's a super serious conversation for two people with stinking hangovers," I say, unable to keep the sarcasm from my voice.

"Oh, very funny," says Jonny, daubing a handful of bubbles on to the end of my nose. I giggle. "Don't giggle," he warns, "otherwise I'll end up breaking my 'no sex with a horrendous hangover' rule."

He receives an overly exaggerated eye roll from me for that remark. "Jeez, you and your many rules. You used to be a rule breaker, Jonny, not a rule maker."

I get a nip on the ass for that remark and I squirm uncontrollably under the bubbles as Jonny starts to punish me for my sarcasm. "And you're a bad influence and a fucking tease," he murmurs into my ear, "always were."

"Right, okay, I surrender," I say, holding my hands up out of the water.

I can't handle being tickled for a minute longer. Even though my headache is easing, I still feel a little iffy and my tummy is now growling away at me from beneath the bubbles, telling me oh so loudly that it really wants some food. I on the other hand can't stand the thought of food right now. That growling stomach of mine will have to wait for a little bit longer.

Noticing that I'm still not feeling quite myself, Jonny finally relents and instead rests me back against his chest once more. "Sorry. You okay?"

"Yeah, just my body reminding me for the millionth time this morning to not drink alcohol ever again."

Jonny brushes his knuckles softly against my left cheek and I sigh into his touch, closing my eyes as I do. After a beat, he says, "So, you going to answer my question or not?"

My eyes flutter open once more and I smile at his persistence. "Of course. I...well, you know my dream job is to perform in the theatre one day. Any theatre really, but treading the boards of Broadway one day would be the absolute dream job for me. However, I know that things like that don't happen overnight, so I thought that maybe Stacey and I could perhaps audition for things like backing dancers at local concerts or shows, or even theatres, though I'm not too sure exactly what they have around here for the likes of us but, it's all about just finding a starting point, right?"

Raking his fingers through my wet curls, Jonny says, "That all sounds really good, but..."

"How did I know there was going to be a 'but' in there somewhere?" I say with a roll of my eyes.

"Hey," he says. Placing his index finger under my chin, he

tilts my face up to meet his gaze. "All I was going to say was, you are way past just starting out, Lauren. Fuck, you were ready to work in theatres years ago, when we were together the first time round, but for some reason, you never went after that dream. You always stood back and supported me and my dream, working in pubs and bars to bring in the regular money while I toured the pub circuit, never really having a consistent wage. You were the home maker and the one who made sacrifices…"

"I didn't make any sacrifices, Jonny, I wasn't ready for the theatre at that point…"

"Of course you made sacrifices, and don't pretend otherwise," he says, his determined eyes now burning down into mine. "You sacrificed your own career so that I could have mine. And now it's time that I repaid that sacrifice by supporting you on your way to finding that theatre career you really and truly deserve."

Breaking eye contact with him, I blow out a breath from between my lips and instead lie back against his chest, deep in thought. As much as I love and adore this man of mine for wanting to love and support me in making that important career leap in to the theatre business, a part of me, a huge part of me, is holding back on him, holding back on it all.

"Jonny, I…I need to make you understand something…"

"Understand what?"

Pulling myself out of his hold, I instead sit upright in the bath. Pulling my knees up to my chest, I wrap my arms around them and rest my head on top. Letting out a heavy sigh, I finally admit to Jonny the very thing that I've been unable to admit to myself. "I didn't just not pursue a career in the theatre because of self-sacrifice, I didn't pursue it because…"

My voice trails off as I grapple with my emotions. I feel

Jonny's chest against my back once more as he sits himself up in the bathtub right along with me. Resting his chin on my left shoulder, he whispers, "It's okay, take your time."

Clearing my throat nervously, I finally find the words that really express how I actually feel about myself and my so called talents. "Because I never thought I was good enough. Not really. I mean, I know I can dance and I know I can sing but, did I ever really think I was good enough to get into a huge theatre production and become the starring role? No. Did I really push myself and try hard enough to get a job in any of the theatres I ever took an interest in working in back in our early days? No. And why? Because I think I'm not good enough. There, I said it. After never admitting it to myself, I've finally said it out loud not only to myself, but to you too. So…"

And now I feel foolish. So bloody foolish. Especially as the tears start to flow, unbidden, down my cheeks, as Jonny looks on sympathetically. And I really don't want sympathy right now. Or ever. "Don't look at me like that," I say, spluttering out my words as I swipe angrily at my eyes. "Please don't."

I turn away from his pitiful eyes, angry at myself for getting so upset over something that is so insignificant. "Hey," Jonny says, wrapping his arms tightly around me from behind once more, "Look at me."

I shake my head at him. "I don't want your pity, Jonny."

"Hey, I don't pity you," he says, sounding offended. "Far fucking from it. I feel sad that you think this of yourself, but not only that, I feel angry at myself for never knowing how you truly felt." He reaches for my chin once more but I snatch my face away from his grip, feeling so upset and embarrassed. "Hey," Jonny says, urging me to look at him. "Please don't turn away from me."

I close my eyes once more. "I just feel so stupid for even

thinking it, never mind saying it out loud to you."

"You are not stupid, and I don't want to hear shit like that come out of your mouth ever again. Baby, try to make me understand. Why...why do you think that you're not good enough?"

I wince inwardly at the pain I feel as I suddenly see my dad in my mind's eye, raining down on me with his fists after he'd been on an all-day bender at the pub. One of many all-day benders, and sadly, one of the very many beatings I took from him over the years. He used to tell me I was useless and pointless, a complete waste of oxygen who would amount to nothing. And he used to tell me that right before he took the money from my pocket that I had earned all by myself, by doing whatever bit of a job I could, just so that I could put some food on the table for myself.

I was working from the age of eleven, when I started high school, whether it be a paper round or just helping out with shopping for the elderly people who lived nearby. Any bit of a job I could do, I found and did, because what other choice did I have? What was the alternative? To go home to the one person who was supposed to love me and look after me but didn't.

I avoided going home as much as possible, using my little bits of jobs as a distraction, a way out from the pain of living with a man as violent as my father was. He never did a day's work in his life, having always played the benefit system to absolute perfection, getting his rent and his bills paid for him. But that wasn't enough for my dad. Oh no. My dad always wanted more. Because he was greedy and selfish and cruel. So very cruel. Which is why I can't bear to think of him. Ever. He reminds me of the weakness within me that endured his violence for far too long, and I hate that. I hate that I'm weak. And I hate even more that he is the reason for that weakness...

"Lauren?" Jonny's voice cuts into my depressing thoughts.

"Lauren, are you okay?"

"Sorry, I was just…" I sigh. In all honesty, I don't really want to carry on with this conversation but I owe it to Jonny to give him a straight answer to his question. After all, I'm normally the one out of the two of us who's always encouraging us both to be open and honest with each other. I just hate talking about my dad, and I hate that it's because of my dad as to why I'm feeling like this.

"Okay, here goes nothing…I don't think I'm good enough because…I was never brought up to feel like I was ever good enough. No matter how hard I tried in school, how well behaved I was at home, no matter how much money I earned or gave to him, my dad just beat me anyway and then told me how pointless I was, a waste of oxygen in fact. So…how does one come back from that? How do you…move on from being told that you're a waste of a life?"

Even though Jonny knows about the full extent of my father's violence, and faced it himself on many occasions in the past, I've never actually told him some of the miniscule details of the sorts of things my dad used to say to me whilst he was beating me with his fists. I suppose, in some ways, at the time, what my dad said to me was irrelevant in comparison to how violent he was, but now, here we are, all these years later, and those god awful, terrible things he used to say to me have suddenly become relevant. Relevant in how I move forward with my life, but more importantly, my career, if there is a career to be had at the end of all of this.

"Oh, baby," Jonny whispers. Pulling my face into the crook of his neck, I feel his mouth press against my forehead, and he sighs. "I'm so sorry," he says to me quietly, "I'm so so sorry."

"Jonny, you don't need to be sorry. It's him who needs to be sorry, and he'll never be sorry. I just want to move on now with my life. *Our* life. I'm just…well, I'm scared. Scared of not being good enough…"

"Baby, you're already good enough. More than good enough. You're absolute fucking perfection to me, but, it's you who needs to believe that about yourself, Lauren. You need to have that belief. I know it won't happen overnight and you may never truly believe that you have what it takes, but maybe, one day in the future, when you do finally make it, which you will by the way, maybe when that day arrives, you'll finally believe in yourself."

"And until then?" I ask, still unsure about how I go about the whole theatre career I've always longed for.

"Until that moment arrives, you fight your way to the top. You work your ass off like you always have done. You audition for parts, you show them your talents and you make damn fucking sure that you go knocking down those doors, because once they see what I see, your life will change forever, I guarantee it."

"My life has already changed in a pretty big way recently," I joke, trying to lighten the mood a little. Pulling my left hand out of the bath water, I hold it up in front of Jonny's face, flashing my engagement ring at him. "A really big way actually."

He grins down at me like a loved up loon. "Well it's going to change a whole lot more when you start knocking down those theatre doors, Lauren Whittle, and I'll be right by your side, knocking them down with you."

I smile up at him. "Have I told you that I love you?"

"Mmm…" Jonny pretends to think about this question for a moment, before finally shaking his head. "No, I don't think you have."

"Well I do," I whisper, my face slowly turning serious. "I

really really do." Reaching up, I place a soft, tender kiss to his lips. When I pull back, I say, "Even if you are giving me special treatment."

I'm met with an eye roll. "Trust you to follow up an 'I love you' with an accusation like that."

"Not an accusation," I say, raising an eyebrow, "just stating a fact."

"Well let me state a fact right back. I am your fiancé. Therefore I stand by your side through thick and thin, supporting you as you go through life, helping you to achieve the things you want to achieve, because that's what supportive partners do. You always supported me back in Manchester, and I always supported you. That hasn't changed. So please don't punish me by telling me you don't need me to help you with your career, just because of the fact that I'm now famous. I'd be doing the exact same thing for you if I wasn't in the band, so please don't push my support away."

"Oh, Jonny, I was only joking," I say, feeling suddenly guilty.

"Were you though?" he asks, his eyebrows raised up at me.

"Okay, so maybe I wasn't fully joking, but, in my defence, I never meant to offend or upset you. I'm just being my usual independent, headstrong self in wanting to go about this whole career thing on my own."

"Well, sometimes, even the strongest and most independent person might still need a little help or a step up towards them achieving their dreams. Does this sound like something you can get on board with?"

Cupping his cheek in my hand, I gaze deeply into the eyes of the man I love, loving him even more in this moment, for being the kind and caring, generous man that he is. "Consider me well and truly on board, Jonny Mathers. And thank you for being the wonderful man that you are. Thank you for looking after me back then, in Manchester, and thank you for looking after me now. You truly are my man in a hundred million."

"A hundred million?" says Jonny in mock surprise, "I kind of like the sound of being your one in a hundred million."

"Oh, you do?"

"Yeah," he says, with a huge grin on his face, "but do you know what you are to me, Lauren?"

"What am I to you, Jonny?"

"To me, you are my one in about six or seven billion."

I chuckle. "So basically, what you're saying is that I'm the only one on this planet for you."

Pushing a wet curl away from my face, Jonny then says, "Actually, scrap that, you're the only one for me in the entire universe, however large that universe is. Am I making my point?"

"Oh, you've well and truly made your point, baby," I say, pressing a kiss to his lips.

Jonny smiles against my mouth. "Good."

I kiss him once more, Jonny's fingers now tangling into my wet locks of hair. I decide right there and then that my hangover is well and truly on its way out, that I want more than just a kiss and a cuddle in this overly bubbly bath of ours. That is until my stomach makes a rather large growling sound, forcing both Jonny and I apart.

"Was that your stomach?" asks Jonny, looking rather amused.

I huff at the interruption. "Oh go on, laugh at me why don't you?"

"Just admit that you're hungry," says Jonny, purposely toying with me.

"Okay," I sigh, "I'm hungry…but not just for food." I give him the look that he knows only too well and he shakes his head at me.

"Feeling a little better are we?" he teases.

"A little." I shrug, trying to play down my sudden rush of hormones.

"Tell you what," says Jonny, "how about we finish in the bath, go and grab some breakfast to stave off any more growling from your stomach, and then…" Brushing his fingers slowly up my arm, he says, "I'll try my best to quell your other hunger."

Hmm, I love the sound of that. Jonny quelling my hunger, it's what true hangover cures are made of I'm sure. Biting down on my bottom lip, I flash him a suggestive smile. "Oh, I have no doubt that you'll try your best with me, baby, I have no doubt whatsoever."

CHAPTER 22

JONNY

"Where is she?! Where is Lauren?!" I scream loudly at everybody and nobody, trying in desperation to get through the crowd of people that have congregated outside our block of flats. I can see the blue lights of the ambulance flashing outside the main entrance to our block and I can hear people gasping in shock at the scene that is unfolding in front of them.

Oh fuck, my world is about to fall apart, I know it. When I got the call from one of my neighbours just a few moments ago, telling me that Lauren had been hurt, I'd luckily been just around the corner in my car, on my way back from a gig at one of the local pubs. But now I'm here, fighting my way through all the people to get to the girl I love with all my heart, and nobody will fucking move.

"Let me through, god damn it!" I shout, "please just let me through!"

Thankfully, the neighbour who phoned me is standing nearby, and she dashes over to me in a panic, telling people to move out of the way so I can get through. "Mandy…" I can barely speak, "is she…where is she?"

Placing a hand on my arm, Mandy looks at me gravely. "Jonny, she's…in a bad way…"

I follow her gaze, my eyes landing on a stretcher being bungled into the back of the ambulance. A stretcher with a badly beaten Lauren lying on top of it. Oh fuck, no, this can't be happening. He can't possibly have got to her. Not after all this time.

"Lauren!" *I scream, running as fast as my legs will carry me, although my legs feel like they have turned to jelly right now. I can't think straight. Fuck, I can't see straight either, everything is beginning to look blurry.* "Lauren!"

I arrive at the ambulance and try to force my way inside but one of the paramedics pulls me back. "Excuse me, sir, who are you?" *The male paramedic looks annoyed with me.*

I push his arm away from me in anger. "She's my girlfriend!" *I shout at him, losing my patience. Shit, I'm losing my grip on reality here. And shit, I might be losing Lauren too. Am I losing Lauren?*

"Is she? Is she..."

My neighbour, Mandy, comes to stand by my side again, talking to the paramedic about the fact that I'm Lauren's boyfriend, giving him my name in the process. I barely register anything else that they're saying, my eyes instead fixated on the state that is now the love of my life, my Lauren, covered in blood, bruised, and so badly beaten that it makes me crumble. Physically crumble.

"She's...pregnant..." *I somehow manage to say those words out loud. At least I think I do.*

"Mr Mathers, I'm afraid we need to get your girlfriend to hospital immediately, she's sustained some potentially life threatening injuries..."

"Let me in the ambulance, I need to be with her," *I whisper, the tears now streaming down my cheeks, all fight from before now completely gone. What if she dies? What if our baby doesn't make it?*

The next thing I know, I'm in the back of the ambulance with Lauren as she's blue lighted to hospital. One of the paramedics is seeing to her, checking her vitals and trying his best to do whatever it is he has to do to allow her to make it through this.

"Is she going to die?" I ask weakly, another tear slipping down my cheek. "Is Lauren going to die?"

When the paramedic doesn't answer me, I repeat the question, over and over again, like a mantra. "Is she going to die? Is she going to die? Is she going to die? Is she going to die?"

I jolt awake with a start, trying desperately to get a grip on my surroundings. The room is swathed in darkness and I'm struggling to breathe, scrambling around like a maniac, looking for her. Where is she? Where is Lauren? Is she going to die? Is she dead? Oh my god, where is she?

"Jonny?"

As soon as I hear her voice, I crack wide open, my emotions overwhelming me all at once. I turn over in the bed I now realise I am in to find her lying next to me in the darkness and I reach for her immediately, pulling her against me. The tears flow hard and fast and Lauren, although taken aback and probably wondering what the fuck is going on with me, just holds me against her, soothing me gently.

"Hush, baby, it's okay," she whispers into my ear, "I'm here."

Thank fuck she is here. Jesus, I really thought I'd lost her there for a minute. Damn the nightmare, damn the nightmare all the way to hell. "I thought you were…" I can't get the words out, they're like acid on my tongue.

I don't understand where that nightmare came from as I haven't had a nightmare now for a good while, but it was so real. So real that I felt like I was back there on that dreaded night. Back in that ambulance with Lauren as she fought for her life after….

I let out an anguished cry as Lauren holds on to me tightly, saying nothing, not needing to at this point. I haven't had a nightmare about that night for a very long time, not since I left Manchester and came over to LA actually. The nightmares that I have had since coming home from hospital have mostly been about me being buried alive, none of them to do with Lauren whatsoever, which is why this one has really disturbed me.

It takes me a good few minutes to feel calm enough to be able to register that I am in fact in my bedroom, in my own bed, in my house in LA with Lauren lying next to me. Shit, I feel terrified. Truly terrified. In fact, I need the light on. "Lauren, please can you put the lamp on so I can see you, make sure you're really here?"

Lauren doesn't hesitate, instead quickly turning over to flick on her bedside lamp before turning back to comfort me. It is only when my eyes land on her beautiful face lying on the pillow next to me that I am finally able to fully relax. Reaching over for her, I pull her close so that her forehead is pressed against mine. "You're really here," I whisper, my heart slowly breaking apart on the inside. Breaking apart for what could have been.

"Jonny, of course I'm here," she whispers back to me, her eyes soft and reassuring. Pressing a tender kiss to my forehead, she then leaves her lips there. "What happened, Jonny?"

I close my eyes as my mind goes back to the hellish nightmare from moments ago. "I…I dreamt about the night that you…the night that I nearly lost…" I can't fucking say the words out loud, and so I don't, but Lauren understands anyway, wrapping her loving arms around me and holding me against her tightly. So fucking tightly that I don't want her to let me go ever again. "Why now?" I croak out through my tears, "after all these years…"

"Hush now," she whispers into my hair, "it was just a bad nightmare, probably brought about by the fact that we were talking about my dad earlier today. But it's nothing more than that, Jonny. I promise."

Lauren is probably right, we were talking at length earlier today about her dad and how he used to make her feel, how he hurt her, both with his words and his fists. God, how he used to hurt her. I bite down hard on the insides of my mouth to try and shut out the pain and anger I feel whenever I think of him. I hate the fact that he still holds that power over both me and Lauren, wielding that violent axe over the pair of us over a decade later, causing us both unbearable pain. Not all the time, obviously, but more often than I'd like to admit.

I suppose as Lauren and I are only just finding our way together again, our past is still bound to play a huge part in our relationship and even though we have vowed to try and put it behind us, the shadows of that painful past are still lurking, and sadly, that is a fact of our lives that probably won't ever go away. Not fully. We as a couple will somehow have to learn to live with what happened to us. But not yet. I'm not quite ready to learn to live with what happened to us just yet, and neither is Lauren.

Lauren pulls back slightly, and gazes deeply into my eyes, showing me that she's here for me, next to me, holding me, comforting me, loving me. But that just isn't enough for me right now. I feel so disturbed by the nightmare, so unsettled about what it all means, about the fact that I was so very close to losing her, that I may very well lose her all over again. Fuck me, I need to feel her. All of her. Every single inch of her. Until I am lost in her to the point where the ghosts of our past no longer exist.

And get lost in Lauren I do as she allows me to kiss her hungrily, stealing her very breath as I practically rip her nightie away from her body and worship her like I've never worshipped her ever before. It's so slow and intense, emotional and overwhelming, all rolled into one.

Oh, the feel of her body being wrapped around mine, the way she looks into my eyes as I move inside her, as though she is looking straight into my soul. It fucking breaks me apart every single time and I find myself almost going mad with the feeling. I can't help it. I don't know how to deal with it. Which is why I shatter apart completely in her arms, the last fragments of my heart splintering into tiny pieces as my love for her washes over me like a tsunami, breaking me wide open on the inside at the realisation of what I could have lost, of what I could still lose.

"Oh, Lauren," I whisper, her name on my lips like a prayer. "I love you, I love you, I love you."

I repeat those three words over and over to her, trying in my own mind to erase the dreaded words from my nightmare earlier, that god awful question I kept asking the paramedic over and over again. Is Lauren going to die? Is she going to die? And I did ask that question over and over apparently, so I got told later on. I just don't remember that part of it at all, almost like I was in a weird sort of trance at the time, shock maybe. My nightmare tonight however has reminded me of it in all its horrifying glory. Which is why I need to erase it again. Erase it in the hope it never comes back.

I consume myself in Lauren, drowning myself in her love and her body as I erase every last shred of that nightmare from my system, Lauren more than willing to drown herself right along with me. I don't know how long we are one for, and I don't much care, all I know is that we devour each other until we can devour no more, both tired and replete afterwards, breathless and spent, lying in each other's arms until a peaceful, dreamless sleep finds us both.

****

"You seem on edge today, Jonny. Any reason for that?"

I deliberately avoid making eye contact with my counsellor, Brian, and instead look out of the window at what should be a relaxing view. The brightly coloured flowers and the palm trees in the sprawling gardens outside of this little therapy room of Brian's are doing nothing at all to make me feel relaxed. Fuck, the five fags I smoked my way through on the way over here did nothing to make me feel relaxed so I hardly think some pretty looking gardens outside are going to do the trick. Although I know what will…. *You don't need the drugs, Jonny. You've got this far without them. All you need is Lauren.*

And therein lies my problem. Whenever I now think of Lauren, I get this weird plummeting feeling in my stomach, like something really bad is about to happen to her, and it's all thanks to that god awful nightmare I had a couple of nights ago. Needless to say that it's set me more than on edge and has resulted in me taking a few steps back with my recovery, much to my dismay. It feels like Lauren has been walking on eggshells around me again too and I just don't want that. For her, or me.

"I…" Shit, I still don't feel comfortable with bearing my innermost fears and feelings sometimes. Admittedly, I've come to really like and trust my counsellor, Brian, however this shit from my past is really beginning to haunt me at the minute, to the point where I just don't want to talk about it. Or deal with it.

"Look, I'm fine. I can deal with it…" I sigh, and then look through the window again, appearing disinterested. Hopefully my ignorance will put Brian off his line of questioning with me today. Sometimes, when he can see that I'm spiralling, he takes his foot off the accelerator and leaves me be, however, as we've only just about got started with our session, Brian is having none of my bullshit.

"I didn't ask if you can deal with it, Jonny. I asked you the reason for your seemingly anxious like state this morning."

Well, looks like Brian isn't mincing his words with me this morning. Fair enough I suppose, at least he's still sticking to his promise of cutting out the whole tiptoeing around me, airy fairy bullshit that I told him I hated right at the beginning of our sessions. And if he's holding up his end of the bargain, I suppose I should hold up mine too.

Heaving out a defeated sigh, I glance over at Brian who is now sitting back in his large, brown leather chair that looks decades old, with his arms folded across his chest. He looks at me expectantly through his large round glasses, the frames of which are black in colour and so thick, he reminds me of some sort of college professor or a teacher.

I can just see Brian giving lessons in a laboratory somewhere in a school, teaching science to kids and showing them exciting experiments. I have no doubt that his science experiments would be as loud and as brash as the clothes he wears. Yep, Brian definitely belongs in a science department. His brown flowery shirt is practically the same colour as his leather chair and is in complete contrast to the lime green pants he's wearing. All he needs is a zany looking cardigan and a white lab coat and he'll be right at home in his very own science lab. Anyway, moving on from Brian and his bad taste in clothing….

"Okay, right to the point then…I had a nightmare, a couple of nights ago, it was about Lauren and how she nearly…" I almost wretch at the thought of saying it out loud, the word getting stuck in my throat, as it always does.

Running a nervous hand through my hair, I then reach for my glass of water from the old oak coffee table that sits between us. I'd rather it was a glass of whisky right now but water will have to do I suppose. Taking a quick sip of the water, I then place the glass back down on to the table and sit forward in my chair.

Placing my forearms on my knees, I lean forward and keep my gaze focused on the coffee table in front of me, taking note of the various knots and blemishes in the oak. The imperfections in the wood that have always been there. Right from the very beginning. But, imperfections or not, I think those knots and warps give the table more character, make it more unique and individual. Much like us humans. Full of very many imperfections and yet each one of us being that imperfectly perfect human to someone else. Lauren is my imperfectly perfect human although in my eyes, she has no imperfections at all. To me, Lauren *is* perfect. Perfect for me in every possible way. And I'll never think differently.

"It's okay, Jonny. I can see that you're struggling, so take your time. Take a few deep breaths, steady yourself, and continue when you're ready."

Brian has deliberately softened his voice with me now, gently cajoling me into opening myself up to him. He's really good at doing that, especially when it comes to working with me. I'm sure I've been one of the hardest nuts to crack for Brian but here we are, nearly three months down the line, and I'm opening up to him in a way I never thought possible. Especially as Brian is the only other person in the world who is managing to get me to open up to him like I am doing. The only other person who has ever been able to do that with me is Lauren. I didn't even open up to my mum like I do with Lauren. I mean, I loved my mum to bits and we always had a great relationship, but for whatever reason, I could never quite open up to her in the same way that I always opened up to Lauren. We were still very close though, me and my mum, and I miss her desperately.

I feel strange whenever I think about my mum, almost like my chest has been hollowed out from the inside, like a part of me died with her. And that part that once existed inside of me is now like an empty chasm in my heart, a part of me that will never be whole ever again.

Steadying myself for what I'm about to say out loud to both myself and to Brian, I take another deep breath in and then slowly but surely, I let the dreaded words fall from my mouth that I've been trying so damn hard to keep in.

"I had a nightmare about the night when Lauren nearly died," I say, trying my best efforts not to vomit right in front of him. Because I feel so sick right now. Sick to the pit of my stomach. In fact, I need more water. Reaching for my glass once more, I gulp down the remainder of my water and then slam the glass back down on the table.

"Do you need a refill?" Brian enquires, but I shake my head at him.

"No, I'm...well I'm not fine, clearly, but...no more water needed for now...thank you," I say to him, grateful for his thoughtfulness.

Brian gives me a nod of the head and then quickly jots something down on his notepad in front of him. Crossing his right leg over his left, he then looks up at me once more, a look of concern etched on his face. "I'm very sorry to hear about the nightmare and how it triggered you, although I'm more concerned about the content of the nightmare itself. You say that Lauren nearly died?"

I must grimace without even realising, Brian immediately putting his hands up in some sort of apologetic gesture. "I'm sorry for making you feel even more uncomfortable but I do need to ask these questions. Some will be very difficult questions. Are you happy for me to continue?"

Am I happy for him to continue? Fuck no, I'm not, but I will allow him to continue because this is slowly eating me up inside and I need to get a level head on it otherwise I'll be going backwards with my recovery and I can't allow that to happen. I won't allow that to happen. "Yes, you can continue. It's okay. I'm okay."

Brian smiles and then picks up right where he left off. "Okay, so, in order for me to be able to work my way through this with you, we need to try and make some sort of sense of it all, but we can only do that if you start at the very beginning."

"At the very beginning?" I ask him, feeling panicked.

Brian nods. "I know it's difficult, Jonny, but in order to help you, I need you to tell me about what happened to Lauren, what happened to you both, when you were first together. You've touched on bits and pieces here and there in our past sessions, but as you know yourself, we've mainly been working through your recent issues following your suicide attempt, such as dealing with your grief following your mom passing away, your negative thought processes and your anxiety, as well as your drug addiction. But this, this is something we've never ever touched on and I really think it's time that we did. If you're willing. Are you willing?"

Am I willing? Again, not really. But I have to do this. Fuck, I *need* to do this. The old me would have cut and run long ago but the new me is willing. Willing to put my faith in a man that has terrible taste in clothes but is damn bloody good at his job.

With a small nod of agreement, I say quietly, "I'm willing."

He gives me a small smile before turning over the page of his notepad so that he has a fresh piece of paper to start writing away on. Peering over his thick rimmed glasses at me, he says, "Okay, Jonny, in your own time and at your own pace, start from the beginning of what happened to Lauren that night."

Taking yet another deep breath in for what feels like the

millionth time in as many minutes, I steel myself ready to tell Brian absolutely everything about what happened that night. The night I will never ever forget for as long as I live and breathe...

****

It's around lunchtime when I arrive home after my therapy session with Brian. I find both Lauren and Stacey sitting at the dining table, poring over Lauren's laptop, the pair of them chatting enthusiastically over something or other. It makes me smile, and right now, after that two hour intense therapy session with Brian, I really could do with something to smile about, because talking about that night when Lauren nearly died was hard. So fucking hard. But I did it.

I sat there and poured my heart and soul out to Brian, almost cracking into pieces as I practically relived that hellish night all over again, but somehow or other, I got through it. And I put myself back together enough afterwards so that I could walk out of there and drive myself home. But as Brian said to me earlier, that session today was just the beginning. He hinted at many more sessions to come surrounding that particular subject, something that clearly triggers me even now, all these years later.

As I gaze over at Lauren, deep in conversation with Stacey, I wonder whether or not she should seek out some help for herself after what happened to her that night, but I talk myself out of even mentioning it to her before I even talk myself into it. Triggering Lauren is the last thing I want to do and so, I push away such thoughts and decide to just deal with my own shit for now, because Lauren is clearly happy and settled over here with me, and I want it to stay that way. And speaking of her being happy and settled....

"Hey, ladies, what you up to over there?" Lauren and Stacey both jump back in their chairs at hearing my voice, the pair of them seemingly so engrossed in whatever it is they've got opened up on the laptop that they didn't even realise I'd returned home. I stroll over to them, a smile spreading across my lips as they both look over at me in surprise. "Sorry, didn't mean to scare you both."

Lauren narrows her eyes on me in jest. "So sorry that you're grinning about it?"

I flash her another award winning Jonny Mathers smile and then gesture towards her laptop. "Maybe if your heads weren't buried in your laptop, you might have noticed your rock star coming home instead of completely ignoring him. He's really upset about that, by the way."

"Well, my rock star is a big guy, I'm sure he can take being ignored for once in his life," jokes Lauren, and then her and Stacey both laugh. Nice comeback from my girl right there. I do love our banter. And now that she's reeled me in….

"Oh, he's a big guy alright, great in bed too, so I've heard."

Stacey bursts out laughing at my smutty remark and I get the usual eye rolling from Lauren. "Trust you to yet again lower the tone, Jonny Mathers."

I walk around the dining table to stand behind them. Placing my hands on Lauren's shoulders, I give them a gentle squeeze. "I'm just stating the facts, Lauren. No smut intended on this occasion." Stacey looks up at me and I flash her a cheeky wink.

"Don't ever change, Jonny," laughs Stacey, "in fact, neither of you change please because watching your banter is always so entertaining."

"Well I'm glad you think of us as entertaining, Stace," says Lauren. She then glares up at me from her chair, but I can see right through her ruse, that glint of amusement sparkling brightly in her eyes.

Leaning down, I plant a soft, tender kiss to her lips, and of course she instantly turns to mush, grinning up at me liked a loved up teenager when she pulls back. "Hey," I whisper, smiling down at her lovingly.

"Hey to you too, rock star," she replies, reaching up for another kiss, which of course I gratefully receive.

Stacey's overly loud and very deliberate clearing of the throat is like a bucket of ice cold water being splashed over the pair of us. Wrenching my lips away from my girl, I throw an apologetic look at Stacey as Lauren stifles a giggle behind her hand.

"Honestly," she says, as if suddenly disgusted by our public display of affection, "you two are sickening sometimes."

My brow creases in mock confusion. "That's funny, because I swear just a moment ago you said we were entertaining."

"I said your banter was entertaining, Jonny. You two making out right next to me? Not so entertaining. Save that for later on, preferably long after I've gone home."

"Oh, I will save it for later on, Stacey, believe me…"

"Anyway," says Lauren, cutting me off, "moving swiftly on… how was it this morning?"

Well that's a conversation changer if ever there was one. And an awkward one at that. As Stacey is here, I really don't want to talk about it and I thought Lauren would have known that. I shrug my way through an answer. "It was fine…"

Lauren soon picks up on my sudden change in demeanour, throwing a silent apology my way. Her eyes look up at me sorrowfully and I know she's now feeling guilty for asking that question, but it doesn't matter. She was trying to stop me and my overly suggestive mouth and she probably didn't even think about the question properly before she asked it. I therefore change the subject as quickly as possible.

"So, what is it on this laptop that's got you two so enthusiastic this afternoon?"

Lauren's face lights up when I say that to her, and my chest constricts. I love seeing her so happy and enthusiastic about something that she's clearly interested in. "So, after our conversation the other day, I talked to Stacey about the whole career out here in LA thing, and so that's what we've been doing on here today. We've been trawling through job adverts in the local theatres, shows that may be up and coming that need dancers or cast members. That sort of thing."

I raise my eyebrows in genuine surprise. "Wow, that all sounds promising. I'm glad that you're finally looking into this. I'm also glad that I kind of kick started the whole thing, you know." I never miss the chance for bigging myself up to Lauren. It's all part of that banter between us that I love so god damn much.

"Never passes up an opportunity to inflate his ego, does he?" says Stacey, chuckling.

"Sadly not," Lauren sighs, "but I suppose that on this occasion, he is actually the reason for kick starting me into doing this. Without that kick, I may not have bothered for a good while longer."

"You see?" I say to them both, "just what on earth would you do without me?"

Leaning down once more, I give Lauren the cheekiest grin I can muster, right before I press another kiss to those luscious lips of hers. Hmm, I could quite happily taste these sweet, full lips of hers forever, but sadly, I have work to do, and, as it turns out, so does she. And I couldn't be happier for her.

"Good luck with the job hunting, baby. I'm off to the label now as we need to get started on recording this new album of ours, but if you need any help with any of this at any point, then you know where I am. I won't interfere with any of it but if you want or need the help, then please come to me. Yeah?"

She smiles at me gratefully. "Yeah. Of course. Thank you."

"Thanks, Jonny," says Stacey with a smile.

I leave the pair of them to it, grab the stuff I need from my music studio and then head out to the label. I am so ready to get back in the saddle over at the record label like you wouldn't believe, and if anything, that nightmare I had has made me realise that even more. I want normality more than anything and getting back to recording music is what I absolutely need to be doing. And I can't fucking wait. I just hope the lads are ready for me, because this new album is going to blow their minds.

CHAPTER 23

JONNY

It's been a month since I had my nightmare. One whole month. And life has been great. Wonderful, in fact. Putting my ongoing mental health issues to one side, because I am now well and truly dealing with those, life, I think, couldn't possibly get any better than it is right now.

Lauren has started to audition for some small parts in the local theatre productions and I've started to record our new album over at the studios along with the rest of the lads. Stacey has also managed to bag herself a job as a backing dancer in one of the local dancing troupes that put on shows and theatrical productions and our house move is drawing ever nearer, which is great. Everything is great.

I can't pretend that things are great with my dad, but then, things haven't gotten worse with him either. He's backed off a bit from hounding me with constant phone calls and he hasn't shown up at my house. Whenever we have spoken over the phone, which has only ever been about all the legal stuff to do with the record label, things have been civil at least. But no more than that. I still can't accept what he did to Lauren, or to me, and therefore I need to just leave it at that for now and try to move on with my life.

Moving on certainly hasn't been easy but it's something that I've had to do. For my own sanity, and for Lauren's too. Without her unwavering love and support, I wouldn't be back to where I am today. I so wish that my dad could see that about

Lauren. See her for the wonderful woman that she is. See how much she has loved and supported me these last few months, how she nursed me back to health and picked me up whenever I fell, how she battled her way through my many storms right along with me, whilst never letting go of my hand. Maybe he does see in Lauren what I see now, who knows? But, as the old saying goes, too little too late in my eyes.

The lads and I are busy working away in our music studio at the record label at the moment, recording the all-important music for one of the tracks I've written for our new album. Whilst I write all of the songs and the music, the lads then like to have their input afterwards. None of them profess to have the song writing talent I have but I like for them to have their say and put in their ideas, because at the end of the day, we are a band after all. They may not want to write any of the songs themselves, I don't even think they like song writing, but they certainly want to 'fine tune' them, as I like to call it, and that is the part about the whole album recording process that I love and have long missed.

Don't get me wrong, the album recording journey isn't always plain sailing. From time to time, things can get, shall we say, a little heated between us all, my overly inflated ego being the usual culprit that causes most of the arguments. I can get a little over protective of my songs and I know that sounds ridiculous, but when you pour all of yourself into writing something that is going to be shared with the rest of the world, then it needs to be right. In fact, it needs to be damn well perfect.

We're just busy finishing up on recording some of the music for one of our new songs when Lara suddenly bursts into the recording studio looking worried. I say worried, more like panic stricken. I immediately stop strumming away on my acoustic guitar, Ben, Will and Zack quickly following suit. Silence descends in the studio like a lead weight and I already know from the expression on Lara's face that something bad has happened. Something really bad.

I knew it. I knew something like this would happen. Just as things had started to settle down for the both of us, something shit has come along to spoil it. I just know it. I can feel it in my bones, in my very blood. Pulling the strap of the guitar over my head, I place my guitar on the floor and stand up.

Walking over towards Lara, I look her straight in the eyes, trying to gauge as to what this terrible thing might be. Is it my dad? Has he launched a lawsuit against me over the record label after all? Or has he been taken ill? Shit, I don't know how I would handle that if he had. I know things aren't great between us right now but I still wouldn't want him to fall ill, or worse still...die? No, I can't lose my dad as well, not straight after losing my mum. Feud or not, I can't lose my dad, I just can't.

"Is it..." I break off from speaking while I try to gather myself for what's coming. *Get a grip, Jonny, maybe you're over blowing things here. Remember what Brian said. Don't do the whole leap frog thing without knowing the bare facts.*

Unfortunately, my brain is more than leap frogging right now. It's leap frogging all the way to my dad's funeral, or something else, something even worse than that. Can there be anything worse than that? I don't know! That's the point. Get your shit together, Jonny. You can do this. "Is it my dad?" I manage to ask quietly, "is he okay?"

Lara's confused expression tells me straight away that whatever this is, it isn't to do with my dad. Well, thank fuck for that. "No, your dad's fine. Jonny, it's..." Lara's voice trails off as she looks over at Ben, Will and Zack sitting behind me, still waiting quietly with their musical instruments at the ready. I get the dreaded feeling in my gut that somehow or other, we won't be finishing off anything in here today.

Turning back to Lara, I say, "It's fine. You can tell me in front of them. They are, after all, my family. You of all people should already know that."

"Of course," Lara says, with a nod of her head. Clearing her throat, she looks me straight in the eyes as she starts to speak. "I don't know how it happened…"

"How what happened?" I ask impatiently. I am seriously not in the mood for waiting around a minute longer. Bad news or not, I need to know and I need to know now. "Lara just tell me what the fuck is going on so I can deal with it!"

Lara sighs heavily. "I'm so sorry, Jonny, but…I've just found out that a news article has been printed in the tabloids this morning, one tabloid in particular. It's also gone viral all over the internet…"

"What article?" I snap, finally losing my patience with her, "another one about me with women? Is my dad trying to throw me under the bus all over again?" And just when I felt bad for him, thinking he had been taken seriously ill! Plunging my hands into my hair, I start to pace around the studio in anger. "I thought you had a handle on this shit, Lara. You told me that you were going to protect me and Lauren from any more shit like this…"

"No, Jonny, you're misunderstanding me. This article has nothing to do with your past with women, and it certainly has nothing to do with your dad…well, not *your* dad anyway."

What. The. Fuck. Surely I just heard wrong. What Lara just said *had* to be wrong. "Whoa! Back up there for a minute, won't you?" I say, turning towards Lara once more. "What the fuck does that mean? Nothing to do with *my* dad anyway? What do you…what do you mean by that?"

I really don't understand what she means by that at all. Okay,

I'm lying to myself here, of course I know what she meant just now, but surely not. Not after all these years. Please god, no. Don't let it be him. It can be anyone or anything else in the whole world, but not him. Please do not let it be *him*.

Lara swallows hard, as if composing herself for the next bit. "Lauren's dad…he's…he's sold his story to the tabloids…"

Fuck. Fuck. Fuck. No, this can't be happening. I don't believe it. In fact, I don't understand it. Any of it. "What story?" That's all I can manage to force out from between my lips right now, because I feel sick. So fucking sick.

Lara hesitates with her answer at first, but then remembers herself and how desperate I am to know more. "He's sold his story about your past, Jonny. Your past with Lauren…"

Oh god, this is my worst fear realised.. And Lauren's too. *Lauren.* Fuck. I need to get to Lauren right now. I need to go home and protect her from this devastating turn of events. "I need to go home. I need to get to Lauren. Does she know?"

Lara looks uncertain. "I don't know, that all depends on whether she's been online or bought a newspaper this morning…"

"We don't buy fucking papers, Lara!" Fuck, I'm really losing my shit right now, and my mind too. "But she does sometimes scroll online although she tends to avoid any gossip columns as she hates reading anything like that."

Ben, Will and Zack soon spring into action when they see I am fast unreeling, all three of them gathering around me and offering their support. But I can't stand around for a second longer. Because I need to get home and I need to get to Lauren before anybody else does.

****

Lauren is singing away at the top of her voice when I arrive home an hour later. The car journey was an hour too long in my eyes but I'm here now, and the fact that she is singing her heart out somewhere in the house tells me that she doesn't yet know. Well, thank fuck for that. Because I need to be the one to tell her. I need to be the one who breaks her whole world apart all over again.

I don't want to be the person who does that to her, but at the end of the day, what choice do I have? I owe it to Lauren to tell her the truth before she hears it from someone else or worse still, reads about it online. But before I deliver this truly devastating news, I needed to see the article for myself. So I read it. I sat in the front seat of Ben's car on the way home and I fucking read it. Out loud. As Ben, Will and Zack listened intently. And right after I read it, I had to ask Ben to stop by the side of the road somewhere so I could throw my guts up. And throw my guts up I did, to the point where I was retching so badly, that my stomach began to hurt.

The lads are as disgusted as I am with the vile newspaper article, at how a person can be as wicked and as cruel as the man who dares to call himself Lauren's father. That lowlife scumbag is worth nothing. In fact, he's less than nothing, and this article, told 'in his own words', is living proof of that.

I use the term 'in his own words' very loosely, due to the fact that nothing about the article is true. Every single poisonous word in this so called 'story of his life' is false. A complete lie. And the most hurtful lie of them all that this heartless bastard has decided to share with the world is the one about how our baby boy died.

This repulsive newspaper article is living proof to me that, yet again, he really and truly will stoop to the lowest of the lows, and all because of money. It's always been about the money with him, and here we are, all these years later, and he's gone and proven that to me all over again.

I bet he commanded a hefty sum to sell this juicy story to the newspapers, but using our stillborn son as a way of reaping in that money is going to be the downfall of this man. Because he will be done for after this. Well and truly done. But I will have to bide my time, because right now, he isn't my priority. His daughter is my priority. Always was, always will be.

That kind, generous, beautiful daughter of his who I look at on a daily basis and wonder how the fuck she turned out to be as beautiful as she is when she came from *him*. I can only thank my lucky stars that it all came from her mother. The mother she never got to know. Again, all thanks to *him*.

Anger like never before bubbles just beneath the surface as I try to compose myself in readiness for talking to Lauren. I can't be angry when I talk to her. I need to be as calm as I can possibly be, so I try to work through my anger by using the techniques that I have come to use regularly throughout my many therapy sessions with Brian.

Once I have breathed my way through my anger for a few minutes, I then decide to be brave, step up, and go and talk to her. I find her by following her beautiful singing voice through the house, that angel like voice that reaches into my heart, my very soul, every time I hear it.

It turns out that she's in the upstairs bathroom, scrubbing away at the bathtub with a cloth as she belts out the lyrics to Empire State of Mind by Alicia Keys.

Now that takes me back a good many months. All the way back to last July to be exact, when I first laid eyes on her after spending ten years of my life without her. And whilst it wasn't quite the reunion I had longed for in my head, Lauren working in a lap dancing club at the time, I wouldn't change that night for the world. Or that song.

She sang it back then as she's singing it now, belting out the high notes to absolute fucking perfection, sounding as happy as can be as she cleans the bathroom.

Honestly, she doesn't need to clean the bathroom in this house, or anywhere in this house for that matter. But she wants to. She doesn't want to get a cleaner or employ a maid or anyone else, she just wants to continue on as she always has done. By being herself.

I have all the money in the world for her and she isn't remotely interested in spending any of it. And I fucking love her all the more for it. Which is why this is so hard. So fucking hard that I almost back away from her before she sees me lingering in the bathroom doorway.

But I don't back away, because I can't. I owe it to her. I owe it to Lauren. This next part is not going to be easy. Far from it. But I am with her. Every step of the way. No matter what.

To be continued....find out what happens next when Jonny and Lauren's story concludes in Fragmented – Book 3 of the Reclamation Rock Star Series.

ACKNOWLEDGEMENT

Thank you for purchasing and reading this book. I am so excited that you are taking this journey with both Jonny and Lauren as they continue to fight their way through to that all-important happy ever after. Jonny and Lauren's story will conclude in the next instalment, Fragmented, which is also told from the perspectives of them both. A release date will be announced in due course so please see below for further information on keeping up to date with all things Reclamation related.

If you did enjoy the story then if you would please leave me a review on Amazon or Goodreads, I would be most grateful. Reviews are so important for authors and most especially, for self-published authors like myself who are trying to build their audience.

For more up to date news and further releases, you can follow me on Amazon, Instagram, Threads and Tik Tok, by following JFrances81author.

Thank you for reading. J x

Printed in Dunstable, United Kingdom